W9-AUK-062

ALABAMA BRIDES

ALABAMA BRIDES

THREE-IN-ONE COLLECTION

SANDRA ROBBINS

BARBOUR
PUBLISHING

The Columns of Cottonwood © 2010 by Sandra Robbins
Dinner at the St. James © 2011 by Sandra Robbins
Blues Along the River © 2011 by Sandra Robbins

ISBN 978-1-61626-459-8

All scripture quotations are taken from the King James Version of the Bible.

This book is a work of fiction. Names, characters, places, and incidents are either products of the author's imagination or used fictitiously. Any similarity to actual people, organizations, and/or events is purely coincidental.

Cover design: Kirk DouPonce, DogEared Design

Published by Barbour Publishing, Inc., P.O. Box 719, Uhrichsville, Ohio 44683, www.barbourbooks.com

Our mission is to publish and distribute inspirational products offering exceptional value and biblical encouragement to the masses.

ecpa Member of the
Evangelical Christian
Publishers Association

Printed in the United States of America.

Dear Readers,

Several years ago I had the idea for a story set in the time the great paddlewheelers plied the rivers of the South. That idea soon grew into three stories set in Alabama in the years following the Civil War.

During that period in American history, a way of life disappeared, but the hardy spirit of the people did not. Those who struggled to survive knew that love for God, family, and the land were the only roads to a renewed future, and the riverboats that hauled freight and passengers up and down the river played an important role in the rebuilding of a tattered society.

Set along the Alabama River, bordered by farmland and cane brakes, *Alabama Brides* tells the stories of three women who lived and loved in the fictional town of Willow Bend, Alabama, during this ravaged period. I hope their experiences will provide insight into life along the Black Belt of Alabama where a determined people worked to rebuild their way of life. May you be immersed in a place and time when the pleasant drawl heard in speech fell sweet on one's ears.

I hope you enjoy *Alabama Brides*.

Sandra Robbins

THE COLUMNS OF COTTONWOOD

Dedication

To Jay, Megan, Katie, Sydney, and Kylie, my wonderful grandchildren. I pray you will always look to God for direction in your lives. No matter where you go and what you pursue in life, you can be assured that He is watching over you.

Chapter 1

August 1871
Outside Willow Bend, Alabama

A low, musical rumble like distant thunder drifted through the afternoon quiet. Savannah Carmichael paused before climbing into the buggy outside her aunt's house and listened. The familiar sound floated from the direction of the river.

The horse hitched to the buggy jerked up his head and whinnied at the deep-pitched drone. Jasper Green, her aunt's handyman, stroked the horse's back and grinned. "There's the whistle. The *Liberty Queen* done docked. I 'spect we's be seein' lots of folks flockin' to town."

Savannah nodded and stepped into the buggy. "I'm sure the merchants will be glad to see the passengers come ashore. They always spend a lot of money."

Excitement washed over her as it did each time she heard a steamboat arrive. The *Montgomery Belle*, the *Carrie Davis*, the *Liberty Queen*, the *Alabama Maiden*—she knew them all and recognized their distinct whistles.

Today she'd get to see the *Liberty Queen*, because her route would take her by the landing. She never tired of watching the passengers from the big paddle wheelers walk from the boat up the hill to the small port town of Willow Bend, Alabama. Her mind would whirl with all sorts of visions as she imagined herself a passenger in unfamiliar locations and disembarking with enough money to buy whatever her heart desired.

She smiled. "Wouldn't it be wonderful to sail away on a steamboat and leave all our problems behind?"

Jasper pushed his tattered straw hat back and gazed up at her. "You'd just have to come back sometime, Miss 'Vanna. Besides, it takes money to ride boats, and I doan think we's seen much of that 'round here lately."

She laughed, smoothed her long skirt, and reached for the reins Jasper held. "Not since the war at least. But one day that will all change, Jasper. I just know it will."

"Yas'm. That's what you been sayin' for a long time now, but I ain't seen no taxes being paid."

A sigh rippled through her body. "No, not yet, but I have faith God's going to provide us with the money somehow."

Jasper shook his head. "I hope you right." He patted the horse's flank and glanced up. "Miss 'Vanna, why doan you let me drive you today? It jest ain't fit'n for a lady to be drivin' by herself. I be more'n glad to go wit' you."

Savannah let her gaze wander over Jasper, and her heart warmed at the kindness in his face. He had been given to Aunt Jane by her father as a wedding present, and Jasper had dedicated his life to taking care of his mistress. Even when he was granted his freedom, he couldn't bring himself to leave.

Now with her parents dead, he was taking care of her, too. Savannah leaned out the side of the buggy and patted Jasper's shoulder. "You're so good to us, Jasper, but I'll be fine. I should be back long before supper."

Jasper frowned and backed away from the buggy. "Be careful when you goes down Main Street. Them folks gittin' off dat boat doan pay no 'tention to where they's goin'."

Savannah laughed and tightened her grip on the reins. "I know what you mean. I saw a man and woman step right in front of a wagon the last time the *Maiden* docked."

"You jest keep a keen eye out for 'em."

"I will." Savannah cast a glance back toward the house. "I left Aunt Jane resting. I don't think she's feeling well today. Will you check on her after a while?"

Jasper's eyes clouded with concern at the mention of his mistress. "Yas'm. I 'spect I best go do that right now."

Savannah flicked the reins and headed down the street toward the docks. With any luck, passengers would still be getting off, and she would get a look at the people traveling the Alabama River in luxury.

The August sun bore down on her as she rode down the dirt street that ran in front of Aunt Jane's house. Dust, stirred by the horse's hooves and the buggy, boiled up around her. The last three months had been hotter than usual, and she welcomed the coming of fall's cooler temperatures.

Of course there was no place she'd rather live than in the Black Belt of Alabama, so named because of the rich, black soil that extended along the Alabama River. She might dream of traveling on one of the big paddle wheelers that stopped at Willow Bend, but she would always be drawn to the canebrakes and farmland that lay along the twisting river.

Her lifestyle had certainly changed when the war began. The once lush fields of Cottonwood had returned to the wild when most of the slaves left, and money had been nonexistent. In the years following the war, her father had been content to sit on the veranda and dream about the past, but that, too, came to an end two years ago when a fire took the house and her parents' lives. Now at twenty years of age, all she had was a deserted plantation with years of unpaid back taxes, but she didn't worry about that. No Southern gentleman would buy another's land for the back taxes. It was an unspoken code of conduct.

She thought of Aunt Jane's two-story whitewashed house where she'd lived since the death of her parents and how different it was from what she'd known all her life. It had come to be home, but it would never be Cottonwood. That's where her heart lay and where her parents were buried.

At the end of the street, Savannah guided the horse through a left turn and headed for the docks. As she approached the landing, she glanced toward the river and the boat moored at the shore. Its white sides glittered in the sun, and crew members hurried along the three decks. Smoke still poured from the two tall stacks near the front as dockworkers loaded waiting goods aboard for shipment to upriver ports.

In the midst of the bustling activity, passengers walked across the gangplank and headed up the hill. In front of her, people already strolled across the street. One woman held a white ruffled parasol over her head to shade her face from the hot sun. As Savannah drew closer, she could see the delicate lace that covered the umbrella.

She squinted and tried to get a better look at the woman. Rows of ruffles draped the back of her blue traveling dress, and its hem swept across the dusty street.

Lost in thought about the elegant lady, Savannah pulled her gaze away and screamed in terror at the sight of her horse bearing down on a man in the middle of the street. He looked around in surprise and jumped back out of the path of the buggy.

The horse, sensing danger, reared on its hind legs as she tugged on the reins with all her might. In the same instant, the man leaped forward and grabbed the horse's harness. He struggled with the animal while she continued to pull on the reins. After a few tense moments, the horse quieted.

When he was able to release his hold on the harness, the man stepped to the side of the buggy and stared up at her. A frown lined his face. "Are you all right, miss?"

Savannah stared into eyes the color of ink. They widened for a moment as she gazed down at him, and she almost gasped aloud at the murky depth she sensed in his eyes. Not only were they dark, but so was the hair sticking out from under his felt bowler. His bronzed skin bore evidence of long hours outdoors, but his calloused hands caught her attention. He might be traveling in luxury, but he wasn't one of the idle rich. This man was used to hard work.

She shook her head to clear her thoughts. "I'm fine, but what about you? I'm so sorry. I didn't see you."

He smiled, and his white teeth offered a stark contrast to his dark features. "It was my fault. I wasn't watching where I was going. I'm sorry to cause you trouble."

She glanced at the steamboat. "Are you a passenger?"

He nodded. "I was, but Willow Bend is my destination."

Savannah tilted her head and studied the man. Willow Bend was just a stopover on the upriver or downriver routes. It wasn't anyone's destination. "Are you visiting someone?"

He chuckled. "No. I've bought some land, and I'm settling here."

She glanced past him to the boat. "Is your family traveling with you?"

He shook his head. "I have no family." His gaze traveled over the stores along the street. "Maybe you can help me. I need to rent a horse. Where is the livery stable?"

She pointed in the direction she'd just come. "Go down this street, and you'll see it on the left."

He tipped his hat and backed away from the buggy. "Thank you. Maybe we'll meet again."

The horse snorted and pawed at the ground. She wrapped the reins around her hands. "I'd better be going. I hope you like living in Willow Bend."

His eyes sparkled. "I'm sure I will."

Savannah snapped the reins across the horse's back. As the buggy surged forward, she chuckled. No family meant he didn't have a wife. The presence of a new eligible bachelor in town should stir the local female interest. She could hardly wait until Sunday to see if he showed up at church.

❧

Dante Rinaldi stood in the middle of the street and watched the buggy disappear in the distance. He'd never seen anyone as beautiful as the young woman he'd just encountered. Her blond hair shimmered in the summer sun, and her blue eyes reminded him of the water off the Gulf Coast.

He wondered how old she was. Perhaps twenty but no more. She was at least ten years younger than he. Her beauty reminded him of what his life had lacked since his parents' deaths sixteen years ago. Each waking moment had been dedicated to work and saving his money for the day he would buy his own land. He'd never had time for love, and now he feared it was too late. He might never find what his parents had treasured.

However, all his years of hard work had paid off, and even better than he thought. He closed his eyes for a moment and thought back to the trip from Mobile to Montgomery before the war, when he'd first seen the plantation homes along the bluff near Willow Bend. One had caught his attention, and it was the memory of the grand house and its columns that had motivated him to work even harder.

Never in his wildest dreams had he dared hope the mansion and its land could be his. Now it was. Or what was left of it. Someday the land would be the great plantation it had once been, and the house would be restored and even larger than before. All it would take was hard labor, and he knew how to do that.

With a smile on his face, he turned in the direction the young lady had pointed. The first thing he had to do was rent a horse and go take a look at his land.

An hour later, Dante pulled the horse to a stop at the edge of what had once been a well-manicured lawn that rolled down the steep bluff in front of an imposing mansion. Now with the area overgrown with thick weeds and brambles, the view of the river was almost blocked.

Underneath him the horse twitched with restlessness, and he leaned forward to pat her neck and whisper in her ear. His gaze returned to the eight smoke-streaked columns that towered above him, the only remnants that remained of the great house. The clerk at the courthouse had told him there had originally been thirty-two of the forty-five-foot Corinthian columns lining the four sides of the home. All but the eight front ones had been destroyed in the fire that consumed the house.

Dante closed his eyes, and for a moment he envisioned the house as it was when he first glimpsed it from the river. Gone now was the mansion with its balconies that circled the house. He remembered a young girl standing on the second floor beside one of the columns and waving to the passengers on the boat. Perhaps she died in the fire that took the lives of the owner and his wife.

"Evenin', suh. You needs some he'p?"

The quiet drawl surprised Dante, and he swiveled in the saddle. A man with skin the color of chocolate stood next to one of the columns. His fixed stare told Dante the man harbored a protective attitude toward his surroundings.

Dante dismounted and tied the horse to a birch tree still standing in the yard. He walked toward the man, who hadn't moved, and extended his hand. "I'm Dante Rinaldi. I just bought this land."

The man's eyebrows arched, and he licked at his lips. "You done bought Cottonwood?"

Dante nodded. "That's right. The plantation's mine, all one thousand acres of it." The man still hadn't taken his hand, and Dante let his arm dangle to his side. "Do you live around here?"

A look of fear crossed the man's face, and he glanced over his shoulder. "Me and my woman, Mamie, we lives in the same cabin we al'ays had when Mistuh Vance be here."

Dante frowned. "You didn't leave when you were given your freedom?"

The man shook his head. "No use us a-doin' that. We doan have no place else. So we stayed and he'ped out."

"But what about after the owner died?"

He shrugged. "Nobody tole us to leave." His lips trembled. "I 'spect you be a-wantin' us gone now, though."

Dante looked at the muscles bulging under the man's tattered shirt and recognized strength in his arms and shoulders. But it was the sadness in his eyes at the thought of leaving his home that touched Dante's heart.

"Tell you what," Dante said. "I'm going to be needing workers here. Would you consider staying on as a tenant farmer? We could work the land together on shares, and you could have a plot of ground to grow your food and keep some animals. Maybe a cow or two and some hogs."

The man's mouth gaped open. "I sho' would like that, and I be a good worker for you. I got me two boys, and they strong. My Mamie, she works hard, too."

Dante held out his hand again. "Then why don't we shake on it, and we'll work out the details later, Mr. . . . . I don't think you ever told me your name."

Unable to pull his stare from Dante's hand, the man reached out and grasped the outstretched fingers. "Saul Clark, suh."

"Well, Saul, I'm looking forward to working with you. Where's your cabin?"

Saul pointed over his shoulder. "Out yonder in the old quarters. We still be in the one we al'ays lived in."

"Is there an empty one I can stay in?"

Saul's eyes widened. "Suh, you gwine live in slave quarters?"

Dante laughed. "It doesn't look like there's any other shelter around here. One of the cabins will be fine until we can build something better for both of us."

Dante didn't think Saul's eyes could get any bigger, but they did. "Both of us? You mean we gwine build somethin' for me and Mamie, too?"

"Of course. The land has plenty of timber on it. We might as well put it to good use."

Saul's legs twitched, and Dante thought he might jump up and down. "I's got to go tell Mamie the good Lawd done answered our prayers."

Dante laughed. "You do that. I want to look around a bit, and then I'll come on to your cabin."

Saul turned and ran, leaving Dante smiling at the retreating figure. He'd thanked the Lord, too, when he found out he could purchase Cottonwood for the back taxes, but he didn't think his happiness could start to compare with what he'd seen on Saul's face.

Dante turned and looked back toward the river. The first thing he wanted to do was clear out the saplings and all the growth that had sprung up. He wanted the view open so he could sit outside on quiet nights and watch the

Alabama River roll by his land.

Now he wanted to walk across the soil he had purchased. Maybe then he'd really believe his dream had come true.

He glanced to the right, and to his surprise he spied a path that ran along the edge of the bluff. Vegetation didn't cover the lane, giving it a traveled appearance. He strode toward it and headed along the bluff on the path.

After walking about two hundred yards, the river swung to the left, and the path veered away from the water. As he rounded the bend of the trail, he stopped in surprise at the sight of a buggy ahead, the horse tied to a tree. Treading as lightly as possible, he eased around the buggy and stopped in astonishment at the sight of a white fence surrounding a small cemetery. Tall water oaks shaded the area where five or six tombstones protruded from the ground.

A woman knelt between two of the graves. She leaned forward, and he could hear her whispered voice. He strained to understand the words, but they were too soft.

"Excuse me," he called out.

The woman sprang to her feet and whirled to face him. Fear etched her face.

Dante's breath gushed from his body as if he'd just been kicked in the stomach. The woman facing him was the one who'd almost run him down in Willow Bend.

Chapter 2

Savannah could hardly believe her eyes. The stranger she'd encountered in town had followed her. Now she was at his mercy.

She took a step back. "Leave me alone, or I'll cry for help."

The man's lips twitched. "You may have to holler really loud. Saul went back to his cabin."

She looked around for an escape route, but the man blocked her path. "You know Saul?"

"Yes." He moved closer. "Please don't be afraid. You surprised me as much as I did you." He smiled, and in that gesture she realized he meant her no harm. She relaxed.

"My name is Dante Rinaldi. I think we met earlier in town."

She nodded. "Yes, we did. Did you follow me here?"

His lips parted, and a deep laugh rumbled from his throat. "No. I was walking along the river. What are you doing here?"

She felt more at ease, so she pointed to the tombstones. "I'm visiting my parents' graves."

His eyes clouded, and he frowned. "Your parents?"

"Yes. I'm Savannah Carmichael. My parents, Vance and Amelia, are buried here."

"Your parents were the owners of Cottonwood?" Surprise laced the words.

She walked through the gate of the white fence surrounding the cemetery and latched it. "The house burned two years ago. My parents died in the fire, but I was able to escape by sliding down one of the columns from the second-floor balcony." She stopped in front of the man. "Did you say your name is Rinaldi?"

He swallowed. "Yes."

She tilted her head to one side. "That's an unusual name."

"I'm Italian."

She smiled. "You don't speak with an accent. Have you lived in America long?"

He nodded. "All my life. My parents came to this country before I was born. I grew up in the Mobile area." His dark eyes seemed to bore into her.

"When I almost ran you over, I thought you told me you had no family."

He shook his head. "I don't. My parents died of yellow fever."

16

She sighed. "I'm sorry. We have yellow fever outbreaks quite often, too."

"So I've heard."

She started to question him further about his reasons for choosing Willow Bend but decided she'd already been too inquisitive. "I'm sorry to be asking so many questions. I'm sure you'll like living here. You'll have to come to church next Sunday and meet all the people who live around here."

"I'd like that." His gaze shifted away from her, and she noticed a drop of perspiration trickle down his cheek.

A warning floated somewhere in the recesses of her mind. Why was he here on her land? She should have questioned him more before she lapsed into conversation with him.

She frowned and gazed up at him. "You haven't told me where you're going to live."

He pulled a handkerchief from his pocket and dabbed at the perspiration that now seemed to be popping out all over his face. "I'm going to live here."

His answer made no sense. "What do you mean? Along the river?"

"No." He bit at his lip and took a deep breath. "I'm sorry. I had no idea you were Savannah Carmichael. I didn't know any of the Carmichaels were still alive."

Her heart began to pound in fear. She knew she was about to receive news that threatened everything she held dear. "What are you trying to tell me?"

He exhaled. "I bought Cottonwood yesterday at the courthouse in Selma."

She heard the words, but she couldn't believe it. A stabbing pain ripped at her heart. "You can't have Cottonwood," she cried. "It belongs to me."

"The taxes haven't been paid in years. The county had the right to sell it." Sympathy lined his face, but she refused to acknowledge it.

She doubled her fists and advanced on him. "But I was going to pay the taxes and come back here to live. You can't do this to me."

He backed away. "I'm sorry, Miss Carmichael. I didn't mean to cause you any hurt, but Cottonwood now belongs to me."

She raised her hand to strike him, but she hesitated. Violence had never solved anything. She should know that after seeing what the war had done to her parents and their plantation. She stepped back and glared. "Well, you can't have it. It's supposed to pass to my heirs. Not some Italian carpetbagger who takes advantage of other people's misfortunes."

His dark eyes flashed. "I'm not a carpetbagger. I've worked for years to get enough money to buy some land. Now I have it. I'm sorry for your problems, but they aren't of my making."

Her chest heaved as she turned, climbed into the buggy, and grabbed the reins. "This isn't the end, Mr. Rinaldi. I intend to get Cottonwood back."

He reached out and grabbed the horse's reins as he had done earlier in town. "Until you do, Miss Carmichael, please feel free to visit your parents' graves anytime you want. Cottonwood will always welcome your visit."

She bit back the retort hovering on the tip of her tongue, snapped the reins, and turned the buggy in a circle. With a heavy heart, she guided the horse down the path toward the ruins of her home.

At that moment, the whistle of the *Liberty Queen* rumbled from the river. She glanced at the sleek paddle wheeler churning its way through the winding channel. She hoped the cargo headed to the upriver ports would be more welcome than what the steamboat had delivered to her. She'd convinced herself this day would never come. Now it had, and the last remnant of her old life had been snatched from her grasp.

As she passed the charred columns, tears rolled down her cheeks. Cottonwood would be hers again. She didn't know how, but it would.

❦

With supper over, Aunt Jane leaned on Savannah's arm as they made their way into the sitting room. Savannah eased her aunt down on the sofa and watched her scoot back into the cushions and settle her long skirts around her.

Savannah took in the faded dress her aunt wore and the threadbare brocade of the couch. Even if it had been six years since the end of the war, everyone she knew was still trying to recover the lifestyle they'd lost in that great conflict. Sometimes Savannah wondered if life would ever be the same again. At the moment, it didn't appear it would be for her.

Savannah settled on the floor at her aunt's feet and laid her head in the portly woman's lap. "I can't believe it," she sobbed. "Cottonwood is gone." She'd spent most of the mealtime wiping away tears with her napkin.

Aunt Jane reached down and stroked Savannah's head. "But darling, you knew the plantation could be bought by paying the back taxes."

Savannah straightened and stared at her aunt. "Not by somebody like him. He's not even a Southerner."

Aunt Jane frowned and picked up her fan from the table next to the sofa. "But, my dear, I thought you said he was born and raised in Mobile. The last time I checked, that was a part of the South."

Savannah waved her hand in dismissal of her aunt's words. "You know what I mean." She shivered in distaste. "I can remember how upset Poppa was when we heard that the ironworks in Selma had fallen to the Yankees and they were raiding the city. We thought they would come to Cottonwood, but we were spared when they turned back to Montgomery. Now there's an Italian, a foreigner, living there. And on land that should belong to me."

Aunt Jane touched Savannah's lips with the still-closed fan. "You're faulting him because of his birth? Talk like that is not worthy of you. Remember, we are all God's children."

Remorse filled Savannah's heart. "I know. I suppose I'm just so shocked to think that someone stole my plantation right out from under me. I believed that God was going to answer my prayer and provide the money to pay the taxes."

Aunt Jane took hold of Savannah's arms and tugged until Savannah rose and sat on the couch next to her. "And how did you think He would do that? I hope you weren't expecting your friend Jonathan Boyer to give you that kind of money. He's only interested in making Oak Hill Plantation productive again."

Savannah blinked in surprise. "Why, Aunt Jane, you sound like you don't like Jonathan."

"I liked his mother, but I had no respect at all for his father. Any man who would treat his slaves like that man did is a disgrace to the human race. I never understood how your father could be friends with him."

"Poppa was a dreamer, Aunt Jane. He loved everybody and didn't believe anything bad about his friends."

Aunt Jane sighed, and sorrow flashed on her round face. She reached for Savannah's hand. "I know, and he let Cottonwood fall apart."

Savannah nodded. "I think the war took the heart out of him."

Aunt Jane touched a lace handkerchief to her nose and sniffed. "We all suffered during the war, maybe the Boyer family more than most. I doubt if Jonathan will ever get over being a prisoner of war at Fort Lookout Prison. That must have been an awful experience. Then to finally come home and find out his brother was killed at Gettysburg and both of his parents had died. . ." Aunt Jane paused and shook her head. "He's not the boy we knew, Savannah."

"I realize that, but you know Poppa and his father wanted us to marry and join the two farms."

"Humph! I don't put stock in folks telling you who to marry. My pa didn't want me to marry my Timothy, but I knew he was the man for me. I was right. I've watched you and Jonathan together, and I know you don't love him. At least not like I loved my Timothy."

Savannah couldn't help but smile. "I don't have too many choices around here. When you take into account how many young men died in the war and how many have left the county looking for a better life, there aren't many eligible men. There's certainly no one left who interests me. I don't think I'll ever marry."

Aunt Jane shook her head. "You don't need to unless you love someone so much that you hurt from wanting to be with him. That's the only reason to marry."

Savannah stood up. "Well, I don't ever see myself feeling like that. Maybe you and Uncle Timothy were the exceptions."

Aunt Jane rose to stand beside her. "No we weren't. There's someone like that for you. Give the good Lord time to show you."

Savannah looped her arm through her aunt's as they walked toward the hall staircase. "Well, if I ever do marry, I won't be living at Cottonwood, because it's been bought by Mr. Dante Rinaldi of Mobile."

Aunt Jane patted her hand. "The plantation may be gone, but you're still alive. And who knows what great things God has planned for you? Don't limit Him, Savannah. Let Him show you what wonderful things He has waiting for you."

Savannah leaned over and kissed her aunt on the cheek. "I don't know what I'd do without you." She glanced at the steep stairs. "Do you want me to help you upstairs to bed?"

Aunt Jane shook her head. "I can still climb my own staircase. You check things before you retire. Make sure all the lamps are out."

Savannah watched her aunt make her way to the second floor of the house and disappear into her bedroom. Walking back to the sitting room, she blew out the lamps until only one was left lit.

She picked it up and studied the flickering flame. The small light held her captive and seemed to grow into a larger blaze the longer she stared at it. A burned smell drifted up the lamp's chimney, and she closed her eyes.

"No, I don't want to remember," Savannah moaned. "I don't ever want to see anything like that again."

❦

Dante sat on the bluff and gazed across the rolling water of the Alabama River. With a contented sigh, he stretched out on the grassy bank, cupped his hands behind his head, and lay down. The stars twinkled brighter than he thought he'd ever seen. Maybe it just seemed so because this was a special night—his first on his own land.

He'd dreamed of this for years. At times he'd think it was in his grasp only to have it vanish like a vapor. Now it was real, and he'd never been happier. At least he told himself so.

Savannah Carmichael's anger still troubled him. It had never been his intention to let his dream destroy another's, but according to her, that's what had happened.

She'd lost so much—her parents, her home, the very existence she'd always known. In some ways, he knew how she felt. He'd lost everything, too, but a man could bury his grief in his work. For a woman, he doubted it was that easy. He hoped she would consider his offer to visit Cottonwood. That might help her some.

"Suh, you all right?"

Saul's voice from behind startled him, and he jumped to his feet. Saul held a tin lantern with a candle in it. The circle of light from it revealed the man's worried face. Dante chuckled and brushed off his pants. "I'm fine. I was just listening to the river."

Saul nodded. "It sho' can be mighty peaceable lis'nin'."

Dante stretched. "I guess it's getting late. I'd better retire if we're to get an early start tomorrow."

Saul tilted his head to one side. "What we gwine be doin'?"

Dante headed toward the house with Saul beside him. "I think we'll go into town for supplies. Tell Mamie to decide what she needs from the store, and I'll get it for her. We also need to purchase a wagon and some horses. Maybe a cow if we can find one. And tools."

Saul stopped and stared at him. "We gwine buy all that?"

Dante nodded. "There's lots to be done at Cottonwood, and the sooner we get started, the better."

Saul shook his head in wonder. "I 'spect this 'bout the bestest day of my life."

Dante smiled. "Mine, too, Saul. Mine, too."

❧

Savannah stepped inside the general store and glanced around. "Mr. Perkins?"

"Just look around. I'll be right with you." The owner's voice drifted from the room in the back.

"I'm in no hurry," she called out. *Just as long as I get out of here before Martha Thompson arrives,* she thought.

She'd come early in hopes of arriving before Martha or any of the other women in town. The news had probably already spread across Willow Bend that Cottonwood now belonged to someone else, and she couldn't bear the pitying glances she'd have to endure. Not yet, anyway.

She set the basket of eggs on the counter and waited. After a few minutes, Mr. Perkins walked from the back of the store. He smiled and wiped his hands on the long apron he wore. "Sorry, Miss Carmichael. I wanted to finish storing some of them tools that came in on the *Liberty Queen* yesterday."

The mention of the steamboat reminded her of what she'd desperately been trying to forget. She pushed the basket forward. "Aunt Jane sent me with these eggs to sell."

He peered at the contents of the basket. "Good. I need these today. I'll put them in the back."

He turned to leave, but the bell above the door jingled as someone entered the store. "Be right with you, mister. Make yourself at home."

"Take your time."

Savannah froze at the sound of the voice. She would recognize the deep tone anywhere. Slowly she turned and stared into the smiling face of Dante Rinaldi.

"Wh–what are you doing here?"

Dante's brow wrinkled as his gaze roved over her. "The same as you, I suppose. How are you this morning, Miss Carmichael? Better than yesterday, I hope."

Her face burned, and she wanted to run from the store. She couldn't until Mr. Perkins came back. She straightened her back and clasped her hands in front of her. "I'm very well, thank you, for someone who has just been robbed of everything she had left."

If her words produced any guilt on his part, he didn't give any indication. A sad smile curled his lips. "I hope someday you'll come to see that was never my intention."

"I hardly expect that will happen."

He nodded. "Maybe not. But remember that I invited you to visit Cottonwood anytime you wish. I would never keep you from your parents' graves."

She arched an eyebrow and stared at him. "Thank you for that at least."

"Good. Then I'll expect to see you there."

At that moment, Mr. Perkins returned from the back room. "I have the amount I owe you figured up, Miss Carmichael."

She grabbed the basket from his hand. "Please apply it to our account. I'll be back with more eggs later in the week."

Without waiting for a reply, she brushed past Dante Rinaldi and hurried out the door. She stopped outside and took a deep breath. Running into the new owner of Cottonwood had been the last thing she'd expected this morning.

"Miss 'Vanna. How's you doin'?"

Her eyes widened in surprise at the sight of Saul sitting on the seat of a wagon and holding the reins of the two horses hitched to it. She took a step toward him. "Saul, where did you get this rig?"

He chuckled. "Hit ain't mine, Miss 'Vanna. Hit belongs to Mistuh Dante."

She shook her head in disbelief. "What are you doing with it?"

Saul's chest expanded with what Savannah thought must be pride. "I's workin' for Mistuh Dante now. He gwine give me money for workin' the land. Ain't that somethin'?"

Savannah's mind reeled from the second surprise of the day. How could Saul and Mamie desert her? Tears sprang to her eyes. She opened her mouth to spew out her disappointment at Saul's betrayal. Then she remembered how Saul had served her father, even when he was free, and how he'd watched over her all her life, how gently he and Mamie had tended her burns the night of the fire. She could never act spiteful to this dear man who'd been so devoted to her family. She sighed and brushed her hand across her eyes.

"I'm happy for you, Saul."

He leaned over the side of the wagon. "Cottonwood gwine be a grand place a'gin, Miss 'Vanna. Jest you wait and see. Mistuh Dante, he a good man."

Savannah's lips trembled. "I'm happy things are working out for you. Give Mamie my love."

Saul and Mamie's lives might be improving, but hers seemed to grow worse with each passing day. She clasped the straw basket tighter and hurried down the street. She had to get to Aunt Jane's house. It wouldn't do for the residents of Willow Bend to see her crying.

Chapter 3

Savannah sat underneath the towering oak trees behind Aunt Jane's house and tried to concentrate on the book she held. Ever since her early morning encounters with the new owner of Cottonwood and with Saul, she'd been restless. She'd hardly touched her noon meal and had come outside to get some air after Aunt Jane lay down for an afternoon nap.

With a start, she realized she had not turned a page in at least ten minutes. Her thoughts kept returning to Dante Rinaldi. Every reasonable thought told her she should hate the handsome Italian, but for some reason, she couldn't. Maybe it was how he had returned her anger with kindness. It had been gracious of him to invite her to visit her parents' graves.

She sighed and raised the book. Perhaps she'd go tomorrow or the next day.

A horse galloped to a stop in front of the house, and a voice rang out. "Savannah, where are you?"

She smiled at the sound of Jonathan Boyer's voice. "In the backyard."

Jonathan ran around the corner of the house and strode toward her. He held his hat in his hand and pointed at her with it as he walked. His brows were drawn into a fierce frown. "I came as soon as I heard."

Savannah rose from the chair and laid her book in it. "Jonathan, what's the matter?"

Anger shone in his blue eyes, and he raked his hand through his brown hair. "Cottonwood has been sold?"

"Yes," she said. "How did you find out?"

"I heard it at the general store. Mr. Perkins said the new owner came in and bought supplies this morning."

She reached out and placed her hand on his arm. "He did. I was there when he arrived."

He stepped back, his eyes wide. "You've seen him?"

She nodded. "Yes. I met him yesterday."

His eyes narrowed. "What's he like?"

Savannah hesitated before she replied. If she was honest, she would say she sensed kindness in him. He'd seemed truly sorry at her distress, and he'd given Saul and Mamie what her family hadn't been able to since the war. Still, he was her enemy, and she needed to remember that.

24

"He's Italian," she finally said.

He stepped back in surprise. "An Italian? I should have known that no Southerner would have stolen your land."

Savannah remembered her conversation with Aunt Jane. "He's from Mobile."

Jonathan's eyes narrowed. "Mr. Perkins said he looked like he was in his early thirties. Mr. Perkins asked him if he fought in the war, and he said he hadn't. Can you believe that? He's not only an Italian, but he let men like me rot in a prison camp and my brother die in battle instead of helping our cause."

The anger in Jonathan's face deepened. It seemed everything that upset Jonathan always related back to the war in some way. Savannah sighed. "We've got to quit fighting the war, Jonathan. It's been over for six years."

Jonathan recoiled from her as if she'd slapped him. "How can you say that after all we've lost? Cottonwood is just one more tragedy of the war's aftermath, and now it's in the hands of an Italian."

Tears flooded her eyes. "Whatever the reason, it's gone."

Jonathan propped his hands on his hips and shook his head. "I can't believe it. How did he get it?"

She wiped her eyes and shrugged. "Paid the taxes."

She sat back down and motioned for him to take the other chair, but he shook his head. He began to pace up and down in front of her. "Cottonwood was supposed to be mine."

"Yours?" Startled, Savannah grabbed the arms of the chair and stared at him.

Jonathan dropped to one knee beside her and covered her hand with his. "I meant *ours*. Isn't that what our families wanted?"

"B–b–but that was just talk between our parents. You and I have never been more than friends."

He reached up and cupped her chin with his hand. "Forgive me, Savannah. I didn't mean to upset you." He stood up and stared down at her. "Don't worry about this. Let me take care of it."

The determined look on Jonathan's face scared Savannah. She jumped up. "What are you going to do?"

He smiled, grasped her hand again, and raised it to his mouth. His lips felt warm to her skin, and pleasure flowed through her. He straightened and let go of her. "I'll do whatever's necessary to get that land back."

Without another word, he turned and rushed across the yard. Within moments she heard the sound of his horse galloping down the road. Jonathan's visit troubled her. He'd never acted possessive or given her orders before. Why would he do it now? Perhaps the loss of the land disturbed him more than it did her.

His words and the tone of his voice troubled her. Maybe a visit to her parents' graves would settle her down. She picked up her book and headed for the house. She'd get Jasper to hitch the horse to the buggy, and then she'd go to Cottonwood.

Savannah stopped before she entered the back door. What would she do if she encountered Dante Rinaldi again? No need to worry about that. He'd probably be working away from the river, and he'd never know she'd been there.

⁂

Dante stooped down, scooped up a handful of soil, and raised it to his nose. The smell of the earth always excited him, but this was something different. This was his land, and it held promise for the future. He spread his fingers and let the dirt sift through them.

"This ground is going to grow some good corn."

Saul pulled off his hat and wiped at the sweat on his forehead. "Yas suh. If'n we evah git this here canebrake cleaned out. We shoulda brought Abraham and Joshua 'stead of leavin' them to clear off the front of where the big house sat."

Dante rose and glanced across the area where they'd worked all afternoon. When he'd first seen the dense growth of the field, he thought it would take no time for Saul and him to clear it. Now he realized how wrong he'd been. Even with the help of Abraham and Joshua, Saul's sons, it would take longer than he'd thought.

The majestic cane stalks with their daggerlike green leaves towered above their heads. He estimated their height anywhere from fifteen to thirty feet, and they grew closely together, forming an almost impenetrable barrier. Even the birds that flew among the branches of the trees along the edge of the canebrake didn't enter the dense vegetation.

"I think you have a point, Saul. We need some help." He thought for a moment before he spoke again. "Do you know any other men who'd like to come to Cottonwood as tenants?"

Saul's mouth pulled into another of his huge grins. "You means like me and Mamie? Workin' on the shares?"

Dante nodded. "That's right. All I can offer them right now is a place to live in the old quarters. But we've got to get some of this land cleared by spring." He glanced down at the rich soil. "I've never seen anything like this fertile earth. We could grow enough corn on it to feed an army."

"I knows lotsa men a-wantin' to work."

"Then we'll start visiting them tomorrow." Dante laughed and slapped Saul on the shoulder. "There's no time to waste."

Saul let out a whoop. "Yas suh, we gwine grow us some corn."

Dante chuckled at the excitement on the man's face. "And lots of cotton, too. But I think we've done about all the good we can here until we get some help. What say we go see what Mamie's cooked us for supper?"

Saul glanced up at the sky and bent to pick up the ax he'd been using. "I s'pose hit 'bout quittin' time."

Together they loaded the tools in the wagon at the edge of the field. They climbed aboard, and Saul guided the horse through the dense growth toward the bluff. Within minutes Dante spied the rolling water through the trees.

As the wagon drove along the bluff, Dante stared across the wide expanse of water and wondered how far it was to the opposite bank. Perhaps someday he'd try rowing across to the other side, but that would have to wait. Right now he had more pressing matters—like clearing additional land.

He'd been disappointed when he first saw the amount of tillable soil left at the plantation. Evidently with no slave labor available after the war, Vance Carmichael had let most of the fields return to their natural state. If Dante was going to bring in more tenant farmers, he would need extra acreage for planting.

The thought of Vance Carmichael brought to mind his daughter. Every time Dante thought of her, his heart stirred. Her anguish at losing the plantation had caused him to lie awake last night. Or maybe it was more than her distress. It could be that he found her to be a fascinating young woman. As much as he tried to fight it, she'd occupied his thoughts ever since he'd stared up at her when she almost ran him down.

With a sigh, he straightened on the wagon seat as they rounded the path leading back to the front of the old mansion. The fence of the cemetery came into sight, and his heart pounded in his chest. Her buggy stood outside the fence.

Saul pulled the horse to a stop. "Miss 'Vanna's heah."

Dante swallowed and looked around, but he didn't see her anywhere. Then he spied her sitting underneath one of the water oaks beside her parents' graves. She leaned against the trunk of the tree, her eyes closed.

Dante climbed down. "I'll check on her."

He walked through the gate and stopped in front of her. His chest contracted and squeezed his pounding heart as he stared down at her. He'd never been affected by any woman the way she stirred him, and it frightened him.

Love had been something he thought he'd never find, and the last thing he needed was to have feelings for a woman who hated him. As he gazed at her, he knew he was helpless to ignore it. No matter what she thought of him, she had cast a spell on him.

She stirred in her sleep, and he backed away.

⌒∾⌒

Savannah dug her knuckles into her eyes in an effort to wake. She hadn't meant to drift off; but the day had been so nice, and it was so peaceful here. Her eyes fluttered open, and she shrank against the tree trunk. A man stood over her.

Fear rose in her as her gaze traveled up the man's body and came to rest on Dante Rinaldi's face. He leaned over her, a worried expression on his face. "Are you all right, Miss Carmichael?"

She scrambled to her feet. "I'm fine."

In an effort to push past him, she took a step but caught the hem of her dress under her foot. Arms flailing, she pitched toward him.

His strong hands grasped her shoulders and steadied her before he released her. He backed away. "I didn't mean to frighten you. I saw you under the tree and thought you might be ill."

Her shoulders burned from the contact with him. Had his touch blistered her skin? Her bonnet lay on the ground next to the tree, and she bent to retrieve it. "I—I sat down for a minute, and I suppose I fell asleep."

The corners of his eyes crinkled. "Then I'm glad I came along. You might have spent the entire night on the ground."

Samantha glanced across the river, and panic overcame her at the sun sinking into the west. "Oh, I didn't realize it was so late. Aunt Jane will be worried." She stepped around him and headed for her buggy. "I need to go."

He followed and closed the gate to the cemetery. Saul, who'd climbed down from the wagon, held the reins of her horse. "Afte'noon, Miss 'Vanna. It sho' is good to see you ag'in."

She smiled. "It's good to see you, too."

Saul pointed over his shoulder. "Me and Mistuh Dante been a-cleanin' out that ole canebrake. Reckon we gwine grow some mighty good corn there."

Savannah raised her eyebrows and turned back to Dante, who'd stopped beside the buggy. "Clearing the canebrakes? That's a big job for two men. I doubt if you'll be able to accomplish it."

He nodded. "I think you're right. That's why I told Saul we needed more tenant farmers."

She narrowed her gaze and studied the self-assured man. "If you want more tenants, you might check out at the Crossroads. There's a shantytown filled with men who need work." She nodded toward Saul. "Saul knows the way."

Dante's eyes sparkled. "Thank you, Miss Carmichael. It's kind of you to tell me."

She could hardly believe she'd given him that information, but anybody in Willow Bend could have told him. Perhaps some of Cottonwood's former slaves who lived there would be able to return.

It was hard to ignore the thrill that she'd felt at the news they were clearing more land. After the slaves had been freed, she'd begged her father to bring in tenant farmers as many of the other planters were doing. He'd refused, and the land had suffered. It seemed the new owner intended to restore the land to what it had once been.

As if Saul could read her thoughts, he spoke. "Big Mike and Pinky live out to the Crossroads. Maybe they's can come back home."

His words pierced her heart. The former slaves might return, but she knew she never would. She fought back tears and climbed into the buggy. Dante took the reins from Saul and handed them to her.

"It's getting late, Miss Carmichael. I'd be happy to follow you home."

In his face she saw genuine concern for her safety, but she couldn't be swayed by his attempts to gain her friendship. He was still her enemy. She turned a cool look toward him. "Home? Haven't you heard? I don't have one anymore."

She snapped the reins, and the horse surged forward.

❧

Saul, a confused expression on his face, turned to Dante. "What she mean she ain't got no home?"

Dante shook his head. "Miss Carmichael's angry at me for buying her land."

Saul's mouth formed a large circle. "Oh."

They walked back to the wagon and climbed aboard. Neither spoke all the way back to the cabins. The sting of Savannah's words echoed through Dante's mind. There had to be some way he could make her understand his position. He'd worked and saved for years, and now he couldn't abandon his dream. Not even for a woman who filled his thoughts and made him long for something that could never be.

The wagon rumbled to a stop outside the still-standing barn. Dante was thankful that Saul and his sons had kept it in good repair.

"Go on, Mistuh Dante. I'll take care of the hosses."

Dante hopped from the wagon and nodded. "Thanks."

He strode toward the cabin where he was living. It sat away from the rows of ramshackle buildings where slaves had once lived, but it wasn't much better than the other houses. He stopped on the front porch and clutched one of the posts that supported the extended roof.

When the additional tenant farmers came, perhaps building new cabins should be one of the priorities. Men worked better when they had adequate housing and food. He'd wanted to have a good portion of the land producing by next spring, but perhaps he needed a new timeline. He had to provide for his workers first.

He stepped through the door and glanced around at the dreary interior of the two-room cabin. And what about himself? He also needed better quarters. What if he decided to marry? A woman would have to love a man a lot to share such a life as his.

Certainly a woman like Savannah Carmichael would want better. She'd been used to the best, not a cabin built of rotting wood.

He raked his hand through his hair and groaned. "Why can't I quit thinking about her?"

Walking back to the front door, he looked out across the hard-packed earth that covered the area where the cabins stood. Mamie would bring him some supper in a while, but she'd go back to Saul and her sons. He'd be alone like so many other nights in the past, but tonight the loneliness crushed him more than ever.

The vision of Savannah Carmichael drifted through his thoughts, and the words she'd spoken sent guilt racing through his body.

"Home? Haven't you heard? I don't have one anymore."

Chapter 4

Dante strode from the cabin as soon as the sun was up the next morning. He ignored the ache in his back and shoulders from the labor in the canebrake the day before. The pain was little enough to bear if it meant his land would be cleared and ready for planting by spring.

Today he and Saul were going to the Crossroads to see if they could enlist more men to join them as tenant farmers. From what Saul had told him, the freed slaves couldn't wait to get away from Cottonwood, but they had found it hard to live on their own. Maybe some of them would want to come back to the land they'd worked for the Carmichaels. This time, though, they would be working for themselves.

"Good mornin', Mistuh Dante."

The voice startled him, and he turned as Saul rounded the corner of the cabin. "I didn't see you there. What are you doing out so early?"

Saul's eyes grew wide. "The sun done come up, so it's time to git to work. Mamie got you some breakfast cooked. Come on over and eat."

Dante smiled. "I hope she's made some more biscuits like those she had last night."

Saul laughed and slapped his leg. "I ain't never seen no woman so happy to have anything as she was what you done bought yestiday. It's been a long time since we had such good eatin'. I 'spect the Lord blessed us when you come to Cottonwood."

Savannah Carmichael's face flashed before his eyes, but he tried to ignore her words that still rang through his mind. "I hope I can be a blessing to more than just your family, Saul. If we can get some more tenant farmers and get the fields ready for planting, we can restore Miss Carmichael's land to what it was before the war."

Saul pulled off the straw hat he wore, held it in front of him, and gazed down at the ground. "I don't means to be speakin' bad about Mistuh Vance, but the land done started to grow wild 'fore the war came. He never seemed to know what to do like his pappy did. Now Miss 'Vanna, she got a good head on her shoulders. After the war, she tried to talk to Mistuh Vance 'bout gittin' some tenant farmers to help clear those canebrakes and plantin' more crops, but he wouldn't listen. Sometimes I thought even if Miss 'Vanna was just a young girl, she ought to be runnin' Cottonwood."

Dante smiled and glanced up at the sun. "We better hurry. After we eat, I want to leave right away for the Crossroads. We've got a big day ahead of us, Saul."

Saul nodded. "I 'spect we do, Mr. Dante. I 'spect we do."

∽

Two hours later, Dante stood in the center of the shantytown known as the Crossroads. The makeshift hovels that dotted the area made the abandoned slave quarters at Cottonwood look like comfortable houses. Saul had told him he didn't know how many people lived in the small community that had sprung up after the war, and he couldn't estimate the number either.

Small children ran along the dirt paths that twisted between the shelters, and a group of older young people sat underneath a tree to his left. Suspicion gleamed in their unblinking eyes. He wondered what memories had made them wary of strangers. He smiled, but they gave no response.

The horses harnessed to the wagon snorted and swished their tails as the August sun climbed higher in the morning sky. Dante patted the one he stood beside and stared down the path where Saul had disappeared ten minutes ago. Perhaps he was having trouble persuading any of the men to come to talk to the stranger from Mobile.

When Dante thought he could bear the stares of the young people no longer, Saul appeared at the end of the path. Four men walked behind him. Dante's eyes grew wide at the sight of a young white man in the group. The others had skin the color of Saul's, and they walked forward with their gazes directed at Dante.

As they approached, Saul broke into a grin that radiated confidence. The group stopped in front of Dante, and he let his gaze drift over their faces.

Saul pointed to a tall, muscular man dressed in overalls and a long-sleeved shirt. "This here Big Mike. He was over the field hands at Cottonwood, and he knows that land better'n anybody in these here parts."

Dante stuck out his hand. "It's good to meet you, Big Mike. I'm Dante Rinaldi."

Big Mike glanced down at the outstretched hand and hesitated before he reached out and grasped it. "Suh," he said.

Saul pointed to the others behind him. "And this here's Pinky. I tole you 'bout him. He kin pick mo' cotton in a day than anybody I ever seen."

Dante pumped Pinky's hand. "Sounds like you're what we need at Cottonwood."

Pinky grinned and shifted from foot to foot. "I sho' would like to pick in them fields agin."

Sweat glimmered on the dark brow of the man standing next to Pinky. He glanced at Dante's hand but didn't pull his from his pockets. "My name Mose.

Mr. Boyer owned me 'fore the war, and I worked his place."

Dante let his hand drift to his side and stared Mose in the eye. "Nobody owns you now, Mose."

The man took a deep breath. "Naw suh, I 'spect they don't."

Dante looked past Saul at the white man, who appeared to be barely old enough to shave. "And what's your name?"

The boy grinned, and Dante noticed two bottom teeth missing. "I'm Henry Walton. Grew up in Georgia. After the war, there weren't nothing left for me there. Folks all dead. So me and my wife started west. Thought we might end up in Texas. We got this far and found these good folks and decided to stay for the winter."

"Are you planning on moving on in the spring?"

Henry shrugged. "Depends on what I find here."

Dante smiled and glanced around at the faces of the men. "I suppose Saul has told you that I need some workers to help me farm my new land. Right now I can't offer you much. I'm staying in one of the slave quarters myself, as are Saul and his family. You'll have to do the same. But we'll build you houses so you can have a little spot that's yours, and I'll let you farm a portion of the land on shares. I'll see that you get some livestock to start off, but it'll be up to you to take care of it. If you prosper, it'll be because of your efforts, not mine. I've worked hard to get this land. I'll expect you to do the same, or I'll find someone to take your place. What do you say?"

Henry Walton nodded. "Best offer I've had since I left Georgia. I reckon as how me and my wife gonna take you up on it, Mr. Rinaldi."

"Good." Dante glanced at the other men. "Anybody else?"

Big Mike looked at Mose and Pinky then back to Dante. "Saul says we can trust you. So I 'spect we be going to Cottonwood if you let us bring our families."

Dante laughed. "Of course. I suppose I thought that was understood. I'm not married, but I want there to be families on the land. I want to hear children running and laughing. I want to bring life back to a grand plantation."

Saul smacked his hands together and giggled. "I guess that what we gwine do, Mistuh Dante. We gwine bring life back to a dead place."

"When do you want to move?" Dante asked.

Big Mike's eyebrows arched. "We be ready in a few minutes."

Dante frowned. "Do we have enough room on my wagon to transport all your belongings?"

"I got a small wagon," Henry said. "Between yours and mine, I think we got enough room."

Dante glanced at his wagon. It wasn't very big. "How many women and children will there be?"

Henry thought for a moment. "We've all got wives, and each family has three children except for Mary Ann and me. We ain't got one yet."

Dante shook his head. "We only have two wagons to transport your belongings and, counting Saul and me, nineteen people. Maybe I need to get some extra help."

Big Mike smiled at Dante. "No need for that. We kin walk."

"But it's at least ten miles from here to Cottonwood."

"That don't matter."

Dante chuckled. "Then we'll all take turns walking. Now go get your belongings, and let's head out."

The men stood still a moment as if they couldn't believe what had happened, and then with a whoop, they ran back the way they'd come. Twenty minutes later, Dante and Saul stood beside the two wagons and surveyed the small number of personal objects the families had placed there. Henry's small wagon was almost filled, but Dante's still had room.

Dante turned to the assembled group. The women stood almost hidden behind their husbands, with their children at their sides. The woman standing next to Mose held a small infant in her arms. Dante wondered how long it had been since she'd given birth.

He turned to Saul and whispered in his ear, "Is that Mose's wife with the baby?"

"Yas suh."

Dante cleared his throat and faced the group again. "We have room for some of the women and younger children to ride in my wagon." He nodded to Mose. "Mose, help your wife into the wagon."

The woman hugged her baby tighter, but Mose shook his head. "Tildy can walk. She strong."

Dante sighed and glanced at Saul, who shrugged. He turned back to the group. "I appreciate the fact that your wife doesn't want any preferential treatment, but she's weak. I won't have it on my conscience that I let a woman who's recently given birth walk all the way back to Cottonwood. Now it's your choice. She rides in the wagon, or you unpack your belongings and stay here."

Mose started to object, but he looked down at his wife. His shoulders sagged, and he faced Dante. "Much obliged, Mistuh Dante. I reckon ain't no white man ever wanted to help one of mine before."

Dante stepped forward. "Things have changed, Mose. It's a new day in the South."

Mose's eyes narrowed. "I reckon for some, but not all."

Dante glanced at Saul, who nodded. "Folks at the Boyer plantation waren't never treated like Mistuh Vance did us what lived at Cottonwood. Oak Hill be a hard place to live as a slave."

Before Dante could question him, Saul stepped forward and picked up a small girl who appeared to be about three years old. Mose lifted his wife and baby into the wagon, and Saul set the child he held next to her.

Dante smiled and glanced at the children still standing beside the wagon. "Now you fathers decide who's going to walk and who's going to ride on the first leg of the journey."

When the wagon was filled, Dante turned to Big Mike. "Saul and I will walk the first leg, and then we'll take turns with the wagon. Do you want to lead the way?"

Big Mike's eyes grew wide. "Suh, you wants me to handle the hosses?"

Dante nodded. "I expect you know how from your years at Cottonwood."

A smile broke out on Big Mike's face, and he climbed into the wagon seat. Wrapping the reins around his hands, he released the brake and cracked the reins across the horses' backs. "Giddap, you hosses. We's goin' home."

Home. The word warmed Dante's heart and stirred him in a way he'd never known. His father's dream had been to own some of Alabama's rich, black farmland, but yellow fever had ended that desire. Now it was Dante's turn to fulfill the hope his parents had when they settled in Mobile.

Dante watched the wagons rumble by, leading the way. He stepped aside as those walking behind passed him. Some of the women, their skin glistening in the hot sun and their hair covered by tattered bonnets, darted a glance his way, but most of them directed their attention straight ahead.

There was no laughter from the children, and this surprised Dante. He was overcome by the realization that he had no idea what these people had experienced in their lives. Now another white man had come with his promises. Perhaps they were too afraid to trust him yet. But they would.

With God's help, he would teach them to trust. And the land was going to help him do that.

Chapter 5

Two weeks after Savannah heard that tenant farmers had come to Cottonwood, she sat in the church where she had worshipped all her life. The pastor had been preaching for fifteen minutes, but this morning she didn't hear his words.

She glanced at the few worshippers who'd gathered. When she was growing up, the church had been filled on Sundays. Buggies and wagons loaded with families streamed into the churchyard. Sundays were reserved for worship and, afterward, for visiting with friends and neighbors. Planters discussed their crops, women shared secrets, and children chased each other across the lawn.

Sunday worship, as well as everything else in her life, changed when the first young men left to join the Confederate forces. Too many familiar faces were with them no longer.

Even six years after the end of the war, its effects haunted each family she knew. She caught a glimpse of the Redmans from the plantation closest to Cottonwood. With both of their sons killed in the conflict, they had long ago moved to Willow Bend and left their land to be sold for back taxes just as hers had been.

Resentment rose up in her throat, and she tried to swallow the choking rage at the thought of Dante Rinaldi living on her land. It had been more than two weeks since she'd seen the man but not since she'd heard about him.

Every time she went to the store to sell their eggs, she ran into Martha Thompson, who couldn't wait to tell her what she'd heard was going on at Cottonwood. The new owner had brought in four families to work as tenant farmers, she had said. One of them was white. At this statement, Martha's eyebrows arched, and her nostrils flared.

"Can you imagine white people living out there in that shantytown?" she said. "All I can say is that they must be white trash."

Savannah had turned away and tried to focus on selling her eggs, but the news hadn't been unexpected. After all, she had encouraged Mr. Rinaldi to go to the Crossroads. Although she would never admit it, she was pleased that the land would be worked again. If only her father had listened to her, she might be the one getting ready for next spring at Cottonwood. Instead, an Italian, with dark eyes that made her breath catch in her throat, would harvest the next crop on her land.

Turning her head slightly, she glanced over her shoulder, and her heart thudded. Dante Rinaldi sat in the last pew. His dark stare bored into her, and he nodded in her direction. For a moment, she froze before she blinked and jerked her head around.

Aunt Jane, who sat on her right, frowned and leaned toward her. "What's the matter?"

Savannah bit her lip and shook her head. She patted her aunt's hand. "Nothing."

Smiling, Savannah straightened her shoulders and directed her attention back to the pastor. Aunt Jane continued to look at her, but after a moment, she unfolded the fan that lay in her lap and began to wave it back and forth in the lazy fashion Savannah had seen her do so many times.

For the remainder of the sermon, thoughts of the man who sat in the rear of the church whirled through her head. What would she say to him? After all, she had invited him to church, but that was before she knew he was her enemy. Even if she didn't like him, she reasoned, she couldn't be rude in a house of worship.

When "Amen" was uttered, she turned to Aunt Jane and stole a quick glance toward the back pew. Her heart plummeted at the sight of the empty bench. She scanned the congregation, but he was nowhere to be seen.

A wave of disappointment washed over her. Why should she care if he left? She should be thankful she'd been saved another embarrassing meeting with him.

As the few church members walked up the aisle, everyone stopped to speak to Aunt Jane before they moved on to Reverend Somers, who stood at the entrance.

When the last one walked by, Aunt Jane stepped into the aisle. "How many were here today?"

"I counted twenty." Savannah shook her head. "No, twenty-one. I forgot the visitor."

Aunt Jane's eyebrows arched. "I didn't see a new face. Who was it?"

Savannah took her aunt by the arm and nudged her up the aisle. "Dante Rinaldi sat in the back, but he's already gone."

Aunt Jane stopped and gazed at Savannah. "I wish I could have met him. Maybe another time."

"Maybe."

Reverend Somers smiled as they approached. "Mrs. Martin, it's so good to see you again." He nodded to Savannah. "And you, too, Miss Carmichael."

Aunt Jane closed her fan and stuck it in her reticule. "Very good sermon, Reverend. I understand we had a visitor."

"Yes, but he left before I could greet him. Maybe he'll come again. Do you know him?"

"Savannah tells me he's the new owner of Cottonwood."

Reverend Somers gave a small gasp. "I had no idea." He cleared his throat. "I need to get something from the front of the church, but if you'll wait, I'll be glad to help you down the steps."

Aunt Jane waved her hand in protest. "No need for that. Savannah and I can make it fine. Have a nice day, Reverend."

"And you, too."

As the pastor walked away, Aunt Jane took a deep breath and grasped Savannah's arm. "Come, Savannah. Let's go."

Aunt Jane's weight sagged against Savannah, and a sense of alarm rose in her. "Do you feel all right?"

"Yes. I'm just a little short of breath. Nothing to be concerned about."

Savannah led her aunt out of the church and stopped to catch a better hold of her arm at the front steps.

"Allow me to assist you, Miss Carmichael."

Savannah straightened and stared into the face of Dante Rinaldi, who stood at the foot of the steps. Her heart pounded, and a slow breath trickled from her mouth. "Thank you, Mr. Rinaldi."

He positioned himself on the other side of Aunt Jane. Together they eased her down the steps. When they stopped at the bottom, Aunt Jane took a deep breath and turned to Dante. "You must be the new owner of Cottonwood. Savannah has told me about you."

A smile curled his lips. "I hope she didn't convince you I'm some sort of ogre."

Aunt Jane chuckled. "Not at all, Mr. Rinaldi. In fact, I've found myself wondering about you. You should call on us sometime so we can get better acquainted."

"I'd like that."

Savannah glanced around at the people who'd already climbed into their buggies. Never had she seen such looks of loathing, and they were directed at Dante. She recognized the silent message her friends were sending. Interlopers who bought land for back taxes weren't welcome in their closed Southern society.

Guilt flowed through her, and her skin burned. Was she responsible for the community's opinion of Dante? She considered the misfortune of losing her land a problem for her, not a cause that her friends should embrace. She tightened her grip on her aunt's arm. "I'm sure Mr. Rinaldi has better things to do than to stand around talking to two women, and you're tired. Let's get you home."

Dante appeared oblivious to her neighbors' glares. "I believe I see your buggy tied to that tree. I'll walk you there."

Savannah opened her mouth to protest, but Dante was already propelling her aunt across the yard. With a sigh, she followed behind.

When they reached the buggy, Aunt Jane turned to Dante. "How do you like living at Cottonwood, Mr. Rinaldi?"

"I find myself enjoying it, even though we're working very hard."

Savannah watched the last buggy pull from the churchyard before she glanced at Dante. "I hear you have more tenant farmers now. How is that working out?"

"Fine. They're all very hard workers. We're going to try and build some better housing for them before winter, but getting the land ready for spring planting is the main goal right now."

Savannah nodded. "I can understand that."

His gaze flitted across her face. "I haven't seen you at your parents' graves lately."

Her skin warmed more under his intense stare. "I come when you're in the fields. I don't want to be in anybody's way."

His eyes clouded. "It's always a pleasure to have you there."

"Thank you." She turned back to her aunt. "Now, let's get—" She stopped in horror at the grimace on her aunt's face. "Aunt Jane, what's the matter?"

She clutched at her chest. "I'm not feeling well."

Before Savannah could react, Aunt Jane's eyes widened, and she slumped toward the ground. In one swift motion, Dante caught her in his arms.

Fear washed over Savannah. "Aunt Jane, what's happening?"

Her aunt's eyelids drooped, and she struggled to breathe. "My heart."

Dante lifted her into the seat of the buggy and helped Savannah climb in beside her.

"Take your aunt home. I'll get the doctor. I know where his office is."

Aunt Jane tried to straighten in the seat. "May not be there. Wasn't in church today."

Dante gave Aunt Jane's hand a squeeze. "Don't worry. I'll find him no matter where he is and follow him to your house."

Dante ran to the tree and untied the reins. As he handed them to her, Savannah couldn't hide the trembling in her hands. "Thank you."

Dante looped the reins around her fingers and covered her shaking hands with his. "Don't worry. I'll be there with the doctor."

Savannah bit her lip and flicked the reins across the horse's back. As the buggy sped from the churchyard, Dante's horse galloped past in a cloud of dust. She couldn't take her eyes off the straight back and broad shoulders of the man riding ahead. He hunched forward as he spurred the horse on, and she clenched the reins tighter.

Her lips thinned into a straight line at the thought of their friends and neighbors leaving them at the church. Some of them must have noticed Aunt Jane's labored steps. If Dante hadn't been there, she didn't know what she would have done.

She might tell herself that Dante Rinaldi was her enemy, but in her heart, she knew better. From their first meeting, she had known this man was different from any she'd met before. Now he rode to get help for them. A thought that she could never voice popped into her head. She was glad he was the one who'd come to their aid.

An hour later, Savannah sat on the sofa in the parlor where she often sat with Aunt Jane. Dante stood at the window and stared outside. He had done as he said. She and Jasper had just gotten Aunt Jane out of the buggy and into the house when Dante arrived with the doctor.

Again Dante had scooped Aunt Jane up and carried her up the stairs as if she were weightless. Jasper shuffled behind, insisting with each breath that he was still able to take care of his friend.

Savannah stood, walked to the foot of the steps, and stared up to the second floor. Jasper paced back and forth in the hallway. Sighing, Savannah headed back to the parlor.

"What could be taking Dr. Spencer so long?"

Dante turned toward her. "I'm sure he'll let us know something soon."

The sound of hoofbeats outside caught her attention. "Who is that?"

Dante pulled the curtain back and looked outside. "A man just rode up. He's coming into the house."

The front door burst open, and Jonathan Boyer strode into the parlor. He crossed the floor and grabbed Savannah's hands. "I came as soon as I heard about your aunt. How is she?"

"The doctor's still with her. Maybe we'll know something soon."

Jonathan started to say something else but stopped when he spied Dante. A frown wrinkled his brow. He stared first at Dante then back at Savannah. "I'm sorry. I didn't know you had company." Turning to Dante, he took a step toward him. "I don't think we've met. I'm Jonathan Boyer, the owner of Oak Hill Plantation. I'm a friend of Savannah's."

Dante stuck out his hand. "I'm Dante Rinaldi."

A red flush started at the base of Jonathan's neck and spread upward. "I've heard of you. You're the thief who stole Cottonwood?"

Dante's hand drifted back to his side. "Bought it, not stole it."

Savannah touched Jonathan's arm. "Mr. Rinaldi helped me with Aunt Jane today. It was fortunate for me that he was at church."

"Quite right, Miss Carmichael." Dr. Spencer stood in the doorway. A deep frown furrowed his brow.

Savannah hurried toward him. "How is my aunt? Is it her heart again?"

He set his medical bag down and reached for Savannah's hand. "Yes, but she's resting now. I'm afraid I've done everything I can. Her body is worn out. I think you have to prepare yourself for the inevitable."

The sympathy she heard in his voice reminded her of how he'd talked with her after her parents' deaths. A tear trickled from Savannah's eye, but she bit her lip and nodded. "I know. It's just that I can't imagine life without her."

"And she's concerned about you, too. I can't tell you how long she has. So put it in God's hands and enjoy each day."

Savannah nodded. "I will."

Dr. Spencer released her hand. "It was a pleasure to meet you, Mr. Rinaldi. I hope to see you again soon."

Dante crossed the room to shake the doctor's hand. "Thank you, Dr. Spencer. I wish we could have met under better circumstances. Maybe the next time we see each other, no one will be ill."

The doctor chuckled. "I hope so." He nodded to Jonathan, turned, and walked toward the door.

When the door closed behind Dr. Spencer, Savannah faced Dante. "Thank you again, Mr. Rinaldi, for your help. I know you must have other things to do this afternoon, so don't let me keep you."

His eyes widened with surprise, and Savannah felt a moment of guilt. He must think her ungracious to dismiss him so abruptly, but she feared his presence was upsetting Jonathan.

She smiled and led the way to the front door. Dante followed.

When she opened it, he stood in front of her for a moment. "If you need me for anything, Miss Carmichael, please let me know."

She extended her hand. "I will. And thank you again. I don't know what I would have done if you hadn't been there."

He looked down at her hand before he clasped it in his. For a brief moment, he squeezed her fingers then released them and strode from the house. He mounted his horse and rode away without looking back.

Savannah stepped onto the porch and watched until he disappeared. The day had produced some strange reactions in her. During the worship service, she had fumed because her enemy had come to her church. Afterward she discovered that a kind soul inhabited the body of the man she wanted to hate.

Now a new realization spread through her: Dante Rinaldi wasn't her enemy. What he was, she didn't yet know, but she looked forward to finding out.

Chapter 6

Savannah stared at the coffin being lowered into the ground. She wondered why there were no tears on her face. Perhaps she had shed them all in the month since Aunt Jane's attack at church. Or it could be that her body was too exhausted from the constant care her aunt had needed in the past weeks.

Whatever the reason, Savannah felt empty inside. The last link to the life she'd known had now disappeared. Her parents, Cottonwood and its inhabitants, and now Aunt Jane were gone. She had nothing left.

Beside her, Jasper wiped at the tears streaming down his face. He had been diligent in his attention to Aunt Jane in her last days, just as he had been all his life. It dawned on her that they shared something in common now—neither of them had anyone or anything left.

She glanced around at the mourners gathered in the cemetery. All the town's residents had turned out for the funeral of one of Willow Bend's most loved women. Her gaze drifted across the people she'd known all her life and came to rest on a lone figure standing behind the group.

Dante Rinaldi nodded a silent greeting. His eyes held her hostage for a moment before she glanced away.

Jonathan stood across the grave from her. He frowned and looked from her to Dante before he directed his attention back to Reverend Somers. Savannah sighed and did the same.

With the graveside service completed, Jonathan stood beside her as she greeted every person there. From time to time, she searched the crowd for Dante, but he had disappeared.

After shaking hands with the last mourner, Jonathan turned to her. "I'll take you home."

She shook her head. "There's no need. Jasper can drive us. You probably need to get back home."

"I always have time for you, Savannah. I thought you knew that."

Savannah inwardly flinched at the words. Since the day he'd encountered Dante in her parlor, Jonathan had returned only once to check on their welfare. Dante, on the other hand, had stopped by at least once a week. She'd found herself looking forward to his visits. It surprised her to find out that he was nothing like she first thought. In fact, she had come to like him.

In the last days of Aunt Jane's life, she often talked about Dante's kind nature, and Savannah realized her aunt had been right. She pushed her thoughts from her mind and smiled at Jonathan. "To tell you the truth, I think Jasper and I need to be alone. These last few weeks have been difficult, and I just want to rest for a while."

Jonathan nodded. "I understand. If you need me for anything, send Jasper to Oak Hill to get me."

"I will. Thank you for coming today."

Jonathan walked to his horse at the edge of the cemetery and climbed into the saddle. With a wave, he galloped away.

Savannah turned to Jasper, who hadn't said a word since they'd left home. "Are you ready to go, Jasper?"

He nodded and trudged behind her toward the buggy. His footsteps rustled in the leaves that had begun to fall from the oak trees rimming the cemetery. Savannah took a deep breath and smiled. Fall would soon arrive, and nature would paint its landscape with all the brilliant colors she loved.

She always looked forward to fall because nature changed so drastically to welcome the cold days ahead. Now she needed to adjust her life to get ready for all the challenges that lay ahead. Everything she'd known was gone, and uncertainty loomed before her.

When they reached the buggy, Jasper helped her climb in and then walked to the tree where he'd tied the horse. His stiff fingers fumbled with the reins. With a sinking heart, Savannah realized Jasper was getting old, too.

As he turned to get in beside her, a flash of color emerged from the tree line at the back of the cemetery. Dante, sitting straight on his black horse, rode toward her. She pressed her hand to her chest to still her thumping heart.

Dante pulled the horse to a stop next to the buggy and removed his hat. "I wanted to offer my condolences."

She clasped her hands in her lap so he wouldn't see how they shook. "Thank you, Mr. Rinaldi. It was kind of you to come. I saw you at the grave site, but I thought you'd left."

His eyes narrowed. "The good people of Willow Bend haven't been very welcoming to me. I didn't want to embarrass you by speaking to you with them present."

She gripped her fingers tighter. "I'm sorry. In time, I'm sure that will change."

"That's not important today. I just wanted to make sure you're doing all right. Is there anything I can do to help you?"

She took a deep breath and forced a smile to her face. "I don't think there's anything that anyone can do at this point. My aunt is dead, my home is sold, and

I'm left penniless and alone. All I can do is put my faith in God, that He will see me through this time."

"Penniless? But won't you inherit your aunt's house?"

Savannah shook her head. "Right after the war, Aunt Jane found herself with little money. My father tried to get her to come to Cottonwood and live with us, but she was very independent. She sold her house to her friend Lucas Hawkins, who is the captain of the *Montgomery Belle*. He gave her the option of living there until her death. Of course, at the time, she had no idea that I would come to live with her."

Dante leaned forward and rested his arm on the pommel of the saddle. "Do you know what you're going to do?"

"As a matter of fact, I do. When the *Montgomery Belle* docked last week on its way upriver, Captain Hawkins came to see me. He knew how sick Aunt Jane was, and he told me I could live in the house a few more years until he decided to return to Willow Bend."

"Are you going to do that?"

Savannah sighed. "There's no use prolonging the inevitable. When I said I would leave, he told me of a family in Mobile who's in need of a governess. He thought I might be interested."

Dante frowned. "A governess?"

"Yes. He said they're a very nice family with two girls. They're looking for a handyman, too, so Jasper and I have decided to go. Captain Hawkins is supposed to arrive in Willow Bend on his return journey to Mobile next week, and we plan to board the ship with him."

Dante's eyes widened in surprise. "You're going to Mobile to be a governess?"

"I don't want to leave, but I have no choice."

"B–b–but what about your friend Mr. Boyer? I assumed you would marry him."

Savannah shook her head. "Our parents wanted us to marry and join the two plantations, but I realized a long time ago that I wasn't in love with Jonathan."

The horse underneath Dante pranced, and he tightened his hold on the reins. "I hope you know I wish you the best. Maybe I'll see you again before you leave."

"Perhaps." She held out her hand. "Thank you again for your kindness during Aunt Jane's last days and for coming today."

He gazed at her hand a moment before he reached out and grasped it in his. "It was my pleasure."

Her heart raced as he grasped her hand. Savannah pasted a big smile on her face and settled back in the buggy. "Good-bye, Mr. Rinaldi. I hope you can restore Cottonwood to what it was before the war."

He regarded her with a somber gaze. "I'll do everything in my power to make it something you'd be proud of. I promise you that."

The seat beside her sagged as Jasper sank down next to her. Turning to him, she blinked back the tears threatening to flood her eyes. "Let's go home, Jasper. We have lots to do before we leave."

Jasper snapped the reins, and the buggy moved out into the road. Savannah looked over her shoulder once. Dante Rinaldi sat on his horse staring after them. Her eyes grew wide at the sudden truth that struck her—she was going to miss him.

His words pounded in her ears. He promised he was going to make Cottonwood something she would be proud of, but she wouldn't be here to see it happen. She'd be miles away on the Gulf coast with a family she didn't know. As she'd done ever since she realized Aunt Jane was going to die, Savannah offered up a prayer.

Oh God, if there's any way possible to keep me from leaving the only place I've ever known, I pray You'll show me. If not, help me to accept what my lot will be. I put my future in Your hands.

Her heart felt lighter as she finished the prayer. She didn't know what the future held, but she knew who held her future. The faith she'd learned from her parents told her she would never be alone.

⟡

Dante paced back and forth across the floor of the small cabin where he'd been living since coming to Cottonwood. From time to time, he stopped and stared into the small fire he'd built. He didn't know if the chill he felt was from cool, evening air blowing off the river or if it was caused by the turmoil within him.

Savannah was leaving in a few days, and he would never see her again. From the first moment he saw her, he hadn't been able to get her out of his mind. He'd told himself he was being silly. She hated him because she felt he had stolen her land, but that did nothing to quell the thoughts of her that ran through his head.

He began to pace again. It made no difference. He knew what was wrong with him. He was in love for the first time in his life, and it was killing him. He'd tried to lose himself in work on the plantation, but it didn't help. Every night he lay awake in this cabin, unable to shake his thoughts of Savannah.

Now she was leaving, and he was helpless to stop her.

A knock at the door startled him, and he strode across the floor. Jerking the door open, he smiled when he saw Saul and Mamie standing on the small porch. Saul pointed to the pot Mamie held. "We brung you some food, Mistuh Dante. You didn't come for supper."

He glanced at the dark sky and realized the sun had set while he was agonizing over his thoughts. He held the door open wider. "I'm sorry. That wasn't very courteous of me to ignore Mamie's fine cooking. Please forgive me."

Mamie giggled. "Land's sake, Mistuh Dante. You sho' got a way with words. Hit ain't no trouble for us to brang this here food over to you." She set a pot on the table in the middle of the cabin. "Abraham kilt some rabbits today. So we gots good eatin' tonight."

Dante smiled, lifted the top off the pan, and sniffed. "Aw, that smells good. And you've brought me some of your good biscuits, too."

She nodded. "Thanks to you, I kin make them biscuits. We ain't seen no flour 'round here in a long time till you buy Cottonwood."

Dante motioned for them to sit. "Want to keep me company while I eat?"

Saul eyed the chairs with a skeptical look. "You wants us to sit at the table with you? That don't seem right proper, Mistuh Dante."

Dante chuckled. "And why not? I sit in your house when I eat with you. You can do the same in my house."

Saul shook his head and slipped into his seat. Mamie had already sat down at the table and was dishing out the rabbit and biscuits on a plate. "Here you goes. Now you eat up whilst we sit here and talk."

Dante's stomach growled from the aroma of the food. With a laugh, he sat down and began to devour what Mamie had brought. With the first bites, he nodded in Mamie's direction. "You're a good cook, Mamie. If I ever have a wife, you're going to have to teach her all you know."

Mamie ducked her head and grinned. A shy expression covered her face. "All I know 'bout cookin' I learnt in the kitchen at Cottonwood. Mistuh Vance and Miss Amelia used to say nobody on Cottonwood could cook like Mamie. Yas suh, that's what they said."

The mention of Savannah's parents reminded him of why he'd missed the evening meal. He laid down his fork. "I went to the funeral of Miss Carmichael's aunt today."

Saul's eyebrows arched. "How Miss 'Vanna makin' it?"

Dante shrugged. "She looked tired, but she's had a lot to contend with in the past few weeks."

Mamie leaned forward. "What she gwine do now that her aunt done died? She gwine live in that house by herself?"

Dante picked up the fork and stabbed at a piece of meat. "No. She's leaving Willow Bend."

Saul jumped to his feet, and his chair tipped back and hit the floor with a thump. "Leavin'? Where she goin'?"

"She's moving to Mobile to be a governess for a family there. She plans to board the *Montgomery Belle* when it goes back downriver next week."

Wringing her hands, Mamie stood next to her husband. "Oh, this bad.

Miss 'Vanna havin' to leave home. It just ain't right. She belongs here with us." She turned to Dante. "Ain't there somethin' you can do to make her stay?"

Dante couldn't tell Mamie that was all he'd thought about since he'd been back from the funeral. "I don't know anything I could do."

Mamie glanced up at Saul and then toward Dante. "But it just ain't right. Me and Saul think Miss 'Vanna ought to be here."

Saul grabbed his wife's arm. "Hush up, Mamie. This ain't none a' our business."

She shook her arm free. "Then whose business is it? We done saved that girl's life the night the big house burn, and we promised her we'd stay here and take care of things till she came back."

Saul shook his head. "That all changed when Mistuh Dante bought this here place."

Mamie propped her hands on her hips and frowned. "You men can't see nothin'. The day Mistuh Dante come here, I see the Lawd makin' a way for Miss 'Vanna to come home."

"What are you talking about, Mamie?" Dante asked.

Saul's eyes grew big, and he tried to steer his wife toward the door. "Don't matter. We goin' to our cabin." He glanced down at Mamie. "We can't go tellin' no white man what he ought to do. You forgettin' your place."

Dante stepped in front of them. "I thought you realized we are all equal here, Saul. If Mamie has something to say, I want to hear what it is."

Mamie straightened to her full height and sniffed. "I jest see the way you look ev'ry time you talk 'bout Miss 'Vanna. It not hard to figure out you done got struck on that girl. If you are, then you got no business lettin' her go downriver. You got to stop her and bring her home to Cottonwood."

Dante spread his hands in amazement. "And how do I do that?"

Mamie smiled. "You a smart man. You kin figure it out." She turned to Saul. "Now I 'spects we can go. Mistuh Dante gots lots of thinkin' to do."

Before he could stop them, the pair disappeared out the door, leaving him to wonder what Mamie had been insinuating. She'd said he was struck on Savannah. *Struck* was hardly the word for what he felt. He loved her with all his heart.

What could he do to bring her back to Cottonwood? She would never agree to accept his charity and live on his land. She wanted the land to belong to her again, but she had no money to purchase it. She also wanted it to pass on to her heirs. How could that be? The land would pass to his heirs.

Understanding flashed into his mind, and he sank down in the chair at the table. The only way she could have the land would be if they shared it. And it could only pass to her heirs if they shared them also.

Marriage? To him?

He shook his head and bolted to his feet. She would never agree to that. She despised him. She considered him her enemy, a person who'd stolen what she thought was rightfully hers.

Yet a marriage between the two of them made sense. Sharing Cottonwood was a small price to pay for having the woman he loved as his wife. And having a child to pass the land to would be the fulfillment of a dream he'd had for years. He would go to her tomorrow and ask her.

He covered his face with his hands and groaned. What could he say that would make her accept him as a husband?

Dante dropped to his knees beside his chair and closed his eyes. "Dear God, You know my heart. I pray You'll give me the right words as I talk with Savannah. Be with me, and give me strength as I face this crucial point in my life. Amen."

Dante rose. Almost immediately he knew what he would say to her. He'd propose a business deal. She needed a home, and she wanted Cottonwood back. He needed a wife who was respected by the community and could help him become accepted by the residents in the closed society of Willow Bend. If they married, their children would inherit the land that had been in her family for years. They both stood to gain a lot from the proposition.

Dante clapped his hands and laughed. Maybe she would say yes. He could hardly wait to find out.

Chapter 7

Savannah swallowed the last bite of her noon meal and glanced around the sparsely furnished dining room. Aunt Jane's survival since the war had depended on the money she'd received from the sale of her house and on selling off her possessions one at a time. However, there were still many items, including furniture and personal belongings, that had to go.

Savannah touched the linen tablecloth that had been one of Aunt Jane's favorites. Even when their money had dwindled to a dangerous low, it was something Aunt Jane hadn't been able to bring herself to sell. It had belonged to Savannah's grandmother, and Aunt Jane had wanted Savannah to have it when she married.

It didn't look as if that would ever happen. Her life seemed set. She would probably serve a family as governess until their children no longer needed her, then she would go to another. And so her life would be until one day she was so old that no one wanted her. Then where would she end up?

The thought sent a chill through her, and she buried her face in her hands. She had to quit thinking like this. God would take care of her. She knew that, but sometimes it was so hard to trust when the future seemed so bleak.

Sighing, she stood and walked toward the kitchen. Jasper turned from stoking the fire in the iron cookstove as she entered. A frown pulled at his face. "Miss 'Vanna, what we gwine do with all this here stuff?"

She shook her head. "I don't know, Jasper. Maybe Mr. Perkins at the store will take some of it against our account there. The eggs and butter we've sold haven't paid all of it in months."

He nodded. "Yas'm. And that reminds me. What we gwine do 'bout them chickens and the cow?"

A feeling of helplessness washed over her, and she closed her eyes. Her head hurt from all the questions that had run through her mind in the last weeks. Now she only had a few days before the *Montgomery Belle* would be back. She had to find an answer to all her problems, but she had no idea what it was.

God, she prayed, *what am I to do?*

Her eyes widened as the answer came to her, and she smiled. "I think I know what we might do with the chickens and the cow." She turned and started from the room but called over her shoulder, "Jasper, hitch the horse to the buggy.

I'm going to Cottonwood. Maybe Saul and Mamie can use them since they're going to have some land of their own."

She rushed to the stairs and hurried up to her bedroom. Once in the room, she threw open the door of the big armoire that had also belonged to her grandmother. She reached for the shawl that hung on a peg but stopped.

Running her hands down the front of her simple day dress, she spied a smudge from taking out the ashes earlier in the day. She'd have to change clothes just in case she ran into the new owner of Cottonwood.

Savannah shook her head. Why was she worrying about making a good impression on Dante Rinaldi? He'd be in the fields today, and she wouldn't even see him.

Just in case, though, she reached for the blue dress with its draped skirt and ruffled jacket. They'd had to sell a lot of eggs and butter to pay for the material, but Aunt Jane had insisted that Savannah needed one fashionable dress.

Savannah pulled the dress from the armoire and crushed it against her. She'd worn this garment to Aunt Jane's funeral. Now she was going to Cottonwood in hopes of giving away some of Aunt Jane's property. If only she were going home!

She squared her shoulders and held the dress in front of her. "Quit bawling, Savannah Carmichael. God's going to take care of you. Now act like you believe it."

New resolve flowed through her. There were many things to settle before she could leave Willow Bend. One of the hardest would be to leave her parents' graves behind. Before she could say good-bye to Saul and Mamie, she had to bid her parents farewell.

Her hands tightened on the dress she held, and she buried her face in the soft material. She hoped she wouldn't see Dante Rinaldi today. Her heart told her saying good-bye to him was going to be more difficult than she'd realized.

<hr>

Dante trudged along the path that led from the large canebrake to the river. He'd gone alone today to that field and sent the men in other directions. He needed time alone to think and pray, although he'd done that nearly all last night. Sleep had refused to come, and he'd sat in front of the fireplace and pondered how he'd present his plan to Savannah Carmichael.

Dante ran his hand through his hair. Whatever made him come up with such an idea? All she was going to do was laugh at him and make him feel foolish. A sinking feeling hit him in the pit of his stomach. He could envision his father and mother, so in love after years of marriage. That's what he'd always wanted, but he wouldn't have that even if Savannah accepted his proposal.

He clenched his fists at his sides and shook his head. He was crazy to ever think he could ask her to marry him. The best thing for him to do was turn around and go back to the canebrake. Labor in that jungle of cane would drive any thoughts of the beautiful woman from his mind.

He turned to retrace his steps, but he couldn't move. It was as if some invisible hand gripped his shoulder and spun him around then nudged him forward. He remembered something else his father had once told him. *"When you think something is impossible, try it anyway."*

Dante took a deep breath. He had to try the impossible even if he regretted it later. Letting Savannah go without at least asking her would be the biggest mistake of his life.

With a new determination, he strode forward and rounded the corner to the path that led by the small cemetery. His eyes grew wide, and he came to a halt. He couldn't believe what he saw. Savannah's buggy sat in front of the cemetery gate.

Swallowing, he eased forward until he could see her. She knelt between her parents' graves, her head bowed and her lips moving in silent conversation.

His glance traveled over her. She had on the dress she'd worn to her aunt's funeral. The vision of how she'd looked in it had haunted him.

Dante stopped at the fence but didn't enter. He waited until she stood before he spoke. "Good afternoon, Miss Carmichael."

Her body stiffened, and she turned to face him. "Mr. Rinaldi. I didn't hear you approach."

"I've been in the canebrake and was on my way back home."

She walked forward and stopped inside the fence. "I came to Cottonwood to say good-bye to my parents and take care of some more business."

His eyebrows arched. "Some business? Is it anything I can help you with?"

She shook her head. "No. I'm trying to dispose of Aunt Jane's property before I leave. I thought Saul and Mamie might like to have our cow and chickens."

"That's very kind of you to think of them."

Her gaze didn't waver from his face. "Saul and Mamie are like my family. I've known them all my life." She looked up into the sky. "It's getting late. I'd better go see Mamie."

He opened the gate. "Then allow me to drive you."

"Thank you."

Dante reached out and took her arm as he assisted her into the buggy. Then he untied the reins, walked around, and climbed in beside her. Without speaking, he turned the horse and guided it back along the river.

When they approached the charred rubble of the big house, Savannah touched his arm. "Would you please stop? I want to look at it for the last time."

His heart thudded as her gaze raked the burned piles of ashes that had once been a grand house. "I saw the house the first time from a riverboat. There was a young girl on the balcony of the second floor. She waved as we passed."

Savannah smiled. "It had to be me. I used to stand out there and watch the riverboats. I knew them all." She glanced at him. "I can still tell their whistles apart."

He tightened his hands on the reins. "I'm sorry the house burned. That must have been very difficult for you."

She nodded. "I still don't know what woke me that night. I remember sitting up in bed and seeing what appeared to be slivers of moonlight dancing across my bedroom floor. But there was a glow I didn't understand. I jumped out of bed and stood in the middle of the room, trying to figure out what had awakened me."

"You must have heard the fire crackling."

"I suppose so." She hesitated a moment and then continued. "Then I felt the heat and saw the smoke. It looked like giant, licking tongues creeping underneath my bedroom door and crawling toward me. The floor was so hot that my feet burned, and I ran onto the balcony."

"What about your parents?"

Tears glimmered in her eyes. "I called them over and over, but there was no answer. The orange flames leaped from their bedroom window, and I knew I had to escape. I climbed onto the iron balustrade and screamed at the searing pain on the bottoms of my feet. I grabbed one of the hot columns and shinnied down. Saul and Mamie, along with a few former slaves who were still living in the cabins, waited at the base and helped me to the ground."

His throat constricted at the pain in her face. "But you survived."

She nodded. "Saul picked me up and carried me to their cabin, where Mamie tended my burns. The fire was so bright that it was seen all up and down the river. Some of the neighbors arrived and tried to save some part of the big house, but it was no use. In the morning, all that was left were the eight columns that still stood facing the river. Then Aunt Jane and Jasper arrived, and I left Cottonwood and all its memories behind." She glanced at him. "Do you mind if I walk around a bit for the last time?"

"Of course not," he croaked.

He climbed from the buggy and helped her down. She walked across the lawn and stopped between two of the still-standing columns. Gently she laid her hand against one of the smoke-stained pillars. Her head drooped, and his heart constricted at the horror she had faced the night of the fire.

A voice in his head whispered that this was the time for him to tell her what he'd been thinking. He tried to follow her, but his feet felt rooted to the ground.

She straightened and stared into the ruins for a moment. "After the fire, the few slaves who'd stayed on left, too, but Saul and Mamie wouldn't go. Not even after I left." She turned to him, and a tear trickled down her cheek. "Promise me that someday a house will stand on this spot."

Unable to stand seeing her in pain any longer, he forced his feet to move. He stopped behind her. "I promise." He took a deep breath. "Miss Carmichael, there's something I'd like to talk to you about."

She wiped at her eyes. "What is it?"

A declaration of how much he loved her hovered on the tip of his tongue, but he knew to utter it would be a terrible mistake. He had to make his proposition appeal to her, and love from an Italian that she equated with a carpetbagger wouldn't do.

He cleared his throat. "I know a way you can stay in Willow Bend."

She shook her head. "No, Mr. Rinaldi. I have nothing in Willow Bend to keep me there."

Perspiration popped out on his head. "I didn't make myself clear. I'm not talking about the town of Willow Bend. I'm talking about Cottonwood."

Her eyebrows drew down into a frown. "I don't understand."

He ignored the trickle of sweat that ran down his cheek. "I know you love Cottonwood and you blame me for taking it away from you. But let me ask you this: How far would you go to get Cottonwood back?"

Her eyes narrowed. "That's a question that has no answer, because I don't have any money, and I would do nothing illegal to regain my home."

He raked his hand through his hair. He was saying this all wrong. "I don't mean anything against the law. Would you be willing to enter into a business proposition if you could regain Cottonwood?"

Savannah sighed. "Get to the point, Mr. Rinaldi. I have no idea what you're talking about."

"All right, I will. But please hear me out before you answer. I've been thinking about your predicament. Your life has taken a sad turn since the war ended. Your father let Cottonwood fail, and you were unable to stop the tax collectors. Now you're going off to work as a governess." He stepped closer. "You aren't the kind of woman who works for another family. You belong here on the land your family farmed."

"And how do I do that?"

He took a deep breath. "By marrying me."

Her mouth gaped open, and her eyes grew wide. She staggered back a step from him. "Marry you? Have you lost your mind?"

He shook his head. "I told you to hear me out. If you became my wife, the land would in essence be yours again. You could run our home and help manage the tenant farmers and whatever else you wanted to do. I would never refer to it again as my land."

A look of disbelief covered her face. "I can't believe you're serious."

"I assure you I am."

She turned away for a moment and then faced him. "And just what do you get out of this business deal?"

"I find I'm an outsider in the community. I want to be accepted by other families, and by marrying you, I figure I have a way of making that happen. Besides, I need a wife because I want Cottonwood to pass to my children, too."

"This is insane," she whispered. "We don't love each other."

Her words sliced his heart like a knife. "You may not love me, but you love the land. Why not marry me to get it back?"

She studied him for a moment. "That's a good point, Mr. Rinaldi. There is one more thing, though. What about Jasper?"

Dante shrugged. "Jasper can come to Cottonwood, too, if he wants. There's always room for one more. And if you agree to marry me, I'll have Saul and the other tenant farmers help me move everything from your aunt's house here. We can store her things until I get a better house built for you."

Tears puddled in her eyes. "I wouldn't have to sell Aunt Jane's possessions, Jasper can come to Cottonwood, and I'll have my land back. You'll do all that just to be accepted by a community of snobs who are still fighting the war?"

He longed to tell her that he would do it all and more just for her. "Yes, and who knows. We may come to love each other, but even if you never love me, I hope you can respect me as a person."

She turned, took a few steps, and stood unmoving. After a moment, her tense body relaxed, and she faced him. "This is all so sudden. I—I don't know what to say."

He tried to ignore the hope that burned in his heart. "If you need more time, I'll understand. This is a big decision. The question you must answer is what do you want: to be a governess in Mobile or to be the mistress of your family's land."

Her lips parted, and she exhaled. "When you put it that way, Mr. Rinaldi, there's only one choice. I accept your proposal."

The breath left his body as if he'd been kicked in the stomach. He'd been prepared for her to scream how crazy he was for thinking she would even consider marriage with such a ridiculous Italian as he. Instead, she uttered the words that made him the happiest he'd ever been. He struggled to keep his excitement from showing.

"Thank you for doing me the honor of becoming my wife. I promise I will take care of you. I don't want you to suffer any more hurts like the past."

She smiled. "Beneath your rough exterior, Mr. Rinaldi, I think there is a very kind person. Thank you for bringing me home."

He swallowed at the sincerity in her voice. "When would you like to have the ceremony?"

"How about tomorrow?"

Dante gasped. "So soon? But I don't have a place for you to stay yet. I'm living in one of the slave quarters. You can't stay there."

"If it's on Cottonwood's land, I can stay anywhere. I'll go back to town and talk with Reverend Somers about performing the ceremony tomorrow afternoon. If it's all right with you, we can stay at Aunt Jane's tomorrow night and start moving my things the next day." She stopped and frowned. "Unless you'd rather wait."

He shook his head. "No, no. It just surprised me that you would want to do it so quickly."

"I want to do this before I have time to convince myself this is all wrong. I've been obsessed with coming back home. The sooner I'm here, the better."

"Then I will go to your aunt's house in the early afternoon tomorrow and escort you to the church."

She nodded. "Will you bring anyone with you to witness the marriage?"

He searched his mind. He knew no one except the people at Cottonwood. "I suppose I could bring one of the tenant farmers."

"Don't worry about it. I'll ask Mrs. Somers and my friend Sarah Morgan. That should be enough." She reached for the reins. "I suppose that's all we need to discuss. I shall expect you tomorrow then."

He nodded, still unable to believe what had just happened. "I'll be there."

Dante watched until her buggy disappeared from view before he turned and hurried toward his cabin. His feet almost skimmed the surface of the ground. All day he'd been telling himself he was being foolish to even think about asking Savannah Carmichael to marry him. But she had said yes.

He ran onto the porch of his cabin and burst through the door. Inside he stopped and looked around at the place where he would bring her. It wasn't what he wanted for her, but for now, it was the best he could do.

Take one step at a time—that's what he had to do. First, he had to make her his wife, and then everything else would fall into place. They could have a good life together, even if she didn't love him. He could be happy just having her near.

⚬⚬⚬

Savannah's mind raced as she rode back to town. What would her friends think when they heard she had married the man who bought Cottonwood? No doubt many of them would denounce her for joining herself to an outsider and accuse her of doing wrong.

Right now she couldn't think about right and wrong. All she knew was that the man whose dark eyes made her heart race had given her a chance to come home, and that's what she wanted.

Dante was handsome and a hard worker. He was also kind. She'd seen that the first day they met, although she hadn't wanted to acknowledge it then. His attention to Aunt Jane over the past month had shown her his gentle nature. Yes, she could do a lot worse in a husband. But the good thing about the whole arrangement was she'd be back at Cottonwood.

It would be different. She wouldn't be Savannah Carmichael anymore. She would have the strange name of Rinaldi. A smile curled her lips. Savannah Rinaldi. She liked the sound of it.

Chapter 8

Savannah, we're back at your aunt's house."

The soft voice penetrated the silence that had hung over her and Dante on their return from the church. While she'd been lost in thought, Dante had climbed from the buggy and waited to assist her.

She stared at Dante. Was he really her husband? Perhaps the last hour had been a dream. Her gaze traveled to the gold band that circled the fourth finger of her left hand.

"It was my mother's."

Savannah frowned and glanced at Dante. "What?"

He cleared his throat. "The ring. It was my mother's. After she died, I knew I wanted my wife to wear it someday."

She flinched at the strange sensation stirring within her. "And now it's mine."

"Yes." The word was little more than a whisper.

This was no dream. Everything had changed with her visit to Cottonwood yesterday. *"For better or worse,"* Reverend Somers had said, and now they were joined for life.

Savannah swallowed the fear that knotted her stomach and tried to smile. "I will try to be worthy of wearing your mother's ring."

"I'm sure you will." He held out his hand again. "Now are you ready to go inside? I imagine there's a lot to do before Saul and the men come from Cottonwood tomorrow."

She slipped her hand into his and stepped to the ground. The pressure of his fingers on hers tightened, but she pulled away once she stood next to him. "Thank you."

"I'll put the horse away and then come inside."

Before she could protest that Jasper liked to see to the horse himself, the man appeared from around the corner of the house. His mouth pulled into a big smile when he saw them. He stopped next to the horse and rested his hand on the mare's back. "Miss 'Vanna, Mistuh Dante, you done got married already?"

"Yes." They spoke at the same time.

"I bet that cer'mony was somethin' to see. Miss 'Vanna, you a purty bride."

Dante nodded. "That she is."

His words surprised her. Did he mean it, or was he just being courteous?

Savannah bit her lip and looked at the ground. Her face burned. How was she supposed to act? A glance at him told her he probably felt the same way.

One's wedding day was supposed to be one of the happiest days of one's life, but hers had been forged out of a need for acceptance in the community and a desire for land. All the time Reverend Somers was reading the words, her mind had whirled with one question: How could this ever work? They were too different. She had grown up in a gentle society that believed life would go on forever in the South as it had for years. The war had put an end to that notion.

He, on the other hand, had been raised in a family who came from a foreign land and worked hard to make a new life in America. Dante had bought Cottonwood with the fruits of their long hours of labor. All he knew was work. At least they had that in common.

She looked back at Jasper, who seemed to be waiting for her to answer. "Yes, Jasper, it was a very nice ceremony." She took a deep breath. "Dante said he'd take care of the horse."

Jasper shook his head and untied the reins from the hitching post. "No'm. I'll do it. It just rightly seems my job."

Savannah regarded the man she'd known since childhood. Her heart lurched at the thought of Aunt Jane and how she would react to what was happening to both her and Jasper now. "Jasper, I wish you would reconsider and come to Cottonwood with us."

Jasper took off the hat he wore and wiped at the sweat on his brow. "I been free a long time, Miss 'Vanna. Miss Jane done give me my freedom a long time 'fore the war and tole me I could go anywhere I wanted, but I jest didn't want to leave home. But now she gone, and Mistuh Dante gwine take care of you. So I reckon it's time."

"But where will you go? What will you do?"

Jasper stared past her, and his eyes held a faraway look as if he were envisioning sights he'd never encountered. "I always had me a hankerin' to see the ocean 'fore I die. So I guess I'll get on the *Belle* when Captain Hawkins comes back, and I'll go on down to Mobile."

Tears welled in her eyes. "I'll worry about you."

Jasper chuckled. "I be all right."

"Well then, I'll give you what little money I have. I've saved up some from the eggs and butter we've sold."

Jasper shook his head. "Ain't no need for that. Mistuh Dante done give me money."

The words shocked her, and she turned to stare at Dante, who had remained silent during her exchange with Jasper. "When did you do that?"

Dante's face flushed. "I talked to Jasper when I came to take you to the church. I asked him to come to Cottonwood with us, but he told me about his plans. So I gave him some money."

Savannah stared at the man she had just married. When she'd first met him, she had thought she hated him and was sure he would always be her enemy. In the weeks since, she had come to see kindness in him. She wondered what other surprises awaited her as she got to know her husband even better.

"That was very kind of you, Dante. I appreciate all you've done for those I love."

He smiled and turned back to Jasper. "I hope you get to see the ocean, Jasper, but if things don't go the way you want, remember you always have a home at Cottonwood."

Jasper clutched his hat to his chest and nodded. "Thank you, Mistuh Dante."

Dante took a deep breath and grasped her arm. "Now, my dear, are you ready to go inside?"

Her skin tingled at his touch, and she pulled away. "Yes."

On the porch, she fumbled with the door latch, and he reached around her to open it. "Allow me."

"Thank you."

They stepped into the entry, and Savannah headed to the parlor. Once inside, she stopped in the middle of the room in confusion. Should she sit or stand? If she sat on the sofa, he might sit next to her, and she didn't want to be that near him right now. Unsure of what to do, she waited until he entered. Then she turned to face him. His eyes clouded, and he stopped in front of her.

"I know a lot has happened since yesterday, and you may be wondering why you ever agreed to my proposal. But however you feel about me, I want you to know one thing." He paused. "Savannah, you don't have to be afraid of me."

She tried to laugh, but the sound stuck in her throat. "A—afraid?"

He tilted his head. "Don't look at me like you're a rabbit that the dogs have cornered. This isn't going to be easy for either of us, but we need to come to some kind of understanding right now."

She backed away from him. "What kind of understanding?"

He took a deep breath. "I will never force you to do anything that makes you uncomfortable. Do you understand?"

Her face burned, but she forced herself to meet his gaze. "Yes."

"The cabin is small. Right now there is only one bedroom. I've been sleeping there, but I will let you have the bed."

Her eyes grew wide. "But where will you sleep?"

"In the main room on the floor." He chuckled. "I've slept in worse places in my life, and a pallet on the floor by a fire doesn't sound all that bad to me."

She nodded. "You're very kind to respect my feelings, and I appreciate it."

He took a step toward her. "We both grew up with parents who loved each other. We may not have what our parents had between them, but we have something else."

"What?"

"We saw how they respected and treated each other. I promise that I will respect you and be kind to you. I will always protect you and see that your needs are met. And when the time comes that you feel comfortable with me being your husband in every way, don't be afraid to tell me. After all, we both want an heir."

The sincerity in his face told her he meant what he said. Peace flowed through her troubled mind and replaced the uneasiness she'd felt moments ago. Perhaps her life with Dante was going to be all right after all.

"Thank you, Dante. I promise that I will respect you. And thank you for giving me some time to adjust to being your wife. I will also do everything I can to make you accepted by the community."

He smiled. "Then I would say we're starting our marriage with more than many couples have."

She nodded. "I suppose we are."

His gaze raked her face and lingered on her lips. He moved closer, and she tilted her face up and closed her eyes. Her heart thudded as she awaited his kiss.

Disappointment flowed through her at the touch of his lips grazing her cheek. "I'm honored to have you as my wife."

She opened her eyes and stared up into his face. Before she could speak, the front door burst open, and footsteps pounded across the hallway.

"Savannah! Where are you?" Jonathan's angry voice pierced her ears.

She stepped around Dante as Jonathan rushed into the room. He cast a look of pure hatred in Dante's direction before he grabbed Savannah by the shoulders. "Tell me it's not true!"

Savannah tried to pull away from him, but Jonathan held her fast. "Jonathan, what's the matter?"

"Tell me you didn't marry this foreigner," he yelled.

Savannah wriggled in his grasp, but his hands clamped down harder. "Jonathan, let me go."

"No! You can't do this to me."

Dante appeared at her side and grabbed Jonathan's arm. She glanced around and quaked at the dark anger lining Dante's face. "Take your hands off my wife," he muttered.

Jonathan let go, and Dante stepped in front of her. His hands were clenched at his sides, and his tense body told Savannah he was ready to strike out. She moved to Dante's side and faced Jonathan.

"It's true, Jonathan. Dante and I were married this afternoon. I'm sorry I didn't tell you, but it all happened so quickly."

Jonathan shook his head as if he couldn't believe what he was hearing. His body sagged, and he regarded her with stricken eyes. "Why, Savannah? How could you have done such a thing?"

"I know what I'm doing. Dante has offered me a home at Cottonwood, and I agreed."

Jonathan's face hardened as if a mask covered it. The hatred he'd directed at Dante when he entered now focused on her. "So you betrayed your parents for a piece of land."

She shrank away from him. "My parents? What do you mean?"

He leaned toward her, but he glanced at Dante and straightened. "You know your father meant for me to have that land, but you've taken it away from me by marrying this carpetbagger."

Next to her, Dante shook with rage. "Now listen to me—"

She laid her hand on his arm. "No, Dante. Let me handle this." She faced Jonathan. "Whatever our parents planned for us was a long time ago. You know there was no way Cottonwood was ever going to be mine again. I had no money, just like everyone else around here. I'm sorry if you think I've betrayed you, but you never offered me any options. Thanks to Dante, I have a home again."

"You could have had a home at Oak Hill."

She reached out and touched Jonathan's arm. "It doesn't matter now. I'm married to Dante."

Jonathan shook free of her grasp. Backing away, he pointed his finger at them. "This isn't over. You've made me a laughingstock in front of all our friends. You'll be sorry."

He whirled and ran from the room. Savannah hurried after him. "Jonathan, come back here."

By the time she got to the front door, he was already on his horse and galloping away. Tears stood in her eyes as she remembered the boy she'd known all her life. The angry man she'd just encountered wasn't the same person. But then, most of the people she knew were different. The war had taken its toll on all of them.

She felt Dante's presence behind her. "I'm sorry about your friend, Savannah."

"It doesn't matter. I don't know Jonathan anymore."

She wiped at the corner of her eye before she closed the door and turned around. He stared at her, and she let her gaze drop to the floor. "I suppose I should get supper started, but I need to change clothes first. Why don't you and Jasper look at the tools in Aunt Jane's smokehouse? You can decide what you want to take with us."

"All right." He pointed to the small valise he'd left sitting in the hallway before they went to the church. "I'll need to change also. Where should I do that?"

She glanced toward the stairs. "My bedroom is to the right at the top of the landing. Go on and get settled in there. I'll change after you're through."

His shoulders sagged as he mounted the stairs, and she wondered if Jonathan's anger had caused Dante to have second thoughts about marrying her. She raised her left hand and gazed at the gold band once more. If he was having second thoughts, it was too late now.

The enormity of what she'd done hit her, and her eyes widened. It was one thing to talk about marrying Dante so she could go home. It was quite different when she remembered the vows made before God.

She glanced up the stairs. Dante had stopped halfway up and was studying her as she stared at his mother's ring. A frown wrinkled his brow before he inhaled and continued to the second floor. Savannah let her hand drop to her side and stared at him until he disappeared into her bedroom.

Dante's words about her not being afraid of him flashed through her mind, and the truth hit her like a kick in the stomach. She feared Dante less than anyone she'd ever known. Peace flowed into her heart, and she smiled. Working together, they might be able to return Cottonwood to what it had once been, but they might also be able to build a good life.

❧

Dante set the valise on the floor in Savannah's bedroom and looked around. The quilt on the bed looked worn, but he could tell it had once been an elegant coverlet. The curtains at the window also appeared to have been in use for a long time. The house's furnishings reflected the lifestyle of a bygone era—both frayed and tattered by a war that tore a nation apart.

A walnut dresser with Savannah's personal items on top sat against one wall. He gazed at the brush with a tarnished silver handle. Golden hair clung to the bristles. He picked it up and turned it slowly in his hand.

His heart had almost stopped when Jonathan told her she could have had a home at Oak Hill. If Jonathan had spoken earlier, Savannah might very well have married him. Dante gripped the brush tighter. Savannah was his wife now, and he was going to do everything in his power to make her happy.

She might never love him, but perhaps she could become content to live with him at Cottonwood. Only time would tell.

Chapter 9

Savannah could hardly believe that nearly four months had passed since her marriage, but all she had to do was look at the world around her to see the passing of time. Summer green had turned to autumn, which gave way to winter. The scarlet leaves of the dogwoods that lined the edge of Cottonwood's forests now lay mingled on the woodland floor with the brilliant gold from the hickory trees she loved. Most days woodpeckers could be heard hammering at the hardwoods, but there was only silence today. Maybe they were resting, too, on the Sabbath.

A chilling breeze rustled the bare limbs of the trees on either side of the road. Savannah pulled her coat tighter against the cold morning air and snuggled back into the buggy's seat. Beside her, Dante guided the horse along the bumpy road that led to Willow Bend.

Savannah glanced at her handsome husband and pulled the buggy robe over her legs.

Dante gripped the reins with one hand and reached over to tuck the heavy covering more securely around her. "Is that better?" The slight smile she'd come to know in the months since their marriage played at his lips.

She nodded. "Yes. Thank you."

He turned his attention back to the horse and took a deep breath. "I love crisp mornings like this. When January comes, I know it won't be long until we can be in the fields and getting ready for planting."

"I know."

In the days since their marriage, they had developed a comfortable relationship. Most of their conversations centered on the land, spring planting, and the new house they would have before next fall, but that hadn't been a bad thing. All in all, she and Dante had gotten off to a good start. He and the men worked hard all day, and he came home exhausted at night. No matter how tired he was, he always had time to listen to her day's activities. Sometimes when she talked, his penetrating gaze would bore into her and take her breath away.

It was times like that when she dreamed of romance. She supposed every girl wanted to be swept off her feet, but for her it hadn't been that way. Now as she got to know Dante better, she had begun to wish for something more in their relationship.

She sensed he was watching her, and she turned to meet his gaze. "What are you looking at in the woods?" he asked.

"Nothing really, and then again everything." She laughed at the absurdity of her remark. "I'm remembering the beautiful colors of fall that are gone and enjoying the winter landscape." She pointed to the forest. "I thought the color of the leaves this year was the most beautiful I'd ever seen."

He smiled and flicked the reins across the horse's back. "Maybe next year you'll walk with me and show me your favorite spots."

Savannah's heart thudded, and she looked at him. Her mouth felt like cotton. She tried to answer, but the words wouldn't come. Before she could recover, the churchyard with buggies and wagons scattered about came into view.

She straightened in her seat. "It doesn't look like a very big crowd today."

Dante guided the horse into the churchyard and pulled to a stop. He jumped down, tied the reins to a tree, and walked around to face her. Extending his hand, he smiled. "Let's see if the local residents are any happier to see me today than they've been in the past."

She gripped his hand and stepped to the ground. "I've told you to be patient. I thought last Sunday several more people spoke to you."

He chuckled. "I suppose you can say that. I thought I never would get away from Martha Thompson, but I had the feeling her conversation was more to find out something she could repeat to the townspeople the next day."

Savannah laughed. "I think you're probably right, but I—"

A loud voice rang out, "Savannah!"

She and Dante spied Jonathan Boyer at the same moment. Dante tensed as Jonathan pulled his horse to a stop in front of them. Jonathan glared at Dante.

"Jonathan," she said, "I'm glad to see you've finally come to church."

He shook his head and climbed down from the horse. "I'm not here for services. I wanted to see you."

Dante stepped closer to Savannah. "I hope you know you're welcome to visit Savannah anytime at Cottonwood, Mr. Boyer."

Jonathan's lip curled into a sneer. "As if I'd set foot on ground you stole."

Dante's fists clenched, and he sucked in his breath. Savannah laid a restraining hand on her husband's arm. "Please, Dante, let's not have a scene in the churchyard. Why don't you go on inside? I'll be right along."

He stared at her. "I don't think you need to talk to him. I don't trust him."

She waved her hand in dismissal. "Don't be ridiculous. I've known Jonathan all my life. I'm perfectly safe with him."

Dante hesitated for a moment before he bit his lip and nodded. "All right. If that's the way you want it."

He whirled around and strode across the yard. Savannah swallowed back the impulse to run after him. He looked as if her words had hurt him, and she didn't want that. She turned back to Jonathan. "Now what do you want?"

Jonathan rubbed the horse's reins that he held. "Savannah, I've been miserable these last few months. I can't believe what has happened to us."

"I'm afraid I don't understand, Jonathan."

He swallowed, and Savannah detected moisture in his eyes. His shoulders slumped. "Please forgive me. I should have helped you more. Ever since the war, I've been so obsessed with getting Oak Hill back to what it was I forgot what our parents wanted. I should have figured out a way to get Cottonwood back."

She reached out and grasped his hand. "You can't blame yourself for what has happened."

"But I do. Even when I knew you were about to leave, I did nothing. I stood back and let another man take what was rightfully mine."

Savannah gasped. "Cottonwood was never yours to have, Jonathan."

He shook his head. "I'm not talking about the plantation. I'm talking about you. I let that man take you away from me, and I did nothing. I should have married you."

Tears came to her eyes, and she wiped at them. "Don't torture yourself like this. It wasn't meant for us to marry. You didn't love me, and I don't love you."

He gritted his teeth and glanced at the church. "And do you love him?"

His question stunned her. She'd barely known Dante when they married, and now she realized he was one of the kindest men she'd ever met. She respected him, but love had never been spoken between them. After four months of marriage, he was still sleeping in the main room, but he'd never complained. Still, she couldn't deny the pleasure she received when his gaze swept over her or the way her heart thudded when she looked into his eyes.

She took a deep breath and spoke. "He's my husband."

Jonathan dropped the horse's reins and grabbed both her arms. "Answer me. Do you love him?"

From behind her, a voice called out, "Take your hands off my wife!"

She turned to see Dante charging across the yard. Jonathan let go of her and tensed. Before he could step around her, she grabbed his arms. "Jonathan, please don't cause any trouble here. Get on your horse and leave before something bad happens." He glanced down at her, and uncertainty lined his face.

"Please go. Now."

He grabbed the reins and swung into the saddle just before Dante reached them. "I'm leaving, but you haven't seen the last of me." He glared at Dante and then Savannah. "I didn't think I'd ever see the day when a Southern woman would turn her back on her people for a yellow coward who wouldn't even fight in the war. You deserve each other."

Jonathan pulled back on the right rein and dug his leg into the horse's right side. The horse turned and galloped away. Savannah watched him disappear. Jonathan had never been the same after the war, but his behavior today bordered on insanity. He was one of the living victims of the war, and she had no idea how to help him.

Fighting back tears, she turned to Dante. "Thank you for coming back."

"I was afraid he was going to hurt you."

She took a deep breath. "Let's go inside. I don't want anybody to know what happened here today."

As they walked beside each other on their way to the church, Savannah was very mindful of her husband's presence. When Jonathan asked her if she loved Dante, she hadn't answered, and she wondered what had kept her from speaking. Could it be that Dante had come to mean more to her than she realized?

When they reached the church entrance, Dante grasped her arm to assist her up the steps. She glanced at him, and the look in his dark eyes sent a ripple of pleasure through her. In his gaze, she detected the unspoken promise that he would always be her protector.

Her heart swelled, and she stepped closer to him. The truth that she'd put out of her mind for the past few months wouldn't be ignored any longer. She didn't know when it had happened, but she had fallen completely in love with her husband.

⌘

Dante could hardly concentrate on the sermon. His mind whirled with what had happened earlier. When Jonathan had grabbed Savannah, Dante thought he would go mad. He couldn't stop himself from charging back.

He had no idea what they had said to each other, but whatever it was, it had upset her. The look on her pale face made his muscles contract. When she'd become his wife, he promised himself he would protect her and take care of her as long as he lived. For him, there would never be another woman. He'd started to tell her many times how he felt, but he still hadn't brought himself to do that. Maybe he would soon.

With a start, he realized that the congregation had stood. He jumped to his feet and joined in the closing hymn. After the "Amen," he grabbed Savannah's arm and steered her from the church before any of the church members could stop them.

When they were in the buggy and on their way home, he could stand it no longer. "Are you going to tell me what Boyer said to you?"

She sighed. "It was just a repeat of past conversations. He feels like he lost what was his."

"Cottonwood?"

"Yes." She paused. "And me."

The words sliced through Dante. "You said your parents had planned for you to marry, but you never said you wanted it."

She sat up straighter. "I didn't. I think Jonathan feels like he lost some kind of battle, and he can't accept it."

"I suppose I'm his enemy for all time."

"I hope not. Jonathan was once a fun-loving young man. He was a wonderful son and brother—and a great friend. The war changed the person I knew."

Dante nodded. "It changed a lot of people."

"Why. . .why. . . ?" She hesitated and cleared her throat.

Dante glanced at Savannah. Her knuckles whitened from her clenched hands on top of the buggy robe. "What were you going to ask?"

She took a deep breath. "Why didn't you fight in the war?"

The memories he'd struggled to erase surged into his mind. "Why do you ask?"

"Because you were the right age to enlist, yet you didn't. How did you get out of going when everybody else was being drafted?"

He took the reins in one hand and rubbed the other over his eyes. "I've never spoken about that to anyone, but maybe it's time I did." He paused for a moment, wondering where to begin. "When I was young, my father worked for a landowner named Thomas Jackson. He had a big plantation near Mobile. He didn't own any slaves, just worked his land with hired men. I helped out, too, and he took a liking to me. In 1855, when I was fourteen, my parents died of yellow fever. I didn't have any family, so Mr. Jackson let me live with him."

"He sounds like a nice man."

"He was. When the war came, I told him I would run away before I stepped on a battlefield and killed men who were trying to free the slaves. He understood my feelings and told me he'd try to help. He knew the people involved in conscripting soldiers, and he begged my case before them. As a favor to him, they agreed to exempt me from serving as a soldier if I would work as a medical helper on the battlefield."

Savannah's eyes grew wide. "What did you do?"

"I agreed. Saving lives instead of taking them seemed the right thing to do."

"Then why do you tell people you didn't serve in the war?"

"Because they ask the question meaning, did I fight? No, I didn't bear arms against another man. But the fight I had was probably as difficult as facing death."

Her forehead wrinkled. "What kind of fight did you have?"

"The doctors, officers, and even some of the wounded didn't like the idea of what they considered a coward helping them. I got the dirtiest jobs in the field hospitals and took the most abuse, but I survived. And now I can face those families living on Cottonwood and know that I didn't fight to keep them enslaved."

"What did you do after the war?"

"I went back to Mr. Jackson and worked for him. He'd kept my money safe, and he paid me a lot more after the war. When he died, his brother inherited the land, but Mr. Jackson left me a large sum of money that helped me to buy Cottonwood."

She sat in thought for a moment before she spoke. "The war changed all our lives, didn't it? I can't imagine what it must have been like for you. I admire you for being true to your beliefs. Thank you for telling me."

He nodded and directed his attention back to the horse. He hadn't ever meant to tell her about that. And he hadn't related how horrible it had been in those battlefield hospitals. He'd never forget all he'd seen.

Perhaps he should have kept those memories to himself. He wanted her to judge him on what he was now, not what he'd been years ago. His story very well could convince her that he was a coward. If she believed that, it would be even worse than what he'd endured on the battlefield.

Chapter 10

Savannah had tried all afternoon to erase the vision of Jonathan's angry face from her mind. She could still see how he'd looked when he called her and Dante his enemies. *He didn't mean it,* she told herself. She'd talk to him soon, and everything would be all right.

When she wasn't thinking about Jonathan, she thought about Dante's revelation about his war experiences. She'd never known another man who had gone to such extremes to stand up for his convictions. When he could have run away or even gone north to fight, he chose to accept a gruesome existence in a battlefield hospital. She could only imagine the horror he'd endured amid the hurt and dying.

Her heart swelled with pride for her husband's actions. If the people of Willow Bend only knew, she was sure they would accept him. However, it was his story, not hers, to tell, and she would never breach his confidence.

The door to the cabin opened, and Dante stepped in. He closed the door, pulled off his gloves, and blew on his hands. "It's getting colder. I wouldn't doubt if it gets down to freezing tonight."

Savannah hurried across the room that served as their combination parlor, kitchen, and dining room and grabbed the back of his coat as he shrugged it from his shoulders. "Freezing? It hardly ever gets that cold here."

She hung his coat on the peg next to the door. When she turned, he was staring at her. "Thank you."

Puzzled, she frowned. "For what?"

"For helping me with my coat."

Her face burned, and she pointed toward the iron cookstove they'd brought from Aunt Jane's house. "I've got a good fire going. Scoot your chair up and get warm while I finish supper."

As he settled in the chair, she turned her attention back to the pots on the stove. "Did you get all the livestock watered?"

"Yes, thanks to Abraham and Joshua. Saul and Mamie have two mighty fine sons. They're some of the best workers I've ever seen."

Savannah replaced the lid on the pot she'd just checked. "They are. Abraham is a little older than me, and Joshua is younger. Mamie used to make us sit while she was scrubbing clothes, and she'd tell us stories. I always thought Abraham was so funny. He loved to laugh and make jokes. I thought he might leave when he got his freedom, but he hasn't."

Dante shrugged. "I think he loves his parents too much to leave. And now there's someone else. A young girl named Hattie. She lives at the Crossroads. Her family hasn't found a place to work yet."

"Maybe they'll find something soon." Dante's face flushed, and she knew it wasn't from the heat of the stove. "What is it? Is there something you haven't told me?"

"Abraham really wants to marry Hattie. So we decided Saul and Mamie's house needed an extra room. He and Hattie can live there for a while. After next year's crop, I think we'll be able to set Abraham up with his own acreage to farm."

Savannah placed her hands on her hips and gazed at her husband. Every day he surprised her with something else he did for the people she'd loved all her life. "You're a kind man, Dante Rinaldi. In the short time I've known you, you've done more for me and those I love than anyone else ever has. Thank you for that."

His gaze raked her face. "I appreciate that, Savannah." He glanced down at his hands and held them out toward the warmth of the stove. "I've been meaning to ask you if you're upset because we're going to build Saul and Mamie's house before ours."

She frowned. "No. Why would you think I'd be upset?"

His gaze traveled around the walls of the small cabin that had once housed slaves. "I know this isn't where you imagined yourself living, and I will build us a better house. But the roof on Saul and Mamie's cabin is the worst on the plantation. I wanted them to have something better first."

"I understand. Our house will come later."

He nodded. "Yes, our house."

The way he said the words sent tremors through her body. Savannah pulled her gaze away from him and reached for the iron skillet that hung on the wall. Her hands shook as she placed it on top of the stove and placed the pieces of ham she'd cut earlier in it.

Dante rose from his chair and moved to stand behind her. As he peered over her shoulder, she could feel his breath on her neck, and it sent ripples up and down her back. "Um, this looks good. Ham and biscuits?"

"Yes. I haven't made the biscuits yet, but I made your favorite—fried peach pies."

He moved closer. "Who taught you how to cook?"

She took a deep breath. "Mamie cooked for us in the big house. My mother didn't know the first thing about the kitchen, but I stayed there a lot. All that I learned came from Mamie."

He chuckled. "Then I owe Mamie a great debt of gratitude."

"That's almost the last of the ham we brought from Aunt Jane's smoke-house, though. Do you think we'll be able to butcher some hogs soon?"

He stepped back to his chair and sat down. "I'll see if I can buy a few from one of the farmers. By next year, though, we'll be able to fill each family's smokehouse."

Savannah glanced over her shoulder at him. "Mamie and I are already talking about the garden we're going to plant in the spring. With the help of all the women, we should be able to grow enough vegetables to get us through next winter. We'll have to take a look at the apple and peach orchards, though. They've been neglected for a long time."

Dante stared at her for a moment, and she thought she detected respect in his eyes. "You surprise me, Savannah."

She frowned. "How?"

"You cook, you're ready to butcher hogs, and you're already planning next spring's garden. I expect you'll have us all out in the orchard pruning and doing whatever it takes to get those trees producing again. I wouldn't have thought a beautiful woman who grew up the pampered daughter of a planter would do those things."

She snorted. "Then you have a lot to learn about me. I told you I wanted to bring Cottonwood back to what it was before the war, and I meant it." She stopped and bit her lip. "Which reminds me, there is one more thing I've been meaning to mention."

"What?"

Savannah took a deep breath. She had no idea how he would respond to her next suggestion. She wiped her hands on her apron and faced him. "I know you've been concerned about transporting our baled cotton next year to Willow Bend to load on the steamboats going to Mobile."

He nodded. "Yes. There doesn't seem to be a good place to build a steam-boat landing. The bluffs along the river on our land are too steep. It'll take a lot of time to take the cotton to Willow Bend by wagon."

"I have an idea. What if we built a slide from the top of the bluff straight down to the water? There's a good place at the bottom of the bluff near that canebrake you and the men cleaned out where the ship could dock. Some of the men could push the bales straight down to the ship, and others could be at the bottom to load it. That would eliminate the need to take it into Willow Bend."

"Savannah, I said a few minutes ago that you surprise me, but that's not correct. You amaze me."

A quizzical expression lined his face, and she felt a pang of regret. He looked at her as if she'd lost her mind. He must think her a silly woman to come up with such an idea.

Her face burned. "It's just a suggestion. If you don't like it, I'm sure you'll come up with something else." She turned back to the stove.

His hands touched her shoulders, and she froze in place. Turning her to face him, he smiled. "Not like it? I think it's a brilliant idea. I didn't realize what a keen mind you have."

Her uncertainty melted away, and she smiled back at him. "You really like the idea?"

"I love it. Saul told me that even though you were a young girl you could have run the plantation after the war. I think if you had, things might be different." He'd no sooner said it than his eyes clouded. "And you wouldn't have had to marry me."

He released his hold on her, and she felt chilled. The breath caught in her throat. "I didn't have to marry you, Dante. I'm glad I did."

His Adam's apple bobbed. "Are you really glad, Savannah?"

She cupped his hand in both of hers. "You're a good man, Dante, and I'm honored to be your wife."

He smiled. "No, I'm the one who is honored." He turned away and disappeared into the bedroom. In a few minutes, he returned, his Bible in his hand. Without speaking, he sat at the kitchen table, opened it, and began to read.

The ham in the skillet sizzled, and Savannah turned her attention back to the meal. She stole a glance every once in a while over her shoulder, but Dante didn't look up. Something about the sight of him sitting there, studying God's Word warmed her heart. Every day she found another reason to respect and like her husband. She wondered what he thought about her.

~~~

Dante tried to concentrate on the scripture, but he found it difficult. Savannah's presence in the room distracted him. The words she'd spoken a few minutes earlier made it almost impossible to think about anything else except her.

He glanced up and studied her as she put the last touches on their evening meal. He still couldn't believe that she was his wife, but here she was. His prayers of thanks were offered each day for God blessing him in such a way. Maybe he should tell her how he felt—let her know how dear she was to him.

A knock at the door startled him, and he jumped to his feet. "I'll get it."

When he opened the door, Abraham, Saul and Mamie's older son, stood on the porch. He held something covered with a cloth in one hand. Dante opened the door wider.

"Abraham, come in."

The young man stepped into the room and grinned. His ebony skin glistened in the light from the oil lamp on the table. "Mamma sent me with these here biscuits for yore supper. She said Miss 'Vanna cookin' ham."

Wiping her hands on a towel, Savannah laughed and stepped forward. "Mamie knows how much I like her biscuits. She's a dear for sending these." She took the pan and set it on the table. "Don't leave, Abraham. I have something for all of you, too. Some of my fried peach pies."

Abraham's eyes lit up. "Fried peach pies? I reckon we ain't had none of them in a long time."

Dante chuckled. "Savannah and her aunt dried these peaches last year, but I imagine we'll all be having peach pies next summer. Savannah told me that we have to get the orchards cleaned up and the trees pruned. Maybe there'll be a bumper crop of apples and peaches to dry."

Abraham nodded. "That sounds good to me, Mistuh Dante. We's gwine make Cottonwood like it used to be."

Savannah handed him the pies and smiled. "Yes we are, Abraham. Maybe even better. Dante tells me that we may soon have another person living with us. A young woman named Hattie. Is that right?"

Abraham backed toward the door, a grin on his face. "Yas'm, I 'spects it won't be long now."

Savannah reached around him and opened the door. "I'm glad. We'll look forward to seeing her."

Dante studied Savannah as she closed the door behind Abraham and walked back to the stove. She hummed a tune under her breath. A sheen of perspiration covered her brow from standing over the hot stove, but Dante thought he'd never seen anyone more beautiful in his life.

Two hours later, with the meal finished and the dishes washed, Savannah sat in her rocking chair mending a pair of socks. Dante glanced up from the passage he'd just read in the Bible and let his gaze drift around the cabin once more. This wasn't where he'd wanted to bring Savannah, but tonight, for some reason, he felt happy just to be here with his wife. He'd never known as much contentment as she'd brought into his life in the last few months.

She glanced up from her sewing and smiled. Laying the socks aside, she rose and picked up Aunt Jane's oil lamp from the table beside her. "It's been a long day. I think I'll go to bed."

He closed his Bible and stood. "Let me get the quilts for my pallet before you go in the bedroom."

Savannah's fingers grasped his arm. "No, Dante. There's no need for that."

He turned to her, a frown on his face. "What do you mean?"

She took a deep breath. "I think it's time you stopped sleeping on the floor. There's no need for that when we have a perfectly good bed."

His eyes grew wide, and he swallowed. "Do you understand what you're saying, Savannah?"

She nodded. "You told me to let you know when I wanted you to be my husband in every sense of the word, and that time has come."

He reached out and trailed his fingers down Savannah's cheek. "You're so beautiful, Savannah, and I want to be your husband. First, though, I must be honest with you and tell you that I have loved you since the day you almost ran me down with that buggy. I know I can't expect you to love me, so you may wish to take back what you've just said. I never want you to feel pressured by me."

Tears filled her eyes, and she pulled his hand to her mouth and kissed his palm. Her long eyelashes fluttered as she gazed into his face. "But I do love you, Dante. I have for a long time. All I want is to be with you for the rest of my life."

His arms circled her and pulled her against him. "That's all I want, too."

She stretched on her tiptoes toward him, and their lips met in the kiss that sealed their marriage vows.

❧

Savannah stared out the window as the first rays of morning light spread across the yard. Lucifer, her favorite rooster, crowed from the henhouse, and it sent a thrill through her. She'd always loved that early morning sound.

Walking to the stove, she picked up the coffeepot and filled Dante's cup. She set the pot back on the stove and caressed Dante's shoulder before she sat down at the kitchen table. The beginning of a new day always excited her, but today it was more. They were beginning a new life together. His eyes sparkled as he gazed at her and talked about what he'd planned for the morning.

"We've cleared the land and marked off the spot for Saul and Mamie's house. I'm going into Willow Bend to order the first building supplies. Do you want to come along?"

Savannah took a sip of her coffee and thought about his invitation. "I'd like that. Maybe I could go by Sarah Morgan's house and visit with her while you're getting what you need. She hasn't been in church for the past few weeks. Her son Seth has been sick."

Dante pushed up from the table. "I like Sarah. She's treated me better than anybody else in Willow Bend."

"She's a good friend of mine and would never do anything to hurt me."

He regarded her with a playful stare. "Are you saying that the way the good people around here treat me is painful to you?"

She made a face at him, stood, and began to stack their dishes. "Of course. I want everyone to know you and like you as I do."

She turned to place the dishes in the dry sink, but he caught her by the arm. "You said last night you love me. Do you really?"

She laughed and swatted at his arm. "How many times are you going to make me say it?"

His grip tightened. "Savannah, I still can't believe. . ." He stopped at the sound of horses galloping to a stop in front of their cabin.

"Hello in the house!"

Dante released her, walked to the window, and peered out. "It's Sheriff Newton and several men."

Savannah grabbed her shawl and followed Dante to the front porch. Stopping behind him, she stared at the men who faced them and flinched inwardly at the ragtag bunch who rode with the sheriff. She'd known most of them all her life, and they were nothing but drunkards and troublemakers. Just the type of men she'd expect their sheriff to have as friends.

"Good morning, Sheriff Newton," Dante said. "Kind of early to come visiting, isn't it?"

The sheriff spit a wad of tobacco to the ground, wiped his hand across his handlebar mustache, and pushed his hat up on his head. "This ain't no social visit. I just need to know where you were last night."

"I was right here with my wife."

The sheriff's gaze drifted to Savannah. "That right, Miss Carmichael? Was he here?"

Savannah stepped closer to Dante. "Yes, Sheriff, he was. And my name is Mrs. Rinaldi."

He glanced over at one of the men, who snickered, and then looked back to her. "Oh yeah, that's right. You did marry this carpetbagger, didn't you?"

Savannah could feel Dante tense, and she touched his arm. "State your business here, please."

The man leaned forward and rested his arm on the saddle. "Somebody rode through that Crossroads shantytown last night and shot it up right good. Probably the work of outsiders. So that's what made me think of Mr. Rinaldi first."

Dante took a step forward. "Was anybody hurt?"

"Some killed. A few hurt. No great loss. They're just a bunch of ex-slaves."

"Ex-slaves?" Savannah gasped. "You're the law, and you're supposed to be protecting everyone." She crossed her arms and glared at him. "But then I remember how you treated all the freed slaves after the war. You're a disgrace to your office."

The sheriff's face turned crimson, and he pointed a finger at Savannah. "Now just a minute."

Dante held up a hand. "You've gotten the answer to your question about my whereabouts last night. Now I suggest you ride on and look for whoever did this horrible deed."

The sheriff glared at the couple for a moment before he whirled his horse and nodded to the men. "Let's get out of here. I smell a yellow-bellied abolitionist."

Savannah and Dante watched as they rode away. When they'd disappeared, Savannah turned to Dante. Tears filled her eyes. "Oh Dante, some of Cottonwood's people are still living there. We need to find out what happened."

He reached for her hand and guided her back inside. "I'll get Henry Walton to ride over there with me. I think it might be safer for the other men to stay here today. I'll come back as soon as I know anything."

He grabbed his coat from the peg by the door and rushed out. Savannah sank down in the kitchen chair and buried her face in her hands. The sheriff's words rang in her mind, but she knew that he spoke only what so many people in the area thought. The war had left some wounds that it might take years to heal. She wondered if it would happen in her lifetime.

Chapter 11

The Crossroads settlement looked nothing like Dante remembered from the day he'd escorted the families from there to Cottonwood. No children played along the dirt paths that snaked between the shacks, and he couldn't see any groups of young people. Instead, deadly silence covered the area.

Dante reined his horse to a stop and climbed down. He stood in the middle of the road and looked around in disbelief. Wisps of smoke curled upward from the remains of several hovels along the edge of the settlement. He counted five others that, although they still stood, had sustained damage from fire.

Henry dismounted and glanced around. "It looks deserted. Where is everybody?"

Dante shook his head. "I don't know."

Henry held the reins of his horse out to Dante. "I'll see if I can find anybody."

"I'll come with you."

"I think you'd better stay here. I 'spect most white men ain't welcome 'round here today. I lived with them, so I think they'll talk to me."

Dante took the reins of Henry's horse. "All right."

Henry nodded and disappeared along the path that led inside the community. A cold wind blew from the river at the edge of the settlement and whipped about Dante's legs. He looked at the makeshift homes the people lived in and wondered how they kept warm.

The residents of Cottonwood might be living in former slave quarters, but he had made sure that each family had what they needed to keep warm this winter. He doubted if the people at the Crossroads were similarly equipped, and now some of them had lost what little they did have.

The longer Henry stayed gone, the colder Dante became. He tied the horses to a tree beside the road and paced up and down in an attempt to keep warm. Crossing his arms, he hugged himself and wished he could be with Savannah in their warm cabin.

As always, thoughts of her made his heart pump faster. She'd said she loved him, but did she? Was she mistaking her grateful feelings to be back at Cottonwood for love? Doubt drifted into his mind. He wanted to believe her, but uncertainty remained. Even though he'd been thrilled to hear her words, he had to be careful. The community still considered him an outsider, and Savannah might very well harbor some of those same feelings. Only time would tell.

Dante glanced at the deserted settlement again and wondered where everyone had gone. He began pacing again, lost in thought. After what seemed an eternity, Henry reappeared. A sad look lined his face.

Dante met him at the end of the path. "Did you find anybody?"

Henry nodded. "Yes. They're all in a field back of here, burying the dead."

"Do they need help?"

"Yeah, they do, but they're mighty upset right now. Don't hardly want to see nobody."

Dante took a deep breath. "How many died?"

Henry's forehead wrinkled, and his chin quivered. "Ten. Two entire families that lived in those huts that burned to the ground."

Dante shook his head in disbelief. "But how did this happen?"

"They said a rebel yell woke them up in the middle of the night. Six men on horses were outside. They had on hoods and held torches. They set fire to some of the houses, and when the people ran out, they shot 'em down."

Dante choked back the nausea rolling in his stomach. "Women and children, too?"

"Yes." Henry wiped at his eyes and blinked. "The folks scattered, but the riders came after them, yelling and shooting. When the men finished havin' their fun, they rode off."

Dante put his hand on Henry's shoulder. "Did you know the ones who were killed?"

Henry blinked back tears and stared at Dante. "Abraham's Hattie, her father, mother, and brother are all dead. How we gonna tell Abraham?"

Dante shook his head. "I don't know." He remembered how happy Abraham had looked the night before when he told Savannah about the young woman he wanted to marry. "You said the men wore hoods?"

"Yes."

"Did anyone see anything familiar about them?"

"They know who done it."

Dante frowned. "But the sheriff came by home this morning, and he didn't know who they were. Why haven't they told him?"

Henry grunted in disgust. " 'Cause they know he won't do nothing to the owner of Oak Hill Plantation."

Dante's mouth gaped in surprise. "Jonathan Boyer? How do they know?"

"Some of the men are former slaves from Oak Hill. They recognized his horse. He was the leader of the bunch."

Dante rubbed his hand over his eyes. "Oh, this is going to be rough on Savannah. Jonathan has been her friend all her life."

"Well, they say he's a right mean man, and they don't want to do nothing else to make him mad." Henry glanced back the way he had come out of the settlement. "They're havin' a hard time diggin' them graves. They only got one shovel. Folks are just scratching at the ground with whatever they got."

Dante took a deep breath. "We need to help. It'll take too long to go to Cottonwood for shovels. I'll go into town and get some at the store. You go on back and tell them. I'll return as soon as I can."

Henry nodded. "Yes, sir. I reckon they'll be much obliged."

Dante untied the reins of his horse and swung into the saddle. "I'll be back as soon as I can."

He dug his heels into the horse's sides and leaned forward as the horse galloped away. He'd known Jonathan Boyer was filled with anger, but he never would have suspected him of murder.

Then there was Abraham. He had no idea how he was going to break this horrible news to him. As he rode toward town, he prayed for the survivors of last night's raid. The people at the Crossroads had suffered for years as slaves. Freedom had only brought them different problems. As free men and women, they hadn't been able to escape the cruelty of men determined to make them suffer.

Men like Jonathan Boyer couldn't believe the changes the war had brought to the South. Instead of accepting the way life was now, they chose to harbor anger that festered like giant sores in their souls. And who better to unleash their anger on than the people they perceived as the ones who caused their way of life to collapse.

Until the ones who raided the Crossroads were caught, no former slaves in the county would be safe. Someone had to put a stop to Jonathan Boyer and his band of murderers.

⤬

Savannah put her sewing aside, got up from her chair, and walked to the window. Dante still hadn't come home, and the sun had already begun to dip behind the horizon. She peered outside, but he and Henry were nowhere in sight.

Ever since he left earlier in the day, she had tried to keep busy, but she couldn't get her mind off what the sheriff had said. If some of the people were hurt, she and Mamie could be of help. But if they were needed, Dante would have sent for her.

She sighed and trudged to the stove to check the beans that simmered in the pot. She stirred them and thought of Aunt Jane's insistence on their having a vegetable garden last summer. Thank goodness for the bounty they'd had. It had come in handy to feed all the mouths that now lived at Cottonwood.

She replaced the lid on the pot and turned back to her chair just as the door opened and Dante walked in. Patches of dirt smudged his face and coat, but it was the look on his face that sent shivers through her.

Her throat went dry, and she tried to swallow. "How bad was it?"

He pulled off his gloves and rubbed his hand across his face. "Ten dead. Henry and I helped dig the graves."

Her hand went to her throat, and her heart pounded. "Were any of them Cottonwood people?"

He shook his head. "I don't think so. It seems that the Oak Hill former slaves suffered more than any."

She hurried across the room and stood in front of him. "Oh no. I knew some of them. How awful this must be for Jonathan."

His face darkened, and his body shook with anger. "Awful? I doubt it since he and his friends were the ones who did it."

She'd never seen Dante so upset, and it scared her. Shaking her head, she reached for his coat. "Let me help you with your coat. I know you're upset, but it's ridiculous to blame Jonathan for something like this."

He pulled away from her. "And why would you think that?"

"Because I know him, and he's not a murderer."

He regarded her with a steady gaze. "Have you forgotten how he's behaved ever since we married? You said the war changed him, and I think it made him into some kind of monster."

Her cheeks burned, but she stared back at him. "He lost his way of life in the war, and he's just rebelling against that. But Jonathan would never commit murder."

Fists clenched at his sides, he advanced on her. "How can you defend him?"

She trembled at his anger. "B—because I've known him all my life. He couldn't kill anyone."

"Well, he did!" Dante shouted.

She took another step back. "Did anybody see him?"

"No, they wore hoods."

"Then how did they know it was Jonathan?"

He leaned toward her. "Some of them recognized his horse."

"His horse? Lots of horses look alike. It could have been anybody with a horse that looked like his."

Dante moved even closer to her, and she backed away until she felt the kitchen table behind her. He stopped in front of her and stared at her for a moment. "So you're choosing to stand up for a killer."

Tears spilled from her eyes. "Please understand, Dante."

His body sagged, and he backed away. "I do. He's an old friend, and I'm an outsider who happened to trap you into marriage. I thought you were different from everybody else in Willow Bend, but you're not. Instead of believing your husband, who talked to the people Boyer attacked, you choose to defend him." He took a deep breath and turned toward the door. "I have to go see Abraham and tell him the news."

Stunned by Dante's last words, Savannah rushed forward and stopped him. "What do you have to tell Abraham?"

He regarded her with an icy glare. "That Hattie was one of the people Jonathan gunned down last night. I dug her grave myself."

She pressed her hand to her mouth. "No, please tell me that's not true."

He took a deep breath. "Oh, but it is. I buried her right next to her parents and her brother while Henry was digging the grave of a woman and her baby."

Tears streamed down her face, and she reached out to Dante. "You're upset over what you've seen today. What can I do to help you?"

He stared at her hand before he pulled away from her grasp. "There's nothing you can do. I don't understand people who hate that much, and I don't understand those that close their eyes to the evil around them." He took a deep breath. "I should never have come to Willow Bend. I'll always be an outsider here."

Before Savannah could respond, he walked out of the cabin. She stared at the closed door a moment before she bent forward and pressed her forehead to the cool wood.

Her heart thudded at the memory of Dante's face and the words he'd said. He sounded as if he thought she'd chosen between him and Jonathan. That wasn't true. She only needed to make some sense out of the whole situation.

Her words hurt Dante. He didn't mean it when he said he never should have come to Willow Bend. If he hadn't come, she never would have met him, and they wouldn't be married. And if they hadn't married, she might never have fallen in love.

Her eyes widened, and she covered her mouth with her hand. The way Dante had spoken sounded as if he didn't believe she really loved him. If that was the case, she had to find a way to show him that he was the most important thing in her life. The loss of Cottonwood was nothing compared to what it would be like to lose Dante.

⁂

Dante stopped on the porch of the cabin and pondered what he should do. He hadn't meant to speak so sharply to Savannah, but her words had ripped his heart. Ever since they'd been married, he'd done everything he could to make her trust him. Just last night she'd said she loved him, yet she still chose Jonathan over him.

He'd spoken in anger, and that wasn't like him at all. He never should have said what he did about not coming to Willow Bend. The best things that had ever happened in his life had occurred here. He'd always dreamed of owning land, and now he did, but he wanted more. He wanted his wife's love.

He raked his hand through his hair. Maybe what he'd feared all along was true. Savannah had married him so she could come back to Cottonwood, and she had played the part of his wife well. But that's all it was—just a role like in a play so that she could keep her end of the bargain.

Dante shook the thoughts from his head. Other things needed to be faced now. He glanced at the cabin a short distance away and knew that Saul's family waited inside for news of friends. With a heavy heart, he stepped off the porch and headed toward their cabin.

Before he could knock on the door, it flew open. Saul stood in the lamplight from inside. A worried expression lined his face. "Mistuh Dante, we's been worried 'bout you and Henry. What you find out?"

Dante looked past Saul to Mamie, Abraham, and Joshua, who hovered in the room behind. He didn't have the words to tell Abraham what he had come to say. That news needed to come from his father.

He cleared his throat and motioned for Saul to follow him outside. When they stood alone on the porch, Dante related the events of the day. As he told of burying Hattie's body, tears burned his eyes, and he wiped at them.

Saul stood speechless, his mouth slightly open. When Dante finished, he put his hand on Saul's shoulder. "I thought it best if this news came from you. You'll know how to tell Abraham."

Saul's lips quivered, and he gazed past Dante toward the remains of the big house. "When we heared the war was over and we was free, we thought life was gwine be good for us, but that ain't the way it's been."

"I know," Dante murmured. "It may take a long time for things to change in the South, but it will, Saul. Someday it will be different."

"Someday ain't gwine help those what died at the Crossroads. All they wanted was to live like ev'rybody else what's free." He paused as if he was remembering the past. After a moment he exhaled. "Bein' owned by somebody is a hard life. My mamma is jest a little picture in my mind 'cause I got sold off when I was 'bout the age of Big Mike's youngest. Don't know nothin' 'bout my pappy."

Pain radiated through the words. Dante thought of his own mother and father and how he would have felt as a boy to be separated from them. "But your life was good at Cottonwood, wasn't it?"

Saul nodded. "Might say that. Leastways, none of mine ever got sold, but others did. When we first heared that Mr. Lincoln wanted to free us, we all talked 'bout where we'd go and what we'd do. Oh, we made big plans, but they warn't no use. Cain't go nowhere without money, and we didn't have none. Just had each other. Now Abraham gwine find out he ain't got what he wanted."

Dante searched for some words of comfort, but nothing came to mind. "Saul, I know how you must feel, but we'll get through this."

Saul stared at him with tortured eyes. He took a deep breath. "You a good man, Mistuh Dante, but I 'spects you cain't know how I feels. Only a man what's been owned by somebody can understand."

Saul turned and walked back into his home. "God," Dante whispered, "watch over this family. Comfort them during this awful time."

A shout from the cabin jerked Dante's attention back to the people inside.

"No! No! No!" Abraham's voice cried out.

Dante stepped off the porch and stared at the soft light coming from his cabin. Inside, Savannah waited. He didn't want to see her right now, and she probably didn't want to see him either. It would be better for them to be apart for a while.

Without glancing at the cabin again, he strode toward the barn. He needed time to think.

Chapter 12

Savannah sat at the kitchen table, holding a book she'd brought from Aunt Jane's, but she couldn't keep her mind on the words. Dante had left two hours ago to tell Abraham about Hattie, but he hadn't returned. Loneliness washed over her, and she wished he would come back.

She glanced around the cabin where she'd lived for the last four months. With Aunt Jane's familiar belongings scattered about, it had begun to feel like home—hers and Dante's.

She touched the surface of the oak table that had once belonged to her grandmother and remembered the times she and Aunt Jane had shared together there. Across the room, the elegant sideboard Aunt Jane's husband had given her before the war stood against the wall. Most of the other furnishings from the Willow Bend house were stored in an empty cabin, but she'd insisted they find room for these. They held many memories for her.

With a sigh, she closed the book and stood. Pulling her shawl from around her shoulders, she hung it on the back of the chair and checked Dante's supper on the back of the stove.

The squirrel stew still simmered in the pot, but it was going to be ruined if he didn't come soon. The memory of his sad face flickered in her mind, and she shivered. She hadn't meant to hurt him. If he would only come back, she would apologize.

A noise from the front porch caught her attention, and she turned. Dante entered the cabin. Relief flowed through her, but she restrained herself from throwing her arms around him. Instead, she clutched at her apron and gathered the material into puckered balls in her hands.

She tried to smile. "I was concerned about you. Where have you been?"

He took off his coat and hung it on the peg. "After I told Saul about Hattie, I went out to the barn. I had a lot of thinking to do."

Her heart pounded, and she struggled to remain calm. "About what?"

"About the war and how it's destroyed so many lives."

She took a step toward him. "We can't do anything about that."

He strode toward her and stopped within inches. His clutched fists dangled at his sides. "But I want to do something. I want to help the people we've brought to Cottonwood, and I grieve for all those who are left drifting without anything—like all those people at the Crossroads. They have families, and they just want to be happy. Why can't they?"

She put her hand on his arm. "I don't know, Dante. Attitudes in the South may not change in our lifetime. All we can do is try to make a difference where we are." She stared up into his face, and her heart longed to bring some comfort to him. "You're a good man. You've brought life back to Cottonwood. It's not what it was, but if we work together, we can make it better than before."

The muscle in his jaw twitched. "Do you mean that?"

"Yes."

"You still want to do that?"

She frowned. "Of course I do. Did you think I'd changed my mind?"

"I thought you might regret telling me you loved me."

"Why would you think that?"

"Because of the way I spoke to you earlier. Do you hate me, Savannah?" His dark eyes burned like coals.

She shook her head. "I don't hate you."

His eyes softened, and his gaze traveled over her face. "I'm sorry for what I said. I understand how you feel about Jonathan. He's been your friend for years. I've never had a friend like that. I envy you."

She smiled. "Don't envy my friendship with Jonathan. I've thought about what you said, and I'm sure you're right. The old Jonathan never would have killed anybody, but the man now living at Oak Hill very well could."

He inched closer. "Maybe *envy* isn't the right word. Maybe I'm jealous of him because I love you so much."

She tilted her head and studied his face. Reaching up, she cupped his cheek with her hand. "I love you, too."

His eyes widened. "Are you sorry about that?"

She stroked his face again and shook her head. "No, why would you think that?"

He reached up, took hold of her hand, and brought it to his mouth. His warm lips grazed the palm of her hand. "Because you're so young and beautiful, and I'm ten years older than you. I'm an Italian and an outsider here. I'm different from all the people you've known all your life."

Her stomach fluttered at his whispered words. "Yes, you are, and I thank God for that."

His Adam's apple bobbed. "Maybe. . ."

They jumped in alarm at the sound of someone pounding on the door.

"Mistuh Dante! Mistuh Dante! You in there?"

Dante whirled and ran to the door with Savannah right behind. She stared over his shoulder at Saul, who stood on the front porch.

"Saul, what's the matter?" Dante demanded.

Tears flowed down Saul's face. "Abraham done went crazy, Mistuh Dante. He kept saying he gwine take him a horse and go find those men what killed Hattie. I tole him he be a thief if'n he took yo' horse, but he did it. He done took my squirrel rifle and gone. What we gwine do, Mistuh Dante?"

Dante pulled the shaking man into the house and closed the door. "Calm down, Saul. You say Abraham took a horse and went after the men who killed Hattie?"

"Yas suh, but he ain't a thief, Mistuh Dante. Doan be mad at him."

Dante reached for his coat. "It's all right, Saul. I know Abraham isn't a thief. He's just upset. Maybe we can catch him."

He turned to Savannah. "Saul and I will go after Abraham. I don't know when we'll be back."

"B—but where will you look?"

Dante's eyes narrowed in thought. "We'll go to the Crossroads first. Perhaps he went there to find out who they thought were responsible for the raid."

"Abraham knows who done it, Mistuh Dante."

Saul's low voice sent shivers down Savannah's back. "How does he know?"

"He say when he went to town with Henry last week, he was waitin' by the wagon for Henry to come out of da store. Mistuh Boyer from Oak Hill walked up and tole him to git in the wagon; folks like him warn't 'posed to stand in the way of white folks walkin' down the street. Abraham tole him he warn't blockin' anybody's path, and Mistuh Boyer got right mad. He tole Abraham he'd be sorry he back talked a white man."

Fear rose in Savannah's throat. "Do you think he might go to Oak Hill?"

Dante shook his head. "I don't know." He walked to the sideboard, opened a drawer, and pulled out his pistol. He stared at it for a moment before he tucked it in the waistband of his pants. "We'd better find him before he gets in bad trouble."

The sight of the gun terrified Savannah. In the months of their marriage, she'd never seen Dante even look at it. Now he acted like a man who wouldn't hesitate to use it. He walked back and stopped beside her. She glanced down at the revolver. "Dante, why the gun?"

He straightened his shoulders and buttoned his coat. "In case we run into any trouble."

She grabbed Dante's hands. "Then hurry and catch him before that happens. I'll go stay with Mamie and Joshua until you get back. And please be careful."

He glanced down at their intertwined hands and squeezed hers. "We'll try." He released her and turned to Saul. "I'll go to the barn and start saddling the horses. You tell Big Mike and the others where we're going. Tell them to keep an eye on everything until we get back."

Saul nodded and dashed out the door.

Dante hurried onto the front porch. Savannah followed and watched him run to the barn. When he disappeared from sight, she stepped back inside, checked the fire in the stove, and grabbed her shawl from the back of the chair. She paused at the door and breathed a prayer for the safety of Dante, Saul, and Abraham before she hurried outside and ran toward Mamie and Saul's cabin.

Dante and Saul rode through the dark night toward Oak Hill. In the months Dante had been at Cottonwood, Savannah had often talked about the Boyer plantation and what a grand place it had been before the war, but he'd never been there. Now he raced in its direction on a mission of life and death.

He didn't want to think about what would happen to Abraham if Jonathan and his friends found him first. Even with a squirrel rifle for protection, a young man would be defenseless against a band of angry killers.

Dante glanced at Saul, but in the dark he couldn't make out the expression on the man's face. He must be worried out of his mind for the safety of his son. Saul had told Dante he could never understand what he felt, and Dante knew that was true. Someone who had never experienced slavery couldn't start to comprehend what Saul and all the others had endured.

A horse whinnied in the distance, and Dante and Saul reined to a stop. "Did you hear that?"

Saul pointed at the forest to the right of the road. "Yas suh. It sound like it comin' from those woods over yonder."

Dante turned his horse's head in the direction of the sound and nudged him forward into the inky darkness. Leaves on the forest floor rustled as the horses moved slowly forward. Dante strained to hear another sound, but even the night animals were silent.

His horse raised its head and snorted in surprise at a figure standing between the bare trees. Dante squinted and recognized the horse from Cottonwood, but there was no rider.

"Mistuh Dante, that the horse Abraham took."

Dante got off and walked toward the animal. "Easy, boy."

The horse didn't move, and Dante grabbed the reins that trailed on the ground. The lather on the horse's back told Dante he had been ridden hard. But where was Abraham?

Dante moved to the side of the animal and stopped. His nostrils flared at the smell that he could identify even in the dark. He'd encountered it innumerable times in the field hospitals where he'd worked. Blood.

He ran his hand over the saddle and felt the sticky substance on his fingers. Saul dismounted and stood beside him.

"Mistuh Dante, what is it?"

"We have to find Abraham right away. Something bad has happened."

Dante grasped the reins of his and Abraham's horses and walked forward. The undergrowth in the forest pulled at his boots, but he ignored it and trudged forward with Saul behind. They'd gone about fifty yards when he stopped short.

Saul halted beside him. "What is it?"

Dante frowned. "I thought I heard something."

A breeze rustled the bare branches of the trees. Dante strained to hear whatever the wind had stirred. It came from straight ahead. He inched forward. The sound, like the creaking of a swaying tree branch, grew louder.

Just as he stepped into a small clearing, the clouds parted, and moonlight filtered down through the trees. Dante stopped and gasped. He saw the rope looped over the limb first and let his gaze travel to the noose at the end. Pain like a kick in the stomach ripped through Dante. Abraham, his hands bound behind him, swung from a branch of an oak tree ahead.

"Saul. . ."

A roar of despair from Saul pierced the quiet of the forest. They dropped the reins of their horses and sprinted toward Abraham's body. Together Dante and Saul grabbed Abraham's legs and lifted him as high as they could.

"Saul," Dante yelled, "hold him while I climb up and cut him down."

Saul clamped his arms around his son's legs and heaved his body higher. Dante pulled the knife from his pocket and opened it before he shinnied up the tree. Easing out onto the branch, he sawed at the rope until it gave way and Abraham's body tumbled downward.

Dante swung his legs off the branch, dropped to the ground, and knelt beside Saul. "Is he breathing?"

Saul frantically tugged the rope from around Abraham's neck and pulled his son to his chest. Tears streamed down his face. "He's dead, Mistuh Dante. They done killed my son. Why they have to go and do a thing like that?"

Dante reached out and grasped the man's shaking shoulder. There was no answer to ease Saul's anguish. All Dante could do was sit beside him as he cried out his grief.

Chapter 13

Savannah stood at the window in Saul and Mamie's cabin and stared into the dark night. Dante and Saul had left hours ago. What if they had encountered Jonathan's men and were lying hurt or even dead on the road to Oak Hill? She gritted her teeth. No, she wouldn't think that way. They'd come riding up anytime now with Abraham in tow.

She glanced over her shoulder at Mamie, who stared into the fireplace's flames. Savannah's heart ached for her. Although Mamie loved her younger son, Joshua, Abraham was her special child, the one who'd always done everything he could to make life easier for his mother.

Savannah's brow wrinkled into a deep frown. Tomorrow she was going to give Abraham a good tongue-lashing. Even though he'd suffered a tragic loss, he should know better than to cause his mother such anguish. After she got through scolding him, he would think before he did it again.

"Where Joshua?" Mamie's voice from behind caught her attention.

"He went to the barn to check on the livestock."

Turning from the window, Savannah walked over to Mamie and put her hand on her shoulder. "Can I fix you something? A cup of coffee? Or maybe something to eat?"

Mamie shook her head. "Don't reckon my stomach would take kindly to nothin' right now, Miss 'Vanna, but I thanks you."

The cabin door opened, and Joshua stepped inside. Savannah gazed at the young man. At eighteen, he was four years younger than his older brother. Savannah had always thought it remarkable that Abraham could be so like Mamie, spirited and fun loving, while Joshua resembled his father in looks and disposition.

Both of Mamie's sons worked hard in the fields during the day, but in other ways they differed. Joshua's serious nature kept him focused on work and family responsibilities, while Abraham loved to sing and tell stories to anyone who would listen. Savannah remembered how the girls in the slave quarters all fell under his spell at one time or another, but he never noticed any of them until Hattie. Savannah wondered how she had been able to capture the wild heart of the young man.

Joshua walked over to his mother and bent over her. "Mamma, I done checked the livestock. I reckon they be all right till morning. Now I thinks I'll jest wait in the other room till Abraham gets home. You need me to do anything else for you?"

Mamie shook her head. "I'm fine. Me and Miss 'Vanna gwine wait right here till they gets back."

Joshua bent and kissed his mother on the cheek. "You calls out if'n you need me."

"I will." Mamie turned her head and watched Joshua enter the small room that served as a bedroom for him and Abraham. When he closed the door, she smiled at Savannah. "Joshua, he a good son. He goin' in there to pray for his brother."

"He and Abraham both are good sons." Savannah knelt beside the woman she'd loved all her life. "Mamie, Dante and Saul will find Abraham and bring him home. We just have to believe that."

Mamie clutched her hands in her lap. "My head tells me that, but it my heart that don't believe it. I feels like my whole insides just torn to pieces."

Savannah covered Mamie's hands with hers. "I can understand how you feel."

Mamie's lips quivered. "He my firstborn. He real special 'cause I had a hard time birthin' him. I don't knows how I can live if'n somethin' done happened to him."

Savannah gasped. "Don't say that. Don't even think that."

Sadness lined Mamie's face. "You don't knows how I feel, but you will when your baby born."

Savannah chuckled. "Don't rush things, Mamie. That won't happen for a long time."

"Don't wait too long, Miss 'Vanna."

Savannah opened her mouth to speak, but the sound of a horse's whinny from outside stopped her. She grasped Mamie's hands. "They're back."

Fear flickered in Mamie's eyes. "You go see, Miss 'Vanna. I don't thinks my feet gwine move."

Savannah nodded and grabbed the oil lamp sitting on the kitchen table. Without waiting to grab her shawl, she ran to the door and bolted onto the porch. She held the lamp high. The small beam flickered across the yard, and Dante's horse moved into its small circle of light. Relief poured through her at the sight of her husband.

She rushed down the steps and hurried to stand beside his horse. He climbed down, but his silence scared her. "Did you find him?"

"Yes." The word, spoken so softly, was almost a whisper.

She glanced over his shoulder and caught sight of Saul, but she didn't see

Abraham. "Then where is he?"

In the dim light she could see Dante's face, and she gasped. She'd seen suffering before, but she'd never encountered anything as horrible as the tortured look on his face.

His lips quivered, and he tried to speak. She looked from him to Saul, who had dismounted. She stepped around Dante and held the lamp up higher. Her eyes widened at the sight of the third horse, a body across the saddle. Her hand shook, and the lamp dipped toward the ground.

Saul stepped forward. "They kilt Abraham, Miss 'Vanna. Them men hung him from a tree and kilt my son."

"My baby." The scream pierced the air, and Savannah turned to see Mamie running toward Saul. "I wants to see my baby."

Saul dropped the reins to his horse and grabbed her. Her eyes had the look of a wild woman, and she beat at Saul with her fists. Saul let her fight at him until her cries turned to whimpers and her hands rested against his chest. Then he wrapped his arms around her and cradled her like a suffering child. "It gwine be all right, Mamie. I here with you."

The doors of the other cabins opened, and the tenant farmers of Cottonwood and their families slipped from their homes to join the mourning family. Savannah glanced back at the porch. Joshua stared at the horse carrying his brother's body. He drifted down the steps and stopped next to his parents.

No one spoke. Savannah looked around the group of mourners. She hadn't seen such sorrow since the night of her parents' deaths. Tears streamed down her face, and she looked up at Dante. "Why would Jonathan do this?"

"I don't know."

Saul reached out to Joshua and drew him into the circle of his arms. Savannah hoped Saul's touch offered some measure of comfort to Mamie and Joshua.

She looked up at Dante and wanted to feel that from him. She stepped closer to him and laid her head on his chest. His arms encircled her and drew her closer. She buried her face in his chest and cried for the war that had destroyed so many lives, for her parents, for Abraham, and for the people whose freedom had only brought them new problems.

❧

Dante entered the cabin, hung up his coat, and opened the drawer of the sideboard. He pulled the gun from his pants waistband and laid it inside. On the ride home, he'd asked himself many times if he could have used it if he'd gotten there before they hanged Abraham.

"Thou shalt not kill."

The words echoed in his mind, but he knew he could have pulled the trigger to save Abraham's life. He clenched his fists and banged them against the wall. It didn't matter now what he could have done. Abraham was dead.

He slammed the drawer closed and strode to the stove. Opening the firebox, he shoved another piece of wood inside and adjusted the dampers to increase the blaze. He closed the door and held his hands over the stovetop. They still burned from the icy cold of the night.

His thoughts went to Savannah and how she had cried when they brought Abraham's body back earlier. Although his heart ached, too, it felt good to have her in his arms.

He sighed and wondered if Pinky and Big Mike had finished the coffin. He'd stayed with them in the barn until they were almost finished, but he'd been unable to help much. Pinky possessed the best carpentry skills at Cottonwood, and he'd been quick to set to work on the task.

Dante walked to the window and looked out. Savannah and the other women must still be at Saul and Mamie's. None of the men or their wives had looked surprised when Savannah took over the arrangements for Abraham's body. Before he knew it, there had been a cover placed on Mamie's kitchen table, and Savannah had supervised the moving of Abraham's body there. Then she'd sent Mamie and Saul home with Henry and Mary Ann Walton while she, Tildy, and Big Mike's wife, Josie, prepared Abraham for burial. He wondered how long it would take.

He sat down at the kitchen table and pulled the piece of paper out of his pocket that Saul had found inside Abraham's shirt. With no light in the dark woods, he hadn't been able to make out the words. Now he unfolded it and spread it out in front of him.

The printed words that spilled across the paper sent an icy chill through his body. His hands shook, and he pulled the paper closer to make sure he read it correctly: "*Cottonwood is next.*"

Abraham's killers had sent a message to him. Dante jumped up from his chair, and it toppled over backward and clattered to the floor. What could he do? Telling the sheriff wouldn't help. For all he knew, the sheriff was as guilty as Jonathan Boyer.

He scooped the note up and stuck it in his pocket. Savannah didn't need to know about this. He would decide how he and the Cottonwood residents could best protect their homes and families before he alarmed her.

The door opened, and Savannah entered the cabin. The red spots dotting her cheeks had to be caused by the cold night air, but the redness of her eyes told him she'd been crying. She set the lamp she carried on the table and sank down in a chair. He eased into the one across from her.

"How are Mamie and Saul?"

Savannah rubbed her eyes and shook her head. "They're in shock. They can't believe this has happened."

"Did you complete the burial preparations?"

Savannah took a deep breath. "Yes. Pinky and Big Mike brought the coffin just as we got through. Big Mike and Joshua placed Abraham's body in it. I went over to Mary Ann's and brought Mamie and Saul home. Mamie nearly collapsed when she saw Abraham. Tildy and Josie are going to stay with them until morning. They don't need to be alone."

"I can understand."

Savannah glanced up at him, and fresh tears ran down her face. "How are they ever going to live with this? Their son has been murdered for no reason." Her eyes hardened, and she gritted her teeth. "And knowing our good sheriff as I do, he'll find every excuse he can to put off looking for the killers. If he looked very hard, he might find them, and he doesn't want to do that."

Dante wanted to take her in his arms and tell her that everything was going to be all right, but the note in his pocket reminded him there still might be battles ahead. The thought that he might lose Savannah as Abraham had lost Hattie and as Saul and Mamie had lost their son terrified him. He had to protect her at all costs.

Dante leaned back in his chair. "You're tired and upset. Why don't you go on to bed? You'll feel better in the morning."

She wiped at her eyes and nodded. "That's a good idea. You're tired, too. Maybe a good night's sleep will help us both." She rose from the table and walked toward the bedroom. At the door she stopped. "Aren't you coming to bed?"

"No. I think I'll enjoy the warmth of the stove for a while. You go on."

She hesitated a moment. "All right. Good night."

"Good night, Savannah."

She closed the door, but he waited until he saw the lamplight underneath the door disappear and heard the bed creak. Then he pulled the note from his pocket again. Smoothing it out on the tabletop, he reread the message.

He stared at the words for a moment before he sighed and stood up. Crossing the room, he drew the gun from the sideboard drawer and pulled his rifle down from where it hung on the wall. He sat at the table and laid the guns on top next to the note. If they had any visitors at Cottonwood tonight, he was going to be ready.

❧

Savannah awoke, her body shaking from the cold. Even though darkness covered the room, she knew Dante had not come to bed. She had no idea how long she'd slept, but she supposed it must be the middle of the night.

She slipped from underneath the covers and reached for the shawl on the chair beside the bed. Her feet touched the cold floor, and her skin prickled at the icy feel. She hurried across the room and opened the door.

The oil lamp still burned on the table. Its glow cast an eerie light across the room and the figure slumped at the table. She eased into the room and stood beside her husband, bent over in sleep. She reached out to wake him, but she spied the note underneath his spread fingers.

She frowned and slipped it free of his grasp. He stirred, and she held her breath. When he settled back into his restless sleep, she picked the paper up and read what was printed on it. Her eyes grew wide at the words, but a greater fear flowed through her at the sight of the weapons on the table.

She didn't know where or when Dante had received the note, but she understood his concern. He'd stayed up to guard their home while she slept, but his tired body had not been up to the task. She slipped the note under his hand and backed away from the table.

Aunt Jane's cedar chest sat against the bedroom wall, and she hurried to it and pulled out a patchwork quilt Aunt Jane had made years ago. She returned to the kitchen, stopped behind Dante's chair, and draped the quilt around his shoulders.

Savannah stared at his handsome face. Even as he slept, she could make out the lines of fatigue caused by his desire to make Cottonwood productive again and to rebuild the lives of the tenant farmers he'd brought there. Guilt pricked at her heart. She, too, contributed to his worries when she had defended Jonathan to him. The responsibilities he'd taken on in the past few months would defeat a lesser man, but not Dante. She'd never known anyone who had the strength of body and of character like he had.

Her heart burst with love for him, and she leaned over and kissed him on the cheek. She pulled her shawl tighter around her, scooted a chair closer to the stove, and sat down. Dante could sleep until morning. She'd keep watch for him.

Chapter 14

A sound jerked Dante from his deep sleep. His cheek lay against a wooden surface. He blinked to remember where he was. The memory of trying to stay awake to keep watch flashed into his mind. He bolted into a sitting position and turned his head in the direction of whatever had awakened him.

Savannah closed the oven door and set down a pan of biscuits on the counter. She wiped her hands on her apron and smiled at him. "I wondered how long you were going to sleep."

His gaze darted across the tabletop, but the note was nowhere to be seen. "H–how long have you been up?"

She kept her attention directed at a skillet on the stove top and didn't look around. "Oh, for some time now. I started to wake you, but I decided not to."

He looked under the table and around the bottom of his chair. The note had disappeared. He straightened and glanced at Savannah. She stood facing him with her arms crossed and a frown on her face. "Did you lose something?"

"Just a piece of paper. I'm sure it's around here somewhere." He bent over and looked underneath the table again.

"Is this what you lost?" The note dangled from her fingers.

He slumped back in his chair. "So you've seen it?"

She walked to the table and sat down opposite him. "Where did you get this?"

He rubbed his hands over his eyes. "It was in Abraham's shirt."

Her eyes narrowed and she nodded. "I thought it must have something to do with the lynching. What were you going to do? Stay up all night, guarding the house?"

He shook his head. "I don't know what I was thinking. I just knew I had to keep watch." He gave a disgusted grunt. "Some sentry I am. I couldn't even stay awake. What if they'd come while I was asleep?"

She smiled. "Oh, I don't know. Maybe I would have heard them since I took over after I found you asleep."

His mouth gaped open in surprise. "You stayed up after I went to sleep?"

She laughed and stood up. "I thought one of us ought to be alert, and you were sleeping so soundly I didn't have the heart to wake you."

"I'm sorry you missed your sleep."

"No need for that." He watched as she went back to the stove and picked up the coffeepot. She poured two cups and scooted one toward him. "Drink this. It'll help you awaken so that we can talk about what we're going to do."

"We?"

She bent over him, her face only a few inches from his. "If I remember correctly, you told me when we married that this land is mine, too. And I don't intend to let anyone harm it or any of its people. Do you understand?"

His heart hammered in his chest as he stared into her eyes. "Yes, I understand. If I didn't know better, I'd think I married a woman determined to have a henpecked husband."

She blushed and turned away. "I don't think you would ever let anybody make you do anything you didn't want to."

He stared at her as she set the coffeepot on the stove. There was something different about Savannah. In the last few days, she'd acted happier than he'd ever seen her. It thrilled him to think her feelings for him might have something to do with that. He sat up straighter and noticed for the first time the quilt draped around his shoulders.

He rubbed his fingers over the cover. "Where did this come from?"

She turned, the pan of biscuits in one hand and a plate of eggs in the other, and set them in front of him. "I put it there. I didn't want you to get cold."

Her face glowed, and he wondered if it was from the heat of the stove. "Thank you."

She sat in the chair across from him, picked up her coffee, and took a sip. He set his cup down and stared into its depth. "Last night seems like a bad dream."

"I know. I keep thinking of how Mamie and Saul looked when they saw Abraham in the coffin." She closed her eyes for a moment, frowned, and shook her head. When she opened her eyes, she blinked back tears. "I need to go over there so Tildy and Josie can go feed their families."

He swallowed a bite of eggs and pointed to her coffee cup with his fork. "Aren't you eating anything this morning?"

She picked up her cup and took a sip. "I ate a biscuit before you woke up."

"You need to eat something else. It's going to be a long day."

"I know." She set the cup down. "What do you have planned for this morning?"

He took a deep breath. "I'm going to see the sheriff first thing and tell him what's happened. I doubt if he'll do anything about it. Then I'm going to the store and buy some extra rifles and ammunition."

"Do you think they'll attack us like they did the people at the Crossroads?"

"I wouldn't doubt it. If they come here, I mean for our people to be ready for them."

"You'll be back in time for the burial, won't you?"

"I will."

"Then eat your breakfast and go to town. We'll be ready when you get back." She pushed up from the table and walked to the door. Her shawl hung on a peg beside it, and she reached for it. She pulled the wrap around her and opened the door. Before she stepped into the cold morning, she turned and smiled. "Be careful, Dante."

Her quiet words set his heart to pumping. Before he could respond, she walked outside. He restrained himself from rushing after her and sweeping her into his arms. Other matters needed his attention. He had to do everything in his power to see that Savannah and the people of Cottonwood were protected.

Savannah stared at her reflection in the mirror of the walnut dresser that had graced her bedroom at Aunt Jane's and now sat crammed into the tiny room she shared with Dante. Her mind wandering, she pulled the silver-handled brush through her hair. Where could Dante be? He'd been gone since early morning, and now it was well past noon.

She laid the brush down and stood to smooth the wrinkles from her dress. As she ran her palms down the length of the skirt, she remembered the last time she'd worn this dress—the day she'd married Dante.

Backing up from the dresser, she twisted at the waist to get a better view of herself. She remembered how uncertain about her decision she'd been that day. Now she couldn't understand why she would have ever doubted saying yes to his proposal.

"What are you doing?"

She jumped at the sound of his voice. He stood in the open door, a puzzled expression on his face.

She reached for the brush on the dresser and pulled it through her hair once more. "I just finished dressing for Abraham's burial, and I thought about when I wore this dress on our wedding day."

His gaze drifted over her. "And you're more beautiful now than you were then."

She moved to stand in front of him. "I'm glad you think so." She frowned at the sadness in his eyes. "How did it go with the sheriff?"

He gave a disgusted grunt. "About like I expected. He brushed the whole episode aside as if it didn't matter. 'After all,' he said, 'it was just a former slave that probably was stealing from somebody, and they decided to teach him a lesson.' "

Savannah's mouth gaped open, and she shook the brush she still held in his face. "Teach him a lesson? By killing him?"

"That's what I said, but the sheriff told me to go on home and let him worry about keeping the peace in the community."

Savannah clenched her fists and stomped her foot on the floor. "He hasn't worried about that since the day he took office. Oh, I'd like to teach him a lesson."

Dante's tired eyes flickered with laughter. "Remind me never to make you mad, my dear."

Savannah's face burned, and she turned away. "Quit teasing me and get dressed. I laid your clothes out."

He followed her to the bed where his Sunday suit lay. He wrapped his arms around her waist and pulled her against him. His warm breath fanned her neck. "Thank you, Savannah."

She twisted in his arms and turned to face him. "For what?"

His arms tightened, and he bent his head. "For being my wife."

Her lips met his in a sweet kiss that set her head spinning. She pulled back and smiled at him. "We're going to be late for the funeral."

He chuckled and released her. "The voice of reason has spoken. I'll change clothes."

She placed the brush on the dresser and headed for the door. "I'm going back to Mamie's. Come on over when you get ready." She stopped and whirled to face him before she left. "Oh, I forgot. Did you get the extra guns?"

"I did."

A frown pulled at her brow. "That probably ran our bill up a lot at the store. Can we afford it?"

He sank down on the side of the bed and ran his fingers through his hair. "We can if we have a good crop next year. Right now I have to do everything I can to protect our home."

She nodded. "Yes, you're right."

He didn't move or respond to her words. His head drooped, and his shoulders sagged. Last night's events had touched him deeply. Savannah wished she could take some of the worry from his shoulders. Since their marriage, she'd come to a new understanding. God had a way of helping His children see what was most important in life. Money, land, acceptance in the community weren't bad things to have, but without love and family, they meant nothing.

Once, she thought being back at Cottonwood was the only thing that would make her happy. Now she realized that her parents and all the people who'd lived on the plantation were what had given her home true meaning.

The land and her goal of returning it to its former glory now took second place in her life to the man she had come to love. For the first time in her life, she had her priorities in the right order. She finally understood that it was the people she loved and who loved her that made life worth living.

Chapter 15

Savannah glanced up from the shirt she was mending and stared at Mamie, who sat across the table from her. Three months had passed since they'd buried Abraham in the small cemetery where Cottonwood slaves had been buried for years, but Mamie still had not recovered.

Savannah laid her sewing aside and reached across the table to grasp Mamie's hand. "Mamie, can I get you something to drink?"

Mamie shook her head. "No, thanks, Miss 'Vanna. I'm fine."

Savannah rose and knelt beside Mamie's chair. "But I'm worried about you. You hardly eat anything. You've got to take care of yourself better."

A tear ran down Mamie's cheek. "I knows that, but it's hard to do."

"Saul and Joshua love you. They're concerned, too."

Mamie nodded. "I know, but I can't get over seeing my baby dead. That ain't 'posed to happen. Chil'run shouldn't die 'fore they mamma and poppa do."

"I understand how you feel, but—"

Mamie held up a hand. "No, you don't know how I feel, but you will soon when your baby come."

Savannah's eyebrows arched, and she stared at Mamie. "I told you that's a long time off."

A smile curled Mamie's face. "Don't you knows you got life in you, Miss 'Vanna?"

Savannah pushed to her feet and stared down at Mamie. "What are you talking about?"

Mamie rose from her chair and pressed her hand to Savannah's stomach. "You with child, Miss 'Vanna. I knowed it some time ago. I reckon we be seeing your baby born this fall."

The breath left Savannah's body. "No. You can't be serious."

Mamie nodded. "It true. You and Mistuh Dante gwine have a baby, and we gwine see new life on Cottonwood. I 'spect Mistuh Dante be right proud."

Savannah's mind whirled with thoughts she'd tried to dismiss for weeks. The tiredness, the queasy stomach in the mornings, and small changes she'd noticed in her body. They all added up to what she'd ignored. She was going to be a mother.

Her eyes grew wide. "Do you really think I'm going to have a baby?"

"I knows you are. I can always tell."

"B—but why didn't I know?"

Mamie chuckled. "I reckon you would real soon."

Savannah opened her mouth to protest, but the words wouldn't come. Laughter rippled through her body, and she threw her arms around Mamie and hugged her. "I'm going to be a mother."

"Yas'm. And Mistuh Dante be a poppa."

At the mention of her husband, Savannah froze. Although there had been no raids on Cottonwood, rumors circulated that the band of murderers who attacked the Crossroads community still roamed the countryside from time to time. She didn't want to add a wife who was going to have a baby to his worries, but he needed to know.

"Don't tell Dante about this yet."

Mamie frowned. "But why? He the father."

"I know, but he's been so worried about what's been happening in the countryside. He's gone into town today to talk to the sheriff. I'll tell him when the time is right. Just not yet. Promise me?"

Mamie's eyes clouded, but she nodded. "All right, Miss 'Vanna. You tell him when you gets ready."

The cabin door flew open, and Dante strode into the room. Savannah could tell from the expression on his face something was wrong.

Mamie gathered up her sewing and hurried to the door. "I gots to get home. Saul be coming from the barn soon. I'll see you later, Miss 'Vanna." She nodded to Dante. "Mistuh Dante."

He smiled at Mamie. "Take care of yourself, Mamie."

Dante closed the door when Mamie left and shrugged his coat from his shoulders. Savannah watched as he hung it up and trudged to the table.

"What's the matter?"

He sat down and motioned for her to do the same. "I want to talk to you."

The tone of his voice frightened her. She eased into the chair. "Dante, you're scaring me."

He clasped his hands on the table in front of him. "I hope I'm wrong, but I'm afraid we may have a visit from the raiders this evening."

Her heart pounded, and she swallowed back the fear that rose in her throat. "What makes you think they'd come now? It's been three months since Abraham's death, and they haven't bothered us."

"It was the attitude of the sheriff today. When I asked him what he'd found out about Abraham's lynching, he told me that anybody who would get upset over somebody hanging a thief might need to think about protecting his own home." His fist pounded the table, and Savannah jumped in surprise. "He knows who they are, Savannah. He as much as said so. For all I know, he could be one of them, too."

"What makes you think it could be tonight?"

He shrugged. "Tonight, tomorrow, the next night—I don't know. But we have to be prepared. I've told the men what I need them to do. Now I want you to listen to me and do as I say."

"What is it?"

He sat up straighter. "If they come, they may set fire to the cabins like they did at the Crossroads, so I don't want anybody in them. I want you to take the women and children to the woods. The men and I will stay hidden here. After all, they believe they're coming after former slaves who wouldn't dare fight back against a white man. We intend to show them differently. With any luck, we'll be able to surprise them."

Her heart pounded in fear, but she didn't want Dante to see that she was afraid. She pushed back from the table and headed toward the stove. "That sounds like a good idea. I'll fix you something to eat. Then I'll get the women."

He followed her and turned her toward him. "Tell the women to take plenty of quilts to keep warm. The nights are still cold."

"I will."

"I'll do everything I can to protect Cottonwood, Savannah. Just take care of yourself."

"You do the same, Dante." Tears burned her eyes. "I can't stand the thought of anything happening to you."

He slid his arms around her and drew her close. The muscle in his jaw twitched as he stared into her eyes. "I love you, Savannah."

After a moment, he released his hold on her and walked toward the sideboard. With a sigh she directed her gaze back to the stove and reached for the frying pan. When she looked over her shoulder, he pulled the pistol from the sideboard drawer.

He walked back to the table and laid it down. "Take this and some ammunition with you. Shoot anybody who threatens you or any of the others."

The frying pan slipped from her shaking fingers and clattered as it struck the stove top. "Sh—shoot them?"

His eyebrows arched. "Do you know how to shoot a gun?"

Fear knotted her stomach as she remembered when and why she'd learned to use a gun. This situation was no different from that one then. "My father taught me in case we ever had to defend Cottonwood during the war."

His lips thinned. "Be careful, Savannah, but if you feel any of you are in danger, shoot to kill."

She stared into his eyes. "I will."

Savannah didn't think she'd ever been so cold in her life. Her stomach rumbled, and she shook her head in disgust. Nausea had kept her from eating all day, but now wasn't the time to be thinking about food. She had to concentrate on something else and get her mind off her hunger.

A cold wind blew through the woods where she and the women and their children hid. They'd been lucky to find a dry place where they could sit and huddle underneath the covers they'd brought. Time had passed slowly since they'd left home hours ago. They'd trudged deep into the forest before stopping. Now they sat silent, hoping that someone would soon come and tell them it was safe to go back home.

Her thoughts turned to Dante, and she wondered where he was. She glanced over at Mamie, who sat on a fallen log, her back straight and her body unmoving. The other women sat silently with their children gathered close.

Savannah pulled her quilt tighter and settled against a tree trunk. She touched the barrel of the gun that protruded from her coat pocket. Fatigue washed over her, and she closed her eyes for a moment. Blinking, she straightened. She couldn't go to sleep. Dante expected her to protect everyone.

She closed her eyes again and hovered on the brink of sleep. A rebel yell pierced the quiet night, and Savannah bolted upright. The other women sat up, but no one said a word. Savannah breathed a prayer of thanks that none of the children had awakened.

Fear radiated from the small group as Savannah strained to hear any distant sounds. Another yell split the air. Then gunshots from the direction of Cottonwood blasted through the night. Savannah's stomach roiled.

The gunshots echoed through the forest for several minutes. Then a deadly calm descended, leaving a silence so eerie that the hairs on the back of her neck prickled. All kinds of thoughts ran through her mind. She could imagine the men from Cottonwood lying in the cabin clearing—all dead from trying to protect the place they called home.

Savannah threw the quilt back and rose to her feet. She glanced around at the women, who huddled protectively near their children. "I'm going to walk to the edge of the forest and see if I can tell what's going on. Don't leave until I get back."

Without waiting for an answer, she hurried in the direction they'd come from when they entered the forest. If she could just get to the edge, maybe she would be able to tell what had happened.

The closer she came to the field beyond the woods, the slower her steps became. She stopped before stepping out into the open and gazed toward home. She couldn't make out the cabins in the distance, but at least there were no fires that she could see.

Pounding hoofbeats alerted her to a rider coming toward her. In the dark, she couldn't tell who it was, but she hoped it was Dante coming to bring them back home. She pulled the gun from her pocket and stepped closer to the forest's edge.

Too late she realized she'd moved right into the path of the horse. She screamed, and the rider pulled back on the reins. The horse reared, his hoofs beating at the air as the rider attempted to get the animal under control. When the horse settled, the rider pulled his gun.

"I hear you in there. Come on out before I start shooting."

Savannah flinched at the sound of Jonathan's voice, and she stepped from behind the tree. Jonathan, a white hood covering his face, sat on his horse, which still pranced in place.

"Jonathan, what are you doing? Have you lost your mind?"

"Savannah?" The word sounded muffled under the hood.

"Why have you turned into a killer and a traitor to your own people?"

He laughed. "Traitor? You're a fine one to talk. I loved you, Savannah, and you left me for a yellow coward who stole your land."

"You never loved me. You loved my family's land."

He shook his head, and the hood swayed. "You're wrong. I loved you, but I waited too long to tell you. You'd already deceived me and married that carpetbagger."

"Don't talk about Dante like that."

"He's no good for you, Savannah. He can't have you."

She backed up a step. "What do you mean?"

He pulled his gun from his holster. "You're a traitor to your people. I'm going to kill you."

Fear gripped Savannah at the sight of the gun aimed at her. Before she had time to think, she raised her hand and fired. The first shot went over Jonathan's head, and the horse reared up again. As he wrestled with the reins, she fired a second shot, and he dropped his gun and cried out in pain.

Jonathan grabbed his leg and bent over the saddle. "You haven't heard the last of me." He jerked the reins and dug his heels into the horse's side.

She watched Jonathan disappear into the night before she collapsed against a tree. Tears ran down her face. She looked at the gun in her hand and replaced it in her coat pocket.

After a few moments, she turned to reenter the forest, but a light across the open field caught her attention. The flickering flame bounced up and down. It had to be a lantern, and whoever was holding it was running.

She pulled the gun out, stepped behind a tree, and stared as the light came closer. A yellow glow from the flame reflected off the face of Dante, and she cried out in relief.

"Dante!"

Savannah ran toward him and threw herself into his arms. His arms encircled her and pulled her close. "Savannah. Are you all right? I heard gunshots." His voice trembled.

She pulled away from him and stared up into his face. "I had to see what was going on. Jonathan found me."

He set the lantern on the ground and held her at arm's length. "Are you certain it was Boyer?"

"I recognized his voice. He hates me for marrying you and wanted to kill me. So I shot him first."

"Did you kill him?"

"I think I just hit him in the leg. But tell me what happened."

He picked up the lantern. "We were able to hold them off. I think we wounded a few. So I've come to take all of you home."

"Good. Let's go get the women and children. They're so cold."

Savannah turned to head back the way she'd come, but Dante grabbed her arm. She glanced over her shoulder at him.

"I'm sorry your friends have turned against you because of me, Savannah."

The sad look on his face told her he meant what he said. She shook her head. "The friends who really count have accepted you. Jonathan's still fighting the war, and I can't do anything about that."

Dante took a deep breath. "Then let's go bring our people home."

She smiled and led the way into the forest. The thought of how she'd thrown herself into Dante's arms returned, and her skin grew warm. She'd never known anyone who had the power to calm her fears like he could. Her heart filled with love for him. Now they needed to build their life together without worrying about protecting their land.

Chapter 16

Dante walked to the bedroom door and looked in on Savannah. After all the excitement of the night before, he'd let her sleep this morning. She'd been exhausted when they got home, and he'd thought she'd go right to bed. She'd surprised him, though, by saying that she had to eat something first. He could hardly believe all she consumed before finally falling into bed.

Now that he thought about it, he didn't remember seeing her eat anything earlier yesterday. He'd never seen her that hungry before.

He stepped back into the kitchen and poured himself another cup of coffee and opened his Bible. The quiet in the early morning hours provided the best time for reading and studying God's Word. He opened the book and found himself transported to another time and place where a young man faced a giant with a sling.

From time to time he took a sip from the cup and had just drained the last drop when he heard Savannah stirring in the bedroom. He started to get up and pour himself another cup of coffee, but he froze at the sound of running footsteps. Savannah, still in her gown and her long hair falling on her shoulders, dashed by him and out the cabin door.

Surprised at her hasty departure, he set the cup on the table, walked to the front door, and peered outside. He couldn't see her, but he could hear her beside the cabin and knew she was in the process of losing everything she'd eaten the night before.

At a loss about what to do to help her, he glanced into the cabin. The quilt she'd taken to the woods the night before lay draped over a chair. He grabbed it and went outside. When he stepped around the corner, his heart pricked at the sight of her leaning against the cabin.

He draped the quilt around her, and she looked over her shoulder and smiled. "Thanks."

Her pallor frightened him. The cheeks that were usually rosy were pale this morning, and her eyes drooped at the corners. "Are you all right?"

She nodded. "I'm better now." She pushed into a standing position but lurched toward him.

Surprised, he scooped her into his arms and carried her back into the cabin. When they got to the bedroom, he laid her on the bed and covered her up. "Last night really didn't agree with you. I think you should stay in bed today."

She pushed up on her elbows. "I'm fine now, Dante. I have too much to do to stay in bed."

He restrained her. "You heard me. You're to stay in bed until you're feeling better. Now is there anything I can get you? Some coffee maybe?"

Her face screwed into a grimace. "The thought of coffee makes me sick. Maybe I'll feel like eating something later."

He stared down at her for a moment. "I have to go into town and tell the sheriff what happened last night. I'll ask Mamie to look in on you."

Savannah shook her head. "No, she's had too much happen in the last few days. I'll be fine. By the time you get back, I should be up and feeling better."

He hesitated. He didn't want to leave, but the sheriff needed to be informed about what had happened. "Well, if you're sure, I'll come back as quickly as possible."

"I'm sure. Now go on."

Dante turned to the door, but he glanced back at her once more. She'd already closed her eyes.

He didn't like leaving her alone when she was ill. All kinds of thoughts tumbled through his head. She might need something and be unable to call out. Or she could get up, faint, and hit her head on something. She could lie there for hours before anybody came to check on her. No matter what she said, he was going to ask Mamie to look in on her in a few hours.

If anything happened to her, he didn't know what he'd do.

The sheriff leaned back in his chair, propped his feet on his desk, and pulled a knife from his pocket. Opening it, he began to clean under his fingernails. He didn't look up at Dante. "How do you know it was Jonathan Boyer? Did you see him?"

Dante tried to control his growing anger at the sheriff. Ever since he'd arrived and told his story of the raid at Cottonwood, the man had come up with excuses why Dante couldn't possibly be sure of the identity of the men behind the masks.

Dante inhaled and tried once more. "I didn't see him, but my wife recognized his voice. She's known him all her life."

The sheriff laughed. "Scared women think they hear a lot of things in the dark. It could have been anybody who sounded like him."

"No. He threatened her and said things only Boyer knew."

"Well, tell you what I'll do. First chance I get, I'll ride out to Oak Hill and question Mr. Boyer. After all, he ain't goin' nowhere. He wouldn't leave his plantation."

Dante walked around the desk and shoved the sheriff's feet to the floor. He bent over until their noses almost touched. "Now I'll tell you what I'm going to do. First chance I get, like maybe this afternoon, I'm going to ride over to Selma and talk to the federal officials there. I'm sure they'll be interested in a sheriff who allows murderers to roam the countryside, killing freed slaves and terrorizing landowners."

The sheriff tried to push up, but the back legs of the chair slipped out from under him, and he tipped backward. His face red with rage, he struggled to get to his feet. "Don't threaten me, you carpetbagger."

Dante looked down at him and grimaced. "You disgust me. You're supposed to protect the people of this county, and you take the side of the lawbreakers. You deserve everything you're about to get."

Dante strode from the room and slammed the door behind him. He shook with anger. How that man ever attained the office of sheriff was beyond Dante. The man was an insult to the office of law enforcer.

After a moment, he took a deep breath and headed toward the general store. Maybe he could find something that would make Savannah feel better.

A bell over the door tinkled when Dante stepped into the store. Mr. Perkins stood at a counter rearranging bolts of cloth. He glanced up and smiled. "Mr. Rinaldi, come in. How're things out your way today?"

"Not so good, I'm afraid. Cottonwood was raided last night."

The man's eyes grew wide. "Anybody hurt?"

"Not any of our people, but a few of our visitors may have been hit. I wonder if anybody's come to see Dr. Spencer today with a gunshot wound."

Mr. Perkins shook his head. "I don't know. Doc hasn't been in here. If I hear anything, I'll let you know." The man pushed one last bolt of cloth into place and stepped back to eye the display. He turned toward the door as the bell tinkled again. "Come in, Mrs. Thompson."

Dante glanced over his shoulder to see Martha Thompson entering. He wondered what gossip she was peddling this morning. He tried to smile. "Good morning, Mrs. Thompson. It's good to see you again."

"You, too, Mr. Rinaldi." She walked over to the counter and picked up a bolt of the material Mr. Perkins had just arranged and laid it on a table behind her. "Now don't you worry about me, Mr. Perkins. You help Mr. Rinaldi, and I'll just make myself at home while I look at this bolt at the bottom of the stack."

Mr. Perkins's eyebrows arched, and he motioned for Dante to follow him. "If you need anything, Mrs. Thompson, let me know." He turned to Dante. "Now what can I help you with?"

"I'm looking for something for my wife."

"Like a present?"

Dante shook his head. "No, she isn't feeling well. I thought I might be able to get some tonic."

Mr. Perkins pointed to a shelf that contained medicine bottles. Dante peered at the labels—some marked tonics, others elixirs. "I don't know which one."

"What are her symptoms?"

Dante searched his mind and realized that Savannah hadn't felt well in several weeks. Although she hadn't complained, he understood now that she was sick. Fear welled up in him. What if it was something serious? Perhaps he should rush home and bring her back to see Dr. Spencer.

"She tires very easily, doesn't have much energy. She's very pale, and her appetite is gone. This morning she lost everything she'd eaten last night." Reciting the symptoms scared him even more, and he turned to Mr. Perkins. "Do you think it could be something serious?"

Before he could answer, a shrill laugh pierced his ears. He turned to see Martha Thompson shaking her head and laughing as if she'd just heard the funniest joke of her life. "Oh you men," she cackled. "You're about as useless as a sick hound dog."

Dante frowned and walked toward her. "What's so funny?"

She roared with laughter again. "You are. And you call yourself a husband."

Dante glanced back at Mr. Perkins, who appeared to be as mystified as he. "I'm sorry, Mrs. Thompson, I have no idea what you're talking about."

She pulled a handkerchief from her pocket and wiped at the tears that streaked her face. "I ain't even a doctor, and I know exactly what's wrong with your wife 'cause I've had the same symptoms five times now."

Dante stared at the woman, who looked healthy. If Savannah and Mrs. Thompson shared the same disease, it must not be fatal. "Then would you mind telling me what it is?"

Martha grinned. "Nothing that nine months won't take care of."

He frowned. "What are you talking. . . ?" His voice trailed off as the meaning of her words dawned on him. "Are you saying. . . ?"

Martha smile and nodded. "Congratulations, Mr. Rinaldi."

Dante glanced over his shoulder at Mr. Perkins. "I—I think I'd better go. I'll come back later."

Without waiting for an answer, Dante rushed from the store and ran to the hitching post where he'd left his horse. Untying the reins, he jumped into the saddle and turned his horse toward Cottonwood. Once outside of town, he nudged the horse into a gallop.

The wind burned his face, but he hardly noticed. All he could think about was that he was going to be a father, but that wasn't the best part. He and Savannah would have something that would bind them together for the rest of their lives.

Chapter 17

Savannah ate the last bite of biscuit and took a sip from her cup. The molasses she'd stirred into the coffee gave it a sweet taste and eased the queasiness in her stomach. She placed her dishes in the dry sink and glanced around the small room.

For the first time, she wondered what it had been like for the slaves who'd lived in this cabin. When she was growing up, she'd hardly given thought to the plight of the people who labored for her family. Now she called this dilapidated house her home, and she understood how bad it must have been for the families who lived in the shadow of the big house.

The small cabin provided just enough space for two people. With the baby, they would be crowded, but they could do it. After all, Mamie and Saul and their two sons shared a cabin just a bit larger than theirs, but their home probably seemed very empty now with Abraham gone.

A knock at the door interrupted her thoughts, and she hurried to open it. Mamie stood on the porch. Her eyes were swollen from crying, but she smiled at Savannah. "How you doin', Miss 'Vanna?"

Savannah reached out and drew the woman inside. She put her arms around Mamie and hugged her. "I'm feeling better. How are you today?"

Mamie sighed. "I 'spects I've been better. I just gotta put this in the Lord's hands and try to get on with my life. I still got Saul and Joshua, and I be thankful for that."

Savannah blinked back tears. "You're a strong woman, Mamie. You'll never get over missing Abraham, but you'll come to a point where you can remember the good times you had with him and be thankful for that."

"Yas'm. I knows that. But I come over to see how you feelin'. Mistuh Dante asked me to check on you, and that's what I'm doin'."

Savannah smiled. "I just ate something, and I'm feeling much better."

Mamie arched one eyebrow. "You ain't tole Mistuh Dante yet, have you?"

Savannah shook her head. "I've tried to, but he's had so much on his mind with all that's happened I didn't want to add to it."

"You have to tell him soon. Cain't keep a secret like this long."

Savannah drew the woman toward the stove and pulled out a chair for her. They sat down, and Savannah basked in the warmth before she turned to

Mamie. "I'm afraid, Mamie."

A look of surprise flashed on Mamie's face. "Why you 'fraid?"

Savannah sat up straight. "What if I'm not a good mother?"

Mamie chuckled. "Oh Miss 'Vanna, you be fine. Lots of women feel that way 'fore their first baby born, but don't you worry none. I been knowin' you since you was born, and you gwine make a good mamma."

"What makes you so sure? I've never taken care of a baby before."

"You can do anything you set your mind to. Just look what you and Mistuh Dante already done. You come back to Cottonwood all ready to make it a grand plantation again, but you not like the girl who left it when the big house burn. You come back with a good man who loves you a lot. I'd shore like to see his face when you tell him about the baby."

Savannah smiled. "You really think he'll be happy?"

"I don't think. I knows it. I thought that poor man gwine go crazy when he heard you want to go on that boat down to Mobile. He couldn't eat or sleep. I knowed all along what he needed to do, so I tole him there was a way to keep you here. And he did it. He got up his nerve and asked you to marry him. When he tole me you done accepted him, he was the happiest man I ever seen." Mamie rose from her chair. "Now you gwine make him so happy he shout."

Savannah laughed and followed Mamie to the door. "Thank you, Mamie. You've always been the one to help me when I needed it. Now I have to decide how I'm going to tell Dante." She stepped onto the front porch and inhaled. "It may be chilly, but it's a beautiful day. I do my best thinking at my parents' graves. I'm going to put my coat on and walk down there."

Mamie smiled and walked down the steps. Savannah stared after her until she had disappeared into her home. Then she reentered the cabin and pulled her coat from the peg by the door. A visit to the cemetery often provided her peace and guidance. She hoped today would be no exception.

She picked up her Bible and started to leave. A warning niggled in the back of her mind. With all the turmoil in the countryside, she probably shouldn't venture so far without protection. She walked to the sideboard, pulled the pistol from the drawer, and stuck it in her pocket.

⌒∾⌒

Dante reined the horse to a stop at Cottonwood's barn and dismounted. He'd ridden harder than he should to get home, but he couldn't wait to see Savannah. One glance at the lather on the mare, though, told him the horse had to be taken care of first.

He led the horse into the alleyway of the barn and pulled the saddle and blanket from its back. A voice from behind startled him.

"Mistuh Dante, I didn't know you got back."

Dante turned to see Saul walking out of one of the stalls at the far end of the barn. "I finished my business and hurried home. I didn't want to leave Savannah alone too long."

Saul stopped beside him and pulled the tattered hat from his head. "She ain't home right now. Mamie went over to check on her awhile ago, and she said she gwine go visit her folks at the cemetery."

Dante frowned. "Did she walk?"

"Yas suh, I thinks so."

The flicker of anger he'd held back on the ride home ignited. She'd kept the news of his child from him, and now she was out walking by herself. After last night's scare, she should have stayed inside like he told her.

Saul coughed, and Dante jerked his attention back to the man beside him. "I'm sorry, Saul. I have a lot on my mind."

"Yas suh."

He handed the reins of the horse to Saul. "Would you mind taking care of my horse? I need to go see my wife."

Saul took the reins and smiled. "I 'spects it 'bout time you got things straightened out in your house, Mistuh Dante."

Dante's eyes grew wide. "Do you know something that I don't? Like the fact that I'm about to become a father, and my wife hasn't told me?"

A sad smile curled Saul's lips. "Yas suh. Miss 'Vanna done tole Mamie, and Mamie tole me. I 'spect it be a happy time here at Cottonwood. The good Lord took away Abraham, but He done give us a new life to bless us. He has a way of makin' things right even when bad things happen."

Dante stared at him. "You can say that with faith after the horrible death of your son?"

Tears filled Saul's eyes. "I thought losing my mamma when I was little was the worstest that could ever happen, but I was wrong. I ain't never gwine git over Abraham, but the Lord done tole me He be right there a-helpin' me each day."

"I know that Saul, but thank you for reminding me."

Dante squared his shoulders and strode toward the river. When he reached the bluff, he stared down into the rolling water and remembered the first night he'd come to Cottonwood and how he'd lain under the stars and listened to its lull. In the time since then, he'd come to love every inch of soil on his land.

Savannah had told him she wanted her child to inherit Cottonwood. Now she said she loved him, but he wondered how she would feel after the baby was born. It scared him to think now that she had what she'd wanted, she would no longer need him.

∽∾

Savannah could tell from the sun's position she'd been in the cemetery for several

111

hours. She rose to her feet and closed her Bible. Glancing down at the graves once more, she put her fingers to her lips and blew a kiss to the parents she loved.

She left the small burial ground and walked along the path in deep thought until she approached the bend that brought her to the river's edge. She stopped on the tall bluff and stared at the water far below.

Once she had wanted to travel the steamboats that plowed this river, but no more. She had found contentment at Cottonwood with Dante. Guilt over her silence about the baby filled her. Even if Dante was worried about the protection of everyone living on the plantation, she had to tell him. It wasn't fair to keep it from him anymore.

The sound of a snapping twig caught her attention. She turned to look behind her. Maybe one of the men had been to the canebrake they'd cleared and was coming back, but she saw no one. Turning to continue home, she jerked to a halt and swallowed the fear rising in her throat. Jonathan Boyer blocked her path.

"Jonathan, what are you doing here?"

His lips curled into a snarl, and he glared at her with hatred. He limped forward. "I came to see you, Savannah." He stopped and grimaced in pain.

She glanced down at his leg. "Are you hurt?"

"Hurt? Don't you remember shooting me last night? You didn't think I'd recovered already, did you?"

She walked closer. "I'm sorry, Jonathan. I didn't want to hurt you. Let me get you back to my house, and I'll send for Dr. Spencer."

He held out his hand to stop her. "Don't you come near me. Because of you and your husband, I've lost everything I ever wanted. Cottonwood, you, and now Oak Hill."

She frowned. "I don't understand. How have you lost Oak Hill?"

He flinched and shifted his weight to the other leg. "Your dear husband made a visit to the sheriff this morning and threatened to go to the federal authorities if he didn't do something. So our good law officer decided he'd better get busy before that happened."

Savannah backed up a step. "What did Sheriff Newton do?"

"He went over to Sam Baker's place and told him he knew Sam was one of the people who attacked the Crossroads. He promised Sam he'd overlook his bad judgment in joining the raiders if he'd disclose the names of everybody in the group. So Sam talked. He told the sheriff how we raided the countryside and how we hung that slave Abraham. Now the sheriff's after me for murder. I expect he wants to hang me so it'll look good for him."

"Then you need to give yourself up. It may go better with you if you go in voluntarily."

He glanced up at the sky and laughed. "You must think I'm crazy. I'm going to finish what I started last night. Then I'm leaving Alabama and everything in it far behind."

Jonathan's laugh sent chills up Savannah's spine. It had the tone of a deranged man. "Please, Jonathan, let me help you."

"Yes, my dear. You're going to help me a lot. I'm going to make your husband wish he'd never come to Alabama."

He stuck his hand into his pocket and whipped out a knife as he advanced on her. Savannah stared in horror at the long blade flashing in the sun. She backed up a step. "Jonathan, what are you doing?"

"You should never have turned against me, Savannah. Now I'm going to kill you."

She wanted to run, but her body seemed frozen in place. The hatred burning in his eyes told her this wasn't the friend she'd always known. She screamed as he advanced, then she pulled the gun from her pocket and fired.

Chapter 18

A woman's scream followed by a gunshot sent an icy chill down Dante's back. It had to be Savannah's voice he heard. He hesitated for only a moment before he bolted in the direction of the sounds.

Near the bend in the road ahead, he saw a man with a knife raised above his head. The man staggered forward, his attention directed to someone in front of him.

"Stay back, Jonathan!" Dante heard Savannah yell. "I'll aim lower next time!"

Dante sprinted forward and grabbed Jonathan's upraised arm. A few feet away, he could see Savannah with a pistol in her hand.

Jonathan whirled in Dante's grip and stared at him. Dante almost felt the heat from the hatred that burned in Jonathan's eyes. Grimacing, Jonathan struggled to free himself from Dante's grip.

"Let me go. I'll kill you both."

Dante could feel Jonathan weakening, and he remembered Savannah had said she shot him the night before. With a new burst of strength, Dante gripped Jonathan's wrist tighter and twisted it away from his body. The knife dropped to the ground.

Letting go of Jonathan's arm, Dante drew back his fist and connected with his assailant's jaw. Jonathan lurched back and fell to the ground. Dante stood over him, but Jonathan didn't move.

Dante turned to Savannah. "Are you all right?"

She bit her lower lip and nodded. "I'm fine. I'm so glad you got here when you did. I don't know what—" Her eyes widened in fear. "Dante," she screamed, "look out!"

Dante whirled to see Jonathan approaching with a large rock held above his head. "I'm not through yet."

Dante ducked, grabbed Jonathan around the waist, and propelled him backward to the edge of the bluff. The ground crumbled underneath their feet, and dirt and rocks rolled down the steep bank toward the river. Dante tried to pull back, but Jonathan gripped him tighter.

A large crack appeared in the earth between Dante's and Jonathan's feet. Dante released his hold, swung his fists up, and hit Jonathan's arms. The force knocked Jonathan loose, and he shifted his weight to swing again. Dante stepped back to avoid the blow he knew was coming.

Before Jonathan could deliver the punch, the edge of the bluff collapsed beneath him. His arms flailed as he struggled to regain his balance, but his footing had disappeared in the earth that slid down the bluff toward the river.

Dante reached for Jonathan, but it was too late. He fell back, tumbling downward amid the rocks and dirt. Dante watched the man's body twist and turn until it came to rest at the edge of the river far below.

A sob next to him alerted Dante that Savannah stood there.

"Oh Jonathan, what happened to the boy I knew?"

Dante turned to her. "It was the war, Savannah. Maybe those who died were luckier than the ones who survived."

She tilted her head. "What do you mean?"

"Men like Jonathan couldn't accept the changes in the South and in their lives. It must have eaten away at him until it destroyed the boy you knew." His shoulders drooped. "I never meant to kill him, though. I hope you believe that."

Her eyes sparkled with tears. "I do."

"Mistuh Dante, Mistuh Dante, what going on here?"

They turned at the sound of Saul's voice. He ran toward them with Big Mike and Henry Walton right behind. When they reached the edge of the bluff, Dante pointed downward. "Jonathan Boyer came back. He's down there."

Saul stared at the body below. "That the man who killed Abraham?"

Savannah nodded. "Yes. He confessed to me."

Saul took a deep breath. "Then let's bring him up."

Dante clamped his hand on Saul's shoulder. "We will. Then I'll take the body into town to the sheriff and tell him what happened."

Savannah reached out and touched Dante's arm. "Do you want me to go with you?"

He shook his head. "No. You go on home. I'll see you there when I get back. We have some things to settle between us."

She wiped at a tear that escaped her eye. "I suppose we do."

She straightened her shoulders and walked down the path toward home. He watched her for a few moments before he remembered the men who were already climbing down the bluff to recover Jonathan's body.

When he bought Cottonwood, he had hopes of finding the happiness he'd been wanting for years. Now he had the land and a wife who said she loved him, but he also had to face the fact that he'd forced Savannah to marry him and then had killed the man she might have married. They had a lot to talk about when he got back from town.

❧

The last rays of sunlight dotted the horizon when Dante stepped onto the cabin's porch hours later. The time at Sheriff Newton's office had taken much longer than he expected, but he'd finally been allowed to leave. Thanks to the questioning of Sam Baker earlier in the day, Dante's accounts of Jonathan's death and of Savannah's presence at the scene compelled the sheriff to accept Dante's statement. He had returned home, but a more difficult task lay before him.

On the ride back from town, he'd pondered what he was going to say to Savannah. He knew from the beginning she only married him for the plantation, but he thought that had all changed. She'd said she loved him. But did she really mean it? If she did, why hadn't she told him they were going to have a baby?

Dante pounded his fist against the post at the edge of the porch. It was time he found out.

He pushed the cabin door open and had no sooner stepped inside than Savannah appeared in the bedroom doorway. She'd already lit the lamps, and the flickering flames about the room cast a glow over her. The anger he'd felt a few minutes before dissolved at the sight of her waiting to welcome him home.

She smiled and hurried forward. "Let me help you with your coat." She moved behind him and pulled the heavy coat from his shoulders. When it slipped from his arms, she turned and hung it next to the door. "Now sit down at the table. I have your supper ready. You've hardly eaten anything today and must be starved."

He grabbed her arm before she could head to the stove. "Eating can wait, Savannah. I think we need to talk."

Her lips trembled. "About what?"

He led her to the kitchen table and pulled out a chair. "Sit down. There are some things we need to settle between us."

Her eyes grew wide, but she eased into the chair without looking away from him. "You sound so serious, Dante. If it's about Jonathan, I want you to know his death wasn't your fault. He came here looking for trouble and meant for us to die. It's because of his actions that he's dead."

Dante sat across from her, stretched his arms out on the table, and balled his fists. "I've tried to tell myself that, but the fact remains he still died at my hands."

She reached across and covered his hands with hers. "Don't think like that. It wasn't your fault."

His skin burned from her touch, and he pulled his hands away. "I've thought a lot today about Jonathan's state of mind. I know he came back nursing horrible memories of the war, but many of us did. Maybe it was more than that. I think he loved you, and his anger turned to violence when I made you marry me."

A look of surprise flashed across her face. "You didn't make me marry you, Dante. I agreed."

He nodded. "Yes, you did. But you never would have married me if I hadn't

116

dangled Cottonwood in front of you."

She straightened in her chair and frowned. "Are you saying that you're sorry you married me?"

"I'm saying that everybody around here thought of me as a foreigner and a carpetbagger. There's no way you would have agreed unless there was something in it for you, and that something was Cottonwood."

Tears pooled in her eyes, and she pushed to her feet. "It's a little late to be reliving the past, isn't it? All you wanted was to be accepted in the community, to have friends. You already had Cottonwood. In time, the people around here would have gotten to know you, and you would have been accepted. When you proposed, I couldn't understand why you would give me so much when you were really getting so little in return."

He stood and faced her. "I told you why, Savannah. I couldn't get you out of my mind from the moment you almost ran me down with that buggy. It was afterward, though, when I saw you here at your parents' graves and witnessed how you tended your sick aunt that I knew I loved you like I would never love another. I thought I'd go crazy when you said you were leaving. I had to find a way to stop. I knew the only thing that would keep you here would be Cottonwood, and I was right. I used your love for Cottonwood to get what I wanted. I'm sorry for doing that."

Savannah exhaled a long breath. "I'm not sorry."

Dante frowned. "You're not?"

She took his right hand in both of hers, brought it to her mouth, and kissed it. Still holding it close to her lips, she glanced up. "If you had let me go, I never would have known the happiness I've had from loving you. I told myself I was marrying you to come home to Cottonwood, but I think I was only deceiving myself. I think I fell in love with you that first day, too. It just took me longer to realize it."

His heart pounded in his chest so hard he could barely breathe. "I know you said you love me, but I've scarce let myself believe it. Are you sure?"

"I am." Savannah still held his hand, and she cupped it in both of hers. "Why is it so difficult for you to believe that I love you?"

He swallowed. "I haven't had anybody who loved me in a long time, Savannah. I've been so lonely, and I didn't dare dream that a beautiful woman like you could see anything worth loving in a man like me."

"Oh Dante. I never realized how lonely you were, but you're not anymore. I'm here with you, and I love you with all my heart." Savannah took a deep breath. "But I think we need to make some changes around here. We need to do what we should have done when we first married. We need to voice our feelings to each other."

"I think you're right." He wrapped his arms around her. "I know we've already stood before a preacher, but I want to start this marriage over. Let's forget about business propositions and concentrate on loving each other. What do you think?"

She nodded. "I don't remember much of what Reverend Somers said the day of our wedding. So I think I should make some new vows to you."

"W–what kind of vows?"

A smile pulled at her lips. "You're the best man I've ever known, Dante Rinaldi, and I love you like I've never loved anyone else. My new vow comes from God's Word: 'Whither thou goest, I will go; and where thou lodgest, I will lodge: thy people shall be my people, and thy God my God: Where thou diest, will I die, and there will I be buried.' "

Shaking his head in an attempt to comprehend what had just happened, Dante pulled her closer. "I've prayed for this, but it seemed impossible that you'd ever love me."

She laughed. "I prayed for the taxes to be paid on Cottonwood, but I thought that was impossible, too. We should have had more faith in God. His plan was the best of all."

Dante roared with laughter, scooped her up into his arms, and whirled her around. "For a day that started out so awful, it's turned into the best of my life."

She squealed and clutched at his chest. "Be careful, Dante."

He stopped and stared at her. "You mean because of the baby?"

Her eyes grew wide. "How did you know?"

"Martha Thompson told me."

Savannah stiffened in his arms. "What?" she shrieked. "I was waiting for the right moment to tell you. How did Martha know?"

"I had asked Mr. Perkins for something to settle your stomach, and Martha diagnosed your condition when she heard your symptoms." He laughed again. "You forget she's the biggest gossip in town. She knows everything."

Savannah relaxed and smiled. "Are you happy?"

"Happy doesn't start to describe how I feel. I can hardly wait to see what else God has planned for us."

Savannah's arms encircled his neck and pulled his head down to meet hers. "Me, too."

Chapter 19

Savannah sat by the window in the parlor of her and Dante's new home and let her gaze travel over the bare branches of the trees, swaying in the December breeze. Christmas was just a few weeks away, and this year she and Dante had a lot to celebrate.

She leaned back in the rocker Dante had bought her and smiled in satisfaction. Her left foot gently rocked the cradle beside her as she thought of the crocks of newly churned butter sitting on a table in the kitchen. She enjoyed the early afternoon when her chores were complete and her child napped beside her.

It seemed impossible that so much had happened in the last year. Sometimes she had to pinch herself to make sure she hadn't dreamed it all. When she looked into the faces of her husband and child, though, she knew it was all true.

Dante appeared at the corner of the house and bounded onto the front porch. He burst through the door and smiled when he saw her. "I thought I'd come check on you."

Without breaking the rhythm of the cradle, she tilted her head and arched an eyebrow. "You're never going to finish that fence if you keep coming home."

He laughed, walked to the cradle, and gazed down at the baby. "For some reason, I just can't stay away."

Her foot stilled, and she hesitated at the question that had hovered on her lips since the baby's birth. She inhaled. "Dante, are you sorry she isn't a boy?"

A big smile covered his face. "A boy? We can have one of those next. Right now I'm happy to have the two most beautiful women in the world in my life."

She laughed. "You do act like she's kind of special."

He dropped to his knees and trailed a finger across their daughter's head. "Amelia Gabriella Rinaldi, you are a beauty."

Savannah smiled. She never tired of seeing Dante with the daughter they'd named after their mothers. She glanced out the window and squinted to get a better view of the person walking toward their house.

"Dante, someone's coming."

He stood and looked out the window. "I can't tell who it is."

"Neither can I, but it looks. . ." She squealed in happiness. "Dante, it's Jasper. He's come home."

They rushed to the door and stepped onto the porch. Dante stood with his arm around her shoulders as Jasper trudged toward them. When he reached the house, Savannah ran down the steps and embraced him.

Tears ran down her face. "Jasper, I'm so glad to see you."

"Good to see you, too, Miss 'Vanna."

Dante followed her and stuck out his hand. "We didn't think we'd ever see you again."

Jasper grabbed Dante's hand and shook it. "Yas suh, I reckon I thought I never would see ya'll, neither."

"What brought you back?" Savannah asked.

Jasper took off the hat Savannah had seen him wear for years and wiped his brow. "Well, I al'ays wanted to see the ocean, and I seen it. Even slept on the beach for a while just a-lis'nin' to the waves roll in. It shore is a purty sight to see."

Dante nodded. "I lived near it all my life. It's hard to understand how big it is until you see it up close."

Jasper chuckled. "You right about that. But it ain't the Alabama." He gazed over his shoulder toward the bluff.

"I reckon there just ain't no water on God's earth like the river I been knowin' all my life, and I wanted to come back. Mistuh Dante done tole me 'fore I left I always have a home at Cottonwood."

Savannah laughed. "You'll always have a home with us, Jasper."

"Thank you kindly, Miss 'Vanna. It's good to be home."

Savannah and Dante watched as Jasper turned and walked toward the river bluff. Dante looped his arm around Savannah's waist. "The Alabama River brought me to Cottonwood, and the best things of my life happened because of it. I don't ever want to leave it either."

Savannah's heart burst with happiness. She kissed her husband on the cheek and glanced over her shoulder at the first wing of their house that had risen from the ruins of her childhood home. Soon they would begin building the next section, and the big columns would stand once again on the riverbank.

"I'm glad the river brought you here, too. Aunt Jane told me that the only reason to marry was because you loved somebody so much you hurt from wanting to be with them."

Dante's lips brushed the top of her head. "What else did she tell you?"

She snuggled closer to her husband. Memories of the war, worries over unpaid taxes, and threats from murdering gangs vanished in his protective embrace. "That God had great things waiting for me. And you know what, Dante?"

"What?"

Savannah stood on her tiptoes and pulled his head down until their lips almost touched. "She was right."

DINNER AT THE
ST. JAMES

Dedication

To Vera, Martha, Nancy, and Jennifer for your service in our church library. You are a blessing to our members.

Chapter 1

May 1878
Outside Willow Bend, Alabama

Tave Spencer, the teacher in the one-room schoolhouse outside Willow Bend, Alabama, sank into the chair behind her desk and blew at a strand of hair that dangled over her forehead. Just minutes before, she'd seen her well-behaved, attentive students transformed into a stampeding herd, each one bent on being the first to escape the classroom and begin the school-free days of summer. They'd dashed out the door without a backward glance at the teacher who'd hammered reading, math, and spelling into their heads for the past nine months.

She glanced around the almost-empty classroom and smiled at the one student who still remained. Gabby Rinaldi, the six-year-old daughter of Dante and Savannah Rinaldi, sat at her desk on the front row, her attention directed to the book she held.

"Gabby, your mother said she was going to pick you up today. I'm sure she'll be here any time now."

The child glanced up, and a smile curled her lips. She tilted her head to one side, her dark eyes sparkling behind the long lashes so much like her mother's. "She wanted to go into town to see the *Montgomery Belle*. Poppa says he can't keep Mama away from the docks when Captain Hawkins's boat pulls up to the landing. I guess she's watching them unload."

Tave chuckled. Everyone in the community knew that when one of the steamboats docked at Willow Bend, Savannah Rinaldi would be somewhere nearby. Picking up her child at school gave her the perfect excuse to stop by the docks.

Tave picked up the books she planned to take home for the summer and nodded. "I'm sure you're right. Why don't we sit outside and wait for her?"

Together they walked from the schoolhouse, and Tave locked the door behind her. A twinge of sadness gripped her heart as she sat down beside Gabby on the front steps. She thought of the boys and girls she'd taught this past year and the progress they'd made.

She'd come to love every one of them and hated to see the school year draw to a close. Some of them, such as Tad Thompson and Johnny Williams, wouldn't return in the fall. They'd be needed on the farms, and their education would come to a halt.

Others, such as Gabby Rinaldi, were just starting their formal schooling and would be back. Tave smiled at Gabby. "When you come back to school in the fall, your brother will get to come with you."

Gabby nodded, and her dark curls bobbed up and down. "He can already read. Me and Poppa. . ." Her eyes grew wide, and she spread her short fingers over her mouth to stifle a gasp. "I mean, Poppa and I have been teaching him."

Tave laughed and slipped her arm around the child's shoulders. "What a good sister you are. And a good student, too."

Gabby smiled up at her and then directed her gaze down the road that led to Willow Bend. Tave leaned back on the steps, closed her eyes, and lifted her face up to the late May sunshine.

Soon it would be hot along the Alabama River that twisted and turned through the Black Belt of Alabama, so called because of its rich, black soil that covered the area. Tave dreaded the hot days that were before them and the mosquitoes that bred in the vegetation along the edge of the river. After the mild winter they'd had, she suspected the annoying insects would emerge in high numbers.

Tave blinked her eyes open as Gabby jumped to her feet. "Mama's coming."

Shading her eyes with her hand, Tave stared in the direction Gabby pointed. Savannah's buggy came into sight, and Gabby hopped to the bottom of the steps to await her mother. When Savannah pulled the horse to a stop beside them, she flashed an apologetic smile in Tave's direction.

"I'm sorry. I ran into Martha Thompson in Mr. Perkins's store, and I couldn't get away." She reached out to pull Gabby into the buggy. Drawing the child close, Savannah planted a kiss on her forehead. "And how was your last day at school?"

"At least I didn't have to walk home today." Gabby snuggled next to her mother. "I don't want to stay home for the summer. I want to come back to school."

Tave laughed. "I wish all my students felt that way. But don't worry, you'll have such a good time at Cottonwood this summer, you'll hardly think of school."

Savannah nodded. "And Vance will get to come with you next fall." She glanced at Tave. "Why don't you let me drive you home? We can visit on the way."

"Are you going my way?"

"Yes. The *Montgomery Belle* still hadn't arrived when I left town. I thought I'd go back and see if it's there yet." Savannah let her gaze drift over the school grounds. "I'll never understand why the town didn't build this school right in the middle of Willow Bend. You have quite a walk coming out here every day."

Tave shook her head and climbed in the buggy. "It's less than a mile, and I like being so close to the river here. We get to see all the steamboats as they pass by."

Savannah turned the horse around and headed back to the small settlement. "I've always liked to watch them, too. I thought the *Montgomery Belle* would dock before I left Mr. Perkins's store, but it still wasn't there."

Gabby glanced up at Tave and grinned. "We thought you might be watching them unload, Mama."

Savannah shook her head. "No, I don't have time for that today. As soon as we let Miss Spencer out and I see the *Montgomery Belle*, we need to hurry home. Mamie is watching Vance, and that boy can be a handful."

Tave scooted back into the leather seat of the buggy. "Thanks for the ride. This last day of school has worn me out. I'm going to fix Poppa and me some supper. Then I think I'll go to bed early."

Savannah flicked the reins across the horse's back. "Are you going to help your father in his practice this summer?"

"Yes. I don't know how he makes it without someone to help run his office, but he refuses to hire anybody. I help out every chance I get, but I have to admit medicine has never appealed to me. I can't stand the sight of blood."

Savannah smiled. "Well, your father is the best doctor I've ever known. We're lucky to have him in Willow Bend."

"I think he's pretty wonderful, too."

Savannah tightened her hands on the reins and cast a sly glance in Tave's direction. "Is there anyone else around here that you think is wonderful besides your father?"

The question puzzled Tave. Her eyes grew wide, and she sat up straight. "No, not that I can think of."

"Not even Matthew Chandler?"

Now she understood. Tave's face warmed, and her breath caught in her throat at the mention of the heir to Winterville Plantation. "What makes you ask about Matthew?"

Savannah took her gaze off the road long enough to cast a knowing grin in Tave's direction. "Don't act so shocked. Everybody in Willow Bend knows he's been calling on you for the past year. That seems like a long time if you're not interested in him. In a romantic way, I mean. But after the way he teased you when you and your father first moved here, I didn't think you'd ever like him."

"I don't know if I've forgiven him or not." Tave turned in the seat toward Savannah. "Do you remember how he made fun of my name?"

Savannah laughed and nodded. "He did until you punched him in the nose at church one day and told him you were named after your grandmother Octavia and that your mother had shortened it to Tave. Then you held your fist in front of his face and dared him to make fun of your name again. Your father was mortified."

Tave cast a glance at Gabby to see if she'd overheard, but her student appeared to be asleep. "I was just a child then, but he left me alone after that." She sighed. "And now he shows up at our house quite often."

Tave wrinkled her forehead in thought about Matthew. It was true Matthew had visited with her and her father many times during the past year. At times she thought he came to argue with her father over their differing opinions concerning the war that had ended thirteen years ago but still produced some of the most heated discussions in west-central Alabama.

An image of Matthew's face flashed across her mind. Was she interested in him romantically? With his dark hair and flashing eyes, he was undoubtedly the best-looking bachelor in the county. And every single young woman she knew prayed to be the recipient of his attention. The fact that he'd picked her from all the available young women thrilled her and yet left her puzzled. After all, she was the daughter of a country doctor, and Matthew helped his father run one of the largest plantations in all of Alabama. The number of tenant farmers they supported was twice what the Rinaldis had at Cottonwood.

Savannah arched an eyebrow and stared at Tave. "Well, are you going to answer me?"

"I—I don't know what to say. Matthew is a friend. He hasn't mentioned anything more than that." Tave sighed. "I suppose I should be flattered that he likes me. After all, I'm not getting any younger, and there aren't that many young men my age in Willow Bend."

Savannah reached out to Gabby, who'd drifted off to sleep, and turned her so that her head rested in Savannah's lap. "Yeah. Twenty years is really old. That was my age when Dante and I married."

Tave always felt a little envious when she thought of Savannah and Dante's marriage. She'd often wondered if she would ever experience such great love in her life. She sighed and brushed at some dirt that had billowed up from the road and settled on her skirt. "You've told me your and Dante's romantic love story. Sometimes I think that's what I want: a handsome young man to sweep me off my feet. My practical side, however, tells me that's never going to happen. I'll probably spend the rest of my life taking care of my father and end up an old maid who wants to talk about how life is changing in the South."

A low-pitched rumble drifted from the direction of town, and Savannah smiled. "There's the *Montgomery Belle*. Maybe I'll get to see Captain Hawkins before I go back to Cottonwood."

The buildings that made up the small settlement of Willow Bend came into view, and Tave strained to catch a glimpse of the towering smokestacks of the big steamboat that plied the Alabama River. As their buggy trotted past the livery stable and the feed and grain store on the right, Tave wondered why no one was in sight today.

As they approached the general store, Tave sat up straight and frowned. Mr. Perkins, the elderly owner, shuffled out the front door of the store and followed several men who ran across the street toward the riverbank where a crowd had gathered. Their attention appeared riveted on the steamboat that sat moored to the dock at the foot of the bank.

"Something's happened," Tave murmured.

Frowning, Savannah pulled the buggy to a stop. She touched Gabby's shoulder, and the child's eyes blinked open. "Stay in the buggy until I get back. I'm going to the *Montgomery Belle.*"

Gabby nodded and closed her eyes.

Tave jumped from the buggy and hurried toward the crowd. She glanced over her shoulder and saw Savannah tie the horse's reins to the hitching post in front of the store before she followed.

Martha Thompson stood in the middle of the group who peered at the boat, and Tave eased up next to her. If anyone knew what was happening, it would be Martha. She had the reputation of knowing everything that occurred in their community.

"What happened, Martha?"

The wrinkles in the woman's face deepened. The bonnet that covered Martha's gray curls wobbled as she shook her head and frowned. "They say it's bad, Tave. Doc's on board right now."

Tave's eyes widened. Her father was on board the boat? "Is someone hurt?"

Martha shifted the basket she held in one hand to the other and nodded. "Dead most likely. Captain Hawkins caught some fellows in a card game on board, and you know he don't allow no gambling on his boat. When he tried to break up the group, one of them gamblers pulled a gun. A young man who works on the boat tried to wrestle the gun out of the man's hand, and he ended up gettin' shot for tryin' to help the captain."

"That's terrible." Tave's worried gaze scanned the big boat from its bow to the stern-mounted paddle wheel at the back, but her father was nowhere to be seen.

Beside her, Martha inched closer. "And that ain't all. They say that, in all the commotion after the shooting, that gambler ran out of the cabin. Some of the deckhands seen him jump overboard."

Tave had no idea who *they* were, but she felt sure Martha had all the facts right. "Do they know what happened to him?"

Martha shook her head. "Last they seen of him, he was swimmin' to the far side of the river. They don't know if he made it though." She shrugged. "So he either drowned or escaped. They don't know which."

Tave looked back at the boat, but her father still had not appeared. "And you think the man he shot is dead?"

Martha arched her eyebrows and directed a solemn stare in Tave's direction. "Now you know I ain't one to start rumors, but I heard one of the passengers who got off say he doubted if the young man could still be alive."

Savannah arrived in time to hear Martha's words. Her eyes grew wide, and she grasped Tave's arm. "Have you seen your father yet?"

Tave shook her head. "No, I don't know what part of the boat he's on." Her gaze drifted over the sleek vessel that bobbed in the water, its gangway already lowered and resting on the bank.

Movement caught her attention, and her father stepped through a doorway onto the lower deck from what she assumed was one of the cabins. He backed up against the railing and stopped as if waiting for someone to exit.

A man, supporting the weight of a man's legs, appeared in the doorway, and he eased onto the deck. Captain Hawkins and another man, who Tave assumed was a deckhand, emerged supporting the injured man's upper body.

They stopped in front of her father, and he bent down to say something then straightened. He pointed up the hill toward the small building that housed his office, strode to the lowered gangway, and headed in the direction he'd pointed. He stopped halfway up the hill to survey the slow procession that followed and then resumed his journey.

When he reached the gathered crowd at the top of the bluff, Tave stepped forward. "Poppa, do you need me to help you?"

Relief flickered in his eyes. "I'm glad you're here. I'm going to have to remove a bullet from this young man, and I need your help. Are you up to it?"

Even after all the years of helping her father, Tave's stomach churned at the thought of assisting in surgery, but it didn't matter. If her father needed her assistance, she would help in any way she could. Before she could speak, the men carrying the injured sailor passed by her, and she glanced at the face of the young man.

She'd never seen anyone so pale before. He must have lost a lot of blood. His wheat-colored hair tumbled over his forehead, and a grimace of pain covered his face. His eyes appeared to be clenched shut, and his teeth bit into his lower lip. A low moan rumbled in his throat.

Tave nodded to her father. "I'll be right there." Turning to Savannah, she clasped her friend's hand. "I have to go. Thanks for the ride."

A worried expression crossed Savannah's face. "I'll be praying that your father can save this young man."

Tave turned and ran past the men carrying the injured sailor as she hurried toward her father's office, her mind in a whirl of what awaited her. She dashed through the front door and was rolling up her sleeves when the men arrived carrying the patient.

Her father took command of the situation right away. He pointed to the other room. "Take him in there and put him on that table."

Tave reached for the apron that hung on a hook by the wall, tied it around her waist, and ran to stoke the fire in the stove. Lots of hot water would be needed in the next few hours. She had just set the big pot on the stove's eye when her father called out.

"Tave, I need you."

Captain Hawkins and the other two men stood opposite her father beside the surgery table when she walked into the room. She stopped beside her father, who had his fingers clamped on the patient's wrist and his gaze directed to the pocket watch he held. When he finished, he glanced at her. "Pulse 114. I don't like that."

Captain Hawkins stared at them. Sorrow lined his face, and his chin quivered. "Dr. Spencer, this boy's name is Daniel Luckett. He saved my life. Take care of him, and I'll pay you whatever it costs."

Tave's father nodded. "We'll do what we can, but there's no telling what kind of internal damage has been done. And he's lost a lot of blood. How long are you going to be in Willow Bend?"

"We'll be leaving for our upriver trip to Montgomery within the hour, but I'll check on him when we come back downriver." Captain Hawkins placed his hand on the injured man's shoulder and squeezed. "Tell him for me that I'm sorry the man who shot him escaped. I'll tell the sheriff when we dock at Selma, and I'll pass the word along to the other ship captains to keep a lookout for him. But I doubt if that gambler will ever show his face on the Alabama River again."

Captain Hawkins and his men turned and left the room, her father following. He called over his shoulder, "I'll be ready to operate on Mr. Luckett in a few minutes, Tave. I'll be right back to get him ready. In the meantime, it might make him feel better if you'd bathe his face with some cool cloths."

Tave hurried to the pitcher on a table against the wall and grabbed a clean cloth from the drawer underneath. Holding the cloth over the washbowl, she poured water over the cloth and wrung it out.

When she stepped back beside the injured man, she glanced down at Daniel Luckett again. Even with the evidence of pain, she realized he had a handsome face. He was young, perhaps about her age, maybe a few years older. She wondered what had made him take a job on a steamboat. Perhaps if he lived, he would tell her.

She touched his forehead with the wet cloth and began to move it gently across his skin. Her fingers moved to his cheeks and across his mouth that puckered with pain. She rewet the cloth and wiped at his mouth and across the lower part of his face. A groan rolled from his throat, and his head twitched.

Without warning, his eyes blinked open, and she stared down into the bluest eyes she had ever seen. They glazed as if trying to focus, and his forehead wrinkled. He tried to push up, but she restrained him with her hand on his chest.

"Don't move. You've been hurt, but we're going to help you."

He frowned and struggled to speak. "H–h–hurt?"

"Yes, you've been shot, but you're going to be all right." She bit her lip after the words were out. Should she have said that? Her father said he was hurt badly.

Daniel stared up at her for a moment then closed his eyes, and his body relaxed. Terrified that he had died, she leaned over him to see if she could detect breathing. His body jerked, and his eyes blinked open again. He stared at her with eyes that held the wild look of one lost in another world. He tried to raise his arm, but it fell back to his side.

He thrashed his head from side to side on the pillow. "Mama! Where are you, Mama?"

Tears flooded Tave's eyes, and she glanced over her shoulder at her father reentering the room. "He's calling for his mother."

Her father nodded. "I've heard ninety-year-old men call for their mother when they're dying. I suppose one never gets too old to want the comfort a mother can give." He sighed and glanced down at his patient. "Well, let's see if we can save this boy for his mother."

Chapter 2

Three hours later, Tave put the last of her father's tools away, placed her hands in the small of her back, and stretched. Working with her father hadn't been nearly as bad as she'd thought it would be. Even the blood hadn't made her queasy like it usually did. Maybe she was getting used to being in a doctor's office. Or maybe her calm in surgery had been brought about by the plaintive cry of a man calling out for his mother. Whatever the reason, she felt hopeful that her father had succeeded in saving Daniel Luckett's life.

She stepped to the door of the small bedroom where recuperating patients stayed. The young man lay on the bed where her father, with the help of Mr. Jensen from the livery stable and one of his workers, had moved him after surgery. Some color had returned to his face, and he appeared to be breathing better. He had survived, but her father had warned her the next forty-eight hours would be critical.

Her father stood beside the bed, watching the rise and fall of Daniel's chest. He turned to her, smiled, and held up the object in his hands for her to see. "Did you see what came on the *Montgomery Belle* today?"

Tave nodded and walked over to her father. "Your new stethoscope arrived. I saw it during the surgery, but I didn't want to distract you by saying anything. How does it work?"

He looked at the instrument and smiled. "You've seen my old stethoscope. It's one long tube that stands upright on the patient's chest. Then I had to place my ear at the top of it to hear anything. A lot of doctors have been afraid this new one with two earpieces would confuse them with different sounds in each ear, but it doesn't. It's great, and just in time for a patient who needs all the help he can get."

Her father stuck the ends in his ears, bent over Daniel, and pressed the stethoscope to his chest. Tave waited until her father straightened before she spoke. "How's he doing?"

"Holding his own right now. We'll have to wait and see. He's young and strong. That should help a lot."

Before Tave could reply, the small bell her father had placed over the front door to alert him to arriving patients jingled. She frowned. Who could be

131

arriving so late in the afternoon?

"Anybody here?" a voice from the waiting room called out.

Tave suppressed a giggle at her father's arched eyebrows. He shook his head. "Martha Thompson's come to see what's going on."

"You want me to go talk to her?"

Her father nodded. "If you don't mind. I'll stay here with Daniel."

Tave hurried into the waiting room and closed the door to the bedroom behind her. Martha Thompson stood just inside the front door, a large basket in her hands. "Hello, Martha. What are you doing here? You're not sick, are you?"

Martha's ample frame shook with laughter. She waved a pudgy hand in dismissal. "Land sakes, no. I thought 'bout you and your pa over here a-workin' to take care of that poor boy that got shot, and I knowed you was hungry. I brought you some supper."

Guilt flowed through Tave. Martha might be the biggest gossip in town, but she also had a heart that looked to the needs of her friends. "That's so sweet of you. I haven't had time to fix anything for Poppa and me. He'll be so excited that you stopped by. He always tries to get whatever you cooked when we have the church dinners."

Martha's face flushed, and she lowered her eyelids. "Oh, hush now. You gonna give me a big head. I's just trying to help out a friend in need." She lifted the cloth covering the top of the basket, and the delicious aromas that drifted from it made Tave's stomach growl. "I fixed chicken and dumplings for our supper and had plenty left over. I stuck in a piece of corn bread, too. So you and your pa enjoy it."

Tave took the basket from Martha. "Let me get the bowls out, and you can take your basket home with you."

Martha shook her head. "No need for that. I'll stop by tomorrow and get 'em. That'll give me a chance to see how the young fellow that was shot is doing." Martha glanced toward the closed bedroom door. "How *is* he doing?"

"He came through surgery. Now it's just wait and see. The next forty-eight hours are critical, Poppa says."

Martha's eyebrows drew down over her nose. "Um, you don't say. Did you find out anything about him? Like where he's from? What made him try to take that gun away from the gambler on the boat?"

"No, Martha. I'm afraid I don't know anything. Just that he's a very sick person right now. We'll all have to pray that he pulls through."

Martha nodded. "I'll be doin' that, and I'll be back tomorrow to check on him."

"I can't thank you enough for the food. I'll have your bowls ready to return tomorrow."

"I'll be back to get them. Maybe you'll know more about him when I come."

Tave tried to suppress the giggle in her throat. "We'll see." She took Martha by the arm, escorted her to the door, and opened it. "I don't want to keep you from your family, and I should see if Poppa needs me. Thanks again, and you have a good night."

Martha stepped onto the porch and turned. "Like I said, I'll see you—" She stopped midsentence, and a slow smile curled her lips. She tilted her head to one side and glanced at Tave. "Well, would you get a look at who's here. No wonder you're trying to get me to hurry off."

Tave frowned and stepped onto the porch beside Martha. Her heart gave a thump as she spied Matthew Chandler coming around the corner of the building. When he saw her, his dark eyes lit up, and he smiled. Stepping onto the porch, he took off the wide-brimmed hat he wore and nodded to Martha, then Tave.

"Good evening, ladies. It's nice to see you." He turned to Tave. "I didn't expect to find you at your father's office. I thought with the last day of school over, you'd be home resting."

Martha grinned. "She don't have time to rest. Not with all that's happened around here today." She reached out and patted Tave's hand. "Well, I know when I need to leave two young people alone. I'll see you tomorrow, Tave."

Tave shook her head and chuckled as Martha walked down the steps and turned in the direction of her home. "That woman never ceases to amaze me. She comes over here to get all the news on my father's latest patient, but she brings us supper. You can't help loving her."

Matthew nodded. "I know. But what did she mean about 'all that's happened around here today'?"

"Come on inside, and I'll tell you."

Matthew followed her into the building, and she related the events that had caused Daniel Luckett to become her father's patient. "At the moment, he's fighting for his life."

Matthew picked up a medical book that lay on a table and flipped to the first page. "That's too bad, but I'm sure he'll be all right. Those deckhands are a resourceful bunch. Not very intelligent, but hardy, if you know what I mean."

An uneasy feeling rippled through her at the unconcerned tone of Matthew's voice. She was just about to say that she didn't know what he meant when the door to the bedroom opened.

Her father emerged. "Matthew, what are you doing here so late in the day? Not sick I hope."

Matthew dropped the book on the table and shook his head. "No, I'm fine. It's one of my tenant farmers, Sam Perry. He almost cut his fingers off this afternoon when he was chopping wood."

Her father looked around. "Why didn't you bring him with you? Wasn't he able to come to town?"

Matthew laughed. "Oh yes. He's with me. I had him wait out back until I told you he was here. I didn't figure you wanted him waiting inside."

Her father's eyes narrowed, and he glared at Matthew. "Waiting outside with his fingers almost cut off? What were you thinking?"

Tave's heart dropped to the pit of her stomach, but Matthew shrugged and smiled at her father. "I know you talk about your oath to help everybody, Dr. Spencer, but this is a black man. The people in this town don't let black people walk through their front doors, and they sure don't want to share a waiting room with them."

Her father clenched his fists and took a step toward Matthew. "Now listen here, young man—"

Tave grabbed her father's arm. "Let's not waste time arguing, Poppa. A hurt man sitting outside needs some help."

Her father took a deep breath, walked to the back door, and flung it open. "Sam," he called out. "Come on in here, and let me look at your hand."

A black man Tave had seen in town several times shuffled through the back door. A bloody rag bound the injured hand. He didn't look up as her father steered him into the exam room. She took a step forward. "Do you need me, Poppa?"

He gritted his teeth and shook his head. "Not now. Keep Matthew company."

After her father and Sam had disappeared, Matthew walked over and stopped next to her. "I'm sorry I haven't had a chance to see you this week, but we've been busy. Things should slow down in a few weeks. I'll make it up to you then."

Tave stared up into the dark eyes that had attracted her to Matthew when she and her father had first come to Willow Bend from eastern Tennessee eight years before. She'd been only twelve at the time, and she'd thought the nineteen-year-old Matthew Chandler was the most handsome man she'd ever seen, and the richest.

He had hardly noticed her then, but that had all changed a year ago when he suddenly developed an interest in the young woman she'd become. He'd been a steady visitor at their home ever since, but on many nights, her father, who'd supported the Union in the war, and Matthew, a staunch supporter of the Confederate cause, had clashed.

She wondered sometimes if they would ever be able to find some common ground in their beliefs. But then, that seemed to be the problem of many people in this part of Alabama. She tried to tell her father that Matthew was a product of his upbringing, but it hadn't changed his opinion of Matthew.

Tave, however, had come to the conclusion that Matthew had many likeable qualities, and when he and her father weren't arguing, she enjoyed his company. As she'd told Savannah earlier, she wasn't getting any younger, and no other young men had come calling.

She smiled at Matthew. "I'll look forward to seeing you more."

The clock in her father's office chimed midnight. Tave shivered in the dark room where she sat beside Daniel's bed and pulled the quilt around her body. She didn't know if there was a chill in the air or if she shivered with concern for the unconscious man. Her father had done all he could to save Daniel's life. Now it was up to God.

The oil lamp on the table beside her flickered and cast shadows on the wall by Daniel's bed. He'd been restless for the past few hours, but her father had warned her that he would be so soon after surgery. If Daniel lived through the night, he would have a good chance of survival, her father had said.

A moan drifted from the bed. Tave jumped to her feet and felt his forehead. Perspiration covered his brow. Wringing out the cloth she'd kept in a bowl of water, she laid it on his forehead.

His head twitched on the pillow, and his hand jerked the cloth from his head. "No, don't do it!"

Tave gasped in surprise at the shouted words. She reached for the lamp and held it up to see if his eyes were open, but they weren't. He groaned again, and she set the lamp down and repositioned the cloth.

His mouth opened, and his body shook. "Leave her alone!" The shout cut through the silent room like thunder.

Tave reached for his hand and wrapped both of hers around it. "It's all right. I'm here with you."

He took a deep breath, but he continued to tremble. A whimper escaped his throat. "Mama, come back. Don't leave me."

For the second time, Tave heard the unconscious man call for his mother, and it touched her heart. She wondered what had happened to his mother and why he called out to her. Tave thought of her own mother, who'd died when she was five years old. Sometimes she had trouble remembering what her mother looked like, but she had never overcome the emptiness of not having her in her life.

Still holding Daniel's hand, Tave dropped to her knees beside his bed and bowed her head. "Dear God, I pray You will calm this man's heart and give him peace for tonight. Let him sleep so that his body may begin to heal. Only You know what causes his heart to ache so, Lord, and I pray You'll ease his pain."

Tave lost track of time as she continued to pray, but the longer she stayed on her knees, the quieter Daniel became. Only when his body relaxed and a soft snore echoed through the room did she rise.

She stared at the handsome young man who'd come so close to death and thanked God again for sparing his life. Then she sat back down in the chair and wrapped the quilt around her.

As she huddled beside the soft light from the lamp, she thought about Daniel's earlier cries and wondered what they meant. Maybe something had happened in his past that had left him deeply scarred. Her father had often told her that wounds to the spirit can be much worse than those inflicted on the body. Perhaps God wanted her father and her to help heal Daniel's spirit, too. Only time would tell.

Chapter 3

Daniel Luckett drifted in a dream world. Time held no meaning. At some point, he'd heard voices. He didn't know who the people were, but something in his soul told him they were discussing him. Snatches of sentences came to him: *"saved my life"*. . .*"lost a lot of blood"*. . .*"we're going to help you."* He didn't know what any of it meant, but the last one comforted him.

"We're going to help you." The voice that spoke those words had sounded like music. It had the same lyrical quality of the songs his mother used to sing. She could always make him feel better, just as that soft angelic sound had.

Who was with him? At times it seemed like many people, and at other times just the comforting voice. It would come to him at odd times, telling him to open his mouth or prodding him to turn his body. Sometimes he could hear a soft whisper beside his bed, as if someone knelt beside him and prayed, and he would strain to open his eyes. But it was no use. His eyes felt glued shut. Just when he would think he was going to be victorious and catch a glimpse of the illusive spirit who hovered over him, quiet would return. And with it, he would descend back into his dream world.

How long he'd drifted like this, he didn't know. He had to wake up. He needed to know what had happened to him.

A groan echoed in his mind, and he wondered if the sound came from his mouth or if it only resonated in his mind. With all the strength he could summon, he blinked. His eyes opened.

He lay still for a moment. Then he rubbed his fingers on the blanket that covered him. The touch was unfamiliar. He turned his head to the left and saw the outline of a window. Beyond the pane, he could only see darkness.

Turning his head to the right, his eyes grew wider. A round table sat a few feet away from the bed where he lay. An oil lamp on top cast an eerie glow across the room. But it wasn't the light that took his breath away. It was the woman in the chair next to the table.

She slept soundly, her auburn hair loose and tumbling over her shoulders. She wore a shapeless, blue housedress with long sleeves and a high neckline. He struggled to focus his eyes on the sleeping woman. His heart pounded. He had never seen anyone more beautiful in his life.

She stirred and opened her eyes. They stared at each other, but then she smiled and jumped to her feet. "Oh, you're awake. I've been waiting for that to happen."

He tried to speak, but his mouth was dry as cotton. "W–water," he whispered.

She picked up a pitcher, poured some water into a glass, and stepped to the side of his bed. Slipping one arm beneath his head, she lifted him up just enough to get his lips on the glass. He sipped at the water until she pulled the glass away from his mouth.

"Not too much just yet. I don't want you getting sick."

He fell back against the pillow and groaned. It surprised him how the little amount of energy he'd exerted had completely tired him. He swallowed and glanced up at the beautiful woman who leaned over him. Her long hair swung close to his face, and he reached toward it.

She didn't flinch as his fingers touched the tips of her hair and caressed a soft curl between his fingers. "Your hair is beautiful."

She chuckled, wrapped her fingers around his hand, and guided it back to the bed. "And you're still delirious."

Daniel glanced around. Was he imagining this beautiful creature? He frowned. "Where am I?"

"You're at my father's office. He's the doctor in Willow Bend."

He tried to turn on his side, and pain surged through his body. "Wh–what happened to me?"

"You were shot on board the *Montgomery Belle*. Do you remember anything?"

He thought for a moment, and he recalled going into a cabin with Captain Hawkins. What happened next seemed fuzzy in his memory. He shook his head. "No."

She tucked the covers around him. "That's all right. It will all come back to you."

"How long have I been here?"

"Three days."

Daniel raised a hand to his forehead and rubbed. "Have you been with me all that time?"

She smiled again. "Either my father or I have been. But you don't need to worry about anything right now. You need to rest."

"Wait," he called out as she turned to go back to her chair. "What's your name?"

She smiled down at him. "Tave Spencer."

Daniel closed his eyes. "Tave Spencer." The name slid like velvet across his tongue and spilled from his mouth. It reminded him of the words of the ballads his mother used to sing. Tave Spencer—a poetic name with the soothing effect of a lullaby. He'd never heard anything lovelier in his life.

He closed his eyes and slept.

❧

Daniel awoke to the sound of birds chirping. He remembered seeing a window when he'd awakened once before, and he turned his head in that direction. Sunlight streamed through the panes and cast dancing rays across the patchwork quilt that covered his body. He lay still and listened to the noisy twittering outside.

A memory of touching silky curls returned, and he smiled at the name he'd dreamed about. *"Tave Spencer,"* that's what she'd said. He glanced at the chair where she'd sat, but it was empty.

He had no idea if it was morning or afternoon. From the busy sounds outside the window, he suspected it was morning. If it was, he wondered where the woman he'd spoken with had gone. Or maybe she'd been a dream. He couldn't be sure.

The door to the room opened, and a man walked in. His brown eyes lit up, and he smiled as he walked toward Daniel's bed. He stopped beside him and peered over the top of the wire-rimmed spectacles perched on his nose. "Well, you're finally awake. I thought you might rejoin us this morning."

Through narrowed eyes, Daniel studied the man, but he couldn't recall having ever seen him before. "Do I know you?"

"I'm Dr. Spencer. I've been taking care of you for the past few days."

Daniel thought of the woman he'd seen and looked past the doctor, but she was nowhere in sight. "There was a woman here."

Dr. Spencer nodded. "My daughter, Tave. She's been helping me look after you." He pressed his fingers to Daniel's wrist and pulled out a pocket watch. He stared at the watch for what seemed an eternity before he smiled and released his hold. "Your pulse is much better. I think you're on the road to recovery."

Daniel tried to lift his head, but the room rotated as a wave of dizziness washed over him. He sank back against the pillow and gasped. "What day is it?"

"Today is Monday. We brought you here last Friday from the *Montgomery Belle*. Do you remember anything?"

Daniel closed his eyes and concentrated. "I remember going with Captain Hawkins into a cabin. There was a card game." He opened his eyes. "There's nothing else until I woke up and saw your daughter."

Dr. Spencer pointed to Daniel's side. "One of the gamblers threatened Captain Hawkins with a gun, and you tried to wrestle it from him. You ended up being shot, but you probably saved the captain's life. He's very thankful, but he was concerned for you. The boat went on to Montgomery, but he said he'd check on you when they returned."

"Captain Hawkins is a good man."

"That he is." Dr. Spencer pointed to Daniel's side. "I need to check on your wound."

Daniel gritted his teeth and tried not to moan as the doctor pulled the quilt back and probed at his side. After a few minutes, Dr. Spencer covered him up and stepped away.

"How am I doing?" Daniel asked.

Dr. Spencer pulled the chair up to the bedside and sat down. "I think you're a mighty lucky young man that the bullet didn't do a lot of internal damage. There was some damage to an artery. That's what caused you to lose so much blood, but I was able to repair that. You should be up and around in a few days."

Daniel heaved a sigh of relief. "Thank you, Dr. Spencer, for all you've done for me." He bit down on his lip. "I don't have any money right now, but I'll pay you as soon as I recover enough to get on up to Montgomery. I'd planned to leave the *Montgomery Belle* and take a job on the docks there."

Dr. Spencer waved his hand in dismissal. "Don't worry about what you owe me, son. Captain Hawkins said he'd take care of everything. Like I said, he's mighty thankful to be alive."

"And so am I." Daniel glanced around the room. "How long do you think I'll be here?"

"Well, that depends on how soon you get your strength back. I'd say—"

A rustling at the door caught their attention, and Daniel and Dr. Spencer glanced in that direction. Daniel's heart pounded in his chest at the sight of the woman with the auburn hair. "Oh, you're awake again." She glided into the room and stopped beside her father's chair. "He looks much better, doesn't he, Poppa?"

Her father chuckled and pushed up from where he sat. "He only had one way to go." He glanced back at Daniel. "I don't mind telling you, son, when you were brought in here, I didn't think you had a chance of living. Glad to see I was wrong."

Tave looped her arm through her father's and smiled at him. "That's because he had a wonderful doctor to take care of him."

Pride showed in her father's eyes as he stared at her. "And a great nurse to coax him back to the land of the living."

Tave stretched on her tiptoes and kissed her father on the cheek. The love between the two was obvious. It reminded Daniel of his mother and how close they had been. There wasn't a day that went by that he didn't think of her and how much he missed her.

He cleared his throat. "I want to thank both of you for what you've done for me." He glanced at Tave. "It meant a lot to me when I woke up and saw you in the room. I knew I wasn't alone."

Dr. Spencer smiled. "I keep telling her she'd make a fine nurse, but she's bound and determined to teach school."

Daniel frowned. "So you're a teacher. Why aren't you there today?"

A soft peal of laughter from her lips stirred his blood, and he stared at this woman he'd first seen in the darkness of his room. What was it about her that excited him? Perhaps it was gratitude for what she had done for him, but something told him it was more.

"School is out for the summer."

Daniel nodded. "Yeah, it is that time of year again."

A bell tinkled in another room, and Dr. Spencer sighed. "I suppose that's a patient. I'll be back to check on you, Daniel."

Tave watched her father leave the room before she faced Daniel again. "So, are you hungry? I made some broth this morning. You need to eat something."

"Have I eaten since I've been here?"

She nodded. "Yes. I'm afraid at times I had to force you, but I did get liquids down you."

The memory of someone forcing a spoon into his mouth returned, and he grinned. "So you're the one who tortured me when all I wanted to do was sleep."

Her eyes held a mischievous glint, and she crossed her arms. "Guilty as charged, but at least you didn't die from hunger."

The realization of how close he'd come to death hit him, and he swallowed the sudden flash of fear that filled his throat. "No, I didn't die. And for that I owe your father and you a great debt of gratitude. Thank you, Tave, for taking care of me."

A crimson flush spread across her face. "You remembered my name. I didn't think you were conscious enough to know what I said to you."

His gaze strayed to the bun on top of her head and recalled how her hair had cascaded around her shoulders. He wished he could pull the pins from her head and let the curls tumble free again. He swallowed and tried to smile. "I remember."

She stared at him for a moment before she reached down and smoothed the apron that covered her dress. For a fleeting moment he believed he saw her hands tremble, but he dismissed the thought. She backed toward the door. "I'll be right back with something for you to eat."

He smiled. "Take your time. I guess I'll be in this same spot when you get back. I'm not going anywhere today."

After she hurried from the room, he settled back on his pillow and smiled. The lines from a ballad his mother used to sing drifted into his mind, and he tried to recall the words. He hummed the melody, but the exact words wouldn't come. They were about a beautiful woman who was peerless in beauty and even a prince could find no sweeter creature.

From what he'd seen of Tave Spencer so far, she could very well have been the inspiration for those words.

An hour later Tave removed the napkin she'd draped around Daniel's neck and laid it on the tray with the remains of his meal. She propped her hands on her hips and stared down at Daniel, whose head she'd elevated with two pillows. "Do you want to lie flat, or do you want to keep the pillows?"

"I think I'll stay like this for a while."

"Okay." She bent to pick up the tray but turned when his hand touched her arm. "Do you want something else?"

"Where are you going?"

"I'm going to take these back to the other room. Then I thought I'd let you rest."

He shook his head. "I haven't done anything but sleep for days. Would you mind coming back and talking with me?"

"I'd be glad to keep you company. With school out, I'm helping my father here anyway." Her eyes twinkled. "And right now, you're my favorite patient. Of course that may change if we get someone else in here."

He laughed. "Maybe I can endear myself to you."

She picked up the tray and carried it into the small room in the back of the building that they used for a kitchen from time to time when her father had to keep a close watch on a patient. A woodstove stood against one wall, and a table and two chairs sat in the middle of the room. A pie safe containing the remains of an apple cobbler Martha Thompson had brought the day before rested against the other wall.

Tave smiled at how well she and her father had eaten since Daniel's mishap with the gambler on board the *Montgomery Belle*. Martha had arrived every day with some new dish in an effort to help with their meals. Although Tave appreciated the thoughtfulness, she knew Martha's main motive had been to glean news about their mysterious patient.

Tave set the tray on the table and dropped into one of the chairs. She rubbed her eyes and yawned. For the last three nights, she'd sat beside Daniel Luckett's bed. Although she'd dozed some, she could feel the results of not sleeping in her own bed. Maybe tonight she could leave Daniel and go home. In his office, her father had a sofa he slept on when he had a patient, so he would be here in case Daniel needed something.

Still, she didn't like the idea of leaving Daniel without someone close by. Her father could be a sound sleeper sometimes, and Daniel might be unable to wake him. Maybe she'd stay another night.

Her eyes grew wide at a sudden realization that flashed into her mind. She had developed a protective feeling toward Daniel that she'd never felt with anyone else before. Perhaps it stemmed from how she had cared for him after surgery, or it could be the memory of his calling for his mother. The fear she'd heard in his voice had pricked her heart. It reminded her of the children she taught and how they wanted their mothers when they fell and hurt themselves.

Her father had once told her that he felt like a protector of the people he cared for. Maybe that's all it was with her. Soon Daniel would be recovered, and he would leave with Captain Hawkins on the *Montgomery Belle*. He would be just another patient to her father, but she knew he would always be special to her. After all, Daniel was her miracle. From the moment her father had first seen Daniel, he had thought the man would die. When she'd seen his pale face, she'd thought so, too. Until a small voice had whispered in her heart that God wasn't finished with this young man.

Some might say she was imagining she heard the voice of God, but Tave knew differently. Daniel needed more than the skill of a surgeon's knife to heal his body. He needed the touch of the Father to repair something much deadlier. She didn't know what Daniel Luckett had experienced in his life. All she knew was that God had told her to pray, and that's what she'd done.

For the last three nights, she'd knelt by his bed and prayed that God would spare him and heal whatever damage life had inflicted. Daniel had lived. Now maybe God would show her what else she needed to do.

Chapter 4

A week later, Tave held on to Daniel's arm as she helped him through the front door and onto the small porch of her father's office. She guided him to a rocking chair that sat in the corner of the porch and helped him ease down into it, then took a step back and smiled at the excitement on his face.

"How does it feel to be outside again?"

"It makes me think I'm really going to recover." He closed his eyes and inhaled. "Ah, is that honeysuckle I smell?"

Tave nodded and dropped down into a chair beside Daniel. "Yes. We have honeysuckle climbing up a trellis on the other side of the building." She inhaled. "I love the smell of it at this time of year before it gets so hot it's hard to breathe."

He settled back in his chair and glanced up and down the street. "So this is what Willow Bend looks like at street level. The *Montgomery Belle* stopped here a lot when I was working on her, but I never got off and came ashore. This is my first chance to get a close look."

Tave smiled ruefully. "I'm sorry you almost had to die to see how we live."

His gaze drifted over her, and his blue eyes twinkled. "If I'd known there was such a pretty nurse living just over the bluff, I imagine I would have been to see you before now."

Her face warmed, and she averted her gaze. "I'm afraid you wouldn't have found me here. I would have been at school or at home."

He sighed. "Just my luck. By the way, where is home? I suppose for the first few days I thought you and your father lived in back of his office. Now that you've deserted me at night to go home, I realize you have a house somewhere else."

"My father and I live in a house at the edge of town. We moved into it when we first settled here. It's small, but it meets our needs."

He swiveled in his chair and stared at her. "Then you haven't lived here all your life?"

"No. My father has a friend who is a doctor over in Selma, and he told us about Willow Bend needing a doctor. So Poppa decided it would be a good place to live. We came when I was twelve."

"And what about your mother?"

"She died when I was a child. We lived in Knoxville. Then when the war came,

Poppa served with the Union army as a doctor. I stayed with my grandmother. After the war, we came to Alabama. We've never been sorry, except Poppa clashes a lot with the residents around here when the war is mentioned."

Daniel chuckled. "I'll bet he does."

She tilted her head and stared at him. "And what about you? Where did you grow up?"

He stared toward the bluff and didn't answer for a moment. When he did, Tave could detect a tremor in his voice. "I guess you could say I'm from Ohio. At least that's where I was born and lived for sixteen years. But I've traveled around so much in the last seven years, I could call a lot of places home."

Tave thought of how he called out for his mother when he was so ill. "Are your parents still in Ohio?"

He shook his head. "I was six years old when my pa joined an Ohio regiment and went off to fight in the war. He died less than a year later at Shiloh. We moved in with my mother's brother for a while, but his wife and children didn't want us there. When the man on the next farm asked my mother to marry him, she did. She figured we'd have a home, and we wouldn't be a burden on her brother anymore."

The wistful tone of his voice told Tave that Daniel's memories were very difficult for him to discuss. She placed her hand on his arm. "You love your mother very much, don't you?"

He stared down at her hand for a moment. When he looked up, a moist sheen covered his eyes. "I did. She died when I was sixteen."

"Is that why you left home?"

"Yes." Daniel's mouth thinned into a straight line, and he tried to push up from his chair. "I'm getting tired. Maybe I've had enough fresh air for now."

Tave jumped to her feet and grasped his arm. "Let me help you."

As Daniel straightened to his full height, his face grew pale, and his knees started to buckle. He swayed toward her. "I. . .I f–feel d–dizzy."

She threw her arms around him and eased him back into the chair. When he was seated again, she dropped to her knees and stared at him. "Are you all right? Do you want me to get you some water?"

Perspiration dotted his head, and he wiped his hand across his face. "I'm okay now. I think I tried to get up too fast. Let me rest for a minute."

"I think I need to get my father." She glanced at him once more before she ran to the door. "Poppa, I need you out here."

Her father came hurrying from his office. "What's the matter?"

"Daniel's dizzy, and I need some help getting him back inside."

Her father's lips thinned into a grim line. Getting on one side of Daniel, he motioned for Tave to take his other arm. When they had Daniel back on his feet, they steered him toward the door.

As they crossed the porch, Daniel glanced from one to the other. "I'm all right. There's no need for all this fuss."

Her father reached out to open the door. "We're not making a fuss. Just taking precautions. I didn't save your life to have you fall and crack your skull. Now, I think you've been up quite long enough for one day."

A footstep sounded on the porch behind them, and Tave glanced over her shoulder. Matthew stood there, his gaze flitting over the three of them.

"Do you need my help, Dr. Spencer?" he asked.

Her father glanced back. "Oh hello, Matthew. We're getting this young man back to bed. Are you here to see me or Tave?"

"Actually, I'm here to speak with Tave."

Tave nodded toward the inside of the office. "Then come on in, and I'll be right with you."

She and her father held on to Daniel's arms as they eased their way across the floor and into the patient bedroom. When he was in bed once more, Daniel smiled up at them. "Thanks. I guess I'm not as strong as I thought."

Tave glanced at her father. "Do you need me, or can I go talk to Matthew?"

He waved his hand in dismissal. "Go on." He cocked his eyebrow and glanced up at Tave. "Doesn't he call on you enough at home without having to come here, too?"

Tave shook her head in dismay. "Poppa, you know you like Matthew."

Dr. Spencer shrugged. "I guess I'll have to like him if you do. Now go on and see what he wants."

Tave opened her mouth to protest her father's words, but the look on Daniel's face made her heart plummet to the pit of her stomach. His blue eyes no longer held the twinkle she'd seen earlier. They'd clouded, and deep lines cut into his cheeks as he bit down on his lip.

She stepped closer to the bed. "Are you in pain, Daniel?"

His chest heaved, and he closed his eyes. "Don't worry about me. I'm just tired." The words had a lifeless quality.

She glanced up at her father. "Do you think sitting on the porch was too much for him? I didn't mean to keep him out so long."

Her father frowned. "Maybe it was. I'll check him out and see." He glanced toward the other room where Matthew waited. "Now you go on. I'll let you know."

Tave backed away from the bed. "Call me if you need me."

She walked to the door and turned to stare back at Daniel. He lay on his back with his eyes closed. He didn't move as her father bent over him and examined the wound in his side. For a moment when she'd stared into Daniel's eyes, she'd been frightened. She'd caught a glimpse of the same look she'd seen when he had called for his mother.

Perhaps he was sorry he'd spoken of his past life today. She'd learned very little, though, and she had the feeling that there was still much Daniel hadn't told her. If it was going to upset him, maybe she didn't need to probe too much into his past. All she could do was pray that he could find some peace.

She pasted a big smile on her face and headed toward the room where Matthew waited.

As she walked through the door, his gazed flitted over her body. The scrutiny in his eyes made her face warm, and she brushed at her hair. "I'm surprised to see you today, Matthew."

He strode across the floor and stopped beside her. "I know. I don't usually drop by during the day, but I came to tell you something."

She gazed up at him. "What is it?"

"I'm going away for several weeks."

His words shocked her. "Going away? Where?"

"You know my mother's sister lives on Dauphin Island near Mobile. She's wanted my mother to visit for a long time, but there never seemed to be time. Now things have slowed down some with the spring planting, and it's a good time to leave. Pa doesn't get along with my mother's family, so he wants me to accompany her downriver. I'll be gone for about six weeks."

Tave wondered why she didn't feel any sadness at the thought of Matthew being gone for such a length of time. Her gaze strayed to the doorway that led to the room where Daniel lay. The thought crossed her mind that his presence might have something to do with her lack of feeling about Matthew's departure. She smiled up at Matthew. "I'll miss you, but I'm glad your mother will get to be with her sister."

A puzzled look crossed his face, and he frowned. "You're not upset that I'll be gone for so long?"

"Why would I be upset? I understand you have obligations to your family."

He stepped closer, and his dark gaze bored into her. "I'm glad you understand how important my family is to me, Tave, but I have other needs in my life besides my parents and preserving the heritage of Winterville."

"What kind of needs?"

"I'm ready to take a wife, a woman who can share my life with me on the land that's been in my family for generations." He reached for her hand, brought it to his lips, and kissed it. Straightening, he stared into her eyes. "You're a wonderful woman, Tave. When I come back, I want to speak to your father. I think it's time we decided about our future together."

"Our future?" She knew the words came from her mouth, but they sounded very much like the nighttime croak of the frogs on the pond behind their house.

He nodded. "After everything is finalized, I'd like for you and your father to accompany my parents and me to the St. James Hotel in Selma for a few nights. We can celebrate our engagement with our families, and you and my mother can visit the shops in town to pick out your trousseau. I'd love to show you the hotel. The view of the river from the balcony is beautiful."

"The St. James?" Tave's heart pounded in her chest. She'd asked her father several times to take her there, but they'd never been able to afford it. Yet this wasn't a trip to be taken lightly. There were decisions to be made first. "I—I don't know, Matthew. Let's talk about all this when you get back."

He released her hand and smiled. "You can count on our talking about it. I'm a determined man, and I always get what I want."

Tave's breath caught in her throat at the intense look in his dark eyes. He was such a handsome man, but in her mind, Matthew's features dissolved, and another's took their place—one with wheat-colored hair and the deepest blue eyes she'd ever seen.

How could that be? She'd known Daniel less than two weeks, yet already he'd found a special place in her heart. It was probably because she'd come to feel so protective of him. It couldn't be more. She knew nothing about the man who cried out in agony when he was delirious.

She had to concentrate on Matthew, who could offer her a life like she'd never imagined. But did she want it? She dismissed her doubts and smiled. "Come to see us when you get back."

❦

Daniel heard the front door of the building close, and he supposed Tave's caller had left. His mind still reeled at what he'd heard. Tave was interested in another man. He closed his eyes and tried to swallow the lump that formed in his throat. He should have known. A beautiful woman like her could have any man she wanted.

How foolish he'd been. Day after day, he'd lain in this bed and waited for her to step into his room and smile at him. Her presence was what had pulled him through the dark nights when he felt like he was going to die. She'd brought him back from the dead, and he'd thought it was because she felt a connection to him.

He'd known the moment he saw her sitting in the chair beside his bed that she was different from any other woman he'd ever known. She was the first person he'd ever talked to about his mother. And all the time he'd been thinking about Tave, she'd been in love with someone else.

Daniel lay still until Dr. Spencer finished his examination, pulled the covers back over him, and sat down in a chair next to the bed. "You gave me a fright, young man. I feared you had an infection setting up, but I don't see any evidence of it. What happened to you?"

Daniel reached behind his head and punched his pillow with his fist. "I guess I was just tired. I'm sorry to cause you trouble."

Dr. Spencer laughed. "Trouble? Son, that's what I'm here for. I want to make sure nothing happens to cause you problems down the road."

Daniel glanced at the man who'd worked so hard to save his life, and his heart pricked at the doctor's tired eyes. Patients had come and gone all week, and many times Dr. Spencer had been summoned to go to some farm along the river. He'd never heard the man complain or resist going where he was needed.

There was a peace about Dr. Spencer that Daniel didn't understand. Tave had it, too. He recalled hearing her pray beside his bed, and he realized there was someone else who had once had that same peace—his mother. She'd trusted God all her life, but in the end, it hadn't done her any good.

Daniel pushed the unwelcome thoughts from his head. "I don't know how I can ever repay you for what you and Tave have done for me."

"I'm glad I could help, and I'm also glad Tave has been here. She's been a lifesaver for me. It's hard to take care of patients in the daytime if you're up all night. It's helped me a lot to have her keeping watch over you at night."

Daniel thought of the man he'd seen on the porch. "What did you say Tave's friend's name is?"

A slight frown creased Dr. Spencer's forehead. "That's Matthew Chandler."

Daniel licked his lips and swallowed. "Are they engaged?"

Dr. Spencer shook his head. "Not yet, but I suspect he'll propose soon. Matthew's been calling on Tave for the last year, but he doesn't seem to be in any hurry about getting married." He shrugged. "Maybe I'm wrong. At least I hope I am."

The words surprised Daniel, and he lifted his head. "Don't you want Tave to marry?"

"Of course I do, but I want it to be the right man. Somehow I don't think Matthew's the one. His family is the richest in the county, and he's a nice enough fellow, I guess, although we have some disagreements about the place of former slaves in Alabama life. But then, Dante Rinaldi and I are in the minority when it comes to their rights."

Daniel sank back on his pillow and thought of his father. "I guess you need to add one more to your list. My father died at Shiloh fighting for the Union."

Dr. Spencer's eyes took on a faraway look. "I was there as a doctor with the Union forces. There were horrible losses on both sides. I never will forget a pond that was there. During the fighting, men from both sides came to it so they could drink and bathe their wounds. Many of them and their horses died in that pond. By the end of the day it was red with blood." He closed his eyes for a moment, and his lips trembled. "The Bloody Pond, that's what they still call it."

Daniel reached out and touched Dr. Spencer's arm. "I'd like to think you were with my father when he died that day."

Dr. Spencer patted Daniel's hand and pushed to his feet. "I don't know. I could have been. I saw enough death that day to last me the rest of my life."

"You must be talking about Shiloh."

They both glanced toward the door where Tave stood. Her father exhaled and nodded. "Yes, but the day's too beautiful to talk about such sad topics. I think I'll go over to Mr. Perkins's store and see how he's doing."

He moved to the door but stopped when a musical rumble drifted from the direction of the river. Tave smiled up at her father. "That must be the *Montgomery Belle.*"

Dr. Spencer glanced back at Daniel. "I guess you'll be having a visitor soon. Captain Hawkins said he'd come to see you when they returned."

Daniel pushed up on his elbows. "Maybe he'll let me rejoin the crew for the trip downriver."

Tave gasped and rushed to his bedside. "Don't you even think about it. You need to stay here longer to regain your strength." She turned to her father. "Tell him, Poppa. He can't leave yet."

Dr. Spencer shook his head. "You're not ready to go. Give it a few more weeks. Captain Hawkins will make a return trip to Montgomery, and you can leave then."

Daniel sank back on his pillow. "Very well. I'll give it a few more weeks."

Tave bent over and tucked the quilt around him. "That's better. Now let's not hear anything else about your leaving before you've completely healed." She straightened and smiled down at him. "I'm going to fix some tea for you and Captain Hawkins to enjoy while he's here."

As she hurried from the room, Daniel's heart thudded. How could he stay this close to her for another few weeks, knowing that she was in love with someone else? She'd awakened something in him that he thought long dead, and he couldn't bear the thought of her marrying another man. As soon as Dr. Spencer released him, he was going to head for Montgomery and leave Tave Spencer far behind.

Chapter 5

Tave knew something was wrong. Daniel had spoken very little since Captain Hawkins had come to see him earlier. With this being his first night to sit at the kitchen table for supper, she had expected a more lively conversation. Instead, Daniel had hardly spoken, and she and her father had spent most of the time discussing the yield she hoped to get from her vegetable garden this spring.

The silence from Daniel began to grate on her nerves, and she stared at him. He glanced up then diverted his gaze back to his plate. He shoveled the last bite of his fried peach pie in his mouth and picked up his coffee cup.

Tave pushed at the last bite of pie on her plate with her fork. "The lady who's been bringing us so much food since you've been ill made these pies."

Daniel took a sip of coffee and nodded. "I'll have to thank her."

Tave waited for him to say something else. When he didn't, she reached across the table, picked up Daniel's empty plate, and stacked it on top of hers and her father's. "I noticed when Captain Hawkins came today he brought all your belongings from the boat."

Daniel nodded. "He said they were in such a hurry to depart the day I was shot that they forgot all about getting my clothes to me." He glanced at Dr. Spencer. "I appreciate you finding me something to wear in the meantime."

The doctor set his coffee cup down and wiped his mouth on his napkin. "No problem. The ladies of the church took care of that. I always call on them when a patient has a need, and they never disappoint me."

"I hope I get to meet them so I can thank them."

Her father chuckled. "Oh, I imagine when word gets out that you're better, they'll all be flocking around." His eyes twinkled. "Several of them have unmarried daughters."

Tave swatted at her father's arm. "Stop it, Poppa. You're embarrassing Daniel."

"Well, I don't want to do that." Dr. Spencer straightened in his chair and turned toward Daniel. "How was your visit with Captain Hawkins?"

Daniel took a sip of coffee and set the cup down. "Fine, I guess."

Tave's father glanced at Daniel. "You guess?"

Daniel leaned back in his chair and sighed. "He gave me some bad news."

Tave set the dishes in the dry sink and sank back into her chair. "What kind of bad news?"

"The *Montgomery Belle* needs some repairs. He probably won't be coming back this way until fall, if then. The company is sending him to New Orleans to work until the *Belle* is ready to go again."

Her father nodded. "He told me that. But why is that bad news?"

"Because it means I'll have to delay going on to Montgomery."

Her father pushed back from the table and stood up. "Not necessarily. There are other boats that stop at Willow Bend. You can go on one of them—when you're well enough, that is."

Daniel picked up his spoon and stirred the coffee in his cup. "I don't have the money for a ticket. I could work on the *Belle*, but there probably wouldn't be a job on another ship. I've been thinking about what to do. Maybe when I'm stronger, I can find some kind of job around here, just temporary of course, and make enough money to get me up to Montgomery."

Tave put her elbows on the table and crossed her arms. "I think that's a good idea. We can help you look for something." She glanced at her father. "Isn't Mr. Perkins always talking about how he needs someone to help in the store?"

"He is. I'll talk to him in the morning." Her father's eyes narrowed, and he studied Daniel for a moment. "If you continue to improve as much as you have this past week, it shouldn't be too long before you could do some light work. Maybe sweeping up, helping customers, that sort of stuff."

Daniel smiled, and Tave was struck once again by how his eyes crinkled at the corners when he smiled. She reached across the table and patted his arm. "Then that's all settled. Now why don't you two go into the other room while I wash the dishes?"

Her father turned to leave, but Daniel reached out and stopped him. "There's something else. I'll need a place to stay. Is there somebody around town who has a room I could use in exchange for doing odd jobs for them?"

Her father clapped his hand on Daniel's back. "Son, you have a place to stay as long as you're in Willow Bend. That bed in the other room is yours as long as you need it."

"But what if you have another patient who needs to stay here?"

"We'll take care of that if it happens. Let's just leave all this in the Lord's hands for now. Since you're feeling better, I think it's time for Tave and me to go back home at night to sleep. You stay here, but we expect you to be at our house for meals. Is that all right with you?"

"That sounds good to me. Thank you, Dr. Spencer. You and Captain Hawkins have been better to me than anybody else ever has."

Her father chuckled. "It's easy to be good to nice people, Daniel, and I can tell you're a fine young man. Now I'm going to work on my accounts. Why don't you stay and keep Tave company until she has to leave?"

Tave watched her father walk through the door before she glanced back at Daniel. "You can talk to me while I wash dishes."

He pushed up from his chair and steadied his legs that appeared to wobble. "I may still be a little weak, but I can help, if that's all right."

She laughed and carried her cup to the dry sink. "I never turn down an offer of help." She set the cup down and reached for the apron she'd hung on a peg by the stove before supper. She glanced over her shoulder and smiled at Daniel. His hair that tumbled over his forehead reminded her of how different he was from Matthew, who was always perfectly groomed. The way they looked, though, wasn't the only difference between the two men.

Matthew didn't have to worry about money. Daniel did, but the fact that he wanted to earn his way made her respect him. There was a lot to like about Daniel Luckett, and she was glad he was going to be in Willow Bend longer.

⚘

Daniel couldn't take his eyes off Tave. She turned from the dry sink and smiled at him, and he thought his chest would burst from the pounding of his heart. He needed to get away from Willow Bend. He was a drifter, a man who hadn't stayed in one place long in the last seven years. In his heart, he knew Tave could make him want to stay forever, but he couldn't allow that to happen. Another man was already in her life, one who could give her all the things she deserved.

He picked up his coffee cup and eased across the floor to where she stood. When he stopped beside her, she turned to him. "Thanks for bringing me your cup."

He started to set it down just as she reached for it, and their fingers touched. The contact sent his blood surging through his veins. Her eyes grew wide as if she felt the same sensation. He placed the cup in the dry sink and stared down into her eyes.

A longing like he'd never known washed over him. She stood still as his gaze moved over her face, lingered on her lips, and moved to her hair. She wore her hair down as she had the night she bent over his bed. He reached up and touched his fingertip to a curl. "Your hair is beautiful."

A nervous laugh escaped her lips. "You told me that once before."

Reason returned to him, and he let his arm drop back to his side. What was he doing? He'd never been this forward with a woman. From the moment he'd opened his eyes and seen her in that chair, he'd felt a connection to her, and his heart told him that would never change.

He took a step back from her. "I'm sorry. I shouldn't have done that."

She smiled. "That's all right, Daniel. I'm not offended."

153

"You should be. I'm not in the habit of being forward with engaged women."

Her forehead wrinkled. "I'm not engaged."

"Well maybe not, but you're spoken for and that's the same."

She smiled and shook her head. "I'm not spoken for, either."

"B–but your father said—"

She laughed, and the sound sent a thrill coursing through him. "I'm sure my father had a lot to say about Matthew. He doesn't really like him."

Daniel eased back to his chair and dropped into it. "Well, he did mention their differences about the war, but I encounter that with a lot of people who are very nice individuals."

She sat down across from him and leaned forward. "That's what I tell Poppa all the time, but it doesn't do any good. He also thinks Matthew flaunts his money." She planted her elbows on the table, propped her chin in her hands, and sighed. "I think it would be a blessing not to worry about money."

Daniel debated whether to ask her the question on his mind, but he wanted to know. "Are you going to marry him?"

Tave crossed her arms on the table in front of her and shrugged. "I don't know. He's going to Dauphin Island for about six weeks. He said he wants to talk to my father when he returns and that he'd like to take Poppa and me to the St. James Hotel in Selma for a few days with his family when everything's decided."

Daniel thought of the hotel on the banks of the Alabama River. "I've seen the St. James before when I was on the *Montgomery Belle*. Captain Hawkins told me that Union troops occupied it during the war. That's why it was saved."

Tave nodded. "Yes. When the city rebuilt after the war, the hotel was sold, and the new owner has redecorated it. It's quite a showplace, I've heard. My friend Savannah Rinaldi and her husband have been there. I've begged Poppa to take me, but we haven't been able to afford it. Savannah says eating in the dining room at the St. James is an experience you'll never forget."

"I've never been inside."

"Savannah says at night the dining room looks like something you might see in a palace. The tables are set with the best china, and candles glow all around the room. It even has a more elegant touch because they serve their biggest meal at night. They call it *dinner*, not *supper* like most Southerners do. She says it's the most romantic place she's ever been."

Daniel shook his head and grinned. "I would never have figured you for a romantic. You seem more like a practical woman to me."

She tossed her head and sniffed. "There are lots of things you don't know about me, Daniel Luckett."

He chuckled. "Like what?"

Tave pursed her lips and tilted her head to the side. "Well for your information, all women want romance. They want to feel like they're special. I want a man who'll show me that I'm the most important person in his life."

Tave's cheeks flushed, and she glanced down at her hands. Daniel struggled to suppress a smile. He realized she was probably telling him something she'd never shared before, and he was thrilled to be getting a glimpse into her heart. "And how will he do that?"

Her face grew redder, and she swallowed. "W–well, he'll talk to me about how he feels, and he'll ask my opinion on issues. He'll value my advice and treat me like I'm more important to him than anyone else. And even if he thinks my wishes are silly, he'll try to make them come true."

A warning flashed in his mind. His happy mood vanished at the thought of what she might want that he couldn't give her. "And just what kind of wishes do you have, Tave? To have dinner at the St. James?"

She straightened and frowned. "I suppose that's one thing I'd like to do."

Daniel's heart plummeted to the pit of his stomach. "And Matthew can afford to give you things like that."

Tave thought for a moment. "He can, but I believe there are more important things in life than what one can buy."

"Like what?"

"Like faith in God and trusting Him to lead you in the direction He wants you to go. That's the greatest wish that I have for the man I marry. I want him to trust God to lead him."

Daniel sat back in his chair and frowned. "If that's what you want, I hope you get it."

She stared at Daniel, and the intensity of her gaze caused his skin to tingle. "I don't know what I'll get, but I believe that God has a plan for me. I'm praying that God will show me what it is. He has one for you, too, Daniel. All you have to do is trust Him."

Daniel shook his head. "You sound like my mother. She used to tell me that all the time. She trusted God, but in the end He didn't do anything to help her. And I haven't seen Him doing anything to help me either."

Tave reached across the table and covered his hand with hers. "He saved your life, Daniel, and He brought two new friends into your life—my father and me. Can't you be thankful for that?"

Her soft words pricked his heart like nothing he'd heard in years. How he wished he could tell her how thankful he was he'd met her. Tears stung his eyes, and he blinked them back. "You're so much like my mother. Maybe that's why I like you."

She smiled and sat back in her chair. "I like you, too, and I'm thankful God brought you to Willow Bend. I'm just sorry it took somebody shooting you to get you off that boat."

The memory of waking to see her sleeping in the chair next to him returned, and he knew that no matter what had brought him here, he was glad he'd come to Willow Bend. "Me, too. Now I know who's at the top of the bluff. I'll never be able to stay on board again when we dock here."

"Good. We wouldn't want to miss seeing you." She glanced over her shoulder at the dirty dishes and sighed. "Well, I'd better get those washed. Then I'm going home for the night."

He pushed back from the table and stood. "I really enjoyed my supper, Tave. You're a good cook."

"Thank you."

Daniel backed toward the door, reluctant to leave. "I think I'll go to my room. Will you be back tomorrow?"

"You can count on it. I'll be here with breakfast early in the morning. But I think my father is right. In a few days, you need to start coming to our house to eat."

"I'm looking forward to it."

Turning, he walked from the room toward his bedroom. Once inside, he shut the door and dropped into the rocking chair where Tave had sat to keep watch over him. The lamp on the table next to the chair cast a soft glow across the room. He sat back, gripped the chair arms, and closed his eyes. He rocked back and forth thinking about the conversation he'd had with Tave.

"Where were You, God?" he whispered into the quiet room. "She trusted You, and You didn't save her. And if You've been around these last seven years, You've been mighty quiet."

He opened his eyes, and his gaze fell on Tave's Bible beside the lamp. During the last week, he'd opened his eyes several times to see her reading while she sat by his bed. Now it was as if the book called his name, and he reached for it.

With trembling fingers, he caressed the leather cover. It had been years since he held a Bible. He opened the book and held it up to read the words. " *'These things I have spoken unto you, that in me ye might have peace. In the world ye shall have tribulation: but be of good cheer; I have overcome the world.'* "

Daniel leaned his head against the back of the chair and laid the Bible in his lap. The words echoed in his mind: " *'In the world ye shall have tribulation.'* " He'd had plenty of that. But if Jesus' words were to be believed, He could help people overcome whatever happened to them because He was always with them.

That's what Tave had been talking about, and Daniel realized she believed the promise he'd just read with all her heart. It seemed to work for her. Could it for him? He doubted it. He closed the Bible and laid it back on the table.

Chapter 6

Three weeks later, Tave stepped into her father's office and knew the moment she entered that no one was there. Frowning, she stepped to the door of Daniel's room and peered inside. The patchwork quilt she'd brought from home covered the bed, and Daniel's clothes hung on the wooden pegs her father had attached to the wall when they first came to Willow Bend. Puzzled, she turned and walked back to the front door. Daniel hadn't said anything at the noon meal about going anywhere, but then he had been taking walks to get his strength back. Maybe that's where he'd gone.

She'd just stepped onto the front porch when she spied Daniel ambling down the street toward her. His rolling gait reminded her of the sailors who came ashore from time to time when their ships docked. He whistled a tune as he walked along, his hands in the pockets of his denim work pants. She recognized the tan shirt he wore, with its white collar. She'd seen it on Dante Rinaldi. No doubt Savannah had donated it to the ladies' auxiliary at church, and it had found its way to her father's office.

Daniel's eyes lit up as he stepped on the porch. "I didn't know you were coming back this afternoon."

Tave held up the basket in her hand. "I was on my way to Mr. Perkins's store, and I thought I'd check on you first. Where have you been?"

"I've been to see Mr. Perkins. Your father told me this morning he'd talked with him about a job for me, and he wanted to meet me."

Tave frowned as she examined Daniel for any hint that he hadn't recovered enough to work. "Are you sure you're ready for this?"

"I'm feeling good. Mr. Perkins said I could start Monday." He laughed and pointed to the chairs. "Let's sit and enjoy the day for a minute." He dropped down in one of the porch chairs and wiped at his forehead. "It sure has gotten warm in the last few days."

Tave settled in the chair next to him and set her basket down. "It's the last of June, Daniel. Can you believe you've been here a month?"

"No, I can't, but I feel stronger every day."

"Well don't try to do too much in this heat. It's only going to get worse." She pulled a handkerchief from the pocket of her dress and mopped her face. "I always dread the hot weather." A breeze drifted from the river, and she smiled. "Then the river reminds me I wouldn't want to live anywhere else."

They sat in silence for a moment, and she studied him out of the corner of her eye. Color had returned to his cheeks, and he looked very different from the man who'd been brought up the riverbank to her father's office. His face didn't hold the gaunt look she'd observed on it in the days after surgery, and he was able to walk farther each day.

He turned his head toward her, and for a moment their gazes locked. Her face grew warm from the scrutiny of his eyes. A slight frown wrinkled his forehead. "What are you thinking?"

Tave struggled to control the increased beating of her heart. "I'm thankful to see you recovering so well. We really didn't expect you to live when we first saw you."

"I know." He gazed back toward the river. "I owe you and your father a lot, Tave."

She reached over and touched his arm. "You don't owe us anything, Daniel. You've given us a lot in just knowing you."

He faced her again. "How could I possibly give you anything?"

His question surprised her. Was it possible he had no idea of his worth? "You've given me so much just by being my friend. I've talked to you more in the past few weeks than I have to anyone else since I came to Willow Bend."

"You have? I would think you and your friend Savannah share all your thoughts."

"Well, she's very busy at Cottonwood, and I'm at school all the time. So we don't get to see each other much except at church."

A frown wrinkled his forehead. "I'm sure Matthew is very important to you, too."

Tave bit her lip in an attempt to keep from grinning. "Why Daniel Luckett," she said, "you remind me of Caleb Thompson, Martha's youngest son. He comes to my desk several times a day to ask if I like his brother Tad better than I do him. I wouldn't have thought a grown man could sound so much like a jealous little boy."

Daniel straightened his shoulders and took a deep breath. The muscle in his jaw twitched. "I'm only saying what is obvious. Matthew must be a mighty fine man if you're interested in him, but we don't have much in common. I've seen a lot of rich people on the *Montgomery Belle*, but they always looked at me as if I weren't really there."

Tave's heart thudded at the sadness she saw in his eyes. She'd never known anyone who put as little value on himself as Daniel did. How could she make him see his worth? She breathed a quick prayer for guidance before she spoke.

"Daniel, you are God's creature. He gave you gifts and abilities that are yours alone. In the time I've known you, I've been struck by the fact that you are a good man who has suffered some terrible tragedies in your life. But God gave you a resourcefulness that got you through those bad times. He gave you a deep concern for other people—enough that you almost gave your life to save another's. Only a brave man would do that. I only wish I could help you with whatever happened in your past that has left deep scars on your soul."

His eyes widened. "What makes you think something happened to me?"

She'd hoped for the opportunity to broach the subject of his past ever since she first heard him cry out in his unconscious state. "I sat by your bed when you were delirious. I listened to your cries and wiped away tears that ran down your face. That first night, you were so agitated that I knelt beside you and prayed that God would calm you. I was afraid you were going to die."

He swallowed, and his Adam's apple bobbed. "I couldn't see you, but I felt you there."

"I'm glad you knew I was praying. That was the worst night. After that, I spent a lot of time on my knees beside your bed." She smiled. "And it worked. Look at you now. You're well enough to get a job."

He took a deep breath. "What did I say that concerned you so?"

"You called out for your mother. Then you yelled for someone not to hurt her."

Daniel nodded. "Yes, I suppose I did." He sat silent for a moment. "I told you that my mother married after my father's death."

"Yes."

"The man's name was Frank Jessup. He'd lost his wife and didn't have any children. My mother thought she was doing the right thing for us. We'd have a home, and I'd have a father. It didn't take her long to realize what a mistake she'd made. Frank had a cruel streak that came out after we moved in. My mother worked from dawn till bedtime, but it was never enough for him. It only got worse when he drank. That's when the beatings began."

Pain flickered in his face, and Tave clasped her hands in her lap. "How terrible."

He glanced at her. "Yeah. It was bad. I was just a child, but I'd try to protect her. Then he'd turn on me. I didn't mind because if he was hitting me, he was letting her alone. Of course she didn't see it that way. She didn't want me hurt. I begged her over and over for us to leave, but she said we had nowhere to go. God would take care of us, she'd say. And then Frank would get drunk again."

"What happened to cause her death?"

He stared out toward the river. "I really don't know how it started. I was sixteen, and I had gone into town to get some supplies she needed. I knew he was drinking before I left, and I tried to hurry back home. When I got there, I couldn't understand why she didn't come out to meet me." A wistful smile curled his lips. "She always came running out when I'd get back from anywhere."

"But she didn't that day?"

He shook his head. "No. I had this awful feeling that something had happened. I didn't even take the horses to the barn. I just jumped out of the wagon and ran inside. She was lying on the kitchen floor. She'd been shot." He clenched his fists. "I knew he'd done it. I ran through the house looking for him. I grabbed the gun I used for hunting. The only thing on my mind was that I had to kill Frank."

Tave's heart pounded. "Did you?"

"No. He was lying in the barn with the shotgun beside him. He'd killed himself, too."

Tave wiped at a tear that rolled down her cheek. "How horrible. What did you do then?"

"I got back in the wagon and rode to my uncle's house and told him what I'd found. He went for the sheriff, and they took care of everything. The next day, we buried my mother, but I wouldn't let them bury Frank next to her. As soon as we finished, I left, and I've been drifting ever since."

"And your heart is still grieving that horrible experience."

His eyes grew wide. "Grief? For my mother, yes. I only feel hate for Frank Jessup. Sometimes I wish I'd found him before he killed himself. At least I'd have the satisfaction of knowing I avenged my mother."

Tave frowned and shook her head. "You should be thankful you didn't get a chance to kill him. You would have been executed, and for what? Vengeance? The Bible tells us that vengeance belongs to God, not to us."

"Yeah, I've heard that before, but it doesn't do anything to make me feel better." He clenched his fists at his sides. "Every time I think of Frank, it's like a knife slices through my heart and leaves me feeling like I've been cut up in little pieces and left to die."

Tave reached over and placed her hand on his arm. "I'm so sorry you've had such bad things happen in your life, Daniel. I can't even start to imagine what it's been like for you."

He stood and raked his hand through his hair. He strode to the edge of the porch, stopped, and turned to face her. "I can barely remember my father before he left for the war. But there are moments when I recall things he said and did. He was such a good man, and my mother didn't deserve to end up with Frank Jessup. If my father had lived, things would have been so different for us."

She rose and walked to where he stood. "Your father couldn't help what happened to him. Your mother did what she thought was best at the time. All you can do is lean on another Father who's waiting to help you."

He stared at her. "I've seen you reading the Bible, and I've tried that, too. I'll read something that gives me some hope I can let go of all this anger I have, and then I remember how my mother's body looked lying on that kitchen floor. I get so angry at God for letting that happen that I want to scream and ask why." He clenched his fists and glared at her. "If your God is so loving, tell me why He let that happen."

She shook her head. "People for centuries have tried to figure out why God lets bad things happen to people who love Him. My mother died when I was so young that I barely remember her, but sometimes I miss her so much that I ache inside. I used to ask my father why God took my mother away."

"What did he say?"

"He said that we aren't supposed to understand God's ways. We are just supposed to trust that He'll comfort us when bad things happen in our lives. I found a passage of scripture a long time ago that helped me cope, and I memorized it. I have to say it quite often to remind myself that God is still in control."

"What is it?"

Tave tilted her head and smiled up at Daniel. "It goes like this: 'That the trial of your faith, being much more precious than of gold that perisheth, though it be tried with fire, might be found unto praise and honour and glory at the appearing of Jesus Christ.'"

"Those sound like a lot of fancy words to me. What does it mean?"

"It reminds me that I can't control what's happening around me. Problems come, and I may be troubled for a while. But these things are necessary because they test my faith. Gold can't survive fire, but our faith is more precious than gold. If we hold on to God, we can survive. When we put our trust in God, He fills us with a peace that can endure forever. So no matter what happens in my life, God is still there, and I have to give it over to Him."

He shook his head. "You make it sound easy, but I don't know if I could ever do that."

"God has given you great trials, Daniel, but I believe He's been preparing you for something greater in your life. If you can trust Him and come out of the fire, you're going to find that God will give you the greatest peace you've ever known. And when you do that, He's going to reveal the plan He has for you."

Daniel's eyes bored into hers. "No one has ever cared enough to talk to me like you have, Tave. You almost make me feel like I'm destined for some great mission in life."

Her gaze didn't waver from his face. "Maybe you are." Then she cleared her throat, glanced around for her basket, and picked it up. "Now, I have to get to Mr. Perkins's store. You're to come to supper with Poppa tonight. Don't disappoint me."

"I won't."

Tave walked down the steps and headed toward the store. When she stopped at the store's front door, she looked back toward her father's office. Daniel still stood where she'd left him. He lifted his hand and waved.

⟨≈⟩

Daniel watched as Tave disappeared into the store. He turned back to the chair and sat down to ponder what he and Tave had discussed. He closed his eyes for a moment and thought about what she'd said.

For the last seven years, he'd moved from place to place in an effort to run away from the memory of what he'd seen the day he found his mother's body. Hatred had burned in his heart for the man who'd destroyed the last person Daniel had in his life, and he didn't know if he could ever let go of the past.

Tave's words returned to him, and he remembered how she looked when she gazed at him. In her eyes, he saw genuine concern for him. She wanted his soul to be at peace, and her words almost persuaded him he could be. His feelings for her made him want to do what she asked, but something still held him back.

When he'd first seen Tave, an emotion he hadn't experienced in years had grabbed his heart. Over the past few weeks as he'd gotten to know her, it had only deepened. There was no doubt about it. He was in love with her. It didn't matter, though. He could never speak of it. He wasn't the kind of man she'd described as the husband she wanted. She deserved so much more than a penniless wanderer haunted by a memory that controlled his life.

He'd never had trouble leaving any other place behind, and when the time came, he'd leave Tave, too. She needed someone like Matthew Chandler, a man with money and family connections. He could make all her wishes come true.

A discreet cough at the edge of the porch caught his attention, and he glanced up to see Martha Thompson standing there. He'd spoken with her several times when she'd brought food to the doctor's office for them.

He had discovered as soon as he met her that she knew everything about all the residents of Willow Bend. He wondered what gossip she was pedaling today. Stifling an inward groan, he stood and smiled. "Mrs. Thompson, imagine seeing you today."

She grinned at him. "I was just on my way back from the store, and I saw you sittin' out here all alone. I thought I'd check on you and see how you're doing."

"I'm fine. And you?"

"Just tolerable, Mr. Luckett. Just tolerable." She frowned and twisted her shoulders. "Been havin' some trouble with my back lately. Walking back and forth to town sure does cause my rheumatism to act up."

His hope that this was going to be a quick greeting vanished. He pointed to the chair where Tave had sat. "Would you like to rest for a while?"

Martha shook her head. "I don't want to bother you none."

Guilt at wishing he'd slipped inside Dr. Spencer's office before Martha saw him niggled at the back of his mind. After all, she had fed him while he was sick. "How could you bother me? Especially after all the good food you've fed me."

She giggled. "Now ain't you a smooth talker? I was just doing my Christian duty to help out folks in need."

"And I appreciate it."

She eased up onto the porch and plopped down in one of the chairs. She exhaled and set the basket beside her. "It sure is a hot day. I reckon I could stand to sit a spell before I take that long walk back home." She glanced at him. "Mr. Perkins tells me you gonna start working for him next week."

Daniel nodded and dropped into the chair next to her. "I am. I need to earn some money so I can get on up to Montgomery."

She tilted her head to one side. "You got family up that way?"

"No. My family's all dead."

"You don't have a wife?"

"I'm afraid not."

"Then what's in Montgomery?"

"I have a job waiting for me there."

"Doin' what?"

"Working on the docks."

The questions had been fired at him with the rapid precision of a Gatling gun. It took Daniel only a minute to figure out that Martha had accomplished her mission. She'd found out what she wanted to know about him.

Martha narrowed her eyes and nodded. "You don't say. On the docks, huh? I know Doc and Tave are gonna miss you. They appear to be quite taken with you."

"I am with them, too. After all, they saved my life."

Martha shifted in her chair and gazed at him, starting at his toes and ending at his head. "You sure look different than you did that day they brought you up that bluff. Me and the other ladies thought you was a goner for sure. Now that you're feeling better, all of us in the ladies' auxiliary hope you'll come to church."

"Dr. Spencer mentioned to me how kind all of you were by bringing clothes for me and of course the food you brought. I'd love to meet everyone."

Martha's face lit up. "Now that'd just be wonderful. I want to make sure you meet my daughter Esther. She cooked a lot of that food I brought over here, and she's just dying to meet you."

Daniel gulped and forced a smile to his face. "I'll be happy to meet Esther and thank her."

Martha pushed to her feet, placed her hands in the small of her back, and rubbed. "That little rest helped a lot." She bent down and picked up her basket. "I guess I can make it home now. Maybe we'll see you Sunday."

"Maybe so."

He watched Martha as she waddled down the street, then turned his attention back to Mr. Perkins's store. Tave stepped onto the street, a blond woman behind her. They chatted as they strolled down the street toward Dr. Spencer's office.

When they reached it, they stepped onto the porch, and Tave pointed to the woman with her. "Daniel, this is my friend Savannah Rinaldi. She and her husband own Cottonwood Plantation."

Daniel had heard Tave and her father talk about the Rinaldis before, but he hadn't had the opportunity to meet either of them. "Captain Hawkins pointed out your home to me once when we passed going upriver. He told me you and your husband rebuilt the house to what it was like before it burned."

Savannah smiled. "Well, almost to what it was like. It's somewhat smaller, but we like it fine. I'm sorry my husband isn't with me today. I know he'd like to meet you." Her eyes lit up as if she'd just been struck with an idea. "Tave, why don't you bring Daniel to the picnic after church on Sunday?"

A shy smile pulled at Tave's lips, and she tightened her grip on the basket's handle. "I was going to ask you if you felt up to doing that. What do you think?"

He hadn't wanted to go to church in years, but he wanted to be wherever Tave was. If that meant going to church, he'd do it. His plans might call for him to leave Willow Bend, but until he did, he intended to spend every minute he could with her.

"I'd love to go."

Chapter 7

Tave and Savannah walked toward the livery stable that sat at the end of the main street. Tave walked past there often on her way back and forth to her father's office and always stopped to look at the horses in the corral at the side of the building. As she and Savannah approached the fence, a chestnut mare with a white star on her head trotted over and whinnied at them.

Tave stopped and stared at the beautiful creature. The mare stuck her head over the fence, and Tave patted her. "Where did you come from, girl? I haven't seen you before."

Savannah stepped up beside Tave. "Dante said Mr. Jensen bought some new horses at the sale in Selma last week. She must be one of them."

Tave took in the sleek lines of the mare. "Whoever gets her is going to be a lucky person." She gave the horse one last pat, and she and Savannah walked on toward the front of the livery stable. Tave darted a glance at her friend. "I'm glad you invited Daniel to church. I wanted to, but I wasn't sure he'd come."

Savannah stopped and stared at her. "Why would you think that?"

Tave longed to discuss her conversation with Daniel, but she didn't want to reveal anything about his background that he wanted to keep private. "Daniel has had some problems in his past, and I've tried to give him some scriptures to help him. I thought he might think I was pushing him too much. It was much better coming from you."

"I don't think you'd have a problem getting him to do anything you wanted."

"Why do you say that?"

Savannah laughed and stared at Tave with a look of disbelief. "What's the matter with you? Are you blind?"

Tave's mouth gaped open. "Blind about what?"

Savannah pursed her lips and studied Tave. "You can't see that he's in love with you, can you?"

Tave pressed her hand to her chest and took a step back. "In love with me? What makes you think that?"

"It's the way he looks at you, Tave. I can see it in his eyes."

Tave could hardly believe what she was hearing. She knew Daniel had developed an attachment to her. But love? No, that couldn't be. Tave shook her head. "You're wrong. I'd know it if that were true."

Savannah looped her arm through Tave's, and they moved toward Savannah's buggy that sat outside the livery stable. "Not necessarily. I remember Mamie telling me that Dante loved me, and I didn't believe it. Later, I didn't know how I'd missed all the signals he'd been sending me."

Tave's stomach churned, and her knees felt weak. "B–but what should I do?"

Savannah stopped at her buggy and placed her basket inside. "Nothing, I suppose. That is, unless you want to encourage him." Savannah turned to face Tave, and her eyes grew wide. "You're in love with him, too, aren't you?"

The question stunned Tave. She reached out and clutched the side of the buggy for support. "I—I don't know. I like him, and I feel very protective of him. I thought that was because I'd taken care of him when he was so sick."

Savannah nodded in the direction of the livery stable. "I need to go pay Mr. Jensen what I owe him. You get in the buggy, and I'll take you home. I think we need to talk about this more."

Tave climbed in and settled on the seat. Savannah's words whirled in her mind as she waited for her friend to return. Was it possible Daniel was in love with her? And what about her feelings? She put her fingers on her temples and rubbed. This was too much to comprehend.

Savannah returned in a few minutes and untied the reins from the hitching post. When she was settled in the buggy, she turned the horse in the direction of Tave's house.

They rode in silence for a minute until Tave's curiosity got the best of her. She turned to Savannah. "How did you know when you fell in love with Dante?"

Savannah arched her eyebrows and flicked the reins across the horse's back. "It's hard to put into words. I think it began with respect. I saw what a good man he was even though he'd had some bad things happen to him in the past. I recognized his strength of character because he was able to survive some terrible experiences, but it hadn't hardened his heart."

Tave nodded. "Daniel's had some horrible things happen to him. He hasn't been able to put some of it behind him yet. I don't know if he ever will." She glanced at Savannah. "He's carrying a lot of anger inside him, but I know he's a good man. He risked his life to save another man's life. Someone who does that has to be brave. Captain Hawkins said he's a fine young man, too."

"Then you can be assured he is. I've known Captain Hawkins since I was a child, and he's a good judge of character. But Tave, you know as well as I do that there are many people who look good in the eyes of the world, but they don't have a personal relationship with Jesus." They rode in silence for a while before Savannah spoke again. "What about Matthew? How do you feel about him?"

With a start, Tave realized she'd hardly thought about Matthew since he'd been away. She bit down on her lip then glanced at Savannah. "I haven't told you what Matthew said before he left with his mother."

When she finished telling Savannah of Matthew's visit, Savannah shook her head. "He talked about marriage, but he never said he loved you?"

Tave gasped. "You're right. I just now realized that."

Savannah grabbed the reins with one hand and reached over to pat Tave's arm. "I'm sure he must, or he wouldn't want to marry you."

Tave nodded, but she wasn't so sure. The first time she'd seen Matthew after coming to Willow Bend she had thought him the most handsome man she'd ever seen, but he'd never noticed her until a year ago. Since that time, she'd often dreamed of what it would be like to be married to the heir of one of the biggest plantations in Alabama. Now she realized she'd ceased having those thoughts some time ago, and she hadn't questioned why.

Why would Matthew talk of marrying her if he didn't love her? And what about Daniel? Was it possible he'd fallen in love with her?

Tave clenched her fists and pounded her knees. "Why is it so hard sometimes to know what God's will is for your life?"

Savannah laughed. "I've often wondered that myself." She pulled the horse to a stop at Tave's house and turned in the seat to face her. "The important thing is for you to pray about it, and search your heart for the answer, Tave. Matthew has a lot of money, but it doesn't mean a thing if you don't love him. On the other hand, Daniel seems like a nice enough young man, but he doesn't recognize the need for God in his life. Be careful. He could end up hurting you. You're my friend, and I don't want to see that happen."

Tave hugged Savannah and smiled. "Thank you. I'll think about everything you've said, and I'll pray about it. For all I know, there may be somebody else God has in mind for me. I'll wait until the Lord reveals what He has planned for me."

"That sounds good to me. We'll talk again. Maybe we'll have a chance to do that Sunday at the picnic."

Tave climbed from the buggy and waved as the horse trotted down the street. When her friend was out of sight, she walked toward the small house where she and her father had lived since coming to Willow Bend.

She stopped at the crepe myrtle bush outside the front door and broke off several branches to arrange in the cut-glass vase that had belonged to her grandmother. The deep pink blooms always added a festive touch to their dining table, and she wanted everything to look special for Daniel tonight.

Her heart quickened at the memory of Savannah's words. Did Daniel love her? She had to admit she harbored special feelings for him, but she hadn't called it love. Not yet, anyway.

❧

On Saturday night, Tave closed the cupboard and turned back to survey the clean kitchen. Every supper dish had been washed, dried, and put away. A burst of laughter came from the parlor, and she smiled. She knew that sound all too well. Poppa had just defeated Daniel in another game of checkers.

She picked up the oil lamp from the kitchen table and walked into the parlor. Daniel gazed down at the checkerboard as if trying to determine which move had proved his undoing in the match. Her father leaned back in his chair, crossed his legs, and tapped his tented fingers together. A smile curled his lips.

Tave set the lamp down on the table next to the rocker that had belonged to her mother and sat down. She plumped a pillow behind her back and sighed. "Don't bother trying to recall the moves, Daniel. I'm sure if you ask Poppa, he can tell you where you made your mistake."

Daniel looked up, a puzzled expression on his face. "How do you know that?"

"Because I've been watching him defeat every guest we've had ever since I can remember. It's an obsession with him. Behind that kind face and loving personality lurks a fierce competitor who shows no mercy."

Her father laughed and pushed to his feet. "You're speaking ill of your father, my dear. I would expect better from my daughter."

The bag that held items to be darned sat on the floor at her feet, and she reached for it. "You forget how well I know you, Poppa." She pulled a sock from inside and cast a glance at Daniel. "I learned a long time ago that checkers is a scientific game, and Poppa plays it well. He's not so concerned about his own moves as he is about waiting for the right moment when his opponent makes a mistake. Then he strikes swiftly."

Daniel rose and stuck his hands in his pockets. "Well, I have to say playing with him these past few weeks has been quite a learning experience."

Her father slapped Daniel on the back. "Keep practicing, son. Who knows? You just might be the one to beat me."

Daniel shook his head. "I doubt that, but I enjoyed the game."

Her father stifled a yawn. "Now if you two will excuse me, I have some work to do. I have a sick patient out at Winterville Plantation, the son of one of the tenant farmers, and I need to do some research about his condition. I'm going to my bedroom and see what I can find in that new medical book that came the other day."

Tave smiled at him. "Don't nod off to sleep in your chair and forget to blow out the lamp."

"I'll be careful."

She watched as her father walked from the room and entered his bedroom before she glanced back at Daniel, who stared at her. He jerked his gaze away from her face and returned to the chair where he'd been sitting.

They sat in silence as she began to mend her father's sock. After a time, Daniel stood and walked over to the mantel. He picked up a daguerreotype and stared at it. He glanced over his shoulder at her. "Your mother?"

She nodded. "Yes, it was made while my parents were on their wedding trip to New York. Poppa's often told me how excited she was that day and how she fussed with her hair. She had trouble picking out which of the embossed leather cases she wanted. She told my father she hoped the likeness would show him how happy she was to be his wife. It's the only picture I have of her, and of course it's my father's greatest treasure."

"She was very beautiful."

"Thank you, Daniel, for saying that." She rose, crossed the room to stand beside him at the mantel, and gazed at the picture of her mother. "That's her wedding dress. I still have it. It's a cream-colored silk-satin dress. My grandmother hand sewed the appliquéd lace you see on the skirt and at the end of the sleeves. Poppa says she looked like a queen when she walked into the church."

Daniel replaced the shiny image to the mantel and turned to Tave. "You look just like her, you know."

Tave shook her head. "No, she was much prettier than I am."

He glanced at the likeness one more time. "Your hair is the same, and so is your smile. I think you're wrong about this picture being your father's greatest treasure."

"Why?"

He took a deep breath. "I think *you* are his greatest treasure because he sees her in you every day."

Tave started to protest, but she remembered how she would often catch her father staring at her, tears in his eyes. He would look away quickly. She wondered if he might be thinking of her mother and the happy times they shared. She turned to face him. "I do look like her, don't I?"

He trailed his fingertips down the side of her cheek. "You're the most beautiful woman I've ever seen in my life. I wish I could tell you. . ."

Tave frowned at Daniel's hesitation. "Tell me what?"

He pulled his hand away from her face and let his arm fall to his side. His eyes that had ignited her heart with the fire she saw in them a few moments before looked as if they were blocks of ice. He backed away from her.

"How much I enjoyed my supper. Now I think I'd better go."

Tave frowned and took a step toward him, but he turned and headed for the front door. It only took her a moment before she reacted. She rushed across the floor and stepped in front of him, blocking his exit from the room. "I think you were going to tell me something else. What is it?"

He licked his lips. "I—I was going to say. . ." He gritted his teeth and raked his hand through his hair. He exhaled and shook his head. "It was nothing important, Tave."

His hand trembled, and she touched his arm. "Daniel, please, if it's something I can help you with. . ."

His eyes grew wide, and he jerked away from her. "It's nothing for you to be concerned about." He pushed past her. "Now I need to leave. I'll be here in the morning to go to church with you and your father. Have a good night."

He'd hardly finished saying the words before the door slammed behind him. Tave stood in the parlor unsure of what had just occurred. One minute, Daniel had reached out to her in a way that could only mean he had some feelings for her. Then he'd shattered the mood with his hasty departure.

She had the impression that his leaving so abruptly meant he wanted to distance himself from her in more ways than one. The reality of what she'd tried to deny hit her. The feelings she had for Daniel weren't caused by how she'd taken care of him when he was near death. What she felt could only mean one thing: she had come to love Daniel Luckett.

Chapter 8

Daniel leaned against the hitching post outside the Spencer home, closed his eyes, and lifted his face to the warm Sunday morning sun. He wondered if Tave would be glad to see him after the way he'd rushed out of the house last night. He had to leave, though, because he was on the verge of making a terrible mistake.

When he'd seen how much she looked like the beautiful woman in the picture, he'd been overcome with a longing to let her know how much she'd come to mean to him. Now in the light of day, he thought he'd put that moment of weakness behind him. He wouldn't think of her that way anymore. From now on, he would think of her as a dear friend, one he was going to attend church with today.

He chuckled at the thought of him in church. If someone had told him two months ago he'd be excited about attending church, he would have denied it. But now that he was about to do it, he knew it was time. He longed to put the past behind him, but every time it almost seemed possible, Frank Jessup's face would flash in his memory. Then the hatred would overflow again.

He'd spent hours reading Tave's Bible in the past few weeks. The scriptures she'd given him, as well as others he'd found on his own, had spoken to his heart. One he'd read last night still lingered in his mind: *"If ye continue in my word, then are ye my disciples indeed; And ye shall know the truth, and the truth shall make you free."*

That's what he needed—to be free of the past.

A creaking sound caught his attention, and he straightened to see Dr. Spencer leading his horse, hitched to a buggy, around the side of the house. Daniel had watched Dr. Spencer leave in the buggy to visit a sick person many times since he'd been staying at his office. Nothing kept the dedicated doctor from going where he was needed. Just last week, he'd watched Dr. Spencer huddle under the buggy's top as he guided his horse out of town in the midst of a driving rainstorm.

This morning, the overhead covering of the buggy lay folded to the rear of the backseat. Dr. Spencer raised a hand in greeting as he approached. "Morning, Daniel. You didn't have to walk over here. I would have stopped to get you at the office."

Daniel inhaled. "I know, but it's such a nice day I wanted to walk."

"It's good to see you've recovered enough that you can walk."

Daniel grinned and thumped his chest. "I've got my strength back just in time to begin my new job tomorrow."

Dr. Spencer looped the horse's reins over the hitching post and walked around to pat the horse's flank. "Ah yes. You're going to start helping Mr. Perkins tomorrow, but be careful. I don't want you overdoing it."

"I will be."

Dr. Spencer pulled out his pocket watch, glanced at the time, and frowned. "Where is that girl? We're going to be late if she doesn't hurry." He cupped his hands around his mouth. "Tave! Aren't you ready yet?"

The front door of the house opened, and Tave stepped onto the porch. She held a basket in one hand as she reached back to close the door. "I'm coming, Poppa."

Dr. Spencer's eyebrows arched, and he sighed. "Daniel, there's something about women you need to find out while you're still single. They're never ready on time. They'll keep a man waiting just to see him squirm."

Tave laughed and glided down the flagstone walkway toward them. "Don't believe a word of what he says, Daniel." She arched an eyebrow. "That is, if you expect to get any of my fried chicken at the picnic today."

Her father laughed, took the basket, and set it in the backseat. "Maybe I'd better rephrase my observation about women, Daniel. The appearance of a beautiful woman can always make you forget your annoyance over her being late." His eyes twinkled. "Especially when she arrives with fried chicken."

Daniel heard the exchange between the two, but his tongue felt glued to the roof of his mouth. All he could do was gape at Tave like a schoolboy. He'd never seen her more beautiful than she was today. The lavender and white dress she wore had rows of ruffles draped down the skirt back, and it swished with every step she took. Her auburn hair pinned on top of her head sparkled in the sun. As she brushed past him, the scent of lilacs filled his nostrils.

As if she could read his thoughts, she lowered her eyelids and smiled. "I'm glad you wanted to come today, Daniel. You'll get to meet all our friends. I hope Dante gets to come with Savannah and the children. I think you'd really like him."

"I hope so, too. I enjoyed meeting Savannah."

She lifted the hem of her dress with one hand to climb into the buggy, and he grasped her other arm to assist. His skin burned from the touch. He bit down on his lip in an effort to keep from revealing the emotions whirling through him.

Once she was seated, she spread her full skirt out and glanced at him. "Thank you, Daniel."

He mumbled something, he had no idea what, and climbed in behind them.

He settled against the leather backseat of the buggy and watched Dr. Spencer turn the horse and guide it along the road toward the Willow Bend Church. The gentle pressure the doctor used to prod the animal gave evidence of how well the horse and handler understood each other, a knowledge that had most likely been acquired by spending untold hours traveling from farm to farm around Willow Bend.

Dr. Spencer chuckled and glanced over his shoulder. "You might as well get ready, Daniel. I expect you're going to be swamped with mothers trying to introduce their unmarried daughters to you. It's not often we get eligible bachelors in Willow Bend, and you've been the topic of conversation ever since you got here."

Daniel's face grew warm, and he squinted up at the sun. "Aw, they won't care about a man like me."

"What does that mean?"

"Just that I'm a drifter, never have settled down anywhere. As soon as I feel like it, I guess I'll be moving on."

His stomach churned at the words he'd spoken. It was true he'd never been interested in settling in one spot before, not until he met Tave, but that didn't do him any good. A woman like her needed someone who could give her a better life than he could.

Dr. Spencer nodded. "Well that's up to you, but we'd like to see you stay around if you'd like to."

"Thanks, Dr. Spencer."

Daniel stared at Tave to see how his words had affected her, but she didn't move or speak. Her rigid back seemed to convey the message that she didn't care whether he stayed or left. With a sigh, he directed his attention back to the road ahead.

The church that Dr. Spencer told him had been built in the early part of the century came into view. Buggies and some farm wagons dotted the area around the front of the building, which sat well back from the road leading out of town. On one side of the church, tombstones marked the graves of past worshippers, and a stand of water oaks fanned across the field on the opposite side. Tables had been set underneath the trees in preparation for the picnic that would follow services.

Daniel hopped from the buggy and helped Tave down. Without looking at him, she held out her hand and grasped his. Once on the ground, she pointed to the basket. "We'll take that inside. I don't want it to sit outside in the heat."

He nodded and reached for the basket. Dr. Spencer walked around the front of the buggy from where he'd tied the horse and put his hands in his pockets. "Well, are you ready to meet all the good folks of Willow Bend, Daniel?"

His stomach churned, and Daniel glanced down at his clothes. Even though they were the best he had, he supposed everybody would be better dressed today than he was. He swallowed and looked up at Dr. Spencer. "Am I dressed all right?"

For the first time, Tave looked at him and smiled. "We don't judge a man by how he's dressed, Daniel." She studied him with a critical gaze before she nodded as if satisfied. "You look very handsome. Now why don't you escort me inside? I'm sure Martha Thompson would love something to talk about tomorrow at Mr. Perkins's store."

He stared down at her small hand resting on his arm, and he thought his heart would burst with love. At that moment, he didn't want to be anywhere else besides right here with Tave. He straightened to his full height and crooked his arm. "I'd consider myself the luckiest man in the world to take you into church."

She looped her arm through his and moved closer to him. "Then let's go hear what message Reverend Somers has for us today."

Daniel's feet felt like they barely touched the ground as they walked to the church and entered. Once inside, Tave pointed to a small room at the side of the entrance where other baskets sat, and he deposited hers inside before they joined the already-gathered congregation.

During the walk down the aisle and as they stepped into a pew near the front, Daniel felt all eyes staring at him. He sat down between Tave and Dr. Spencer and jumped when someone tapped him on the shoulder. He turned to see Savannah Rinaldi behind him. "I want to introduce you to my husband. Dante, this is Daniel Luckett, the young man who saved Captain Hawkins's life."

A broad-shouldered, dark-complexioned man leaned forward, his hand outstretched. "Glad to meet you, Daniel. Captain Hawkins is a friend of our family. Thank you for what you did."

Daniel stared into the darkest eyes he thought he'd ever seen. He grasped Dante's hand. "Anybody else would have done the same."

Dante shook his head. "I doubt that." Dante glanced toward the front of the church where Reverend Somers was about to take his place at the pulpit and whispered to Daniel, "There's something we need to talk about, but we'll do that later at the picnic. Glad to have you here today."

Daniel's body tensed. What could this man he'd only just met have to talk about with him? With a nod in Dante's direction, Daniel swiveled in the pew to face forward.

Next to him, Tave leaned close and whispered in his ear, "I'm glad you've already made a friend."

He started to reply that this new friend had said something that puzzled him, but Reverend Somers's voice rang out. "Let's begin our service today by standing and repeating the Lord's Prayer together."

Daniel rose to his feet with the rest of the congregation and gazed at the small wooden cross on the table in front of the pulpit. An open Bible lay beside it. Peace flowed through him at the sight. He hadn't been in a church since his mother had taken him when he was a child, but it felt natural to be here.

He bowed his head and closed his eyes. He didn't move as the familiar words spoken by the congregation washed over him. "Our Father, who art in heaven, hallowed be Thy name. . . ."

Daniel could hardly believe all the food the ladies of the church had brought, and each one insisted he have some of hers. He'd felt like the guest of honor at a big celebration ever since they'd left the church for the picnic grove.

He finally escaped all the attention when Tave and Savannah rescued him and led him toward a towering oak tree where they had spread a quilt on the ground. Dante already sat there, his plate piled high with enough food to feed two men. He grinned and motioned Daniel to sit beside him.

Now with his plate empty, Dante set it aside and rubbed his stomach. "I don't think I'll be able to eat another bite for a week after that good meal."

Savannah arched her eyebrows and tilted her head to the side. "Is that so? Then I assume that means I won't have to fix you any supper."

He grinned, leaned over, and planted a kiss on his wife's cheek. "I wouldn't want to deny you the pleasure of cooking for your devoted husband."

She swatted at his arm and glanced at Tave. "Do you see what I have to deal with? He's a charmer, and I'm helpless to resist him."

Tave nodded. "I see what you mean."

Daniel watched the couple stare into each other's eyes like there was no one else around. Their feelings for each other were evident for everyone to see, and he thought how fortunate they were to love like that. He glanced at Tave and saw her studying him. She dropped her gaze and reached for the dirty dishes.

"We'd better get this cleaned up before Martha comes around to find out what's taking us so long."

Savannah pushed to her feet, and Dante handed her their dishes. She smiled down at her husband. "While we're gone, I think you have something to talk to Daniel about."

"I do."

Daniel watched Tave and Savannah walk across the picnic area to the table where the ladies were in the process of putting food away and gathering up dirty dishes before he turned back to Dante. "You said something in church about wanting to talk with me. What is it?"

Dante pushed to his feet. "Do you mind if we walk and talk? I've been sitting about as long as I can stand it."

"Fine with me. I was about to get stiff from sitting on the ground."

They walked toward the front of the church and stopped at the edge of the small cemetery. Dante pointed to a grave. "That's Savannah's aunt. I only met her a few weeks before her death, but she was a great lady."

Daniel nodded. "She must have had a big influence on Savannah. She's one of the nicest women I've ever met."

Dante grinned. "Nicer than Tave?"

Daniel almost choked on the surprise that clogged his throat. "Wh–what?"

Dante slapped him on the back and grinned. "Sorry. I couldn't resist. It's plain to see how you feel about Tave, but that's not what I wanted to talk to you about."

"Then what is it?"

He stared back at the grave. "Savannah's aunt Jane was a good friend of Captain Hawkins. When she needed money so badly, he bought her house with the understanding that she could live there until her death. He felt by that time he'd be ready to retire to Willow Bend, and he would take over the house then."

"But he never has."

Dante nodded. "That's right. Aunt Jane died seven years ago, but Captain Hawkins can't leave the river. He will someday, but not yet." Dante motioned for Daniel to follow him, and they strolled toward the back of the church. "Anyway, when Captain Hawkins came ashore to see you a few weeks ago, he left a letter at Mr. Perkins's store for me. I had to take care of something before I could tell you what the letter said."

Daniel stopped and stared at Dante. "Was it about me?"

"Yes. He's very thankful to you for saving his life. Since he's not going to be coming back for a few months, he wanted to do something to help you."

Daniel held up his hands in protest. "He doesn't owe me anything. He always treated me like I was somebody when I worked for him. He wasn't like other men I've known."

Dante's dark eyes narrowed. "Captain Hawkins treated you like you were somebody because you are. He knows, as I do, that you're a child of God, and because of that, you have great value."

A nervous laugh escaped Daniel's mouth. "That's what Tave says."

"Well, she's right. Anyway, Captain Hawkins was worried that you might lose your job in Montgomery if you stayed here too long. He talked to the man who hired you there and told him what had happened. So they're holding your job for a while, but it won't be there if you wait too long."

"There's nothing I can do about that right now. I don't have the money to get to Montgomery. I could walk, but I'm not sure I'm strong enough for that yet."

Daniel nodded. "That's what Captain Hawkins thought. So he left me enough money to buy you a horse and saddle and to pay for the horse's upkeep until you decide to leave. Mr. Jensen at the livery stable found me one last week, and he's taking care of it for now."

Daniel gasped. "Captain Hawkins bought me a horse?"

Dante chuckled. "Yes. She's a pretty thing. Chestnut with a white star on her forehead, and gentle. I think you're going to like her." Dante reached into his pocket and took out a piece of folded paper. "And there's money left over for you to have. This is to help you get on your feet."

With trembling fingers, Daniel unfolded the paper and stared at the money inside. He'd never seen so much in his life. He struggled to speak, but he was afraid he was going to cry instead. "Th–th–this is too much. Did Captain Hawkins leave all this?"

Dante glanced down to the ground and kicked at a tuft of grass. "Well, Dr. Spencer and I helped out a little bit, too."

Daniel folded the paper back and frowned. "I don't understand. Why would you do something for me? You don't even know me."

Dante stared past Daniel as if he were remembering something. "When I was young, Daniel, there was a time when I was alone in the world. Just like you. A kind man in Mobile helped me, and because of him, great things happened in my life. This gift we're giving you is to let you know that there are better things waiting for you, too. You just have to let God lead you to where they are." He pointed to the money in Daniel's hand. "Someday you're going to come across somebody who needs help. When that happens, remember your friends who helped you."

Daniel had never known people like those he'd met from Willow Bend. There was something in their lives that was different from what he'd seen in the lives of other people he'd met in his travels. He clutched the money and tried to control his trembling lips. "Thank you, Dante. It's been a long time since I've met anyone like all the friends I've made in Willow Bend. I appreciate everything you and Captain Hawkins have done for me. And of course, I wouldn't even be here if it wasn't for Dr. Spencer and Tave."

Dante laughed. "Speaking of Tave, I think we'd better get back to the ladies before they come searching for us."

They ambled back to the picnic grove, and Daniel spied Tave and Savannah coming toward them. His pulse quickened as it did every time he saw Tave. She smiled, and something told him it was for him alone.

He thought of the people who were making changes in his life—Captain Hawkins, Dr. Spencer, Dante Rinaldi, but most of all Tave. He didn't want to think about Matthew Chandler and how she might feel about him. At the moment, all he knew was that he loved her. If God really wanted to help him, then maybe Tave wasn't unattainable to him after all.

Chapter 9

With the meal over, the congregation drifted into small groups across the picnic area. Women clustered in the shade of the trees and fanned themselves as the afternoon grew warmer. The men stood in groups discussing the weather and its possible effects on the crops.

Tave and Daniel drifted from group to group, stopping long enough for Daniel to be introduced to those he hadn't met. Tave glanced at him out of the corner of her eye as Martha Thompson waddled toward them, her daughter Esther following behind.

Martha waved in greeting. "Daniel. Come here and meet my daughter Esther. I told you 'bout her. Remember?"

Daniel stopped in front of Martha and smiled. "Of course I do." He nodded in Esther's direction. "I understand I have you to thank for some of that good food I ate while I was recuperating."

Esther looked down at the ground and dug the toe of her shoe in the dirt. "Yeah. Me and Ma was glad to help out."

Daniel thumped his chest. "Well, it worked. I'm back to good health."

Martha nudged her daughter. "Didn't I tell you he was a smooth talker?" She turned back to Daniel. "What you gonna do now that you're well? Still going to Montgomery?"

Tave's heart raced when he cast a quick glance in her direction. "I'm not sure when that will be," he said.

Martha pulled her daughter closer. "Well, don't you go off without visiting us sometime. You hear?"

"I won't."

Daniel glanced at her, and Tave almost giggled at the silent plea in his eyes for her to help him. She stepped forward. "It's good to see you and Esther today, Martha. Now if you'll excuse us, I want to introduce Daniel to some more of our friends."

She took Daniel's arm and pulled him toward a group that sat near one of the tables. Before they reached them, a whoop sounded from nearby, and the girls from her school ran toward them and surrounded Tave.

"Miss Spencer," Sarah Jensen said, "we want you to come play hopscotch with us."

Tave laughed. "You're not serious."

Katie Tyler nodded. "Yes, we are. All year at school you said you'd play one day, but you never did. Now we want you to do it."

Tave shook her head and tried to back away from the girls surrounding her. "I haven't played hopscotch since I was a child."

Gabby Rinaldi looked up at her with a mischievous grin. A gap where the six-year-old had lost a tooth a few days before flashed behind her smile. "You can do it, Miss Spencer."

"Please, please." The chorus of voices rose on the afternoon air.

Some of the boys who were chasing one another across the far end of the picnic area stopped and stared in the direction of the girls' voices. One of them whistled and pointed to Tave. With a shout, they ran forward and converged at the spot where the girls circled Tave.

"You gonna play hopscotch, Miss Spencer?" Tad Thompson shouted.

Hoping for an ally, Tave cast a glance at Daniel. "Aren't you going to help me?"

He spread his hands in resignation. "Far be it from me to go up against a group of determined children."

Tave smiled as her gaze drifted over the children she'd taught for the past year at the Willow Bend School. Bending over, she reached out and cupped Gabby's chin in her hand. "All right, I'll play. But if I fall, somebody had better catch me."

A shout went up from the group. "We will. We will."

Tave glanced at Daniel who ambled along behind the group leading her to the hopscotch course. "A fine friend you turned out to be."

Daniel stuck his hands in his pockets and grinned. "I'm enjoying this. Just like you seemed to enjoy my visit with Martha and Esther."

She glared at him. "Traitor."

Gabby eased up beside Tave and slipped a smooth, flat stone in her hand. "Use this one, Miss Spencer. It's my lucky marker."

They reached the hopscotch course, and the children fanned out around it. Silence descended over the group. Tave glanced over at Daniel, who had walked to a nearby tree and leaned against it. He gave her a small salute, and she frowned at him.

Stepping to the first square, Tave gazed at the slightly crooked lines of the course that two of the older girls had scratched into the black dirt with a sharp stone. Three single squares lay one on top of another with two lateral squares atop them. Another single square with a double square on top of it completed the course. Stones lay in the first square.

"Hey, Miss Spencer, you know you can't jump in the squares that have markers, don't you?" Tad giggled and punched Johnny Williams in the ribs. Laughter rippled through the assembled group.

Tave arched an eyebrow and stared at him. "I know, Tad."

A hush fell over the children as Tave bent forward at the waist and lobbed her stone to the second square. A puff of dust drifted upward as it plopped to the ground.

Tave took a deep breath, balanced on one foot, and began her journey by easily hopping over the first two squares. She reached the end and planted both feet in the two squares there, whirled around, and hopped on one foot back toward the beginning.

When she entered the third box, she stopped and held one arm out to balance herself. With deliberate movements she bent toward the stone resting in the second square, clasped it in her fingers, and looked up with a victory smile. The minute she did she realized her mistake. Her body swayed, and she struggled to keep from falling. It was no use.

A high-pitched squeal pierced the air as the children scurried back. Tave toppled forward and landed facedown in the dirt, her arms spread out to the sides. No one moved. Then a dozen hands pulled at her until she pushed herself up into a sitting position. The girls knelt in a circle around her, and the boys hovered behind.

"Miss Spencer, are you all right?" Their voices all seemed to speak at once.

Dust covered the front of the lavender and white dress she'd worn in an attempt to impress Daniel. She blew at a strand of hair that hung in her eye and let her gaze drift over twenty worried faces. "I thought I told you to catch me."

Gabby dropped to her knees. "I tried, Miss Spencer, but Tad got in my way."

Tave brushed the dirt from the front of her dress and started to get to her feet. A strong hand gripped her arm, and she stared up into the twinkling blue eyes of Daniel. "Allow me." He bit down on his lip, but he couldn't suppress the laughter shaking his body.

She allowed him to pull her up. When she'd regained her balance, she brushed her hair out of her eyes. Unable to help herself, she smiled down at the children clustered around them. "Well, it looks like I'm going to have to practice if I'm going to win at hopscotch." She bent over and chucked Gabby under the chin. "I tell you what. When school starts, I'm going to challenge all of the girls to a contest. Then we'll see who the hopscotch champion of Willow Bend School is."

The children's cheers echoed across the picnic grounds. Several adults glanced in their direction, smiled, and turned back to their conversations.

"Come on. Let's go play," Tad cried, and the boys raced after each other toward the tree line at the back of the picnic area.

Daniel pulled a clean handkerchief from his pocket and offered it to Tave. "You want to use this?"

She nodded and took it from his hand. "There's a well in back of the church. Let's go draw some water so I can wash my face and hands. I'll worry about my dress later."

Tave glanced over her shoulder on the way to the well. The girls had already resumed their game. She glanced at Daniel. "Now you have a small sample of what my day as a teacher is like."

He smiled at her. "I wish I'd had a teacher like you when I was a child."

They reached the well, and within minutes, Daniel had lowered the bucket and drawn cool water from the dark depths. A dipper hung on a peg at the side of the well, and Tave filled it with water and poured it over Daniel's handkerchief.

She wiped at her face then turned to him. "Do I have all the dirt off?"

He laughed and took the handkerchief from her. "There's a little bit left on the side of your face. Let me get it for you."

He stepped closer and bent forward as he wiped at her face. She closed her eyes and lifted her face. When he drew his hand away, she opened her eyes and stared up at him. His blue eyes stared into her, and in their depths she detected a longing that equaled the one she felt. His gaze went to her lips and lingered there.

A thrill raced through her at the thought of their lips meeting. She reached up and cupped his face with her hand. "Daniel," she whispered.

He pulled her closer, and her heart almost beat out of her chest as she waited for his kiss. Before their lips met, he groaned and backed away. "No, Tave," he muttered. "I won't do this."

He released her with a slight shove, and a chill raced through her at the anger she detected in his eyes before he whirled and strode toward the far side of the church. Speechless, she stared at Daniel's back.

It only took Tave a few seconds to recover and dash after Daniel. She caught up with him at the cemetery and grabbed his arm. "Daniel, what's the matter with you? You looked at me like you hate me. What have I done?"

He stopped and whirled to face her. "You haven't done anything. I did. I almost kissed you. That would have been the biggest mistake of my life."

"Mistake?" She shrank from him. How could he say such a terrible thing? She wrapped her arms around her waist and blinked back tears. "Are you telling me you don't have any feelings for me?"

He raked his hand through his hair and groaned. "I do have feelings for you, but I'm not going to take advantage of you and give you false hope."

"False hope about what?"

"That anything's ever going to come of it. I'm not the man for you, Tave."

She straightened to her full height. "Don't I get to decide that on my own?"

He shook his head. "No. I'm going to decide it for you. I'm a drifter with no money or family. I want you to understand I have nothing to give you."

She stared at him. "Can you give me love?"

His eyes grew wide. "Wh–what?"

She squared her shoulders and clenched her fists at her sides. "Savannah told me she could tell that you're in love with me. As embarrassing as it is for me to ask, I have to know. Do you love me?"

He hesitated for a moment, and she held her breath. His shoulders drooped as if his whole body had deflated. "Yes, I love you. More than I ever thought it possible to love someone else."

Her heart pounded, and she frowned. "Then what's the problem? I've fought my feelings for you, but I can't anymore." She stepped closer. "I love you, too, Daniel."

He held up his hands as if to warn her to stay back. "No, I won't saddle you with a man who can't give you everything that Matthew can."

"Matthew? What does he have to do with this? I don't love him. I love you."

He reached out and grabbed her by the shoulders. "It doesn't matter. I won't keep you from the life you deserve." He released her with such force that she stumbled back. "I have to leave."

Icy fear gripped her. "Leave?"

"Yes. When I'm gone, you'll know I was right."

Tave watched in disbelief as he headed toward the road. She ran after him and grabbed his arm. "Where are you going?"

He shook free of her. "I'm going back to your father's office right now. I think it would be better if we stayed away from each other until it's time for me to leave Willow Bend. I told Mr. Perkins I'd be at work tomorrow, and I won't go back on my word. I'll help him a few weeks; then I'm going to pack my belongings, get on my new horse, and go on to Montgomery."

"Please don't do this to me, Daniel."

He turned back to her, and Tave's heart broke at the agony in his face. "I'm doing it *for* you, Tave, not *to* you. From the very beginning, I've been honest with you. I can't stay anywhere very long before I get the urge to move on again. Sooner or later, I'd leave you, too. Matthew is here to stay, Tave. I'm not. You'll see that I was right."

It was no use. Nothing she could say would change his mind. She nodded. "All right. Run away, Daniel. That's what you always do. But before you go, there's something I want to say."

"What?"

She took a deep breath and prayed she'd speak the right words. "Matthew's not the problem. I think you're just using him as an excuse."

He shook his head. "I only want the best for you."

Anger welled up in Tave's heart, and it frightened her. She jutted out her chin and stepped closer to him. She hoped her eyes conveyed the fire she felt in her soul. "The problem is that you're a man who's given his life over to hate for so long that you don't know how to open up to love. You think the answer to your problem is to give up and run from the hate that's gnawed at your heart for the past seven years, but it hasn't worked because you just carry it with you to the next place. Maybe one day you'll finally see that you're never going to have any peace or be able to return anyone's love until you let God's love replace all the hate that's killing you."

Tave couldn't control the tears that puddled in her eyes any longer, and she whirled away from him before he saw them running down her face. She didn't look back as she walked toward the picnic grounds. Laughter echoed from the people who'd been her friends for years. She spied Savannah talking with some women, but she didn't want to see her now. There was only one place she wanted to be.

She stepped onto the porch of the church and went inside.

Two weeks later on a hot July morning Tave sat in a chair in the shade of a tree in the backyard of their house. A pan of tomatoes sat at her feet, and she tapped the metal pot with the toe of her shoe. She'd picked the tomatoes from her garden and planned on canning them, but for some reason, she was restless today. Maybe it was because she hadn't spoken to Daniel since the day of the picnic.

He didn't come to meals at their house anymore, and she stayed away from her father's office and Mr. Perkins's store. When her father mentioned Daniel, she changed the subject.

She thought about how few people she'd seen lately. Savannah had come by once or twice, but Tave couldn't bring herself to discuss her heartbreak with her friend, who had such a wonderful husband and family. This was a burden she was going to have to bear alone. She hadn't even been able to share it with her father. Tave could see the concern in his eyes, and he kept asking her what was troubling her. She kept hoping Daniel would come to see her, but so far, he hadn't.

She sighed and bent to pick up the tomatoes. A familiar voice rang out: "Hello. Anybody home?"

Martha Thompson. Tave didn't know if she was up to a visit from the woman today, but she pushed to her feet. "I'm out back, Martha."

Martha shuffled around the side of the house and directed a grin in Tave's direction. "There you are. I was afraid you was sick. I ain't seen you around much lately. Anything wrong?"

Tave shook her head and pointed to the tomatoes. "No. I've just been busy with my garden."

Martha slapped her leg and laughed. "Land sakes! Don't I know about gardens. Me and Esther have 'bout worked ourselves to death with ours. It takes a heap of food when a family's got five children."

Tave nodded. "I can imagine it does."

Martha cocked her head and smiled. "I was just on my way home from Mr. Perkins's store and thought I'd check on you."

"Well, I'm glad you did. Would you like to have a cup of tea before you walk home?"

"No, I ain't got time. I've gotta get home and ask my boy Tad if he wants to go to work for Mr. Perkins. He needs some help, you know."

Tave's heart pounded in her chest. "No, I didn't know that."

"Oh yeah. That nice Mr. Luckett is leaving today. Going to Montgomery, he says. We sure gonna miss him around here." Martha's eyes narrowed, and she looked at Tave as if checking the effect her words produced.

Tave grabbed the back of the chair for support and tried to smile. "Yes, we are."

Martha continued to study Tave for a moment before she glanced down at the tomatoes. "I'd better get out of here so's you can get to work. Just wanted to say hello."

The woman turned and walked from the backyard. It took Tave a moment to collect her thoughts. She raised her hand, waved, and called after her, "Thanks for stopping by, Martha."

When Martha had disappeared, Tave dropped down in the chair and buried her face in her hands. Anger washed over her, and she sat up straight. What was Daniel thinking? Was he just going to sneak out of town without even saying good-bye after all she'd done for him? No, he was going to face her and tell her good-bye.

She jumped to her feet, jerked off the apron she wore, and threw it in the chair. With her fists clenched at her sides, she stormed from the backyard and headed toward her father's office.

Chapter 10

D aniel had just stuffed the last shirt in the bag his clothes had arrived in from the *Montgomery Belle* when he heard the door of Dr. Spencer's office open. He froze in place and held his breath. Soft footsteps tapped across the wooden floor of the waiting room. They stopped outside the bedroom, and a knock sounded at the door.

"Daniel, are you in there?"

A relieved breath escaped Daniel's throat at the sound of Dr. Spencer's voice. At least Tave hadn't come to see him. He hoped he could get out of town without her knowing. "Yes, come on in."

The door swung open. Daniel pulled the drawstring that closed the top of the bag and turned. Dr. Spencer's gaze appeared riveted on the bag. He took a deep breath and looked up. "Is that your horse tied to the hitching post out front?"

"Yes."

He glanced down at the bag again. "So you're really leaving."

He nodded. "It's time I moved on." He pointed to the lamp table. "I was hoping you'd be back from Cottonwood before I left, but I wrote you a note in case you weren't."

Dr. Spencer rubbed his tired eyes. "It's been a long night. The wife of one of the tenant farmers had a baby. It took a long time, but everything turned out all right."

The front door of the building opened and slammed shut. Someone stomped across the waiting room floor. Daniel's heart almost stopped when Tave appeared at the door to the bedroom. He couldn't tell if it was anger or hurt in her eyes, but he realized that whatever it was had to be directed at him.

Her chin trembled. "Martha tells me you're leaving."

He turned back to the bed and pretended to secure the top of his bag. "That's right."

Dr. Spencer cleared his throat. "I think I'll go into my office and let you two say your good-byes." He stopped beside Tave and patted her shoulder. "I'll be in the next room."

She bit her lip and nodded before her father left the room. After a moment, she inched closer. "Weren't you going to tell me you were leaving?"

Daniel pointed to the lamp table. "I left a note."

A strangled laugh came from her throat. "After all these weeks, I only get a note. You were going to leave without telling me good-bye."

He willed himself not to move toward her. He had to keep his distance. "You know why I couldn't see you."

"I know what you said, but I can't believe you'd leave town without at least thanking me for sitting by your bed and nursing you back to health, for cooking your meals, for—" She swallowed. "I suppose whatever else I might feel doesn't matter."

His heart told him to close the distance between them, to take her in his arms and tell her he didn't want to ever be parted from her, but he didn't move. "Don't make this any harder than it already is, Tave. I'm going, and there's nothing you can say to change my mind."

"I guess I knew that when I came." She glanced at his packed bag and back to him. "Will you do one thing for me, Daniel?"

He swallowed. "What?"

She pointed to the lamp table where her Bible still lay. "Take my Bible with you and read it. Maybe you can find the peace you're looking for."

"If you want me to take it, I will."

She stepped back from him. "I want you to stick it down in your bag; then I want you to leave. I've done a lot of thinking in the past two weeks, and I've come to realize it would never have worked out for us. I want a man who can love me, not someone whose heart is shriveled up with so much hate that he's turned his back on God. If the day ever comes that you turn your life over to God and allow Him to take away all that hate, think of me, Daniel, a woman who loved you for the man she could see waiting to be released from the past. I'll think about you often, and I'll pray for you every day."

She whirled and ran out of the room. He wanted to go after her, but he knew he couldn't. She'd forget him in time.

Daniel closed his eyes and bit his lip. The front door slammed, and he realized he was alone again, just as he had been for years. A discreet cough at the edge of the room caused him to open his eyes. Dr. Spencer walked in and stopped at the foot of the bed. "Do you have everything you need?"

"Don't worry. I'll be fine."

Dr. Spencer frowned. "I hope so. Just be careful of your side for a while."

"I will."

Dr. Spencer pushed his glasses up on his nose and took a deep breath. "I saw Tave leave. She didn't ask me to stop you, and I won't try."

"Thank you. You couldn't change my mind."

"I know. If I've learned anything in this life, it's that you can't change folks from whatever they're bound and determined to do. Only God can do that."

Daniel's shoulders slumped, and he dropped down on the bed. He clasped his hands between his knees and stared at the floor. "I don't want to go, but I feel like I have to."

Dr. Spencer eased down beside him. "Because of Tave?"

Daniel jerked his head around to stare at Dr. Spencer. "How did you know?"

He shrugged. "I thought something was wrong when she wanted to leave the picnic early that day. Then when we got home, she told me you were leaving and ran into her room. She's hardly gotten out of the house since then. I figured something had happened between the two of you."

Fear at telling Dr. Spencer what had happened washed over him, and Daniel averted his gaze. "Tave is a wonderful woman. She's too good for me. I can't give her the things that Matthew can, and she deserves to have a good life."

"Did you tell her that?"

"Yes."

"What did she say?"

Daniel swallowed before he spoke. "That she doesn't love Matthew."

Dr. Spencer laid his hand on Daniel's shoulder. "Do you love my daughter, Daniel?"

He bit his lip and nodded before he turned back to face Dr. Spencer. "With all my heart, but I'm not going to stay here and ruin her life."

Dr. Spencer rose, clasped his hands behind his back, and walked across the room before he stopped and retraced his steps. "You would ruin her life if you stayed."

Daniel thought he'd heard the doctor wrong. The realization that her father hadn't thought him good enough for Tave hit him like a kick in the stomach. All he could do was try to disguise his disappointment. "Then you think it's best for me to leave?"

Dr. Spencer peered over the rims of his spectacles. Sadness shadowed his eyes, and Daniel felt as if the man could see into the depths of his soul.

"I'm just a country doctor who's devoted his life to healing folks' ailments. Sometimes, though, I see someone who has a sickness that I can't do anything about, and I have to rely on a higher power to take over."

"You're talking about God."

Dr. Spencer nodded. "I am. Tave told me you've had a lot of bad things happen in your life, things that have hardened your heart and made you doubt God. She thought maybe you were beginning to see the truth, but I can tell you haven't quite reached that stage yet. So I think you're right about leaving. You and Tave never would be able to have a life together."

Daniel rose to his feet. "Thank you for seeing it my way."

Dr. Spencer held up his hand. "Hold on there, Daniel. I didn't say I see it your way. I said you were right to leave. By that I mean that Tave needs someone who has a deep faith in God, a man who'll turn his life over to Him and follow whatever path God leads him on. I don't want anything less than that for my daughter."

A frown pulled at Daniel's brow. "You mean you wouldn't mind the fact that I don't have any money or any prospects of getting any?"

Dr. Spencer sighed. "Daniel, there's a lot more to life than what money can buy. Jesus once spoke about that to a large group of people and told them to look at the lilies of the field and the sparrows in the air and see how God took care of them. He ended by telling the crowd not to worry about what they should eat or what they wear. Then He spoke some words that I carry with me every day. He said, 'For all these things do the nations of the world seek after: and your Father knoweth that ye have need of these things. But rather seek ye the kingdom of God; and all these things shall be added unto you.'"

"What does that mean?"

"It means that when you open your heart to God's love, He's going to take care of you. You may never be rich, but when He's working through your life, those things aren't the most important anymore. We see other things that mean so much more."

Daniel nodded. "I've been reading the Bible, and I felt so peaceful when I went with you and Tave to church. Then I remember what happened to my mother, and I can't let go of the past. It's just too hard."

Dr. Spencer smiled. "It is for all of us. It was hard for me to let go of the terrible things I saw men do to each other during the war. If I hadn't put my faith in God, I don't think I could have survived that time. Until you come to the place where you can turn the past over to God, you're never going to have any peace. You've got an ache that I can't fix, but God can." He pointed to Tave's Bible on the table. "The best medicine for you is found in that book. Read it, Daniel, and let the words speak to your heart. Only then are you going to be ready to have a relationship with any woman."

Daniel stared at the Bible, walked over to the table, and picked it up. "Tave told me to take it with me."

"Then do it." Dr. Spencer stuck out his hand. "I'm glad I met you, Daniel, and I'm going to be praying you find the peace you need in your life."

They shook hands, and Daniel watched as Dr. Spencer walked from the room. He heard him cross the waiting room and the sound of the front door closing as he left. A vast emptiness consumed Daniel, and he staggered back. He'd left many places in the past and had never given it a thought. Now he knew he didn't want to leave the people he'd come to know here. He'd never felt more alone in his life.

What was it Tave had said to remember? The words flashed across his mind:

"If the day ever comes that you turn your life over to God and allow Him to take away all that hate, think of me, Daniel, a woman who loved you for the man she could see waiting to be released from the past."

The urge to unpack his clothes overcame him, and he reached for the bag. He opened the top and reached inside but stopped before he pulled out a shirt. "No!"

Gritting his teeth, he shoved the Bible in the bag, pulled the opening closed, and ran from the room. His horse waited outside at the hitching post. He tied the bag to the saddle horn, climbed on, and turned the horse north. It was time for him to go to Montgomery.

⬥

Two days after Daniel left, Tave strolled down the main street of Willow Bend. She wondered where he was at that moment and if he was thinking of her. Tears flooded her eyes at the memory of their last conversation. She couldn't erase it from her mind.

She wiped at her cheeks and glanced around to see if anyone had seen her momentary lapse. No one appeared to be paying her any attention. Straightening her shoulders, she opened the door to Mr. Perkins's store and stepped inside.

At the sound of the bell over the door, Mr. Perkins hurried from the back room. His face lit up when he saw her. "Tave, come in. How can I help you today?"

She handed him the list she'd written before leaving home. "These are the items I need."

He scanned the list and nodded. "I have all this in stock. I'll get it right away for you." He turned to walk to the other side of the store but stopped. "Oh, I almost forgot. The *Liberty Queen* docked today, and there was a letter for you."

A letter? Could it be from Daniel? Tave's heart pounded as Mr. Perkins strode to the counter at the back of the store that served as the post office for Willow Bend. An open cupboard with mailbox slots sat behind it. He pulled a letter from one of them, hurried back, and handed it to her.

"Here it is. Now if you'll excuse me, I'll go to the storeroom to get some of the items that are on your list."

"Thank you."

She held her breath and didn't move until he'd left the room. Her fingers shook as she raised the letter to get a better view of it. Tears sprang to her eyes, and her heart plummeted to her stomach. The letter wasn't from Daniel. It was from Matthew.

She grabbed the edge of one of the display tables to steady herself and bit her lip. After a moment, she took a deep breath and opened the letter. Her eyes widened with each word that she read. By the time she finished, her mouth hung open and her face burned.

Unable to believe what it said, she reread the words:

Dear Tave,

I feel the need to offer you an apology for my behavior the last time we talked. At that time, I mentioned the possibility of speaking to you of marriage when I returned. I realize now how presumptuous that was, because your father would never consent to our union. I also shouldn't have assumed that you would even consider such a proposal. Having reached this conclusion, I hope you will soon find some young man who will be worthy of your affection.

As for me, I have met such a woman in the person of Miss Portia Davenport of Dauphin Island. We will be married by the time this letter reaches you. I look forward to introducing you to my new wife when we arrive home.

Regards,
Matthew Chandler

Tave crumpled the letter in her hand. "Of all the nerve," she muttered. "Dismissing me like that. I've got a good mind to—"

She stopped midsentence and arched her eyebrows. What was the matter with her? She didn't love Matthew. She hadn't wanted to marry him and would have turned him down if he'd asked. If she was honest, she'd have to admit the only thing that was hurt was her pride. As her true feelings regarding Matthew surfaced, a sense of relief flowed through her body. She wouldn't have to worry about Matthew showing up to relive the war and play checkers with her father anymore.

Glancing down at the wrinkled letter, she began to laugh. She needed to go tell her father right away. "Mr. Perkins," she called out, "I have to go to my father's office. I'll be back for my purchases."

Without waiting for an answer, she ran out of the store and up the sidewalk. She stopped outside her father's office as another thought struck her. A few weeks ago, there had been two men in her life, but she loved only one of them. All she could do now was pray that somehow God would bring Daniel back.

◆◆◆

Three days later, Tave sat in the parlor of Savannah's house at Cottonwood Plantation. She studied the fragile china cup and saucer with pink flowers painted on the sides before she took a sip of tea and set it back on the serving tray.

"Thanks for inviting me this afternoon, Savannah. I don't mind telling you this has been a hard week for me."

Savannah set her cup down and grasped Tave's hand. "I couldn't believe it when I heard Daniel had left. The two of you seemed so happy the day of the picnic."

Tave scooted back onto the sofa and propped a brocade-covered pillow behind her back. "It was such a wonderful day until I fell playing hopscotch."

Savannah reached for her cup and took another sip. "What happened?"

For the next few minutes Tave told her friend about the argument she and Daniel had after he almost kissed her. When she finished, she brushed a tear from her eye and tried to smile. "I didn't see him again until the day he left. I wouldn't have known he was leaving if Martha hadn't come by to tell me."

"Bound for Martha to bring the latest news."

Tave reached for one of the napkins on the tray and wiped at her eyes. She thought by this time all her tears would be gone, but they still popped out at unexpected moments. "In this case, I was glad she did. At least I got to tell him good-bye and give him my Bible to take with him. Poppa talked to him, too, before he left. Poppa hasn't told me what all was said, but he did say he told Daniel that he didn't think we could be happy together until he turned his life over to God."

Savannah nodded. "He's right, you know. Marriage is difficult even when you love each other. If two people aren't in agreement about God's place in their lives, it'll just bring unhappiness to both of them."

"I know. I've prayed about this, and I know everything is going to turn out all right for me. God's got something else in mind."

Savannah stood up. "Good for you. You don't need to waste your time thinking about what might have been with Daniel Luckett. You need to occupy yourself with other interests." A coy grin pulled at her mouth. "Like Matthew."

Tave's eyes grew large. "Oh that's right. You haven't heard, have you?"

"Heard what?"

"Last Tuesday when the *Liberty Queen* docked at Willow Bend, it brought a letter to me from Matthew."

Savannah reached to pick up the tray. "When's he coming home?"

Tave sighed. "I don't know. He wrote to apologize to me for speaking of marriage before he left for Dauphin Island. It seems he's met a young woman down there whom he's quite smitten by. He's going to bring her back as his wife."

The cups and saucers rattled as the tray slipped from Savannah's hands and thudded back to the table. She dropped back to the sofa, her eyes wide with surprise. "His wife?"

Tave laughed. "Yes." She tilted her head to the side and tapped her chin with her finger. "I wonder if I'm the only woman in Willow Bend who's ever lost two men within two days."

Red spots, a sign of her anger ever since Tave had known her, appeared on

Savannah's cheeks. "Of all the nerve. He writes to tell you he's taking back his proposal. I can't believe he'd be such a coward."

"I have to admit it was quite a shock."

"Well, all I can say is good riddance to Matthew Chandler." Savannah grabbed Tave's hands. Her eyes brimmed with tears. "But I'm sure that makes the loss of Daniel only worse. I'm so sorry."

Tave squeezed Savannah's hands and shook her head. "Don't be. Neither one of them were meant to be. I wouldn't have married Matthew anyway, but. . ." She couldn't suppress the tears anymore, and she covered her face with her hands. Her body shook with sobs.

Savannah placed her arm around Tave's shoulders and drew her closer. Tave collapsed against Savannah's shoulder and cried out the hurt she'd tried to keep inside all week. Savannah patted her shoulder. "Go on and let it all out, Tave. It'll make you feel better."

She pulled back and wiped at the tears on her cheeks. "But I love Daniel so much. How can I get him out of my heart?"

Savannah shook her head. "I don't know. I shudder sometimes when I think how close I came to leaving Willow Bend and losing Dante. I believe God knew what was happening in our lives, and He made everything work out in the end."

A hiccup shook Tave's body, and she placed her hand over her mouth. When the urge had passed, she closed her eyes and sighed. It didn't seem possible that only a few months ago she'd been so happy. Now she wondered if she would ever smile again. "I've always said I believed God would lead me where He wanted me to go, but I never thought putting Him in control could be this hard. It sounds so easy to say you'll do it, but it sure does put your faith to the test."

Savannah leaned back on the sofa and drew Tave's head to her shoulder. "I know it's hard. God told us we'd have problems, but He promised He would be with us when we were passing through those times. Don't lose your faith, Tave. My aunt Jane once told me that God wasn't through with me, that He still had plans for me. I know He has the same for you."

"I'll try to hang on to that thought, Savannah. When things get bad, I'll think of what you said. I don't know what I'd do without you as a friend."

"Don't worry. You're going to be all right."

Tave's thoughts turned to Daniel. Surely he'd made it to Montgomery by now since it was only about three days away by horse. He was probably already working on the docks and making new friends. Some of them were probably women. Maybe he'd already forgotten about her. She wondered if she would ever forget him. She breathed a silent prayer for him.

❧

Daniel walked into the second-floor room he'd rented in a house close to the docks and tumbled onto the unmade bed. The late-afternoon September sun cast a shadow across the floor. He opened the small window in an effort to get some air into the hot room. He needed to rest. He hadn't slept well in the two months since he'd arrived in Montgomery, and the oppressive heat would probably keep him awake all night. His only consolation was that fall would soon arrive with cooler weather.

Before he'd climbed the steps to his room, Mrs. Whittaker, who owned the boardinghouse, had called out that supper would be ready in an hour. He didn't know if he could eat or not.

A soft knock at the door caused him to sit up. Even though he was sure he knew who stood there, he called out anyway. "Who is it?"

"It's Jacob Whittaker, Daniel. I thought I'd check on you."

There was something about Jacob that reminded Daniel of his grandfather who had died when he was young. Like his grandfather, Jacob never missed an opportunity to share his love for God and His Word.

Daniel opened the door and smiled at the white-haired, elderly man facing him. Pain pinched his face, and he leaned heavily on a cane. Daniel opened the door wider. "Come in, Mr. Whittaker. I didn't think you saw me come in."

Jacob hobbled into the room and sank into the chair next to a small table by the open window. "I was in the kitchen, but I heard my daughter-in-law speaking to you. I thought I'd come up here and see if you did what I asked."

Daniel glanced at the table beside Jacob. Tave's Bible sat on it. Picking it up, he opened it to the passage Jacob had told him about and read aloud. " 'Love your enemies, bless them that curse you, do good to them that hate you, and pray for them which despitefully use you, and persecute you; That ye may be the children of your Father which is in heaven: for he maketh his sun to rise on the evil and on the good, and sendeth rain on the just and on the unjust.'"

Jacob planted his cane in front of him, rested his hands on top of it, and closed his eyes. "Beautiful words."

"Love your enemies?" Daniel asked. "How is that possible?"

"It's only possible if God has control of your life. The day you walked in our front door, I told my daughter-in-law you were a man with deep scars. Over the last two months, you've shared your past with me. I know you've suffered, but you can overcome it. You're never going to be happy until you let go of the hate in your heart."

"Someone else told me that, but she made it sound so easy."

Jacob's eyebrows arched. "Ah, a young woman told you the same thing I've been telling you ever since you've been in Montgomery. She's right. All you have to do is pray and ask Jesus to take control of your life. He'll take away the hate and replace it with peace." Jacob closed his eyes again and breathed deeply. "I can feel His presence every time I come into your room, Daniel. He's here, waiting for you to open your heart to Him."

Daniel looked back at the words he'd just read. Love, bless, do good to your enemies? Why should he? The veil that had covered his mind for years parted, and the answer hit him like a kick in the stomach. So he could be a child of God.

Suddenly, everything Tave and her father had said and all of Jacob's words made sense to him. They had been trying to make him see how his life would be changed if he opened his heart to God.

He gasped aloud at the great wave of emotion that poured through his body. He closed his eyes and let his senses soar with the recognition of an emotion he'd never felt before. Was it really as easy as Jacob said? If it was, why did he hesitate? He dropped the Bible, fell on his knees, and buried his face in his hands. "God, help me. I can't carry this hatred anymore. Help me to let it go. I want some peace in my life. Show me what to do."

The Bible lay on the floor where he'd dropped it. He picked it up and stared at the page where it had fallen open. The words of a verse almost stood out from the page, and his skin prickled as he read it: *"And that he died for all, that they which live should not henceforth live unto themselves, but unto him which died for them, and rose again."*

He clutched the Bible to his chest. From his seated position, Jacob stared down at him. "How do you feel, Daniel?"

The greatest peace he'd ever known washed over him, cleansing every bit of hate from his body. With tears on his cheeks, he smiled. "Like a great weight has been lifted from my shoulders. I feel so light, I think I might be able to fly."

Jacob laughed. "I remember that's how I felt when I accepted Christ. What are you going to do now?"

Daniel stuck out his hand, and Jacob grasped it. "There's still a lot I don't understand, Mr. Whittaker. Will you teach me more about the Bible and God's ways?"

Tears stood in the old man's eyes. "There's nothing that would make me happier."

Chapter 11

Daniel buttoned his coat in an effort to ward off the chill from the brisk wind that swept across the docks. With Christmas Eve only two days away, there wasn't much activity on the river, and most of the workers had already gone home.

He thought of his warm room at Mrs. Whittaker's boardinghouse and shivered. If he wasn't on a mission right now, he would be sitting in the dining room, having a hot cup of coffee and a piece of apple pie with Jacob. His stomach growled, and he pushed the thought away. Eating would just have to wait until he talked with Mr. Smith, the owner of a riverfront warehouse.

As long as Daniel had been in Montgomery, Mr. Smith had been a regular Saturday visitor to his business. Regular until today, that is. Daniel had stood in the cold for hours, hoping the man would appear, but so far he hadn't.

He was just about to give up and go back to his room when he spied Mr. Smith's carriage coming down the street. A black man in a long coat and a top hat guided the horses along the cobblestone street toward the riverfront. Mr. Smith huddled in the backseat underneath a heavy buggy rug.

The carriage pulled to a stop in front of the warehouse. With slow movements, Mr. Smith pushed the lap covering to the seat beside him and heaved his portly body up. He grunted as he stepped to the ground. Leaning on a cane, he spoke to the driver, who nodded, and then he hobbled into the building. The man in the front seat of the carriage didn't move or look around as Daniel stepped from the docks and headed toward the building.

Daniel stopped at the door and said a quick prayer before he pushed the sliding door to the side and stepped into the musky darkness of the warehouse. The interior of the building with its huge floor space reminded Daniel of a cave. Very little cargo sat inside the building, but that didn't surprise Daniel. In the months since he'd been in Montgomery, he'd seen a drastic reduction in goods shipped by river. The railroads could deliver faster, and those who made their living on the river were beginning to worry how much longer their businesses could survive.

Daniel glanced around and spotted the warehouse office to his left. The soft glow of an oil lamp cast a shadow underneath the office door and sent flickering patterns rippling across the floor. Overhead, more light filtered in through the small windows lining the top of the walls.

Daniel stepped to the closed office door and knocked. Footsteps shuffled inside before the door opened. The warehouse owner gripped the handle of his cane and propped himself erect. His eyebrows arched. "Yes? Can I help you?"

Daniel pulled off the hat he wore and held it in his hands. "Good afternoon, Mr. Smith. My name is Daniel Luckett. I wonder if I might have a word with you."

The man's gaze raked over Daniel, but he finally moved aside and motioned him to come into the office. He closed the door behind him and turned to Daniel. "Haven't I seen you working on the docks?"

Daniel nodded. "Yes, sir."

The man moved to a chair behind his desk and lowered himself into it. He motioned for Daniel to have a seat in a chair facing him. "What is it you want to talk to me about?"

Daniel sat down and scooted to the edge of the chair. He took a deep breath. "Mr. Jacob Whittaker told me that you are a good Christian man. I've come hoping you might help me with a problem I have."

Mr. Smith nodded and opened his desk drawer. "Oh I see. You've heard that I'm the person a dockworker needs to come to when he has a problem." He pulled out a roll of money. "Do you need to buy food for your family for Christmas?"

Daniel's eyes grew wide, and he held up his hands and shook his head. "No, sir. I don't want your money. It's quite another matter."

A puzzled expression crossed the man's face as he stuffed the money back into the drawer and closed it. "Then what is it you need?"

Daniel cleared his throat. "Well you see, sir, a few months ago, I accepted Christ as my Savior, and Mr. Whittaker has been teaching me about the Bible. A few of the men who live at the same boardinghouse saw us reading the Bible, and they began to ask questions. Mr. Whittaker encouraged me to start a Sunday morning Bible study in my room. Then some other fellows heard about it, and they came, too. Soon, we'd outgrown my room, and we had to use the boardinghouse dining room. But sometimes we have to finish early so Mrs. Whittaker can serve the noon meal."

Mr. Smith chuckled. "How many do you have attending now?"

Daniel wrinkled his brow and mentally counted the men who'd been attending regularly. "About ten or twelve, but this week I had four more men tell me they'd be there tomorrow. The problem is we need another place to meet."

Mr. Smith stared at him. "But how can I help you?"

Daniel glanced over his shoulder. "Well you see, sir, I asked the men if they'd like to start going to a regular church, but they said they didn't think they'd fit in at a city church. They want to keep our group together. You have a mighty big warehouse here. I wondered if you would let us meet here for Sunday services. We wouldn't bother anything, and we'd clean up after ourselves. I'd be glad to pay you each week when I get paid."

Mr. Smith picked up a pen from his desk and studied it for a moment before he looked back at Daniel. "No need for you to pay me anything. I'll be glad for you to hold services here." His gaze wandered over Daniel. "So you're a preacher?"

Daniel frowned and shook his head. "No. I'm just a man who's learned a lot from Mr. Whittaker, and I promised God I'd go wherever He led. These men have a real hunger in their hearts to hear God's Word. Some of them are far from home, and they're lonely. They need to know that God can give them peace."

"It appears Mr. Whittaker has taught you well."

Daniel nodded. "Yes, sir, he has, and I'm still learning. But God did a miracle in my life, and I have to tell other people about it."

Mr. Smith leaned back in his chair and smiled. "Well, tell your friends to come here tomorrow and every Sunday afterward for services. You're welcome to use my warehouse as long as you need it."

Daniel stood up and backed toward the door. "Thank you, Mr. Smith. Mr. Whittaker said you were a kind man who loves the Lord. I appreciate your helping us out."

Mr. Smith held up a hand to stop him. "Tell me, Mr. Luckett, do all of the men have Bibles?"

"No, sir, but the ones who do share with the others."

Mr. Smith's stubby finger tapped on his desk for a moment. "Tomorrow when you get here, there will be a box filled with Bibles inside the front door. Tell every man who doesn't have one to take one as a Christmas present from me."

Daniel couldn't believe what he'd just heard. He shook his head in disbelief. "I've been praying I could find enough Bibles for all the men to have one. I shouldn't be surprised when God answers my prayers, but I still am."

"That's a natural reaction we all have, because we can't begin to understand God's love." Mr. Smith glanced down at his desk and then motioned for Daniel to leave. "Well, go on now. I have some work to do. I hope you have a good service tomorrow, and tell the men I wish them a merry Christmas."

Daniel grinned. "I'll tell them, and I hope you have a merry Christmas, too."

Daniel pulled his hat on and hurried from the building. When he was on the street again, he stuck his hands in his pockets and stared up into the sky. "Thank You, Lord. You've provided for us again."

He whistled a tune he'd heard one of the men singing the other day, a song of the river, the man had said. For some reason, the melody made him think of Tave. He wondered what kind of Christmas she was going to have. She was probably married to Matthew by now and planning a celebration at her new home.

The memory of her smile and her long auburn hair stirred a longing in him that he knew would never go away. He wished he could tell her she was right about how he needed God in his life. He'd started to write her several times to tell her God had brought peace into his heart, but each time he'd torn up the letter and thrown it away.

It would do no good to stir up old memories. She had a new life now, and he prayed she was happy.

⌘

Tave left Mr. Perkins's store and hurried toward her father's office. Christmas Eve was only two days away, and she still had so much to do. She'd baked the jam cakes yesterday, but she still had to make the gingerbread she'd promised to take with them to Cottonwood on Christmas Day. She also had to finish the scarf she was knitting for her father to wear when he made house calls outside of town in cold weather.

She rushed through the doorway of her father's office. "Poppa, are you here?"

He appeared from the small kitchen, a cup in his hand. "I'm right here. Would you like to join me for some coffee?"

Tave shook her head. "I don't have time. I've been over to Mr. Perkins's store. Savannah was there, and she reminded me that we needed to be out at Cottonwood in time for Christmas dinner on Tuesday."

"Did you tell her we wouldn't miss it?"

She laughed. "I did. She said she and Mamie are planning a feast. My mouth watered just listening to her talk."

Her father smiled and motioned for her to follow him into the kitchen. "I just put some wood in the cookstove. It'll be warmer in here."

They sat down at the table, and Tave glanced around the room. Since school had started, she'd had little time to come by her father's office except for quick visits to check on him. She had hardly been in this room since she'd last cooked the meals that she, her father, and Daniel had shared.

Her gaze fell on the dry sink, and she recalled how Daniel's hand had once touched hers while standing there. Her chest tightened, and she blinked to keep tears from forming in her eyes.

Her father leaned forward, a worried expression on his face. "What's the matter? Don't you feel well?"

She laughed and touched the corner of her eye. "It's nothing."

He took a sip of his coffee and set the cup back on the table. He reached across the table toward her. "We don't talk much about Daniel, darling, because I don't want to upset you. But I want you to know that I'm here for you anytime you need me."

She smiled and patted his hand. "I know you are. Having you and Savannah to give me moral support has gotten me through these past months." She sighed and pressed her fingertips to her temples. Closing her eyes, she tried to massage away the pain that seemed to hover at the back of her eyes all the time. "For a long time, I kept thinking he'd come back, but I'm about to give up hope."

"Do you want him to come back?"

She'd asked herself that question many times. "I don't want him to come back the way he was. I keep praying that something we said finally got through to him, and that he's changed. If he has, then I hope he does."

Her father's forehead wrinkled. "How long are you going to wait? I don't want to see you waste your life, hoping for something that may never happen."

"I know you don't, but I can't answer your question. My heart's not ready to give up on him yet."

Her father grinned. "Well, I have to admit I haven't had to go looking for opponents who want to beat me at checkers. There've been several young men who'd like to get to know you better. I especially like Joshua Tucker. He's not much of a checkers player, but he loses well."

"Joshua is a good friend, and I've enjoyed getting to know him. That's as far as it will ever go with us." Tave crossed her arms and rolled her eyes. "But you needn't worry about me ever finding a husband. I'm never going to get married because you scare off all the men by crushing their spirits when you beat them."

He laughed and pushed to his feet. He came around the table, placed his hand on her shoulder, and kissed her on the cheek. "I'm glad you can joke about it, darling. But I can see in your eyes that your heart is broken over Daniel. I wish I could help you, but I can't."

She turned her head and kissed his hand. "Thank you for caring, Poppa. I don't know what I'd do without you."

The bell over the front door of the office jingled, and a man's voice called out, "Doc, you here?"

Her father sighed. "It sounds like I have a patient. You go on home, and I'll see you there."

Tave waited until her father took the man into his office and closed the door. Then she stood up, picked up her basket, and walked to the bedroom where Daniel had lain when he was so ill. She stood in the door and recalled the times she'd prayed beside his bed.

A longing to see him ripped through her, and she grasped the door frame to keep from collapsing. "Oh, God," she whispered, "when am I going to stop missing him?"

She stared into the room for a few more minutes, and then she squared her shoulders and left the building. As she passed the livery stable, Mr. Jensen waved to her from the corral. "Merry Christmas, Miss Spencer."

She smiled and waved back. "Merry Christmas to you, Mr. Jensen."

Christmas had always been her favorite time of year since she was a child. This year, though, she felt no joy in her heart. It had disappeared the day Daniel Luckett rode out of Willow Bend.

Chapter 12

July had come again and with it the blazing heat that threatened to cause every plant and blade of grass to shrivel and die.

Tave could hardly believe a year had passed since Daniel's departure. Another school year had drifted by, and the summer break was half over. There hadn't been much excitement in Willow Bend in the last twelve months unless she could count the June wedding of Esther Thompson to Joshua Tucker, Tave's friend and a tenant farmer out at Winterville Plantation. Martha hadn't quit talking about her new son-in-law for weeks, but everybody else went about their business, content to let one day blend into another. Before Tave knew it, she was one year older.

Sometimes one of her students would remind her of the day she fell playing hopscotch, and she would smile as they recalled last year's church picnic. At times, thoughts of Daniel would flash through her mind and be gone before she had time to dwell on them. At other times, the memory of his deep blue eyes and the way her skin had tingled the day he almost kissed her would sweep over her and leave a desolate emptiness in her heart. Today was one of those times.

The thoughts had probably been brought on by her task of cleaning the patient bedroom at her father's office. The patchwork quilt had been taken back to their house months ago, and she had packed it away. She couldn't stand to see the covering—a reminder of another time in her life.

With a sigh, Tave grabbed the broom she'd brought into the room and began to whisk it back and forth across the wood floor. Work was what she needed. Anything to take her mind off the memories this room evoked.

The front door opened, and her father's familiar footsteps echoed through the empty building. "Tave? Are you here?"

She stepped from the room and smiled. He'd been gone all night, and the rumpled shirt and trousers he wore told her he'd been busy. "I was beginning to worry about you."

He set his medical bag on a table, dropped down in a chair, and closed his eyes. "I'm exhausted. I've been to three different farms along the river since I left here yesterday afternoon."

Tave set the broom aside and hurried to stand behind him. Placing her hands on his shoulders, she rubbed the tight muscles as she often did when he was so tired. "Three? That's a lot of families to have sickness at one time."

He nodded. "Yes, and I'm afraid they're just the beginning."

Tave's body tensed, and her fingers stilled. "Why? What's the matter?"

"Yellow fever," he whispered.

Tave flinched at the words that could cause panic in the strongest of hearts. She pulled her hands from her father's shoulders and walked around the chair to face him. "Yellow fever? Are you sure?"

He rubbed his hands across his eyes. "I wish I wasn't."

She swallowed back the fear building inside her. "How many cases so far?"

"Two at a tenant farmer's home at Cottonwood, one over at the new Oak Hill owner's house, and Mrs. Somers."

Tave could barely believe what her father was saying. "Are any of them critical?"

"The only one who is right now is Mrs. Somers. I don't know what made them wait so long to let me know. Reverend Somers said she kept telling him she was going to be all right. By the time I got there, she had already developed jaundice."

"Oh no." Tave's mind raced at what the next few weeks could bring to their quiet little town. "Do you think I need to go over to help with Mrs. Somers?"

Her father jerked upright in the chair, and his eyes widened in fear. "No. You need to stay away from any of the sick. I don't want you coming down with this."

She smiled and patted her father's hand. "If I remember correctly, you're the one who's always believed this terrible disease is caused by some kind of insect, a gnat you said."

He nodded. "I know. But I've been ridiculed by every medical group I've ever presented my theory to. Until somebody finds out the real cause of it, I want you to take every precaution." Tears filled his eyes. "You're all I have in this world, and I couldn't stand it if something happened to you."

"And neither could I if you became ill. You're the one who's going to be with all these sick people. I'd think you'd be more at risk than I would be."

He sighed. "If this becomes an epidemic, and I pray it won't, I may need you. But not until that time. Do you understand?"

She leaned over and kissed him on the cheek. "Yes. Now I want you to lie down on the sofa in your office and get some rest. I'll stay here in case someone comes for you."

He pushed to his feet. "I think I'll do that." He walked toward the door to his office but stopped and turned toward her before he entered. "Tave, please pray that we'll only have a few isolated cases."

She smiled. "I will, Poppa."

The look in his eyes, however, told her that he didn't think they'd escape this disease so easily. She had the feeling dark days awaited the residents of Willow Bend.

A week later, Tave knew she'd been right. Nearly every home along the river had reported at least one case of yellow fever. Her father was nearing exhaustion from little sleep, but he wouldn't refuse any call for help. With the death toll at fifteen, the first being Reverend Somers's wife, and more cases being reported every day, he moved like he lived in a dream world.

Tave glanced around her father's office that had been converted into an emergency hospital for the most serious cases. The community had responded to the call for beds, and all ten that had been donated were filled with patients. Tave didn't know where they would place the next victim. She prayed there wouldn't be another one.

The mothers of three patients hovered near the children's beds, and Tave was grateful for their help. Most people were afraid to venture into the midst of the disease. She'd found herself giving aid to the other seven people near death.

She had even become immune to the stench in the room from the constant vomiting of those so sick. It never ceased to amaze her how much strength God could provide when it was needed.

A whimper from one of the beds caught her attention, and she hurried to kneel beside an elderly man who lived alone in a small house at the edge of town. He didn't mingle with the town folks much and appeared to live off his garden and the fish he caught in the river.

As Tave bent over him, she realized how she'd failed in the past to make an effort to know this man. Maybe he'd lived a lonely life, waiting and hoping for someone to act as if they cared. She wet a cloth and rubbed his face.

He opened his eyes, and Tave flinched at the yellow tint that had even invaded his pupils. She reached for a glass of rice-water on the table beside his bed. She lifted his head from the pillow and placed the glass on his lips, but he was unable to drink. Lowering him, she picked up a spoon and began to feed him the water.

She'd just completed the task when the front door opened. She glanced over to see Savannah and Mamie Clark walking inside. Tave jumped up and rushed across the room. "What are you two doing here?"

Savannah pulled her bonnet from her head and her nostrils flared. For a moment, Tave thought Savannah was going to be sick, but she straightened her shoulders and turned a determined look on Tave. "From the looks of things, you and your father need some help. Mamie and I have come to volunteer."

Tave shook her head. "No, you can't do that. You have children to take care of. What if you get sick?"

Savannah waved her hand in dismissal. "Mamie and I had this conversation with Dante and Saul. We can't go through life being afraid of what might happen. We have to trust God to take care of us. We're here to do His work with these people in need."

Mamie smiled, and her eyes lit up her dark face. "Miss 'Vanna's right. We gwine help any way we's can. So jest tell us what needs a-doin'."

Tave grasped their hands. "Thank you so much. Come with me. I'll show you."

She led the way to the kitchen and explained how they were treating the patients with plenty of liquids, the only known treatment to counteract the fluids they were losing from vomiting. "They're all running high fevers, and they're restless from aching muscles. Poppa says we should keep cool cloths on their heads and try to get some liquids down them. We're using black tea with a little sugar in it and rice-water. We need to keep a supply of each of those."

Mamie nodded. "I kin take care of that."

Tave took two aprons from the pegs by the stove and handed one to each of the women. "Savannah, are you sure you're up to this? Some of the patients are still in the acute stage of the disease. They're running a fever and having terrible aches with some vomiting. The ones in the toxic stage are much worse. In addition to the vomiting, some of them are hemorrhaging. This is not going to be an easy task."

Savannah tied the apron around her waist and took a deep breath. "Don't worry about me. I'm ready to help."

"Then come with me." Tave led her friend into the waiting room and directed her to the bed of a young woman who moaned aloud before Tave headed back to the bedside of the man she'd been helping. As Tave bent over him, she wiggled her shoulders. The back of her neck itched. She reached over her shoulder and scratched her skin then straightened. Just a mosquito bite—a summertime hazard of living on the river.

❧

"Hey, Preacher. We need you over here."

Daniel glanced over his shoulder at a group of dockworkers who stood at the gangway of a steamboat tied to the pier. Daniel walked toward the men he'd worked with and come to know in the past year.

"What can I do for you?"

One of the men pointed to the ship. "There's a sick man on board who's calling for a preacher. We told him we had one working on the dock."

Daniel chuckled. "Did you tell him I'm not a licensed preacher?"

The dockworker's eyes grew wide. "What difference does that make? You're the one that holds Sunday services over at that warehouse, and I ain't seen nobody else preaching except you."

Daniel nodded. "Sometimes I think you fellows railroaded me into leading the services in case none of you could show up after a night of living it up in that saloon all of you frequent."

A sheepish grin covered the face of Augie, the man Daniel had been trying to reach for the past six months. "Aw, Preacher, you know that ain't true. You're the only one who knows 'bout the Bible."

"Only because I study it, Augie." He glanced at the ship. "Now where is this man who wants a preacher? Maybe I can say something that will help."

Augie pointed to a cabin on the lower deck. "Right there, but you may not want to go."

"Why not?"

"They think he has yellow fever. They're waitin' for somebody to come take him off the boat. Nobody on board wants to touch him."

Daniel frowned. "Is he near death?"

Augie shrugged. "That's what they say."

A memory of being near death on a boat returned, and the faces of those who had helped him flashed into Daniel's mind. "Then he's in need of comfort." Daniel walked onto the boat, stopped at the door, and knocked.

The door was opened by a middle-aged woman. A worried expression covered her face. "Yes, may I help you?"

Daniel pulled the cap from his head and smiled. "I work on the docks, ma'am. Some of my friends said you were in need of a preacher. I'm not a licensed one, but I do hold services for the dockworkers every Sunday."

Her face relaxed into a smile. "My name is Lydia Collins. I think my husband, Herbert, may have caught yellow fever." She glanced over her shoulder. "He's very ill. I'll understand if you don't want to come inside."

Daniel stared past her at the writhing form on a bed across the cabin. "I'd be glad to come in if I can be of any help, ma'am."

She opened the door wider and smiled. "Then please come in. We've called for a doctor, but he hasn't gotten here yet. Herbert asked if I could find a preacher to pray with us. Thank you for coming."

Daniel stepped into the darkened cabin. The man groaned in agony, and his fingers clutched the side of the bed. Daniel knelt beside him and placed a hand on the man's trembling arm. "My name is Daniel Luckett. I've come to pray with you."

He nodded, and Daniel bowed his head. "Dear God, I come to You today on behalf of Herbert. He's in a great deal of pain right now and needs the assurance that he's not alone. Give him peace as only You can, and let him know that You are still in control. We can do nothing except place our lives in Your hands. Father, Your Word tells us there is a season for all things. We pray that this will be a season of rejoicing at Herbert's returned health. Be with this loving wife who stands ready to help her husband, and comfort her in this difficult time. We thank You for what You're going to do in Herbert's life today, and we give You praise, Lord, for loving us and caring for us. Amen."

Daniel opened his eyes, and Herbert Collins turned his head on the pillow. A weak smile curled his lips. "Thank you," he whispered.

The door opened, and the ship's captain ushered a small man holding a medical bag into the room. Daniel rose and backed away from the bed as the doctor bent over Herbert.

A hand touched his arm, and he glanced at Lydia Collins, who stood beside him. "Thank you, Mr. Luckett. You were a great comfort to my husband and me today."

Daniel smiled. "I'm glad I could be of service." He looked back at Herbert. "Yellow fever is a bad disease. Do you have any idea where he might have caught it?"

She nodded. "Actually I do. We live in Selma, but we've stayed the past few weeks with our dear friend Reverend Thomas Somers in Willow Bend. He lost his wife to the disease."

Daniel reeled from her words. "Willow Bend? I know Reverend Somers. You say his wife died?"

"Yes, she was the first. There have been many more since then."

Daniel almost doubled over from the pain that ripped through his body at the thought of Tave in the midst of that illness. He struggled to speak. "Did you happen to meet Dr. Spencer while you were there?"

She nodded. "Yes, once. He was very busy with so many sick people in the area. Right before we left for home I heard he'd set up a hospital at his office for the worst cases."

"And his daughter? Did you hear of her?" He could hardly speak the words.

She shook her head. "I'm sorry. I didn't meet her. We went back to Selma and caught the boat to Montgomery because none of the steamboats are stopping at Willow Bend right now. My husband is the pastor at a church in Selma, and he was supposed to speak at a meeting of church leaders here."

Daniel backed toward the door. "I hope your husband recovers. I'll go and let you talk with the doctor now."

Daniel bolted onto the deck of the ship, rushed to the railing, and grasped it. He couldn't believe what he'd just heard. Why hadn't he known about the yellow fever outbreak in Willow Bend? Surely it had been in the newspapers. Somehow he'd missed it.

He thought of Tave and wondered if she was all right. And her father. What about him? An uneasy feeling washed over him, and he knew he had to find out about them some way. How could he do it?

He lifted his eyes toward heaven and breathed a prayer for God to show him what to do. Just give him some assurance that she was all right.

A door to a cabin down the deck from where he stood opened, and a man stepped out. He glanced back inside and spoke in a loud voice: "You look beautiful enough. Now quit wasting time, and let's go. This boat's going to be ready to depart before I can get you onshore."

Daniel's forehead wrinkled. There was something familiar about the dark-haired man's profile. Where had he seen him before? He turned, and Daniel gasped in recognition. This was the plantation owner he'd seen at Dr. Spencer's office, the man interested in Tave—Matthew Chandler.

Matthew approached and glanced at Daniel. A slight frown wrinkled his brow. He stopped and stared at Daniel. "You look familiar. Have we met?"

Daniel swallowed and nodded. "Last summer in Willow Bend. I was a patient of Dr. Spencer's."

Matthew nodded. "Oh yes. I remember."

Daniel took a step forward. "I've just heard the news about the yellow fever outbreak there. How bad is it?"

Matthew sighed. "Terrible. I think about twenty people have died so far." He looked back over his shoulder toward the cabin he'd exited. "I took my wife to Selma so that we could board the boat there. We're going to stay in Montgomery until the epidemic is over."

Daniel breathed a sigh of relief. Tave was safe. "I'm glad to hear that. How is your wife?"

"She's fine."

"And her father?"

Matthew frowned. "How would you know her father?"

The question surprised Daniel. "He was my doctor."

Matthew laughed. "Portia's father isn't a doctor."

"Portia? I thought you married Tave Spencer."

Matthew shook his head. "Oh, that's right. I'd come to visit Tave the day I saw you there. No, it didn't work out for us." His eyes clouded. "I was very sorry to hear that she was ill."

Daniel felt as if he'd been slapped. "Sick? With yellow fever?"

Matthew nodded. "Right before we left, one of my tenant farmers went to town. When he came back, he told me Tave had gotten sick with yellow fever."

Daniel staggered back. "How bad was it?"

Matthew hesitated before he spoke. "I think she was near death."

Panic seized Daniel. "I've got to get to Willow Bend right away."

"I don't know how you'll do that. The disease is traveling upriver. I heard that this is the last boat Montgomery is allowing in, and they're setting up blockades to keep anyone from going south."

Daniel heard the words, but he didn't care. He turned and ran from the boat. No matter what it took, he had to get to Willow Bend. He prayed he wouldn't be too late.

Chapter 13

Tave groaned and tried to turn on her side, but it was no use. Her back hurt, and her head ached. She'd never felt so helpless in her life. A soft hand touched her forehead, and she opened her eyes. Savannah stood over her, a smile on her face.

"Are you awake?"

Tave tried to answer, but her throat was too dry. Maybe she could nod, but she didn't even have enough energy to move her head. There wasn't a place in her body that didn't hurt. Her eyes drifted closed.

Footsteps approached her bed, and she tried to smile. She would recognize her father's steps anywhere. She could sense his presence, and she felt him lift her arm. "Her skin is turning quite yellow. That means the disease is attacking the liver."

He sounded so sad, and she wished she could tell him everything was going to be all right. She tried, but she couldn't reopen her eyes.

"What do I need to do, Dr. Spencer?" Savannah's voice drifted into her ear.

"Just keep up the liquids. Everything that comes up has to be replaced with even more in hopes that some of it will get into her body."

"I'll do my best, Dr. Spencer."

A soft sob sounded, and she wondered if her father was crying. She'd never seen him cry. He was so strong.

"Thank you, Savannah. I don't know what I'd do without you."

They moved away from the bed, and a chill shook Tave's body. She waited for it to pass and tried to think of something to make her happy. Daniel's face drifted into her mind, and she smiled inwardly. She wondered where he was and if she'd ever see him again. She hoped so.

❧

Augie held the reins of Daniel's horse and waited for Daniel to tie the saddlebags on the mare's flank. "Are you sure you want to do this, Preacher? I hear those barricade guards are shootin' before they ask any questions. Just 'cause it's midnight, don't make the mistake they'll be asleep. You most likely won't make it a few yards past them before you get a bullet in the back."

Daniel patted the horse and took the reins from Augie. "I've gotta try. Thanks for coming to see me off."

Augie pulled his cap down on his forehead and scowled. "Aw, don't go making such a fuss. I just wanted to see you one more time while you was still breathin'."

Daniel laughed and shook Augie's hand. "Thanks for everything, Augie. Tell all the fellows that I talked with Mr. Smith, and he's going to see that services continue at the warehouse. And I told the Whittakers not to hold my room." He gazed into the face of the man he'd been praying about for months. "If I don't make it back to Montgomery, I want you to know I'll never forget you, and I'll never quit praying for you."

Augie tilted his head to the side and studied Daniel with a probing gaze. "I'll remember you, too. I ain't never known anybody like you before. I'll think about all those things you've been talking to me about."

Daniel smiled. "Good. I've turned you over to Jacob now that I'm leaving. He wants to help you like he has me." He put his foot in the stirrup and swung himself into the saddle. "Good-bye, friend."

Augie backed away. "Now remember what I told you. Follow the river until you get out of town. Once you're past the barricade outposts, I reckon it'll be safe enough to get back on the road."

"I'll remember."

"And one more thing. It's gonna be dark out there in the woods along the river. It might be good for you to lead the horse. You don't want her to step in no holes. Last thing you need is a horse with a broken leg."

Daniel rested his arm on the saddle horn and gazed down at Augie. "You're beginning to sound like a mother hen."

Augie grinned. "Can't help it. I done come to think a lot of you. Be careful, Preacher. I hope your woman friend is all right."

Daniel nodded and urged the horse forward. He glanced up at the sky and said a prayer of thanks for the cloudy night. With the moon obscured, he might be able to blend into the shadows better. Now if the Lord would just provide his horse a clear path, everything would be all right.

Daniel rode through the deserted streets of Montgomery. The *clip-clop* of the horse's hooves sounded like a drumbeat to his ears, but no one stirred in the dark houses they passed. As he approached the outskirts of town, he guided the horse off the road and into the trees that lined the riverbank. He slowed the horse to a walk and peered into the darkness before them. After a few minutes, he pulled the horse to a stop and dismounted. Taking the reins in his hands, he pressed his weight into the ground with each step before he led the horse forward. Inch by inch they began a slow advance that would take them past the barricades.

Only once did Daniel pull to a stop. Voices drifted through the trees. He stood still, his hand gently stroking the horse that seemed to sense the nearby danger. She didn't move as Daniel's fingers gently calmed her.

After what seemed an eternity, the voices quieted, and he moved on down-river. Three hours later, the clouds parted, and the moon reflected on the rippling water of the Alabama River. Daniel looked for landmarks that he remembered from his days on the *Montgomery Belle* and spotted a scraggly tree he'd often seen on the riverbank. He breathed a sigh of relief. They had cleared the barricades and were well south of the city.

He led the horse back through the trees, and within minutes they were on the road he'd traveled when he came to Montgomery. He offered a silent prayer of thanks for safety through a dangerous night and urged the horse south. If all went well, he would soon be in Willow Bend.

Someone was crying again, but Tave couldn't tell who it was. She tried to call out, but her throat refused to work. Voices echoed in her ears. It reminded her of how she used to yell into the depths of her grandmother's well and hear her voice vibrate.

"How is she?" someone asked.

"I think she's dying." That almost sounded like her father, but the voice trembled more than her father's.

"Is there anything I can do?"

"Pray, Savannah. That's all that will help now."

Relief washed over her. Savannah was here. Maybe she could comfort who-ever was crying. No one should be sad today. She'd had a dream that had made her so happy. She'd seen Daniel again, and he wasn't angry anymore. The hatred was gone from his life.

She was glad. So glad. Now she wanted to go back to sleep and dream again.

On the second day after leaving Montgomery, Daniel rode into Willow Bend. The town looked like a ghost town with no one on the deserted streets, and he wondered if he was too late. Maybe everyone had died.

He rode into the livery stable and was relieved when Mr. Jensen stepped from one of the stalls. Daniel dismounted, tossed the reins to the man, and grabbed his saddlebags. "I'm Daniel Luckett. You took care of my horse when I was here last summer. I need you to do that again. I'm going to Dr. Spencer's office, but I'll be back later to pay you."

Without waiting for an answer, he ran out the door and down the street toward the familiar building. When he charged onto the porch, he grabbed the doorknob. Fear like he'd never known gripped him, and he couldn't open the door. What if she was dead? How would he be able to forgive himself for the way he'd talked to her the last time he'd seen her? He should have told her how much he loved her instead of pushing her to marry someone else.

But that hadn't been God's plan. Daniel had come to understand that God had sent him to Montgomery so he could meet Jacob Whittaker. Alone with Tave's Bible in his small room at the boardinghouse, he had digested everything Jacob had told him about God, and it had given him a new life. Now he realized that he had to trust God to take care of him no matter what he found in Dr. Spencer's office. He took a deep breath and pushed the door open.

A sour stench overpowered him, and he almost stumbled backward to the porch. His stomach rumbled in protest, but he forced himself to walk into the room.

The neat waiting room he remembered now resembled a battlefield hospital. Beds, each occupied by a patient, sat side by side with narrow walk spaces between them. Low moans joined together in a deadly chorus that chilled him.

In disbelief, he took in the scene before him. A woman, a scarf covering her blond hair, leaned over one of the beds. She turned toward him. Surprise flashed in her tired eyes. "Daniel, what are you doing here?"

Daniel took off his hat and let his gaze wander over the beds again. "Hello, Savannah. I heard about the epidemic. I came to see if I could help."

She wiped her hands on a cloth and hurried across the room. "I'm so glad you're here. Dr. Spencer needs anybody willing to volunteer."

He studied the faces of the patients again, but Tave wasn't among them. He had to know about her, yet he was too frightened to voice the question. The brim of his hat curled between his clenched fists. "Tave? Where is. . . ?" He choked on the last word.

Savannah glanced toward the patient bedroom where he'd stayed just a year ago. "In there."

Daniel tried to take a step, but his legs felt as if they had large weights attached. His mouth thinned into a straight line, and he willed his body to move. Slowly, he made his way to the open door and peered inside.

She lay on the bed where he'd spent his days after surgery. Her face was obscured by the form of Dr. Spencer sitting in a chair next to her. Daniel eased across the room, stopped behind the man he'd come to respect during his time in Willow Bend, and placed his hand on the doctor's shoulder.

Dr. Spencer swiveled in the chair and looked up into Daniel's face. The broken person staring at him wasn't the strong man who'd spoken to Daniel of God's love just a year ago. Dr. Spencer's eyes held a vacant look as if he'd witnessed unspeakable horror. Gray stubble covered his face, the result of days without shaving.

When he saw Daniel, tears came to his eyes, and he pushed to his feet. "Daniel, I can't believe it's you."

Daniel wrapped his arms around the man who'd been the closest to a father he'd ever known and hugged him. Dr. Spencer's slight frame shook, and Daniel wondered how much weight the doctor had lost.

Daniel released him and stared into his eyes. "How's Tave?"

A tear trickled from the corner of Dr. Spencer's eyes. "I think she's dying. I'm glad you got here in time."

Although he'd known he might hear those words, they still stabbed at his heart. He stepped around Dr. Spencer and gazed down at Tave. Her beautiful auburn hair fanned out on the pillow, and he remembered the first time he'd seen it. Her eyes were closed, but the yellow tint of her skin sent chills through him. Her mouth opened, and her body tensed in a violent contraction.

Dr. Spencer shook his head. "She's lost so much fluid there's nothing to expel anymore."

Daniel bit down on his lip and studied her for a moment. "Then we have to get more into her."

"We've tried over and over, but it's done no good. She loses everything we get down her throat."

Daniel glanced at Dr. Spencer out of the corner of his eye. The gaunt figure looked little like the robust man he had known last summer. Dr. Spencer might not have contracted yellow fever, but the dreaded disease had taken its toll on the man. "You look worn out. Why don't you go lie down? I'll take over here. Can you get me whatever you're feeding her and a spoon? I'll see what I can do."

Dr. Spencer rubbed his eyes and nodded. "I'll be right back."

When Tave's father had left the room, Daniel knelt beside the bed and took her hand in both of his. He leaned close and whispered in her ear, "Tave, it's Daniel. I've come back. If you can hear me, I want you to know that I love you more than I can ever tell you. I'm sorry I hurt you when I left, but God needed me to go away for a while. Now He's brought me home, and I need you here with me."

Tave's body twitched, but she didn't open her eyes.

Daniel grasped her hand tighter and bowed his head. "Dear God, please look down on this woman today and touch her body. If it's Your will, Father, purge her of this terrible disease and return her to the people who love her. And give me the strength to face whatever may come our way. I love You, Lord." His lips trembled, and he struggled to speak. From the bottom of his soul a desperate wail burst from his mouth. "Oh God! Please don't take her away from me. Not now." He pulled her hand to his chest and shook with sobs.

Behind him someone gasped, and he straightened to see Dr. Spencer and Savannah standing in the doorway. Dr. Spencer's face held a questioning expression. "Daniel, you're praying?"

Daniel wiped at his tears and pushed to his feet. "A lot has happened to me since I left here. I'm not the same person I was."

Dr. Spencer's eyes grew wide. "What happened?"

Daniel pointed to Tave. "She came into my life and showed me how to trust God. Then I met a man in Montgomery who wouldn't give up on me, either. The hate I had is gone, and I have the peace I'd wanted for years."

Savannah frowned. "Then why didn't you come back? Tave's been unhappy ever since you left."

"I thought she had probably married Matthew, and I stayed where I thought God wanted me. The fellows I work with in Montgomery even call me Preacher because I conduct services for them every Sunday."

Dr. Spencer's mouth gaped open. "You're a preacher?"

Daniel shook his head. "Not a licensed one who's been ordained. But my friend Jacob Whittaker says he thinks God's already ordained me."

Dr. Spencer and Savannah exchanged surprised looks before they both smiled at Daniel. Dr. Spencer shook his head. "God sure does work in strange ways sometimes."

Daniel nodded. "That He does. It took me getting shot to make the most important decision of my life." He reached for the pitcher Dr. Spencer held. "Now you two go on about your work. I'll take care of Tave."

He turned back to the bed and sat down in the chair beside it. He leaned toward her and patted her hand again. "You took care of me when I was sick. Now it's my turn to help you, but you've got to do your part, too. Fight to live, Tave. I need you."

Setting the pitcher on the bedside table, he dipped the spoon in, filled it, and lifted her head with his free hand. Slowly he brought the spoon to her mouth and forced it between her lips. Half of it trickled down the side of her face, but a sip went down her throat.

Daniel shook his head in disappointment before he reached for the pitcher and refilled the spoon. He had no idea how long it would take to get a sufficient amount of liquid into her body, but he knew it didn't matter. As long as she was breathing, he wouldn't give up.

Chapter 14

Twenty-four hours later, little had changed in Tave's condition. Daniel pulled himself up from the chair where he'd sat since arriving and stretched. Footsteps at the door caused him to turn.

Savannah stood there, a pan of water in her hands. "Mamie has some food in the kitchen. Why don't you get something to eat while I bathe Tave?"

He stared down at her, unwilling to leave. "She's better, don't you think?"

Savannah put the pan on the table next to the bed and placed her hand on Tave's forehead. "She does seem cooler." She looked up at Daniel. "I know she'd be so happy to have you here. She's missed you this past year."

Daniel nodded. "I've missed her, too. I almost came back once. I wanted to tell her she was right, that I had found God and I was at peace. But then I knew I couldn't stand to see her married to someone else."

"And all that time she was waiting for you to return. Well, you're here now, and she would be happy to know you've been preaching in Montgomery."

Daniel's face grew warm. "It's not really a church. Just a group of workers who need a place to worship."

"And you've been leading them. I'm very proud of you, Daniel."

"Thank you." Loud sobs rang out from the waiting room, and Daniel turned to see where they were coming from. "Who's that?"

"Martha Thompson. Her son Tad has taken a turn for the worse."

"Oh no." Daniel walked to the door and glanced into the room.

Martha Thompson, trying to force liquids down her son Tad's throat, sobbed with each sip he took. "There now, Taddy boy, you open your mouth for Mama. You gonna feel better when you drink this."

Daniel walked over to Tad's bed and touched Martha's shoulder. "How is he, Mrs. Thompson?"

She looked up at Daniel with stricken eyes, clamped her teeth onto her bottom lip, and shook her head. Tears rolled down her cheeks.

Daniel knelt beside her. "We just have to keep praying."

Martha nodded. "I know." She stared back at her son. "He's such a good boy. He works so hard to please his daddy. And he's smart, too. I always wished he had the chance to do something more than farm. He used to say he was gonna be a doctor when he grew up. Now I just want him to have the chance to grow up." Her body shook with sobs.

Daniel took her hand in his. "Then let's pray for that, Mrs. Thompson."

They bowed their heads, and Daniel began to pray: "Dear Lord, we come to You with heavy hearts because of all the suffering and death the good folks of Willow Bend have seen. I pray that You will give us peace to face what may be ahead of us. Bless this dear mother, Father, who watches beside the bed of her son. Give her strength, and I pray that You will touch Tad and restore him to those who love him so much. We pray that You will lift this dreaded disease from our midst and heal those who are ill. These things we ask in Your name. Amen."

When he'd finished, Martha looked up at him. "Thank you, Daniel, for praying for my boy."

He squeezed her hand. "Savannah is bathing Tave. If you need me, I'll be in the kitchen."

She smiled. "When I saw your face that day they brought you up the bluff to Doc's office, I thought you was gonna die. I'm glad the Lord saved you. You've been a blessing to me today."

Her words pricked his heart. "And everybody in this town has been a blessing to me. Being shot was well worth what I gained from coming to Willow Bend."

He stood and started to the kitchen, but a whimper from another bed caught his attention. He walked over and stared down at the young man lying there. Dropping to his knees, he began to pray for him. When he'd finished, he went to the next bed and the next until he had prayed beside every bed in the room.

Only then did he make his way to the kitchen.

⬥

Tave wanted to open her eyes, but they wouldn't obey her. She didn't feel like struggling anymore. She would just lie there and try to understand the sounds around her.

Something cool touched her head. It felt so good. "You look so pretty today with that clean gown on."

Tave's heart beat faster at the familiar sound. Savannah was with her.

A foggy memory returned. Someone else had been with her, and she tried to remember what was said. *"I need you."* Now she remembered.

Someone needed her. But who?

She couldn't worry about that now. It hurt her head to think. All she wanted was to sleep.

⬥

Three days later, Daniel stood at the foot of Tad Thompson's bed. Martha alternated between spooning broth into her son's mouth and squeezing his hand. She glanced up at Daniel, and he thought he'd never seen a happier expression on anyone's face. He wished he could have seen that from others who'd had loved ones in Dr. Spencer's office. Since he'd been there, two of the patients had died.

He glanced toward Tave's room, where Savannah sat with her. Dr. Spencer thought her condition had improved some in the past few days, but she still hadn't opened her eyes.

Daniel rubbed his hands over his face and sighed. He had slept very little since returning to Willow Bend, but he wanted to be awake in case Tave regained consciousness.

"Ain't he lookin' good?" Martha's voice broke into his thoughts.

Daniel glanced at Tad and nodded. "He is indeed."

Tad squirmed as his mother squeezed his hand once more. "Aw Ma, I'm all right now. You don't have to keep carryin' on so."

Martha leaned over and kissed Tad on the cheek. "Well, I know when we get back home and you're back to your normal self, you won't let me fuss over you none. So while I got you flat on your back, I'm gonna take advantage of the situation."

Daniel's heart filled with gratitude to God that Martha had her son back. "Tad, I lost my mother when I was just a little older than you are. Don't ever take yours for granted. You're a very lucky boy to have someone who loves you so much."

Tad grinned and winked at Daniel. "I know. I just like to give her a hard time sometimes."

Martha laughed and stood up. "Land sakes, this boy is something else. Takes after his father. They both just love to tease me." She reached over and smoothed Tad's hair. "Now I'm gonna take this bowl back to the kitchen and get me something to eat. I'll be back before long."

"Take all the time you need, Ma. I'm not goin' anywhere."

Daniel watched Martha leave before he glanced back at Tad. "I'm glad you're doing so much better."

"Thanks, Mr. Luckett." He glanced toward the other room. "How's Miss Spencer?"

"About the same."

Tad settled back on his pillows, and a smile pulled at his lips. "Do you remember when Miss Spencer fell playing hopscotch?"

The memory of their argument after the incident flashed across his mind, and he nodded. "Yes. That was at the picnic."

Tad's eyes clouded. "She's such a good teacher. I sure hope she gets better."

Daniel sighed. "So do I."

"You know," Tad continued, "Pa had told me I couldn't go to school last year. He said I had to start working on the farm. But Miss Spencer came to see him and Ma. She told them I was one of her smartest students. She said it would be a shame for me to have to quit school. After she got through talking to them, Pa finally agreed. Of course, it was Ma that really made him change his mind."

"Your mother told me that you used to say you wanted to be a doctor."

Tad lifted his head, his eyes wide. "She did? I haven't said that to anybody in a long time, except Miss Spencer and her father. They told me that if God wanted me to be a doctor, He'd make a way for it to happen."

"They're right. I'll pray for you, Tad."

"Thanks, Mr. Luckett."

The front door opened, and Dr. Spencer trudged inside. His stooped shoulders and tired eyes looked as if they should belong to a man twenty years older. He stopped at Tad's bedside and set his medical bag on the floor. "How are you feeling today?"

"Much better, Dr. Spencer."

"Good. That's what I like to hear." He glanced at Daniel. "You know this young man is going to take over my practice someday. We're already working on it. Aren't we, Tad?"

Tad's pale face lit up, and he grinned. "We are."

Dr. Spencer looked around the room and frowned. "Where's your mother? She hasn't gotten three feet away from you since you got sick."

"I'm right here." Martha bustled from the kitchen and hurried toward them. "We were beginning to get worried about you."

Dr. Spencer rubbed the back of his neck and stretched. "I visited all the homes that have sickness. I was glad to see most of the patients are improving. There's a few that I'm still worried about, but things are beginning to look better. We haven't had any new cases in two weeks."

"Maybe that means it's about over," Daniel said.

"Could be. We'll just have to keep praying. Which reminds me. . ." Dr. Spencer turned to Daniel. "I stopped by to see Reverend Somers. We haven't had any church services since this thing started. Some of the folks have said they'd like to have worship on Sunday, but Reverend Somers says he doesn't know if he can preach or not. He's taken his wife's death really hard."

Martha's eyebrows arched, and she turned to Daniel. "Then why don't you preach for us?"

"Me?" Daniel looked at Martha as if she'd lost her mind. "I'm not a preacher."

Martha shrugged. "You coulda fooled me. The way you been spouting Bible verses and praying by everybody's beds around here, you sure look like a preacher to me."

Dr. Spencer chuckled. "I guess we agree, Martha. That's exactly what I told Reverend Somers. He thought it was a great idea."

Tad pushed up on his elbows. "I sure wish I was well enough so I could be there to hear you, Mr. Luckett."

Daniel held up his hands in protest and took a step back. "I'm telling all of you I'm not a preacher. Maybe somebody else will do it."

Martha shook her head. "No, we want you to preach."

"But I don't feel like I'm qualified. I still have so much to learn about the Bible."

"We never stop learning, Daniel." Dr. Spencer cocked an eyebrow and peered over the top of his spectacles. "You said you've been studying the Bible. Have you ever run across a verse in the Bible where Paul is talking about how he's learned to be content in whatever state he's in?"

Daniel swallowed. "Yes sir."

"What did he say?"

Daniel closed his eyes and recalled the verse that had helped change his life. He quoted, " 'I can do all things through Christ which strengtheneth me.'"

Dr. Spencer chuckled and spread his hands as if declaring victory. "Right. So what do we need to tell Reverend Somers about Sunday?"

The lump in Daniel's throat grew larger. "Tell him I'll be glad to lead the services," he whispered.

Martha clapped her hands and smiled. "Good. Now that Tad's better, I'll be able to leave him to come hear you. I know we gonna have a great day at church."

Daniel could only nod. When he'd attended Willow Bend Church the summer before, he would never have believed that he would ever stand in the pulpit and tell the people of Willow Bend how much God loved them. Dr. Spencer was right. God's ways were too mysterious for anybody to understand. All Daniel could do was accept them in faith and obey.

He opened his mouth to thank Dr. Spencer, but the sound of running footsteps caused him to whirl and face Tave's room. Savannah stood in the doorway, her face white.

"Dr. Spencer, Daniel, come quickly."

Fear rooted Daniel to the spot, and he didn't know if he could move. Clenching his fists at his sides, he rushed forward past Savannah and hurried to Tave's bedside. If she was dying, he had to tell her one more time how much he loved her.

Chapter 15

"Wh–what is it, Savannah?" Dr. Spencer's strained voice held the fear Daniel felt in his heart.

"I think she's waking up."

Daniel dropped to his knees and cupped Tave's hand in both of his. He stared into her face. Her eyelids fluttered and then were still. He looked up at Dr. Spencer, who stood beside him. "What's happening? Is she all right?"

Dr. Spencer nudged him to scoot aside. "Let me check her."

Daniel hardly breathed as Dr. Spencer pulled his stethoscope from his bag and listened to Tave's heart. After a moment, he grasped her arm and checked her pulse. A slow smile covered his lips. "Her heart rate is better." He turned to Savannah. "Has there been any hemorrhaging today?"

Savannah shook her head. "Not since yesterday. And she's kept down everything we've fed her today."

He smiled and pushed to his feet. "Good. Maybe we've turned a corner here. We'll keep a close watch until we know for sure."

Daniel exhaled and covered his face with his hands. "I was so scared when I came in here. I thought she might be dying."

Dr. Spencer put his hand on Daniel's shoulder. "If she lives—and now I think she will—we will have to give God the thanks for bringing you back here, Daniel. Even if she hasn't indicated it, I think she knew you were here."

Tears blinded Daniel. "Do you really think so?"

"I do." He took a deep breath and turned to Savannah. "Now, if you think you can spare me awhile, I'm going to lie down in my office. I think I can sleep now."

Savannah put her arms around Dr. Spencer's shoulders and hugged him. "You go on. Daniel and I will keep watch over Tave."

With one last glance at his daughter, Dr. Spencer shuffled from the room, and Daniel sank down in the chair next to the bed. He leaned forward and touched her forehead. It felt cool to his touch, and he smiled.

"I think her fever's down."

Savannah placed her hand on Daniel's shoulder. "I really think we've reached the turning point. She seems to be sleeping peacefully. I'm going in the kitchen to help Mamie with supper. If you need me, call out."

"I will." He reached out and caught Savannah's hand as she turned to leave. "I want to thank you again for taking care of Tave while she's been sick. I know it hasn't been easy for you being away from your children."

"I've been home more than you realize, but I'm blessed to have good friends at Cottonwood who are taking care of Gabby and Vance while I'm gone. I know Tave would have done the same for me."

"Yes, she would have."

Savannah walked from the room, and Daniel leaned over and grasped Tave's hand. "It's time for you to come back to us, Tave. I need you. Open your eyes and look at me."

There was no movement. He took a deep breath and began to talk to her as he had done so often since he'd been back. He related every memory he had of their time together the summer before, from the night he awoke to see her sitting beside his bed to the day he left for Montgomery. He told her how beautiful she'd been in the lavender and white dress the Sunday they went on the picnic, and how funny she looked when she fell playing hopscotch. He leaned closer and whispered how he had lain awake nights and wished he had kissed her that day. It would have been a memory to treasure.

The longer he talked, the more his heart ached. She teetered between life and death, and he wanted her to live so badly. A thought struck him. Maybe God had need of Tave. Even though it would be difficult, that thought could prove comforting if she died.

Something told him, though, that she wasn't going to die. She was going to live, and they were going to have a full life together.

He brought her hand to his lips and kissed her fingers. Still holding it tightly, he leaned closer. "You're going to live, Tave, and as soon as you feel like it, we'll be married. And when we are, I'm going to take you to Selma for a wedding trip. When we get there, I'm going to find a studio and have a daguerreotype made of you to set on our mantel. We'll tell our children that it was made on the happiest day of our lives. Then when we get through at the studio, we're going to do something else you've always wanted. We're going to dinner at the St. James."

He kissed her fingers again. "I know I'll be the envy of every man in the hotel when I escort my beautiful wife into the dining room. So you've got to get well. I've got plans, and you have to help me get ready. How about it? Does all this sound good to you?"

Her lips twitched, and then her fingers pressed against his. His breath caught in his throat. He wasn't sure if he'd imagined it or not. He squeezed her hand, and her fingers responded with gentle pressure. His heart nearly burst with joy. "Good," he whispered. "Now you get some rest, and we'll talk about it when you wake up."

There was no more movement, and after a few minutes, Daniel slipped to his knees. As he had done so often since he'd returned to Willow Bend, he prayed and begged God to spare the woman he loved.

∞

The clock in Dr. Spencer's office chimed midnight, and Daniel stirred in his chair. He hadn't meant to drop off to sleep, but he must have. In a rocker beside him, Savannah slept soundly. She'd dropped off soon after sitting down.

He didn't know how she'd kept going for the past few days. She hardly slept and had devoted every minute to those so ill. Mamie had done the same, as well as Martha and several other ladies from the church.

Working together to care for the sick these past few days had forged a bond between all of them. For the first time in years, Daniel felt like he'd found a place to call home with the people of Willow Bend. Because of the people he'd met here a year ago, he'd also come home to God, and that was the best part. Now if Tave would only recover, life would be perfect.

The bed creaked, and he straightened in his chair. Had she moved? He picked up the oil lamp that they kept burning all night and held it closer to her face. She frowned as if the light caused her pain, and he set it back down.

He knelt beside her bed and stroked her forehead. "Tave, do you need something? Open your eyes, and tell me what you want."

Her mouth twitched, and her eyelids fluttered. He grabbed her hand and squeezed it.

"You can do it. Open your eyes, and look at me."

She frowned as her eyelids fluttered again, and then her eyes popped open. She stared up and blinked several times. Her tongue licked at her lips, and she turned her head toward the window as if she was staring into the darkness.

He pressed her hand again. "Tave, it's Daniel. Look at me."

The frown on her face deepened, and she turned her head toward him. Even in the soft light, her face, framed by her hair spread out on the pillow, appeared pale and almost lifeless. She blinked several times before recognition flashed in her eyes.

Her mouth spread in a weak smile. "Daniel," she whispered, "is it really you?"

He fought to hold back tears and grasped her hand tighter. "I'm here."

She frowned again. "Wh—where am I?"

"At your father's office. You've been very sick, but you're going to be all right now." He kissed her fingers. "Everything's going to be all right now."

Behind him, Savannah stirred in the rocker, and he touched her arm. "Savannah, wake up."

She jerked upright at his touch. "What's wrong? Is she worse?"

He smiled. "No, she's awake. Stay with her, and I'll get her father."

Savannah dropped to her knees beside the bed, tears running down her cheeks. "Oh Tave, I'm so glad you're back with us. I've missed you so much."

Daniel started to rise, but Tave held on to his hand. "You're not leaving me, are you?"

He put his hand on her head and stroked her hair. "I'm going to get your father. He made me promise to wake him the minute you opened your eyes." He leaned closer and stared into her eyes. "You don't have to worry about me ever leaving again. I plan on staying with you for the rest of my life."

&

Four weeks later Tave sat on the porch of her father's office. Upriver she could hear the rumble of the *Liberty Queen*'s whistle announcing its arrival at the Willow Bend docks. With the yellow fever epidemic over, travel had commenced on the Alabama River once again. Tave wondered if there would be any passengers getting off today.

The office door opened, and her father stepped onto the porch. He walked over to one of the posts that supported the roof and leaned against it as he stared toward the river. "I heard the whistle."

Tave nodded. "That should be the *Liberty Queen*. It's about time for her trip downriver."

Her father smiled. "I don't think we're going to see the steamboats for very much longer."

Tave rose and went to stand beside her father. "Why do you say that?"

"Like you're always telling me, for everything there is a season. The railroad is going to replace the steamboats." He straightened and took a deep breath. "But we've got a few years left with them, I think. I'm sure going to miss them when they're gone."

Tave had never given a thought to the fact that the sleek ships she loved might disappear, but she now realized it was possible. She looped her arm through her father's. "I'll miss them, too."

He patted her hand and glanced around. "Where's Daniel? I haven't seen him since early this morning."

Tave laughed and went back to sit in her chair. "He's visiting out at the Ramsey farm. They haven't come to church since they moved here, and he thought he'd give them an invitation."

Dr. Spencer shook his head. "He's quite different from the young man who came to us last summer. I knew God could change his life, but I have to admit I didn't expect such a drastic difference. Can you believe he's preaching?"

Tave smoothed her skirt and chuckled. "I think that was one of my biggest surprises. But he does a wonderful job, and I'm so proud of him I could burst."

"Well, Reverend Somers was happy to have him fill in for him. I think a trip was just what our pastor needed. His wife's death has hit him hard. You know, he'd asked the church to be looking for his replacement this year so he and his wife could move closer to their children. Now I wonder what he'll do."

"I do, too."

Tave looked down to the far end of the street, and her heart thudded at the sight of Daniel riding toward them. He reined the horse to a stop in front of the office, dismounted, and tied the horse to the hitching post. Taking off his hat, he pounded it against his pant leg. Dust swirled from the clothes.

Grinning, he stepped onto the porch. "The roads are mighty dusty today."

Dr. Spencer cocked an eyebrow. "You don't say. Who would've thought Alabama roads would be dusty in August?"

Daniel shook his head, walked over to Tave, and kissed her on the cheek. "Your father's making fun of me."

She smiled up at him. "Only because he likes you so much."

He smiled. "That's good, because I'm hoping he'll let me marry his daughter."

Dr. Spencer cleared his throat. "I've heard a lot about that wedding, but nobody's told me what the date is. Haven't you two decided yet?"

Tave nodded. "We talked about it last night. If it's all right with you, we'd like to have it the first Sunday afternoon in September."

Dr. Spencer pursed his mouth. "That sounds good to me. After all we've been through in the past few months, I think a wedding celebration is just what we need."

The *Liberty Queen*'s whistle rumbled from the docks, and Tave stared toward the big boat. Daniel turned to look at the impressive steamboat, and Tave rose to stand beside him. She put her hand on his arm. "Do you miss the river, Daniel? Do you want to go back to it?"

His eyes registered surprise. "No. Why would you think that?"

"Well, you're going to have to find work somewhere. I thought maybe you wanted to do that."

He put his arm around her waist and drew her close. "I'm never going to do anything that will take me away from you again. I don't know what the Lord has in mind for me, but He'll provide for us, Tave. I have faith that He'll show me what I'm to do."

She snuggled closer to him. "That's good enough for me."

They stared back at the boat that had now docked and the gangway that had lowered. Passengers began to stream up the hill toward Mr. Perkins's store. Dr. Spencer put his hands in his pockets and studied the people walking up the bluff. "I guess Mr. Perkins can expect an increase in sales today. He always likes to see the boats dock."

Tave's eyes grew wide, and she pointed at a man who appeared at the top of the bluff. "Look, it's Reverend Somers. I didn't know he was coming back today."

"I didn't either," Daniel said.

She started to wave to him, but she felt Daniel stiffen next to her. She glanced up at him. "What is it?" she asked.

He pointed to a man and woman who walked behind Reverend Somers. "That's the couple I told you about in Montgomery, the Collinses. They're the ones I prayed with on the boat."

Reverend Somers spied them, and a big smile covered his face. He turned to the man and woman behind him and pointed to the office porch. All three of them headed that way.

When they stopped on the street in front of the office, Dr. Spencer went down the steps and stuck out his hand to Reverend Somers. "Glad to have you back. We've missed you."

Tave tried to hide her shock at how the preacher had aged since she last saw him. His hair seemed whiter, and his cheeks appeared sunken. He gestured toward the people behind him. "These are my dear friends Lydia and Herbert Collins. You may remember meeting them when Mary was so sick."

Dr. Spencer shook hands with the man. "I do. It's good to have you folks visit Willow Bend again."

Lydia Collins's eyes lit up when Daniel and Tave stepped to the street. She turned to her husband. "Herbert, you may not remember because you were so ill, but this is the young man who prayed with you in Montgomery."

Herbert clamped his hand on Daniel's. "I remember it well. It gave me so much peace. I'm sorry I'm so late in thanking you."

Daniel shook his head. "There's no need for thanks. I was glad I could help. I'm glad to see you recovered." He turned to Tave. "This is Dr. Spencer's daughter, Tave."

Mrs. Collins smiled. "Ah yes, the young woman you asked if I knew. I see you found her."

Daniel's face turned crimson. "Yes, ma'am, I did."

Dr. Spencer chuckled and patted Daniel on the back before he directed his attention to the Collinses. "How long are you folks planning on staying in Willow Bend?"

Reverend Somers and Mr. Collins glanced at each other, and Mr. Collins cleared his throat. "That depends on a few things. I wonder, Dr. Spencer, if you would allow my wife to visit with your daughter while Thomas and I have a few words inside with Mr. Luckett? Of course, you may join us if you wish."

A puzzled expression crossed Daniel's face, and he glanced at Tave, then her father. "You want to talk to me?"

"Yes. We have some things we'd like to discuss."

Dr. Spencer stepped back on the porch and opened the door. "Feel free to use my office. And Tave will entertain you, Mrs. Collins, but I'm not sure I should join you."

Daniel walked to Dr. Spencer. "I don't know what they want to say to me, but I'd like to have you with me. After all, you're the only father I've ever known."

Tave's heart thudded at the moisture her father blinked from his eyes before he turned and walked through the door.

"Then come on in, son. Let's see what these men want to talk to you about."

Chapter 16

Tave fidgeted in her chair and tried to concentrate on what Lydia Collins was saying, but her mind was on the conversation going on behind the closed door to her father's office. She wanted to get up and burst through the front door, but that would embarrass Daniel and her father. Difficult as it was, she was going to have to wait to find out what was being discussed inside.

She directed her attention back to Lydia, who continued speaking as if she hadn't noticed Tave's distraction. "I can't tell you how much we appreciated Daniel coming on board when we were in Montgomery. No one else wanted to come near us. They were afraid of catching yellow fever." She reached over and touched Tave's arm. "And Thomas tells us that you have been ill with it also."

"I have been, but I'm recovering. We lost a lot of friends during the epidemic, but we're thankful that it seems to be over now."

Tave glanced at the door, pushed up from her chair, and took a few steps toward it before she changed direction and went to stand at the edge of the steps. Lydia laughed and came to stand beside her.

"I know you're wondering what's going on, but I'm sure they'll be through soon. Then Daniel will tell you all about it."

Tave nodded and smiled. "Daniel and I are going to be married, you know."

Lydia's eyes lit up. "Thomas told us that. I'm very happy for you. Maybe you and Daniel will visit Herbert and me in Selma sometime."

"Maybe." Before she could say more, the door opened, and Reverend Somers and Lydia's husband stepped onto the porch. Daniel followed them outside and stuck out his hand. "I still can't believe what's just happened, but I promise I'll pray about it."

Reverend Somers shook Daniel's hand. "Let us know as soon as you reach a decision. Herbert and Lydia will be staying with me for a few days."

"I will."

Lydia took Tave's hand in hers. "It was so good to meet you. I hope we'll see more of each other in the future."

"I hope so, too."

Tave watched as the three guests walked down the steps and headed for the livery stable. She was about to ask Daniel what had happened when her father stepped onto the porch. "I think you two have a lot to talk about. I'll be in my office if you need me."

Daniel took her hand and led her back to the chairs. When they were seated, he faced her. "I can't believe what has just happened."

Tave didn't know whether to be scared or excited. She frowned and squeezed his hand. "If you don't tell me what's going on right now, Daniel Luckett, I'm going to start screaming."

He leaned back in the chair and laughed. "Reverend Somers has wanted to leave Willow Bend Church for a while, but he didn't know who could take over as pastor. He told Reverend Collins how I'd filled in, and Reverend Collins remembered me from our meeting in Montgomery. They want me to take Reverend Somers's place."

Tave's mouth gaped open. "They want you to be the pastor?"

He nodded. "Reverend Somers said that all the people really like me, and he thought they needed somebody young to take over."

"What did you say?"

Daniel shrugged. "Well, I told them I wasn't a real preacher. I'm not ordained. I just study the Bible, and I still have a lot to learn."

Tave scooted to the edge of her chair. "And?"

"And they said that didn't matter. They still learned something new from the Bible every day. I told them we were getting married in a few weeks, and they thought that would be perfect. Reverend Collins said if we'd come to Selma, he would plan an ordination service for me at his church. Then I could come back and start the work here. Reverend Somers said his house belongs to the church, and we can live there. He doesn't want to take all his furniture, and he'll leave some of it for us."

Tave stood up and pressed her hand to her forehead. "I can't believe this." She paced across the porch, turned, and retraced her steps. "A preacher? I never expected this." She stopped in front of him. "Did you give them an answer?"

He rose and took her hand. "I told them I'd pray about it, but I wanted to talk to you first and see what you thought."

His blue eyes stared at her, and she recalled the day he'd been shot and had looked up at her. She'd stared into the depths of his eyes and had somehow known God had great plans for him. She'd prayed for him, and God had proven her right by bringing them to this moment.

She cupped his face with her other hand. "I think you'll make a wonderful preacher."

He bit his lip. "But what about you? It won't be easy being the wife of a pastor."

She smiled. "I know, but if that's what God has planned for us, we'll make it fine."

He pulled her to him and hugged her then held her at arm's length and smiled. "I wish I knew where that gambler that shot me is right now. I'd sure like to shake his hand and thank him for doing me a favor. The day he shot me was the luckiest day of my life."

~

Daniel ran his finger around the inside rim of his shirt collar and then tugged at the tie knotted at his neck. He didn't know if it really was the hottest day of the year, or if he was perspiring because he was so nervous. Across the room, Dante Rinaldi leaned back in a chair and scraped underneath his fingernails with the tip of a pocketknife. He didn't appear hot at all.

Dante glanced up and grinned. "It won't be long now. The bride and her father should be arriving outside the church any minute."

Daniel rubbed the back of his neck and took a deep breath. "Is it hot in here to you?"

Dante laughed and stood up. "It's just nerves. I doubt if there ever was a man who wasn't nervous on his wedding day."

Daniel ran his hands down the front of the new suit he'd bought at Mr. Perkins's store. "Do I look all right?"

Dante slapped him on the back. "You look fine, but don't worry. Nobody's going to be looking at you. Everybody's eyes are going to be on Tave."

The thought made him smile, and he felt his face grow warm. "Yeah, I guess you're right. I think I am a little scared. A lot's happened to me in the past few weeks. I'm about to become the pastor of a church, and the most wonderful woman in the world is marrying me."

Dante nodded. "You remind me of how I felt when Savannah and I got married. I was scared to death that day. We didn't have any family, and I had to drive her to the church. All the way to her house, I was scared she'd changed her mind."

"But she didn't."

Dante's eyes grew wistful. "No, she didn't. And I thought I had to be the luckiest man in the world. Just like you feel today."

They both grew silent, and Daniel knew Dante had to be thinking of his wife just as Daniel was now thanking God for Tave. "Dante, I appreciate your standing up with me today. You're a good friend."

Dante smiled. "And so are you, Daniel. Of course from now on, I guess I'm going to have to be on my best behavior around you."

"Why?"

"Because you're going to be my pastor. I don't want to come to church and hear you preaching to me about all the bad things you see me doing."

A vision of standing in the pulpit and lashing out at the congregation over their sins flashed into Daniel's mind, and he laughed out loud. "Don't worry. I'm sure God just wants me to preach His Word."

"Sounds like you're going to make it fine, my friend."

The door opened, and Reverend Somers stepped into the room. "Well, Tave and her father are at the front door of the church. Are you ready to go meet your bride, Daniel?"

The heat he'd felt a few minutes earlier disappeared, and his spirit calmed. What he'd dreamed about and thought impossible was about to happen. Tave was going to be his wife. He breathed one more prayer of thanks and took a deep breath.

"I'm ready."

⌘

Her father crooked his arm and smiled down at Tave. She slipped her arm through his and gazed up at the dear man who had dedicated his life to caring for her. Soon she would be Daniel's wife, and perhaps someday she would be someone's mother. But in her heart, she would always be her father's little girl.

Tears flooded her eyes. "Oh, Poppa, I'm scared."

He smiled and patted her hand. "You shouldn't be. You're about to start a wonderful new life with a man who loves you very much, and you're going to be the wife of a preacher. How could I want any more for you?"

"But what about you? Who will take care of you?"

He chuckled. "Don't worry about me. I can take care of myself. Besides, it's not like you're moving off to the far side of the earth. You're going to be right outside of town. And you'll come to my office and help out some."

"I will." She tilted her head and stared up at him. "Do you think I did the right thing giving up my job at the school?"

"I think so. Daniel's going to need a wife to help him, and I know God's going to use you in a great way."

The church door opened, and Tad Thompson grinned at them from inside. "Miss Bonnie's about to start playing the pump organ, Miss Spencer. Are you ready?"

She nodded. "I am." She stood on tiptoes and kissed her father on the cheek. "I love you, Poppa."

He stared into her face, and a tear glistened in the corner of his eye. "I love you, too, darling. You look just like your mother today. I just wish she could be here to see you."

The first chords wheezed from the organ, and Tave and her father stepped to the door. At the end of the aisle, Daniel stood waiting for her.

⌘

Nothing could have prepared Daniel for the vision Tave presented as she walked down the aisle on the arm of her father. She wore her mother's wedding dress, and to him, she looked like a queen, just as Dr. Spencer had thought of his bride many years before.

Her gaze locked with his, and the assembled friends vanished from Daniel's vision. In the stillness of the church, he saw only her. His soul reached out to her in that moment, and he felt a bonding like he'd never known in his life. This was the woman God had chosen for him, and he would cherish her for the rest of his life.

Daniel's breath caught in his throat as they stopped beside him. He smiled at her before he directed his attention to Reverend Somers.

The pastor stepped forward and looked from Tave to her father. "Who gives this woman in marriage?"

"I do," Dr. Spencer replied. He leaned over, kissed Tave on the cheek, and placed her hand in Daniel's. With a smile on his face, he turned and walked to his seat on the front pew.

Tave's hand felt warm in his, and Daniel's pulse pounded. He wrapped his fingers around hers and directed his attention back to the pastor.

"Dearly beloved," Reverend Somers said.

Daniel heard the drone of the pastor's voice, but he could only concentrate on Tave next to him. He had little recollection of the responses he made to the questions asked, but from the shy smile Tave directed at him, he knew he answered.

Then with the final vow taken, Reverend Somers uttered the words that sent Daniel's heart soaring, "I now pronounce you man and wife."

Daniel and Tave turned to face the congregation, and she slipped her arm through his. They walked up the aisle, nodding to those on each side, and made their way to the door. Outside, Dante and Savannah waited in their buggy to drive them back to her father's house. There they would receive all their friends who'd come to share this day with them.

Daniel helped Tave into the backseat and climbed in beside her. Savannah reached back and squeezed Tave's hand. "It was a beautiful wedding. You look so happy."

Tave's eyes sparkled, and she gazed up at Daniel. "I've never been happier."

Daniel stared into his wife's eyes and marveled at how God had blessed him. He had left home after his mother's death and wandered for years. In all that time, he'd been consumed with hatred that threatened to destroy him. Tave and her father had shown him how to find peace through faith in God, and he had been blessed more than he would ever have thought possible.

He leaned over and whispered in his wife's ear, "I can still hardly believe it. We're married."

She grinned. "Yes we are, Mr. Luckett."

He pulled her close. "I love you, Mrs. Luckett."

Mrs. Luckett. No words had ever sounded sweeter to him.

❧

Tave stood on the balcony outside their room at the St. James Hotel and stared at the river that wound past. Two boys, their fishhooks in the water, sat on the bank not far upstream. They hadn't moved since she'd been watching them.

The door behind her opened, and she sensed Daniel's presence. He walked up behind her, circled her waist with his arms, and drew her back to rest against his chest. He bent forward and whispered in her ear, "What are you doing out here?"

His breath tickled her ear, and she smiled. "I'm looking at the river. I think it's so beautiful when the sun's going down and the last rays are reflecting off the surface."

He tightened his arms around her. "That's not the only beautiful thing I see out here."

She laughed and patted his hands. "I'll assume you're talking about me, so I'll take that as a compliment."

"You should." He rested his cheek against her, and they stared across the water.

She laid her head back against his chest. "I thought the ordination service was beautiful today. I was so proud of you. I shed a few tears when you addressed the group afterward. I know you're going to be a great pastor."

"We won't have a lot of money, but we'll be happy because God will take care of us. We'll always have what we need. I have faith that God will provide for us."

"I do, too." A thought flashed across her mind, and she laughed. "I just remembered something."

"What?"

"The day I first saw you, Savannah had driven me from the school to Poppa's office. We were talking about falling in love. I told her that sometimes my romantic side wished that I could meet a handsome young man who would sweep me off my feet, but I doubted that would ever happen. Less than five minutes later, I saw you for the first time."

He nuzzled her ear. "And what did you think?"

She laughed. "I gave you up for dead. But then you opened your eyes. When I stared into those blue eyes, it was as if God told me I had to save you. It was as if I knew God had great plans for you."

"For us, Tave." He kissed her hair. "We had a visitor while you were out here enjoying the scenery."

She turned in his arms to stare up at him. "Who?"

He released her, reached in his pocket, and drew out an embossed leather case. Her eyes grew wide with excitement. "My daguerreotype came."

He nodded and opened it. "What do you think?"

She took the picture in her hand and stared at the shiny portrait they'd had made the day before. She was seated in a chair, her wedding dress spread out and her hands clasped in her lap. Her chin trembled, and she fought to hold back the tears. "I look just like my mother."

"Since your father gave you the one of your mother, I think we need to put the two of them side by side on the mantel in our new home. What do you think?"

She threw her arms around his neck and drew him close. "Thank you, Daniel, for having this made for me. I love you so much."

"And I love you."

Downriver, a steamboat whistle sounded, and Daniel glanced at the river. "That sounds like the *Carrie Davis* coming upriver."

"I wonder if some of the passengers will stay here tonight."

"We'll soon know." He pulled out his pocket watch. "It's almost time to eat. Are you hungry?"

She closed the daguerreotype case and pressed her hands to her stomach. "I'm starved, Mr. Luckett."

He smiled, and her heart leaped at the love she saw in his eyes. "Good. There's a table waiting for us in the dining room." He crooked his arm and extended it to her. "Mrs. Luckett, it would be my honor to escort you to dinner at the St. James."

BLUES ALONG
THE RIVER

Dedication

This book is dedicated to the memory of my wonderful father, who bought me my first piano and started me on a lifelong appreciation for all types of music. I miss playing for you, Daddy.

Chapter 1

The whistle of the *Alabama Maiden* pierced the afternoon quiet. Victoria Turner stopped in her stroll along the deck of the steamboat and peered toward the riverbank to her right. Two boys, each holding a fishing pole, jumped up from the ground, grabbed the straw hats from their heads, and waved to the passing boat.

Victoria leaned against the railing and waved in return. The wake of the ship rippled across the surface of the Alabama River and washed across the boys' bare feet on the shore.

She turned to her mother, who had stopped beside her, and pointed toward the edge of the water. "Look, those boys are barefooted already, and it's only the first of May. They must be looking forward to summer."

Her mother laughed and waved to the boys. "The days are getting warmer. I always loved spring when I was growing up in central Alabama. This is the time of year when the farmers prepare their fields for planting. In fact, they may already have a lot of their cotton planted."

Victoria cast one more glance at the boys and let her gaze wander up the bluff behind them. The thick green leaves on the trees rustled in the warm breeze that blew from the river. The memory of the tall oak tree in their backyard in Mobile flashed in her mind, and she blinked back tears. She wished she could be sitting under it right now.

The azalea bush outside the parlor window in their house would be in full bloom by now. Each spring since she was a young child, she'd watched every day to get a glimpse of the first blossom to appear. This year someone else would enjoy the deep pink flowers she loved. She'd be living above a general store on the main street of a small river town, miles from the only world she'd ever known.

"Oh look, there's another one!" Her mother grabbed the steamship deck railing with one hand and pointed with the other to the top of the bluff and the white-columned plantation home that gleamed in the sunlight.

It was the third mansion they had seen on their journey upriver from Mobile to Willow Bend. Victoria's breath caught in her throat at the sight. "It's the most beautiful one yet," she whispered.

Victoria had never seen anything like it. Six colonnades towered across the front of the two-story house, and a cupola with a walkway around it sat on the roof. She could imagine a large veranda with a table and comfortable chairs for relaxing and sipping cool drinks on the rear of the house.

Her mother stared in the direction of the house and nodded. "I remember going to a dinner there when your father and I came to visit my brother years ago. The man who owned it was a friend of his. I don't remember his name, though."

"May I be of assistance to you ladies?"

Victoria glanced over her shoulder and smiled. "Captain Mills, I didn't hear you come up behind us."

The white beard and mustache that covered the man's face wiggled as his mouth curved into a friendly smile that he directed toward her mother. "I hope I didn't startle you, Mrs. Turner. I was coming along the deck and thought there might be some way I could be of help."

Victoria covered her mouth with the handkerchief she held to hide her smile. Ever since they had boarded the *Alabama Maiden* in Mobile, Captain Mills had been very attentive to her mother. Although she insisted that he treated all his passengers the same, her mother appeared to be enjoying the man's attention.

Victoria pointed to the plantation home on the bluff. "We were just admiring that beautiful house. Mama was a guest there once, but she's forgotten the owner's name."

Captain Mills stood straight with his shoulders back and his hands clasped behind his back. He nodded toward the towering mansion. "That's the big house of Pembrook Plantation."

Victoria stared at the imposing structure. A door in the center of the second floor opened onto a balcony that ran the length of the front of the house. She couldn't help but compare the mansion's size with the small house she and her mother had shared in Mobile. Theirs would probably fit in one corner of the structure. "With its size, it's no wonder they call it the big house."

Captain Mills chuckled. "No matter how large or small, the planters have always referred to the main plantation home as the big house. It doesn't have so much to do with size as it does the symbol of authority the house reflects. Pembrook's big house is indeed one of the most beautiful along the river. The former owner's name was Sebastian Raines. He died a few years ago, and now his son, Marcus, runs the plantation."

Her mother nodded. "Oh yes, I remember now. Mr. Raines and his son, who was a small child at the time, lived there when my brother took us for a visit." Her forehead wrinkled in thought. "That must have been at least twenty-five years ago."

Victoria studied the mansion as the steamboat plowed on through the Alabama River waters and left the big house of Pembrook behind. She wondered what it would be like to live in a house like that. There had to be servants who catered to the residents' needs. Not like the life she and her mother had lived in the year since her father's death. They had barely scraped by on the money Victoria had earned working in the kitchen of a boardinghouse in Mobile.

She glanced down at her red hands and curled her fingers into her palms. She'd scrubbed more pots and pans in the last year than she could count, but at least she'd been in Mobile, where there were lots of people, not in a small river landing town like Willow Bend in the middle of Alabama's Black Belt. There might be a lot of large plantations around, but her only hope of ever seeing the inside of one of those houses was if she ended up working in one of their kitchens.

"So you're going to live with your brother in Willow Bend?" Captain Mills's voice caught Victoria's attention.

"We are," her mother replied. "He lives above the general store he owns in Willow Bend. He has an extra bedroom that Victoria and I can share, and I'll keep house for him. Victoria will help out in the store when she's needed. I think we're going to enjoy living in a small town after the hustle and bustle of Mobile."

Victoria's heart sank at her mother's words. Her mother might look forward to life in Willow Bend, but Victoria couldn't imagine anything more depressing. She'd lived in the city all her life, and there was nothing that would make her like the little river town.

Her mother had told her she would probably meet some young women her own age at church. She didn't want new friends. No one could take the place of Margaret and Clara, who had been her friends ever since she could remember. The three of them had shared childhood secrets, and for the past few years their main topic of conversation had been the men they would marry. Now she was miles away from the friends who seemed more like sisters, and she'd never felt more alone.

She closed her eyes and tried to banish the vision that had occupied her mind ever since her mother announced they were going to live with her uncle. The years would drift by with her working in the town's general store, and before she knew it, she would be an old maid who no man would have an interest in marrying.

Captain Mills glanced in Victoria's direction. "Tell me, Miss Turner, have you visited Willow Bend before?"

"Once when I was a child. I remember the landing where the paddle wheelers docked and the main street that ran along the river bluff. My uncle's store faced the river, and there were a few more businesses. A livery stable, I think, but I don't remember the others."

Captain Mills laughed. "That's about all that's there now. The church and the school are on the outskirts of town."

Victoria's heart sank at the man's words. She'd hoped that Willow Bend had grown since she'd last visited, but it hadn't. She sighed. "It doesn't sound like there's much activity."

"Oh, on the contrary. The congregation at the church has really grown in the last few years. I hear it's because the people in the region have such respect for the pastor. His name is Daniel Luckett, and his wife's name is Tave. She's not much older than you, Miss Turner. She'll take you under her wing and introduce you to all the young people in the community."

For the first time since her journey to Willow Bend began, Victoria felt a sliver of hope. Maybe she would meet some people who could make her exile to Willow Bend more tolerable.

She glanced back downriver, but Pembrook's big house had disappeared from view. With a sigh, she pushed away from the railing. "How long before we dock?"

"About thirty minutes." Captain Mills turned back to her mother, and his gaze raked her face. "I hope you've enjoyed your trip upriver with us, Mrs. Turner. I'll have one of the deckhands take your luggage to your brother's store when we arrive. In the meantime, if you need anything, please let me know."

Her mother's face flushed. "Thank you, Captain Mills. You've been very attentive to our needs, and we appreciate it."

He bowed slightly, turned, and strode down the deck. Victoria watched him go before she looped her arm through her mother's and guided her back toward their cabin. "I think you've got an admirer, Mama, and I have to say I really like him."

Her mother waved a hand in dismissal. "Captain Mills is just being helpful. We'll probably never see him again after we leave the ship."

At their cabin door, Victoria glanced over her shoulder and caught a glimpse of the captain staring at them from the far end of the deck. When he saw her look at him, he whirled and disappeared around the end of the walkway to the other side of the ship. With a chuckle Victoria shook her head. "I wouldn't be too sure about that."

Her mother opened the door to the cabin and turned to direct a stern glare in Victoria's direction. "Quit teasing and come make sure you have everything in the trunk before we close it. We'll be landing at our new home in a few minutes."

Victoria paused in the doorway and winced. "Home? I doubt if I'll ever feel that way about Willow Bend."

Her mother's shoulders slumped as she sat on the edge of the bed. "Victoria, you know there was nothing else we could do. The small amount of money you made at that boardinghouse didn't start to cover our living expenses. We've used up everything your father left. We're fortunate my brother is willing to help us."

Victoria fought back the tears that threatened to fill her eyes. "I understand, and I promised I would make the best of the situation for your sake. But I want more out of life than being an unmarried woman living with my mother and uncle over the store where I work."

Her mother held out her hand. Victoria grasped it and sat beside her. "You're young, and it's natural you should worry about what life has in store for you. I was the same way when I was your age, but things worked out for me. I met your father, and one of these days you're going to meet a nice young man, too."

Victoria gave a snort of disgust. "In a little river town in the middle of Alabama? I doubt it."

Her mother smiled. "You never can tell what the future holds."

The boat's whistle rumbled, and Victoria pushed up from the bed. "We're almost there. We'd better get the trunk ready." She glanced at her mother, who still sat on the bed. "Don't worry, Mama. I'm thankful that Uncle Samuel is willing to offer us a place to live, and I've come with you. I've told you from the beginning, though, that I don't expect to be there long."

Her mother shook her head. "Ever since you were a child, you've been so impulsive. Be careful, darling. The things that look so good on the outside can sometimes contain the biggest flaws on the inside."

Victoria stared at her mother for a moment before she stepped to the trunk to prepare for her arrival in Willow Bend.

∽≈∾

Marcus Raines hopped down from the seat of the wagon the minute James Moses pulled the horses to a stop in front of Perkins General Store. He pulled the straw hat from his head and wiped at the perspiration on his forehead. The last month had been hotter than usual for this time of year, but that had been good. It had given him the time needed to get the fields ready for spring planting and some of the cotton in the ground. If his new purchases arrived on today's boat, the tenant farmers at Pembrook ought to have the entire cotton crop planted by the end of next week.

He squinted up at the young man who still sat on the wagon seat, the reins in his hands. James kept his gaze directed toward his feet and didn't move to wipe at the sweat that covered his chocolate-colored skin. Neither of them had spoken on the drive into town, and Marcus wondered what the young man, the son of one of his tenant farmers, was thinking. His facial expression gave no hint of what went on behind James's dark eyes, which never focused on Marcus.

But then, Marcus had no idea what any of the tenant farmers thought. The ones who'd been slaves before the war regarded him as if he was the enemy at times, and others appeared to tolerate him as the owner of the land they farmed. He wished he had a relationship with his tenant farmers like the one Dante Rinaldi had at Cottonwood, but he didn't know how to go about getting it.

Ever since his father's death, Marcus had tried to get his tenant farmers to treat him the same way they had his father, but it was no use. His father had ruled Pembrook with an iron hand, and he knew how to deal with the men who farmed his land. None of them ever approached his father unless they held their hat in their hand and spoke with respect. For some reason, he hadn't been able to teach Marcus the secret to wielding power on the large plantation.

Marcus had agonized over the problem for many sleepless nights, but a solution hadn't presented itself yet. Perhaps he was the one at fault, for he had never learned the art of conversation. As a child, he'd lived in isolation on the plantation with his father and had only known the tutors his father had hired to educate him. He'd never had a friend, and no woman had ever given him more than a passing glance. How he wished he could laugh and talk with his neighbors like Dante did, but he never felt as if he had anything worthwhile to add to the conversation.

With a sigh, Marcus walked away from the wagon and headed toward the landing where the paddle wheelers docked on their way up and down the river. The whistle of the *Alabama Maiden* pierced the air, and he smiled. He turned and called out to James. "The boat's coming around the bend. Go on down to the landing and be ready to help unload those cotton planters I ordered."

Without speaking, James set the wagon brake and climbed down. After tying the reins to a hitching post, he walked down the bluff to the landing.

Behind him, Marcus heard footsteps as the people of Willow Bend hurried to the landing intent on seeing the big ship dock at their little town. Fewer steamboats plowed the river now than when Marcus was a boy. Soon, he suspected, the railroad, with its faster means of transportation, would spell the doom of the beautiful ships he'd watched from the bluff in front of his home all his life.

"Good afternoon, Marcus. Are you meeting someone on the boat?"

Marcus turned at the sound of a man's voice beside him. Samuel Perkins, the owner of the general store, peered at him over the rims of the spectacles that rested on the bridge of his nose. Marcus shook his head. "No. I'm expecting some cotton planters that I ordered from Mobile."

Mr. Perkins shoved his hands in the pockets of his pants and rocked back on his heels. "Dante Rinaldi was in the store the other day. He said he bought some last year. Are yours like the ones he has?"

Marcus nodded. "They are. My father never would buy any. He said he liked to see men in the fields planting. But from what Dante says, a man using one of those plow-type cotton planters can plant eight acres of cotton in a day. Planting that much by hand takes at least ten to fifteen men."

Mr. Perkins cocked an eyebrow and stared at Marcus. "Your pa didn't like change. Wanted everything to stay the way it was. I'm glad to see you're trying to farm more efficiently. You listen to Dante. When he bought Cottonwood after the war, nobody around here thought he'd make it profitable again, but he did. Now it grows some of the best cotton and corn in Alabama. You're gonna do the same with Pembrook."

Marcus's face flushed. "I don't know about that."

"Well, it sounds to me like. . ." Mr. Perkins paused and pointed to the big ship that glided around the bend. "There she is. I guess they finally made it."

"They?" Marcus turned a questioning glance toward the man.

Mr. Perkins laughed. "Haven't you heard? I'm gaining two new family members today. My sister's husband died a year ago, and she and her daughter are arriving from Mobile to live with me. They've had a hard time since my brother-in-law's death."

Marcus hoped his face conveyed a sympathetic look as he turned to stare at the ship that eased up to the landing at the base of the bluff. He caught sight of James, who stood talking to Henry Walton, one of the tenant farmers from Cottonwood. Henry laughed at something James said and slapped him on the back.

Henry was one of the few white tenant farmers in the area, but he was accepted by all the others, some of whom had been former slaves. Marcus wondered about Henry's secret to having a good relationship with all the other farmers. Maybe sometime he'd get up his courage and ask the man.

"There they are!" Mr. Perkins's excited voice cut through Marcus's thoughts.

He glanced in the direction the store owner pointed and spotted two women standing at the railing of the deck. He knew there were two women because Mr. Perkins said so, but the vision of only one penetrated his mind.

She wore a blue traveling dress with a jacket that reached below her knees and a hat made of the same material as the coat. The ribbons dangling from the hat had been tied between her throat and ear on the left side of her face, and the jaunty bow rippled in the breeze. Dark hair stuck out from under the hat, and she stood on deck like a queen. He'd never seen anyone more beautiful in his life.

"Wh–what is your niece's name?" Marcus frowned at the stammer in his voice.

"Victoria. Victoria Turner." Mr. Perkins turned to him. "That's my sister, Ellen, beside her. I'll introduce you to them with they come ashore."

Marcus glanced at Mr. Perkins's sister before he let his gaze settle once again on the niece. *Victoria.* The name sent a tingle of pleasure through him. It sounded like it might belong to an angel.

As he watched, Victoria waved, and Marcus raised his hand to respond until he realized the greeting was for her uncle, not for him. Embarrassed and fearful someone had witnessed his blunder, he glanced around. No one appeared to be paying any attention to him.

The crew on the ship lowered the gangplank, and the passengers began to come ashore. He didn't move as he watched her follow her mother onto the bank and hurry up the bluff toward her uncle. When she reached Mr. Perkins, she waited while her mother and uncle embraced before she stepped forward and gave her uncle a quick hug.

"Uncle Samuel, it's so good to see you." The lilting drawl of her words made his pulse race.

Mr. Perkins pointed to him. "Ellen, Victoria, I'd like to introduce you to Mr. Marcus Raines of Pembrook Plantation. Mr. Raines, my sister and niece."

Marcus pulled off his hat and held it in front of him. "Mrs. Turner, your brother told me that you were coming here to live. I hope you enjoy Willow Bend."

She nodded. "I'm sure we will, Mr. Raines." She glanced at her daughter. "This is Victoria. I'm afraid she's not as happy as I am about our move to this small town."

Dark eyes bored into his soul when he turned back to the young woman. He swallowed and tried to speak. "Miss Turner, I'm sure you'll like living here. There are many young women who'll help make you feel at home."

She smiled, and his heart flipped. "Thank you, Mr. Raines. So you're the owner of Pembrook? We saw your house from the boat. Mama says she was a guest there years ago."

His eyes widened. "Is that right? Well, you must come again."

Victoria stepped closer to him. "Mama and I would love to meet your wife."

His face grew warm, and he gave a nervous laugh. "I'm afraid that won't be possible since I'm not married. But I'd still like for you to visit my home."

A smile curled her lips, and she tilted her head to one side. "We would be delighted."

At that moment, he caught sight of James and several deckhands bringing his cotton planters up the bluff. He backed away and put the hat back on his head. "I'm afraid I have to be going now. It was nice to meet you, Mrs. Turner. And you, too, Miss Turner."

He started to turn and head up the bluff, but she called out to him. "Captain Mills told us about the church and the pastor and his wife. Mama and I will be attending on Sunday. Maybe we'll see you there also."

Marcus stopped, uncertain what to say. His father hadn't been a believer and had never seen the need to take his son to church. Marcus had never been to the Willow Bend Church and had no idea what went on inside the building. A sudden thought struck him—he wanted to be there if Victoria Turner would be in the congregation.

He smiled. "I'll see you then."

The look of surprise on Mr. Perkins's face sent guilt flowing through him. Who was he trying to fool? He hadn't been brought up to be a churchgoer, and he had no desire to become one now.

A lot of pretty women lived along the river of west central Alabama, and he'd never given a thought to any of them. How could a woman he'd barely spoken with make him want to attend church when he'd never wanted to before?

He shook his head and hurried toward the wagon where James waited. Before he climbed in, he glanced over his shoulder. Victoria, her hand in the crook of her uncle's arm, glided across the street toward the store. She glanced in his direction, smiled, and gave a slight nod.

Marcus tipped his hat and climbed into the wagon. He didn't know what had happened to him today, but he did know one thing. There was no need to waste his time thinking about Victoria Turner. Their brief meeting at the dock would probably be the only conversation they'd ever have.

Chapter 2

Two mornings later, Victoria leaned against the sales counter in her uncle's store and blew at a stray strand of hair that dangled in front of her eyes. "Is it always this busy on Saturday mornings?"

Her uncle chuckled and picked up the bolt of cloth he'd cut some yardage from for a customer earlier and walked to the table where the dress goods were displayed. "Most folks around here try to get to town on Saturdays. If you think this morning's been busy, the afternoon will be worse. That's when the farmers load up their families and drive into town. By noon you'll see wagons and buggies tied up all along the main street, and children will run in and out of here all afternoon."

Victoria opened her mouth to express her apprehension, but a sudden thought struck her. Smiling, she turned to her uncle. "All the farmers? Do you think the owner of Pembrook will come?"

Her uncle lay the bolt down and shook his head. "I doubt it. Marcus Raines is a private person, a loner you might say. He hardly ever comes into town. If he needs something from the store, he sends Sally Moses. Her husband's a tenant farmer on Pembrook, and Sally is the housekeeper in the big house."

Disappointment surged through Victoria. She hadn't been able to get the man out of her mind ever since she'd met him the day she arrived, and she couldn't understand it. If she'd passed him on the street, she probably wouldn't have noticed him, although she had to admit he was quite handsome. That wasn't the only thing about him that appealed to her, though. He was also wealthy and unmarried.

But one thing about him puzzled her. There was a vulnerability that radiated from his deep blue eyes. Even the way he stood with his hat in his hand had given the image of someone unsure of himself. She couldn't imagine why he would feel that way. After all, he was the owner of a grand plantation.

With a sigh she picked up the feather duster from a shelf behind the sales counter. She was being silly trying to analyze a man she'd only seen once and might not see again for a long time if what Uncle Samuel said was true.

She turned to the display shelves along the wall and had taken one swipe with the duster when the bell above the front door jingled. She turned to see a young woman coming in the door.

Her uncle looked up from rearranging the bolts of cloth and smiled. "Good morning, Tave. I thought it was about time you came in. I can almost set my watch on Saturday mornings by your arrival."

The woman laughed and stopped next to him. "I'm a little late today. I had to go by my father's office." She glanced across the room and spied Victoria. A big smile curled her lips, and she hurried forward. "You must be Victoria. Your uncle has told me all about you. I'm Tave Luckett."

The name sounded familiar. Victoria searched her mind and then smiled. "You're the wife of the pastor at the church. Captain Mills told us about you and your husband when we were on the boat. We're looking forward to coming to church tomorrow."

Tave smiled. "Good. Everybody is excited to meet you and your mother. We want to make you feel welcome in Willow Bend."

For the first time since coming to Willow Bend, Victoria felt a sense of relief. Maybe it wasn't going to be as bad here as she had thought. If everyone was as friendly as Tave, there might be hope for finding some friendships in the small town.

"Are there any unmarried young women my age who live nearby?"

Tave thought for a minute. "We have a few. Becky Thompson isn't married yet, but she's engaged. Also Katherine Wainscott over at Oak Hill Plantation is still home with her parents." Tave's eyes lit up, and she glanced over her shoulder. "Mr. Perkins, I have an idea. We need to have some kind of gathering to introduce your sister and niece to all the people around here."

Victoria's heart pumped. "Oh, that sounds wonderful."

Her uncle walked back to where they stood and frowned. "No need to do that. They'll meet everybody soon enough."

The bewildered look on her uncle's face sent Victoria's hopes crashing down. Before she could say anything, Tave patted her uncle's arm and laughed. "Men usually don't understand a woman's need to make friends quickly. With the good weather we're having, everybody's been talking about how it's almost time for a dinner after church. We'll announce it at church tomorrow and have the dinner next week." She glanced back at Victoria. "How does that sound?"

"It sounds wonderful."

Tave nodded. "We can eat after church and spend the afternoon visiting. We don't get the opportunity to do that very often. And you can meet everybody from all the plantations and farms."

A thought struck Victoria. "I've already met one person who I hope will come."

"Who's that?"

"Marcus Raines. He was at the landing when Mama and I got off the boat."

Tave and her uncle exchanged quick glances. "I don't know if I'd count on that," Tave said.

Victoria felt her eyes grow wide. "Why not?"

"Marcus doesn't attend our church. My husband has tried to get him to come, but he won't. He keeps to himself and doesn't encourage friendships."

Victoria glanced at her uncle. "Why not, Uncle Samuel? Is there something wrong with him?"

Her uncle cleared his throat. "I've only had dealings with him in the store, and he's always been fair and paid his bills. But a lot of the farmers don't like him. They think he sees himself as better than they are."

Victoria shook her head. "I didn't think that at all when we met."

"I think he's just shy and unsure of himself," Tave added. "But it doesn't make any difference, because I doubt he would come."

"Maybe he would if your husband asked him again." Victoria hoped she didn't sound like she was pleading.

Tave shrugged. "I'll tell him to, but don't be disappointed if he doesn't show up."

The more she heard, the more her hopes that she would get to know the handsome owner of Pembrook were dashed. He was probably just being polite when he said she and her mother must visit his home sometime.

The bell over the door jingled, and the three of them turned to see who had entered. Victoria's breath caught in her throat at the sight of Marcus Raines standing just inside the door. He wasn't dressed in the work clothes he'd had on the last time she'd seen him. Today he wore a pair of high-cut black trousers that accented his small waist. A pair of suspenders stretched over his white shirt emphasized his broad shoulders. He pulled a wide-brimmed black felt hat from his head and held it in front of him.

His gaze flitted over the group before it came to rest on the store owner, who cleared his throat and stepped forward. "Marcus, what a surprise. I expected to see Sally today. She usually does your shopping."

Marcus nodded. "I know, but I told her I'd do it today." He took a deep breath before he fumbled in his pants pocket, pulled out a piece of paper, and held it out. "Here's the list of things I need."

Her uncle scanned the items. "Most of this stuff is in the storeroom. I'll get it for you. Victoria will help you with anything else you need."

As her uncle left the room, Victoria could only stare at the man she'd met a few days ago. He was even handsomer than she remembered. She finally managed a smile. "It's good to see you again, Mr. Raines."

He bit his lip and nodded before he glanced at Tave. "It's nice to see you, too. And you, Mrs. Luckett."

Tave smiled. "I just came in to meet Victoria." She sucked in her breath and frowned. "Oh, I left my list over at my father's office. I'll go get it and come back later." She turned to Victoria. "I'm glad you're living here, and I can hardly wait to get started on the plans for the church dinner."

When the door closed behind Tave, Marcus eased across the floor in Victoria's direction. "Mrs. Luckett's father is the town doctor. His name is Dr. Spencer."

"I didn't know that."

The brim of his hat curled as his fingers tightened on it. "Are you settled in your new home yet, Miss Turner?"

Victoria moved back behind the counter and smiled. "Almost." When he didn't say anything else, she placed her hands on the counter and leaned forward. "Is there something else I can help you with?"

He shook his head. "I don't think so." He licked his lips. "It's good to see you again."

"I'm glad to see you, too. Tave and I were just talking about you. She said you don't attend Willow Bend Church."

"I don't."

"Have you ever been?"

"No."

"Do you think you might not like it?"

He shrugged. "I suppose I've never thought about it much. My father didn't see the need of attending church, and I never have, either."

His words struck a warning in her heart. Her father had seen to it that she and her mother attended church every Sunday. Since her father's death, they hadn't gone as regularly, but her mother had already told her that the church in Willow Bend would be their best opportunity to socialize in the tiny community. If Victoria was to make friends, she'd find them there. "Maybe if you came, you'd find out differently. And you did tell me at the dock the day I arrived that you would see me at church."

His eyebrows arched, and a smile tugged at the corners of his mouth. "You're right. I really shouldn't go back on my word. So I suppose I'll see you tomorrow."

She smiled. "I'm glad. You know you're the first person I met here, and I hope we can be friends."

He shoved his hands in his pockets. "Maybe we can. I don't have many friends."

Victoria almost gasped aloud as she stared into Marcus's blue eyes. Loneliness flickered in their depths. "Then we have to do something about that. The church is going to have a dinner next Sunday to introduce my mother and me to the community. I hope you'll come then, too."

He hesitated a moment. "I don't know. . . ."

She held up a hand to silence him. "I won't take no for an answer."

His Adam's apple bobbed. "Do you want me to come, Miss Turner?"

Victoria arched an eyebrow. "Mr. Raines, did you not hear me say I hope you'll come? I wouldn't have said it if I hadn't meant it." Her mouth curled into a smile. "I expect to see you there."

"Then I'll be there, Miss Turner."

"Good." She inhaled. "Now one more thing. If we're going to be friends, I want you to call me Victoria. *Miss Turner* makes me sound like an old woman."

His gaze flitted over her. "You're certainly not old. If I'm to call you Victoria, then you must call me Marcus."

She smiled. "It's nice to have a friend in Willow Bend."

"I agree."

At that moment Victoria's uncle reappeared from the back of the store. "I have everything you need at the loading dock out back. You can pull your wagon around there, and I'll help you load it."

Marcus shook his head. "There's no need for that. James and I will get it." He turned toward Victoria. "It's good to see you, Victoria. I'm looking forward to church tomorrow and attending the dinner next Sunday."

"And I am, too, Marcus."

"You're coming to church tomorrow?" Her uncle's voice held a hint of surprise.

Marcus smiled. "Yes. Maybe it's time I got to know my neighbors better. I'll see you then." Without another word, he whirled and hurried toward the door.

When Marcus left the store, Victoria's uncle turned to stare at her with wide eyes. "That was quite a surprise."

A surge of energy shot through Victoria. She hadn't felt so happy in years. "I don't know why you and Tave think he's so strange. I like him very much."

Her uncle reached out and put a restraining hand on her arm. "I said that the other farmers feel he thinks he's better than they are. I doubt if anybody knows him well. That's what concerns me. You're a beautiful young woman, and I only want the best friends for you. Don't be swayed by the fact that he's wealthy. Make sure you choose friends who have the same beliefs your parents have instilled in you."

She laughed and patted her uncle's hand. "Don't worry. Besides Tave Luckett, he's the only person I've met in Willow Bend."

"I'm just telling you to be careful around Marcus."

"I will. Now I'm going to finish dusting before the afternoon customers get here."

She hurried across the room in order to distance herself from her uncle. His warning about Marcus lingered in her mind. Her father also had cautioned her many times about choosing friends who shared her belief in God. Even if Marcus had never attended church, that didn't mean he was an unbeliever. Perhaps her uncle's concerns were unfounded.

At the moment she didn't want to think about that. She wanted to recall how the handsome owner of Pembrook Plantation had stared at her. She didn't understand why Marcus Raines stirred her heart, but he did. He reminded her of a small boy who needed someone to offer comfort. From what, she didn't know, but she intended to find out.

⁂

Marcus Raines strode down the street toward the hitching post where he'd left James with the wagon. He clenched his fists as he walked and tried to make some sense out of what he'd just done. He'd never had any desire to attend church, and now he had committed to two Sundays and a dinner afterward.

When he'd gotten out of bed this morning, he'd known he couldn't wait until tomorrow to see Victoria Turner again. Sally Moses had looked surprised when he'd announced at breakfast that he would go to town in her place today. She hadn't tried to dissuade him. Instead, she had told him what she needed, and he'd made note of it.

All the way to town, he'd asked himself if he should have come. He'd almost backed out of stepping into that store, but when he opened the door and saw her standing there, he knew he'd made the right decision. She was even more beautiful than he remembered. He hadn't dared hope that he would get the opportunity to speak with her alone, but he had. He usually became tongue-tied when he talked with a young woman, but it hadn't been that way with Victoria. He had said more to her than any other woman he could remember.

Not only had they talked, but she had also invited him to a dinner in her honor. Then the best thing of all had happened. She had asked him to be her friend. When he answered her that he, too, was glad to have a friend in Willow Bend, he knew she had no idea what he meant. In truth, she was the first friend he'd ever had, and the thought made his heart pump.

The image of his father flashed in his mind and sent his good mood plummeting. His father had told him often enough that he should stay away from women. They couldn't be trusted. But there was something about Victoria that made Marcus question his father's words. He shared some kind of connection with the woman with the dark eyes. He doubted anything would ever come of it, though. When she got to know him better, she would find a reason to keep her distance from him.

Chapter 3

A s soon as the last prayer was said on Sunday morning, Marcus made a dash for the back door of the church, but he was too late. Pastor Daniel Luckett and his wife, Tave, had beaten him up the aisle. They must have quietly slipped to the back when the man in the front row was saying the benediction.

His plan had been to escape to the yard where his horse was tied and wait for Victoria and her family to come outside. Then he would go and speak to them, but the truth was that he was scared to death.

All through the sermon from three rows behind her, he had stared at the woman he hadn't been able to get out of his mind. He couldn't concentrate on what the preacher was saying for worrying that when he spoke to her after church, he wouldn't be able to carry on an intelligent conversation. What if she thought him dull and boring?

The crowd jostled him from behind, and he glanced around to see if there was another exit from the church, but it didn't matter. His retreat was blocked by people coming up the aisle behind him. Perspiration popped out on his head, and he pulled a handkerchief from his pocket to wipe it away. In front of him the pastor greeted his congregation with a smile and soft-spoken words.

It wasn't that he minded speaking to Reverend Luckett and his wife, but he didn't want anyone to make a fuss over the fact that he had come to church today. Maybe they would welcome him and let it go at that.

The pastor smiled and extended his hand as Marcus stopped in front of him. "Marcus," he said, "I've been praying for this day for a long time. It's so good to have you with us today."

Marcus grasped the man's hand. "Thank you."

"I hope you'll come again," Tave Luckett said before her gaze flitted over his shoulder.

Before he could respond, a voice behind him set his heart to pumping. "Not only did he come today, but he's coming next Sunday for the dinner."

Marcus turned and stared into Victoria Turner's face. His heart skipped a beat at how beautiful she looked today. He wanted to say something, but his mind had suddenly gone blank.

After a moment, Tave cleared her throat. "That's even more wonderful,

Marcus. We'll look forward to seeing you then."

Marcus pulled his attention back to the pastor and his wife. "Thank you."

Reverend Luckett smiled. "Have a good day, Marcus."

Marcus offered a weak smile before he hurried to the rack across the back wall of the church and grabbed his hat. On the porch, he took a deep breath and glanced around at the people climbing into buggies and wagons. No one appeared to be paying any attention to him, and he relaxed. He made it to the bottom of the steps before his escape was halted by a familiar voice.

"Marcus, don't rush off before I get a chance to welcome you to church."

He turned to see Dante Rinaldi, his young son in tow, coming around the corner of the building. Of all the planters in the area, Marcus liked and respected Dante most. The man had come to Willow Bend a few years after the war, bought Cottonwood Plantation when it was in ruins, and restored it to the grand plantation it once had been. Considered an interloper at first, he was now one of the most respected residents in the Black Belt.

Marcus placed his hat on his head and waited for Dante to approach. There was a quality about Dante Rinaldi that Marcus envied. He seemed so sure of himself, and in all the years he'd known him, Marcus had never seen him lose his temper. When Dante and his son stopped beside him, the man glanced down at the young boy who Marcus thought must be about six or seven years old. Dirt smudged the boy's face and pants, and his shirttail hung over the waist of his pants.

Dante grinned down at the boy. "I had to break up a misunderstanding, and I was afraid you'd be gone before I got back to the front of the church."

Marcus shook his head. "No, I was waiting to speak to Mr. Perkins and his family."

Dante's smile grew bigger. "I'm glad you came today, Marcus. I've told you that you need to get out and meet people. You've stayed cooped up on that plantation all your life. You need to see what goes on outside of Pembrook. I think going to church and meeting people is a good start for you." He glanced toward the front door of the church and nodded to his son. "You'd better watch out. Here comes your mother."

Savannah Rinaldi stepped from the church with Victoria beside her. As they came down the steps, Savannah smiled at Marcus. "Victoria and I were discussing the dinner next Sunday. She tells me that you—" Her eyes narrowed as she caught sight of her son. "Vance Rinaldi, have you been fighting again?"

The boy hung his head and dug his toe into the dirt. "Yes, Mama."

Savannah grabbed a handkerchief from her reticule, wet it with her tongue, and scrubbed at the boy's face. "What am I going to do with you?" When she'd rubbed most of the dirt away, she held him at arm's length and scowled. "Go get in the buggy and wait for us. Your father and I will deal with you when we get home." The boy ran toward the buggy, and Savannah turned back to Marcus. "I'm glad to see you at church, Marcus. Please come again. Now if all of you will excuse me, I think we need to get home—that is, if I can find my daughter."

When she'd hurried off in search of the girl, Dante turned to Marcus and Victoria. "I guess I'd better go. Have a nice afternoon."

Dante strode toward the buggy where a dejected Vance sat. "I'm afraid Vance is in trouble," Marcus said.

Victoria laughed. "I think you're right, but Savannah and Dante seem like nice people."

"Oh they are. My father met Dante soon after he came here. Most of the people didn't like him, and my father didn't for a long time. But he's a good man." Marcus watched Dante help his wife and daughter into the buggy and then pull out to the road. He'd always envied families that appeared happy, and Dante's family certainly did.

"What are you thinking?" Victoria's voice startled him.

He jerked his attention back to her. "Nothing." He let his gaze drift over her. "It's good to see you again, Victoria."

"It's good to see you, too. Thank you, Marcus."

He frowned. "For what?"

She smiled, and his heart raced. "For making me feel so welcome in Willow Bend. I really dreaded coming here. I didn't think I'd have any friends. Then I got off the boat, and you were standing there as if you'd come to welcome me. I knew we were going to be friends."

He wanted to respond, but the words wouldn't come, especially when he looked into Victoria's eyes. He silently berated himself.

Ducking his head, he nodded. "I have to be going. Maybe I'll see you this week."

Before she could respond, Marcus strode to where he'd tied his horse, mounted, and turned toward home. He glanced back at Victoria, who stared after him from the churchyard. She had seemed happy to see him, but he couldn't think of anything to say. Anger flared within him, and he dug his heels into the horse's side.

Dante was right. He needed to get out and meet people. When he was a boy, his father had company all the time, but Marcus had always been banished to the upstairs and not allowed to listen to adult conversation.

By the time he'd reached his teens, his father wasn't well, and company at Pembrook became a thing of the past. Even though his father suffered from poor health for years, he ran Pembrook as if he would always be there. When Father died, Marcus realized he hadn't been prepared for the responsibility he'd inherited. Ever since he'd become the master of the plantation, he'd struggled to find his way and keep the land productive.

Now a woman he'd met less than a week ago made him want something more than his lonely life at Pembrook. It surprised him that he had enjoyed being in the group of people at church today, especially with Dante Rinaldi. Best of all was that he'd gotten to speak to Victoria again. Maybe before too long, he could invite her and her mother to Pembrook. He wanted to show them what his father had created along the banks of the Alabama River, but most of all he wanted Victoria to like it.

His only hope was that she would never discover the secret that haunted him—he would never be able to measure up to his father as the master of a large plantation.

Late that afternoon Marcus pulled his horse to a stop in front of the big house at Cottonwood Plantation. He'd struggled with whether or not to ride to Dante's home ever since he'd gotten back to Pembrook from church. Finally, he had given up. He needed advice, and Dante was the only person he could ask.

He tied his horse to the hitching post at the side of the house and walked to the door. Before he had a chance to knock, a dog ran around the side of the house with Vance Rinaldi right behind. "Get back here, Jake." The boy stopped in his tracks when he spied Marcus.

Marcus smiled. "Hi, Vance. I came to see your pa. Is he home?"

Vance nodded. "Yes, sir. I'll go get him." Before Marcus could move out of the way, Vance darted in front of him, pushed the front door open, and ran inside. "Pa, there's somebody here to see you," he yelled.

"Vance, not so loud. Your father isn't deaf." Footsteps tapped on the wooden floor, and Savannah Rinaldi appeared in the house's entry. She smiled in greeting. "Marcus, it's so nice to see you again. Are you here to see Dante?"

Marcus hesitated on the porch before stepping into the house. What was he doing here? He should turn around and go home right away. When he didn't answer, Savannah directed a questioning gaze at him. Marcus swallowed and tried to smile. "I am."

She backed away from the door and motioned for him to enter. "Then come in. He's in the parlor. I'll show you the way."

He pulled the hat from his head and stepped inside the house. His gaze darted around the spacious entry and to the curving stairway that led to the second floor. "This is my first time in your home. It's beautiful."

"Thank you. I'm sorry you haven't visited us before. We must make sure you come more often in the future." Savannah glanced over her shoulder as she led the way into a room just off the hallway. "Dante," she said as they entered,

"Marcus Raines is here to see you."

Dante and his daughter sat facing each other at a small game table. A chessboard rested on the tabletop between them. Dante glanced up as Savannah spoke, and a smile lit his face. "Marcus, you're just in time to save me from having to concede defeat. It's embarrassing that a nine-year-old girl can beat her father at chess." He reached over and chucked the girl under her chin. "I shouldn't have taught you so well."

The girl giggled, and Marcus stopped, unsure if he should enter. "I'm sorry. I didn't mean to disturb you."

Dante pushed up from his chair and strode forward. "It's always good to see you. Come in and have a seat. Would you like something to drink? Some tea maybe?"

Marcus shook his head. "No, I wanted to speak with you for a moment. If you're busy, I can come back later."

The girl stood and came across the room. She looped her arm through her father's. Her dark eyes lit up with a smile. "Don't worry, Mr. Raines. Our games go on forever. We'll finish later."

Dante planted a kiss on his daughter's forehead. "Thanks, Gabby. Now go see if you can find your brother. I think your mother wanted to do something with the two of you this afternoon."

"Yes, I do. Come on, Gabby." Savannah held out her hand, and her gaze drifted over her daughter before it settled on Dante. A smile pulled at the corners of her mouth, and her eyes sparkled with a silent message meant only for her husband.

Dante smiled at Savannah and hugged their daughter again before he released her. "We'll finish our game later, darling."

When Gabby and Savannah had left the room, Marcus turned to Dante. "I'm sorry to intrude."

Dante laughed and led the way to a sofa in front of the marble fireplace. "I've told you many times that you're always welcome at Cottonwood. I'm glad you finally took me up on my invitation." A large ornate mirror with a gilt frame hung over the mantel, which held several daguerreotypes of Vance and Gabby. When Marcus had settled on the sofa, Dante eased into a chair facing him. "Now, is there a particular reason you've come this afternoon?"

The room felt stuffy, and Marcus wiped at the perspiration on his forehead with a handkerchief. "I. . .I need some help."

Dante leaned forward, a worried expression on his face. "What is it? Are you having problems at Pembrook?"

"No, nothing like that. It's. . ."

Dante frowned. "Go on. Tell me."

A large breath of air gushed from Marcus. "It's a woman."

"A woman? I don't understand." Dante's eyebrows arched.

Perspiration rolled down Marcus's cheeks. "Victoria Turner. I don't know what to do."

Understanding dawned in Dante's eyes, and he smiled. "Why, Marcus," he said, "I do believe you've come under the spell of a beautiful woman. Am I right?"

Marcus bit his lip and nodded. "Ever since I saw her get off the boat at the landing, I haven't been able to get her out of my mind. I've never had this feeling before, and it's disconcerting, to say the least."

Dante laughed. "But it's very normal. I felt the same way when I saw Savannah. I thought I would go mad from thinking about her."

Marcus scooted to the edge of the sofa. "You're the only one I felt comfortable talking to about this. That's why I've come. What do I do?"

"The question is, what do you want to do? Do you want to rid yourself of your obsession, or do you want to get to know her better?"

"I don't think I can rid my thoughts of her."

Dante laughed again. "Then you have to call on her, talk to her, see what you have in common."

Marcus stared at Dante. "Is that what you did before you married your wife?"

"No, our situation was quite different. I'll tell you about it sometime. But now I'm a father, and I'll tell you what I would want a young man to do if he was interested in my daughter."

"Good. That's what I need to know."

Dante took a deep breath. "You should go to Mr. Perkins and his sister and ask their permission to call on Victoria—that is, if the young woman wishes it. Then go to their home at night, sit in their parlor, and visit with them, get to know them, and let them see what an upstanding young man you are."

"Visit with them? Talk to them?" The thought scared Marcus. "I don't know how to do that."

Dante leaned back in his chair and studied Marcus. "Your father kept you at home too much. You've got to learn to be more open with people. You're going to find most of them are very nice. If you're kind to them, they'll return the favor. You're going to have to make yourself likable if you ever hope to win any young woman."

Marcus raked his hand through his hair. "I know that, but it terrifies me."

Dante reached over and slapped him on the knee. "Just think of the prize. Don't be afraid. You may find that Victoria will like you as much as you do her. But there is one more thing that I would advise you to do. It made all the difference in my relationship with Savannah."

"What's that?"

"Pray about it, Marcus. You should never enter into any kind of relationship without letting God lead you."

Marcus's eyes grew wide. "Pray? I don't know how to do that."

"It's not difficult. You close your eyes and talk to God."

"That sounds too easy. You close your eyes and talk to an empty room?"

Dante leaned forward. "The room isn't empty, Marcus. You heard Daniel speak about the love that God had for us when He sent His Son to be the Savior of all mankind. Before Jesus went back to heaven, He promised that even though He would no longer be walking the earth, He would still be with us. The Bible tells us that He will never leave or forsake us."

"How is that possible?"

"When you accept Jesus as your Savior, He comes into your heart and stays there. You can feel His presence all the time."

Marcus's mouth gaped open, and he swallowed before responding. "Are you saying that I'll feel Him inside me even though I can't see Him?"

"Yes. I feel God's presence in my life all the time, and He guides me in everything I attempt. I pray over every decision I make, whether it concerns my family or the tenant farmers who live on our land. You're a shy young man, Marcus, but God can make you bold and give you strength to face whatever comes your way."

"My father never had time for God, and I suppose I haven't, either."

Dante's eyes clouded. "I spoke to your father many times about accepting Christ, but he refused. I don't want that for you. All you have to do is believe, ask Him to come into your heart, and turn your life over to Him. When I was a boy, my father taught me a Bible verse that has stayed with me: 'For God so loved the world, that he gave his only begotten Son, that whosoever believeth in him should not perish, but have everlasting life.' I hope you'll think about that verse and come to believe in the power that Jesus has to make your life right."

Marcus pondered what Dante had said before he pushed to his feet and held out his hand. "Thank you, Dante, for talking with me today. I'll think about everything you've said."

"Good." Dante stood and grasped his hand. "Don't be a stranger around here. Come again. And I wish you well with Miss Turner. Let me know how things turn out."

Marcus shrugged. "I will, but there probably won't be anything to tell. She may not even want me to call on her."

"Don't sell yourself short. You have a lot of good qualities that you try to keep hidden from people. I happen to be able to see them."

Marcus's heart pumped at the kind words. He wished his father would have said something like that to him. "Thank you, Dante. Again, I'm sorry for interrupting your Sunday afternoon at home with family."

"Nonsense. We're glad you came."

A few minutes later, Marcus mounted his horse and nudged him onto the road that led away from Cottonwood. He glanced over his shoulder at Dante and Savannah's home. The house was beautiful, but no more so than the big house at Pembrook. There was one difference that he'd noticed from the moment Savannah Rinaldi appeared in the doorway.

Cottonwood's big house was a home. Dante, Savannah, and their children loved each other. For the first time in his life, he realized what a home should be.

Pembrook had never had what he'd experienced during his short visit at Cottonwood. The only way his house would ever be a home was if love lived inside it.

He closed his eyes and envisioned walking to the front door of Pembrook and having it opened by Victoria. His blood raced through his veins at the thought. He opened his eyes, and the feeling subsided.

What was he thinking? There was no way a woman like Victoria Turner would ever be interested in him. No matter how much he longed to have a woman look at him the way Savannah had looked at Dante, he knew it wouldn't happen. His father had told him that often enough. He was destined to end up like his father—a lonely old man living in a big house with no one who loved him.

Chapter 4

Victoria sat on the sofa in the small parlor of the quarters above her uncle's store. She glanced around and wondered how he'd been able to live in such cramped quarters all these years. He'd built the store five years before the war broke out and had brought his bride there to live with him until he made enough money to build a larger house. When she died two years later, he couldn't bring himself to move anywhere else. So he'd stayed on, connected to his work every hour of the day.

A stairway in the back room of the store made the upper level accessible when he was working. For after-hours visitors, a steep staircase on the back of the building led to a small landing and another entrance into the area.

When her mother first told her they would be living above the store, she had imagined the living area to be small, but she'd had no idea how little space there would be. The one good thing about their accommodations, however, was the fact that the kitchen was quite large. Her mother had been right at home in it from the moment they arrived, and the meals they'd shared around the big oak table in the middle of the room had been pleasant.

The small bedroom where she and her mother slept was quite a different story. A bed, a dresser, and an armoire they shared for storing their clothing crowded the floor space and left little room for them to navigate around each other. To make matters worse, the warm weather for the past few days had made the room quite stuffy, but the cool breeze that blew from the river through the open window had been refreshing at times.

There was no doubt about it. Victoria had no desire to spend the rest of her life living over Uncle Samuel's store.

Sighing, she directed her attention back to the book in her lap. With Uncle Samuel living alone, he'd spent much of his time reading, and his assortment of books had kept her entertained for the past few days.

This Sunday afternoon, though, she couldn't concentrate on the story she'd been reading. Her thoughts kept returning to Marcus Raines and how glad she was to see him at church. With everyone speaking to her after the sermon, she'd been delayed in leaving the building. She'd worried that he might already have left. When she saw him talking with Savannah's husband, she'd breathed a sigh of relief.

She couldn't understand why he hurried away so quickly. Most young men she knew in Mobile would have stayed longer and talked, but he seemed eager to be gone. He said he would come to the dinner after church next week, and she hoped he would. With another sigh, she picked her book up again and stared at the page where she'd stopped reading.

A knock at the outside door startled her, and she glanced up at her uncle and mother who sat in chairs facing her. Frowning, Uncle Samuel pushed to his feet. "Who could that be? I don't get many visitors on a Sunday afternoon."

Her uncle walked from the room and into the small hallway that led to the door. She listened as the door opened. "Marcus," Uncle Samuel said, "come in."

Startled at her uncle's greeting, Victoria sat up straight and tensed.

"I don't want to interrupt if you're busy." She could barely hear Marcus's words.

"Do you need something from the store?" her uncle asked.

"No, sir. I'd like to speak with you and Mrs. Turner if I may."

Victoria's heart pounded in her chest. She glanced at her mother, who directed a questioning stare at Victoria. Uncle Samuel walked into the room with Marcus right behind him. Marcus came to an abrupt stop when he saw her sitting there. She smiled, and he moved into the room.

He turned to her mother. "Good afternoon, Mrs. Turner. I hope I haven't inconvenienced you by coming unannounced."

She shook her head. "Not at all, Mr. Raines. I heard you tell my brother you wanted to talk with us." She pointed to the chair where Uncle Samuel had been sitting a few minutes before. "Please have a seat."

"Thank you."

Her mother turned back to her. "Victoria, perhaps you should leave us alone."

Marcus had started to sit in the chair, but he bolted upright. "No, please. I'd like for Victoria to stay."

Her mother glanced at Uncle Samuel. "Very well."

Uncle Samuel took a seat on the sofa next to Victoria. "Is something wrong, Marcus? I'm afraid I don't understand why you need to speak with us."

Marcus's blue eyes flickered over Victoria's face, and in their depths she could sense his fear. His whole demeanor suggested he might rush from the room at any moment. The muscle in his jaw twitched, and perspiration rolled down his face. He swallowed, and his Adam's apple bobbed.

"Mr. Perkins, Mrs. Turner," he began, "I'm not very good at making speeches. I don't know any way to say what I've come for than to tell you right out. I want to ask your permission to call on Victoria." His face turned crimson, and he gazed at her. "That is, if Victoria is agreeable to the idea."

Victoria's breath caught in her throat. Her eyes grew wide, and she stared at Marcus. Her uncle cleared his throat and glanced at her mother, then at her. "I appreciate the fact that you've included me in this request, but I feel like my sister and Victoria are the ones who should make the decision." He swiveled in his seat to face her. "How do you feel about what Marcus asked, Victoria?"

"It makes me very happy. I would be honored to have Marcus call on me." She stared at her mother. "Is it all right with you?"

Her mother clasped her hands in her lap and glanced at Uncle Samuel, who gave a slight shrug. "My brother tells me you're a very hardworking young man, Mr. Raines. You own one of the largest plantations in the area, but you seem to have few friends. Is this true?"

Marcus nodded. "I've lived all of my life at Pembrook, but I can assure you I'm trustworthy. And I will treat your daughter with respect."

Uncle Samuel gave an almost imperceptible nod, and her mother sank back against the cushion of the chair. "Very well, then. We give our permission for you to call on Victoria."

The smile he directed at Victoria sent ripples of pleasure floating through her body. The handsome owner of Pembrook wanted to call on her. From what she understood from Tave and Savannah, he had never shown any interest in anyone before, and now he promised her mother he would respect her.

Marcus rose from his chair and smiled at her mother. "Thank you, Mrs. Turner. I'll look forward to visiting with all of you one night this week. Tuesday, if that's all right."

"That will be fine. Victoria," her mother said, "it appears Marcus is leaving. Why don't you walk him to the door?"

His gaze followed her as she rose and brushed past him. "I'll show you out, Marcus."

She led the way to the door, opened it, and stepped back. "Thank you for coming, Marcus. You've made me very happy today."

"Have I? You may be disappointed when you get to know me better." His forehead wrinkled, and the sadness she'd seen in his eyes before returned. "I'm not like the young men you probably knew in Mobile."

She laughed. "Thank goodness for that. I'm glad you're who you are."

"I'll try not to disappoint you, Victoria." He stepped onto the landing at the top of the staircase and turned back to her. "Good day."

"Good day, Marcus. I'll expect to see you Tuesday night."

He nodded, turned, and headed down the stairs.

Victoria watched until he'd disappeared around the corner of the store before she closed the door. She stood in the hallway with her hand on the knob and thought about what had just happened.

In her wildest dreams she never would have thought a wealthy planter and owner of one of the largest plantations in the area would be interested in her. Yet he was. Marcus Raines might be shy, but he liked her. And the truth of the matter was that she liked him, too.

On Tuesday night, Marcus stared at Victoria from his seat in the same chair where he'd sat on Sunday afternoon. It felt like a repeat of their previous visit, with everyone seated as if they'd been assigned specific places. Perspiration trickled down the small of his back, and he ran his finger around the inside of his shirt collar. He hadn't thought the evening that warm until he'd entered the parlor and stared into Victoria's dark eyes.

Once again he tried to determine what it was about her that fascinated him. She was beautiful, to be sure, but there was something more. Perhaps it was the lilting quality of her voice that made his heart quicken, or it could be the elegance and grace with which she moved. Whether or not he ever discovered the mystery of her hold on him, he knew he would never feel about anyone else the way he did about her. From the first moment she'd directed her sultry stare at him, he knew he was powerless to fight his attraction.

Out of the corner of his eye, he saw her mother reach toward the table beside her where a tray with a tea service rested. She glanced at his empty cup. "More tea?"

He shook his head and handed her the cup and saucer he'd drained within seconds of its being offered. "No thank you. That was delicious."

Her mother collected the other cups and stood. "I'll take the tray into the kitchen if everyone is finished."

Marcus jumped to his feet. "Allow me to carry it for you."

She shook her head. "There's no need for that. Samuel can help me."

Mr. Perkins stood up, his eyes wide. "Of course."

As they disappeared out the door, Marcus glanced at Victoria and swallowed the panic that roiled in his stomach. "It—it's good to see you again, Miss Turner."

She frowned and picked up a fan that lay beside her in the chair. She snapped the ribbing of the fan open in front of her face and peered over its semicircular top. Her dark eyes bored into his. "I thought we'd agreed to call each other by our first names."

His throat constricted. "W—we d—did. I'm sorry, Victoria."

She lowered the fan and smiled. "That's better, Marcus. She inclined her head in the direction of the kitchen. "You know they went to the kitchen so that we could visit without them in the room."

He darted a glance toward the door and back to her. "I didn't think about them leaving us alone."

Victoria tilted her head to one side and smiled. "You are so serious and so formal. How am I ever going to get you to relax and just talk with me?"

He exhaled. "I haven't had much practice talking with a woman."

"Are you scared of women, Marcus?"

"I've never given it much thought. I don't know that many women."

She studied him for a moment. "Then maybe you're afraid of me."

His gaze drifted over her face, and in that moment he knew she wasn't the one who scared him. He shook his head. "It's not you. It's myself that I fear the most."

Her eyes grew wide. "But why?"

"I grew up at Pembrook with my father. The only women around were the wives of the tenant farmers, and I didn't know any of them well. So sitting here talking with you is a new experience for me. I want to do everything I can to impress you and make you like me, but I'm afraid I'll fail."

"And what makes you think that?"

He scooted to the edge of his chair and clasped his hands between his knees. "Even though I've lived at Pembrook all my life, I feel like an outsider in the community. Dante Rinaldi is the only man who's ever talked to me—besides the preacher, that is. Every time I see him, he invites me to church. I think he was shocked I came last Sunday."

"I'm glad you came, too. But it doesn't matter what other people think about you. I make up my mind about my friends based on how I feel. I like you, Marcus."

"You do now, but if you change your mind, I'll understand. You see, we've had very different lives. You've lost your father, but you have a wonderful mother. I can tell how much love there is between the two of you by the way you look at each other. I never knew my mother. My father met and married her when he visited Boston and brought her back to Pembrook. She hated life in Alabama almost as much as she disliked being a mother. She deserted us right before the war and returned to her family. I never heard from her again."

A small frown pulled at her eyebrows. "I'm so sorry. That must have been very hard for you."

"It was. My father saw that I had the best tutors, but they were paid to be nice to me. They really didn't care about me. No one has ever asked me to be their friend until you did. The truth is, I don't know much about friendships or how to talk with people. Especially with a beautiful young woman."

Her mouth curled into a smile. "Do you think I'm beautiful, Marcus?"

He couldn't tear his gaze away from her lips. "You're the most beautiful woman I've ever seen. You're young and full of life, not at all like me. I've inherited a plantation that I'm trying to run like my father did, and I spend all my time thinking about cotton and corn crops. You must have had interesting friends in Mobile."

"I did have a lot of friends. Two of them, Margaret and Clara, were more like sisters. Not only did we attend church together, but we also lived on the same street. I didn't want to leave them."

Marcus hesitated before he asked the question that had been on his mind for days. "Was there also a special gentleman friend you didn't want to leave?"

A smile pulled at her lips. "No, Marcus. There was no man in my life."

Her words made his heart beat faster. "I hope living in Willow Bend won't be too much of a disappointment for you. I'm sure you'll make all kinds of friends soon."

"All the way up the river I tried to think of some way I could get back to Mobile. Then I saw something that excited me."

"What was it?"

"Pembrook. It took my breath away when I spied that beautiful house on the bluff. I wondered about the people who lived there. Then we arrived in Willow Bend, and you were on the dock. It was almost like you were waiting for me to arrive. I knew right away we were going to be great friends."

Her long lashes fell over the dark eyes that stirred his heart, and he leaned back in his chair. She was right. Without knowing it, he had been waiting for her to arrive and had been for years. Now that he had found her, he wasn't going to give her up.

Chapter 5

On Sunday when the final "Amen" was said, Marcus waited at the back pew in hopes of speaking with Victoria as she left the church. Tom Jackson nodded as he and his wife passed by. "Good to see you today, Marcus."

"Thank you," he mumbled and directed his attention back to Victoria walking up the aisle toward him.

She smiled at him as she approached and stopped beside him. "I'm glad you're here, Marcus."

Several women clustered together in a pew near the front of the sanctuary. They held their fans in front of their mouths as they talked, but they didn't take their eyes off him. He felt sure he was the topic of conversation with many of the churchgoers today.

"My presence seems to have stirred quite a bit of interest today."

"I'm sure everyone's happy you're here." She glanced to the foyer where the pastor and his wife stood. "Let's go speak to the Lucketts; then you can walk me out to the picnic grove where the ladies are getting the food ready."

Reverend Luckett's face broke into a smile when they approached. "Marcus, I can't tell you how pleased I am. You've been here two Sundays in a row." His eyes twinkled as he glanced at Victoria. "If you'd moved to Willow Bend a long time ago, Marcus might already be a member of our church."

Victoria laughed and gazed up at him. "We'll have to work on him harder now, I suppose."

She cast a glance at him, and he followed her out the church and down the front steps. When they reached the bottom, he stopped. "Were you serious about our walking together to the picnic area?"

With a sigh, she opened the white lace parasol in her hand and raised it to shade her face. "Marcus Raines, for a man who runs a large plantation, you act like a scared schoolboy. In the last week, you've been to my home three times counting your visit last Sunday. I think that makes it official that you're calling on me. Now don't you think the next step is to let the good people of Willow Bend in on the news?"

He couldn't help laughing. His heart felt lighter than it had in years. "Oh Victoria," he said, "you're the most delightful woman I've ever known."

She held her hand at her waist and gave a quick curtsy. "Thank you, kind sir.

And may I say that you're the most fascinating man I've ever known."

He could hardly believe what she'd said. He threw his shoulders back and puffed out his chest. "Then let's go see what the good ladies have fixed for us to eat today."

They walked toward the tables that had been set up under the trees in the churchyard. He spotted Dante Rinaldi sitting on the ground, surrounded by a group of children. He handed a kite to his son, Vance, and the boys jumped up and ran off. Dante stood and joined one of the groups of men scattered across the yard. With the exception of his encounters with Dante, Marcus had had very few conversations with any of the men. Imbeciles, his father had called most of the planters in the area—except Dante. There was a quality in the man that demanded respect, and even his father had recognized that.

Marcus glanced at the woman beside him. He didn't want to think about his father today or the mother he'd never known. He wanted to concentrate on Victoria and the hold she already had on his heart. She was like a breath of fresh air that had entered his life, and he wanted to enjoy every minute he was with her.

⤛⤜

"I see Dante and Marcus have settled under that tree where I spread out some quilts. Let's go join them." Savannah didn't wait for Victoria to answer but led the way toward where the men sat.

Victoria's skirts skimmed the surface of the grass as she followed Savannah to the spot. She had waited with her food until Savannah had finished helping serve all the children, who were the last to line up at the tables. Now she looked forward to getting to know the woman who had welcomed her into the community.

The men jumped to their feet as Savannah and Victoria approached. Dante took his wife's plate and waited for her to sit and settle her skirts before he handed the food to her. Victoria tried to hide her amused smile as Marcus studied Dante's movements before he turned to her and took her plate in his hands.

When she was seated on the ground, Marcus dropped down beside her and handed her the food. He'd taken off the black coat he'd worn to church and rolled up the sleeves of his white shirt.

Even when she'd met him on the docks, she'd detected a formality in his manner, and she had seen it during his visits to see her. Today he appeared more relaxed. He seemed to really be enjoying himself, and it made her happy.

Dante shoveled another forkful of potatoes in his mouth, chewed, and swallowed. "This is mighty fine eating. We ought to have dinner every Sunday after church."

Savannah chuckled and raised her eyebrows. "You wouldn't think so if you had to cook."

He leaned closer to his wife and patted her hand. "Why would I want to when I have the best cook in the county living in my house?"

Savannah sniffed and sat up straighter. "Mamie doesn't live in our house."

Dante threw back his head and roared with laughter. "No, she doesn't. I was talking about you, but I forgot who taught you how to cook."

Victoria smiled at the exchange between the two and turned to Savannah. "Who is Mamie?"

"She and her husband were slaves at Cottonwood," Savannah said. "Even after they were freed and my parents had died, they wouldn't leave me. When Dante bought Cottonwood, Mamie's husband, Saul, became the first tenant farmer. Mamie has been my second mother all my life, and now she's getting older. But she can still cook better than anyone else in the county."

Dante nodded. "She sure can. I'm fortunate that Savannah learned from her." He leaned closer and whispered in a loud voice to Marcus, "Sometimes I slip off to Saul and Mamie's house just so I can sit down and eat with them."

Savannah laughed and glanced at Victoria. "He thinks it's a secret, but I've always known it."

Victoria turned to Marcus, who'd sat wide-eyed through the exchange between the couple. "Who cooks for you at Pembrook?"

Surprise flashed on his face, and he glanced around at those who stared at him. "S–Sally M–Moses," he stammered.

Dante nodded. "Oh, I know who that is. She's the wife of Ben Moses. Her son, James, is a friend of Henry Walton, who lives at Cottonwood."

Marcus frowned. "I've never understood how they can be friends. Henry's white, and James. . ."

"Isn't," Dante finished for him. "At Cottonwood we look at each other as equals. The color of a person's skin doesn't matter to us. We work together to make all our lives better."

"I see," Marcus said and directed his attention back to his plate.

"Uh-oh," Dante moaned and jumped to his feet. "Savannah, it looks like our son is engaged in battle again. We'd better go break up his fight before somebody gets hurt."

Savannah jumped to her feet and hurried toward a group of boys who minutes before had been playing together. Now Vance and another boy rolled and tumbled on the ground.

Victoria laughed. "Poor Vance. I think he's in for it now."

"I think you're right." Marcus chuckled.

They watched as Savannah and Dante pulled Vance off the boy and marched him toward the church. When they'd disappeared around the back of the building, Victoria leaned forward. "Are you having a good time, Marcus?"

He shrugged. "I guess."

The answer made her gasp. She had expected him to say that spending time with her was always fun, but he hadn't. "Aren't you happy to be with me today?"

He set his plate down and nodded. "Of course I am. I was just thinking about what Dante said about the tenant farmers at Pembrook. He acts like they're almost family. I've never known anyone who felt that way."

Victoria waved her hand in dismissal. "Don't think about things like tenant farmers and crops today. I want us to have some fun. You're always so serious. I want to hear you laugh and tell me what a good time you're having."

"I always have a good time with you, Victoria."

"Then you might show it by relaxing a little."

He smiled. "I thought I was relaxed."

She tilted her head and studied him. "No, I think your problem is that you don't laugh enough."

"I'm a serious person, but I do laugh when something's funny." He pushed his plate aside. "I'll give you a challenge. Make me laugh."

She chewed on her lip for a moment before her mouth pulled into a grin. "I could tell you about some of my adventures when I was a child, but you might decide not to call on me anymore."

"Were you a mischievous little girl?" He cocked an eyebrow at her.

"Oh, worse than that." She looked over her shoulder, leaned toward him, and whispered, "I was horrid."

A tiny smile pulled at his lips. "I can't believe that."

"Oh, but I was. For instance, one time my mother sent me out to gather the eggs from the henhouse. I started back inside with a basketful, but for some unknown reason I walked behind the henhouse, took an egg from the basket, and threw it against the back of the building. I watched the yolk and the whites of the egg trickle down the wood, and it amazed me how slowly they moved. So I threw another one to see if its contents would move faster. Then another and another until every egg in the basket lay broken on the ground."

He chuckled. "I'll bet your mother didn't like that."

"No, she didn't. But she wasn't as upset as she was the time I threw a broken plate at her best friend's son, who was five years older than me."

Marcus's eyes grew wide. "Was he hurt?"

Victoria grinned. "I thought he looked good with a two-inch gash over his eyebrow."

A soft laugh rumbled in Marcus's throat.

"But I suppose the worst thing I ever did happened when my parents and I visited Uncle Samuel when I was about six years old. I was bored and wanted to go home. I'd been whining all day, and my mother was about to lose her patience.

Finally, I told her if they weren't going to take me to Mobile, I would go on my own. She told me she was going to spank me if I didn't quit nagging. I went in the bedroom, crawled under the bed, and hid."

"What happened?"

"They missed me and started looking. I heard them calling, but I didn't say a word. After they checked the bedroom and didn't see me, they went back to the store to look for me. I fell asleep. When they couldn't find me, my mother became upset. She was afraid I'd run away. Then she began to think things like I'd fallen in the river and drowned. The whole town turned out to look for me. When I woke up and crawled out from under that bed, they were so glad to see me. That is, until they realized I'd been hiding."

"And?"

"And my father gave me the worst spanking of my life. I never pulled that trick again."

Marcus threw back his head and laughed. "Oh Victoria. You are the most interesting woman I've ever known. I don't think anyone's made me feel this good in my whole life."

Victoria watched him for a moment before she spoke. "Maybe it's good I've told you these things, Marcus. My mother has always told me I'm too impulsive. I do things and think about the consequences later. You may not like that in a woman."

His hand inched across the quilt, and she slid hers toward it until their fingertips touched. "I like everything about you. Don't ever change. You make me happy."

She glanced across the yard and saw Savannah and Dante returning. She jerked her hand away, picked up her plate, and took a bite. He did the same, but Victoria noticed that he smiled as he ate. She hoped what he said about her making him happy was true, because she'd been happier than she could ever remember since meeting Marcus. She could hardly wait to see where their relationship would take them.

❧

An hour later with all the food eaten and the dishes cleared away, the congregation drifted into groups across the picnic grove to spend an afternoon visiting. Marcus and Dante had left the tree where they'd been sitting while Victoria and Savannah helped clear the tables. She caught sight of Marcus standing next to Dante in a group of men beside the church. At times a loud voice would erupt from within the circle, but she couldn't make out what was being said.

Seated on a quilt again, Victoria placed her arms behind her, flattened her palms, and leaned back. "What do you suppose those men are talking about?"

Savannah chuckled and smoothed her skirts. "The main topic of conversation around here is the weather. Our crops depend on whether we get too much or not enough rain. We can't control it, so we talk about it."

Victoria studied Marcus, who appeared to be taking in everything that was being said. She didn't see him participate in the exchange, and she wondered why. She smiled at Savannah. "Life in a farming community is so new to me. It may take me some time to get used to it, but today has been a great start. I can't thank you and Tave enough for planning this outing so I could meet everyone."

Savannah stared past Victoria's shoulder. "Speaking of Tave, here she comes now." Savannah patted the empty spot on the quilt beside her. "Come and join us."

Tave dropped onto the quilt and sighed. "I don't mind if I do. Martha Thompson caught me just as I was about to come over here. I thought I'd never get away from her."

Victoria narrowed her eyes and stared at the women seated in chairs near the tables where the food had been earlier. She tried to remember which one was Martha, but it was no use. Remembering all of their names had proven to be a bigger task than she thought.

Victoria frowned and turned back to Tave. "Is something wrong with Martha that makes you dislike her?"

Savannah grinned and leaned closer to Victoria. "Now don't misunderstand. We love Martha. She is always the first to be there when someone is in need. But sometimes it seems like she may have an ulterior motive."

"What?" Victoria asked.

Tave sighed. "She wants to be the first one to get all the facts about everyone's personal business."

"Oh," Victoria said, "she's the town gossip. Did she want you to tell her something today? Is that why you couldn't get away from her?"

Tave nodded. "I'm afraid she didn't want to know anything different than what every other woman here today is dying to find out."

"And what's that?"

Tave glanced at Savannah. "What in the world have you done to get Marcus Raines interested in you?"

The question stunned Victoria, and she stared at her two new friends. "I have no idea what you're talking about."

Savannah arched her eyebrows. "Come now, Victoria. Marcus is almost a recluse out at Pembrook. His whole life revolves around that plantation. He hardly ever comes to town, and when he does, he completes his business and hurries home. He doesn't accept invitations, and he doesn't extend any. All of a sudden, you show up in Willow Bend, and Marcus is a different person."

"How is he different?"

Tave scooted closer to her. "Daniel has been the pastor at the church for nearly three years now. He's prayed for Marcus ever since he's known him and invited him to church every time he's seen him, but he never would come. You arrive, and he's attended for the last two Sundays."

"Not only that," Savannah added, "but he came to Cottonwood last Sunday to talk to Dante. He wanted to know what he should do to get to know you better. Dante advised him to speak with your mother and uncle and ask their permission to call on you. Did he do that?"

"Yes," Victoria murmured.

"How many times has he been to see you?"

"Three."

Stunned expressions covered the faces of both women. "Three?" Tave said. "I've never heard of him going to see anybody once, and you say he's been to visit you three times."

Victoria's face warmed, and she directed her gaze to the quilt. She ran her hand over one of the squares that made up the quilt top. "He's only been to see me twice, but I counted last Sunday when he came to ask permission to call on me."

Savannah laughed. "He must have gone straight there after leaving Cottonwood." She leaned forward and patted Victoria's hand. "I would say you have yourself a serious suitor."

Tave's eyes narrowed. "And what do you think about that, Victoria?"

She squirmed under the intense scrutiny of Tave's eyes. "I. . .I really don't know. I suppose I feel honored that a man who owns a large plantation would be interested in me. I don't have any money, and I'm not sophisticated. I have no idea why he'd like me."

Tave glanced at the men across the yard and back to Victoria. "Be careful. No one knows Marcus well. I don't want to see you hurt."

Victoria laughed. "I won't be."

"There's something else that concerns us, Victoria." Savannah glanced at Tave and took a deep breath. "Marcus isn't a believer. That may seem like a small thing right now, but it can cause big problems if your friendship with Marcus gets stronger."

"He's been to church for the last two Sundays. That should show you that he's not a bad person."

Tave sighed. "I'm not saying he's a bad person, but he's told Daniel several times that he has no need for God in his life. The Bible warns Christians not to become yoked to unbelievers. You really need to be careful. Hasn't your mother ever discussed this with you?"

Victoria shook her head. "No. My father often spoke to me about choosing friends who were believers, but my mother has always been concerned that I would marry a man who could provide for me." She smiled. "Besides, Marcus is a friend. It's not like he's asked me to marry him."

Savannah narrowed her eyes and leaned forward. "You can never tell where a friendship will lead. Be careful, Victoria. I wouldn't want to see you get hurt."

Victoria sighed. Marcus was handsome, and he was rich. And he was attending church with her. What more could she want?

She was sure, however, that her new friends only had her best interest in mind. Both women possessed a gentle quality that made her feel as if she'd known them forever, and they seemed genuinely concerned about her relationship with Marcus.

She glanced over at the group where Marcus still stood. As if he felt her eyes on him, he turned and stared at her. A smile creased his mouth, and her heart pumped. In that moment, she knew it made no difference what her new friends said.

Since the moment she'd seen him on the docks, he'd been in her mind, and he said he'd thought about her. If that was true, she had been offered an opportunity like she never would have imagined. All she had to do to escape her lifetime sentence as a clerk in a general store and become the mistress of a great plantation was to make Marcus Raines fall in love with her. Something told her that wouldn't be too difficult.

Chapter 6

Marcus tried to concentrate on the conversation of the men around him, but all he could think about was Victoria seated underneath a tree across the picnic grounds. He glanced at her every chance he got so that he could memorize what she looked like today. It would give him something to think about as he drifted off to sleep tonight.

With a sinking heart, he realized the conversation around him had halted and that all the men stared at him as if they waited for him to speak. He had no idea what had been said during the last few minutes or what was expected of him.

He darted a pleading glance at Dante. "I'm sorry. What did you say?"

Dante's mouth twisted into a grin. "We were discussing our crops. How many acres would you say your tenant farmers will plant this spring?"

Marcus swallowed back the panic that had risen in his throat and cast a grateful smile in Dante's direction. "Altogether I think we'll probably have about a thousand acres in cotton and corn. We'll leave the rest of the acreage for livestock forage."

Dante nodded. "Last summer was so hot the fescue didn't do well in the pastures. Maybe this year will be better."

The men mumbled their agreement. Dante opened his mouth to say something else but stopped when his son ran up beside him. "What is it, Vance?"

Vance closed one eye, tilted his head to the side, and stared up at his father. "Mama says it's time for us to be going home."

Dante patted the boy on the head and laughed. "Go tell her I'll be right there."

"Yes, sir." The boy scampered back toward his mother.

Dante watched until Vance stopped beside Savannah before he addressed the group again. "I suppose I'd better get going." He shook hands with each man. "Have a safe week, and I hope to see all of you next Sunday."

Marcus turned to look back at Victoria, but she was no longer sitting under the tree. She walked toward the church beside Savannah, who held Vance's hand. He fell into step beside Dante. "I'll walk back with you."

As they ambled across the picnic grounds, Dante pulled a watch from his pocket. "It's later than I thought. I was having such a good time I forgot all about the chores waiting at home. Livestock don't take Sundays off. They expect to be fed on schedule."

The words surprised Marcus. "You don't feed your own livestock, do you?"

Dante laughed. "Of course I do. Who else would?"

"Your tenant farmers. They feed mine."

Dante frowned. "Even on Sundays?"

"Yes. Why should Sunday be any different?"

Dante stopped and faced Marcus. "At Cottonwood, I like for my tenant farmers to have Sundays with their families. They have chores at their homes that have to be done, and I don't want to take up their time doing mine, too. Everybody works hard all week, including the women and children. I believe they deserve some time to be together and enjoy the day."

Marcus stared at Dante in amazement. "But you have so many cows, not to mention the hogs and horses. How do you feed all of them by yourself?"

"During the week, some boys whose fathers are tenant farmers do the feeding for me. On Sundays, Savannah, Gabby, and Vance help me."

Marcus's mouth gaped open. "You make your family work?"

Dante laughed. "You make it sound like it's something horrible. There's nothing wrong with honest work, Marcus. Savannah and I have struggled to bring Cottonwood back, and we want Gabby and Vance to understand the value of hard work and to appreciate the people who help to make their life more comfortable."

"You make it sound like the tenant farmers are your equals. Surely you don't believe that."

"Oh but I do, Marcus. The Bible tells us that we're all God's children. No one is more important than another. I want my children to understand that."

Marcus shook his head. "You certainly have some strange ideas, Dante."

Sadness flickered in Dante's eyes. "I tried to talk to your father many times about my beliefs, but he always dismissed me. I hope you'll be more open to what God teaches about loving each other."

He glanced at Victoria's retreating figure and smiled. "I'm certainly open to love."

Dante followed his gaze and turned to frown at him. "I'm not talking about the romantic love a man feels for a woman. I'm talking about the kind of love that is voluntary and unconditional. It allows a person to look at his enemy and love him because God does."

"That sounds impossible. I couldn't love an enemy."

"Maybe you have to start closer to home, Marcus. I've heard rumors that some of your tenant farmers are looking for somewhere else to go next spring. They say living at Pembrook is a lot like slavery."

Marcus's heart pounded from the temper that flared inside him. "So they're looking for somewhere else. Who are they? Tell me, and I'll take care of them."

Dante shook his head. "I don't know any names, and I wouldn't tell you if I did. I've only told you this because I know how difficult it will be to farm your land if you lose tenants. Think about how you treat the people who work with you, and try to make them feel like they're an important part of your success. In reality, they are."

Marcus straightened to his full height. "They'd better realize how good they have it at Pembrook."

Dante put his hand on Marcus's shoulder. "I don't want you to be angry. My only reason for talking to you like this is to help you. Please believe me. I know it hasn't been easy since your father died. You have big responsibilities that require great strength of character. I want you to be successful."

No one had ever spoken to him in such a forthright way before. Yet Dante's words were tempered with compassion. A few days ago, Marcus had told Victoria he'd never had a friend in Willow Bend. He realized now that wasn't true. Dante Rinaldi had been there all the time, but he hadn't recognized the friendship he offered.

Marcus swallowed and nodded. "Thank you for speaking so frankly with me. I'll think about what you said."

Dante smiled. "Good. Now why don't we catch up with the ladies? I'm sure Victoria would like to say good-bye to you before you leave."

Marcus followed Dante as he headed toward where his wife and Victoria had stopped. When they reached the two women, Savannah smiled at her husband. "I have everything in the buggy. If you'll hold on to Vance, I'll see if I can find Gabby."

Dante cocked an eyebrow and grabbed the boy's hand. "You heard your mother. Let's go wait in the buggy." He turned to Victoria. "Let me welcome you to Willow Bend again and tell you how glad we are you've come to live in our town."

She reached out and grasped Savannah's hand. "Thank you for planning this wonderful gathering. I feel much more at home now that I'm getting to know folks."

Savannah squeezed her hand. "Good. I'll try to get into town this week and stop by the store."

Dante rolled his eyes and grinned. "She'll be there Wednesday afternoon, Victoria. I believe that's the day the *Montgomery Belle* is expected on its trip back downriver. Savannah will make sure she gets to see the boat."

Vance put his hand over his mouth and snickered, but Savannah only squared her shoulders and sniffed. "I'm going to find Gabby," she said and disappeared around the side of the church.

Marcus watched Dante head toward the buggy with his son before he glanced back at Victoria. "They're quite a couple, aren't they?"

Victoria smiled. "Yes they are." She shaded her eyes with her hand and stared toward the picnic area. "Now where did Mama go?" she murmured.

A slight frown pulled at her eyebrows, and her mouth opened just enough to expose her white teeth. He couldn't take his eyes off her. She had to be the most beautiful woman he'd ever seen.

His eyes grew wide. What was wrong with him? His father had warned him that women would beguile a man and make him believe they offered love. All they ever wanted, he had said, was a man's money. If that's what Victoria wanted, maybe he should stay away from her for a while, just until he had rid himself of the spell she had cast on him. He cleared his throat. "Victoria."

She lowered her eyelids and smiled. "Yes, Marcus."

"I know I came to call on you last Tuesday and Friday nights, but I don't think that's going to be possible this week."

The lips that made his heart race drooped into a pout. "Don't you want to see me, Marcus?"

His heart pricked at the sight of moisture in her eyes. Was it possible that his words had hurt her to the point of making her cry? He felt as if her tears had seeped through his pores and flooded through his body. He was drowning in the need to be with her, and there was nothing he could do about it.

He took a deep breath. "Of course I want to see you. I wondered if your mother would mind if I came three nights this week."

Victoria smiled, and she inched closer to him. His heart soared. "My mother wouldn't mind, and it would make me very happy. In fact, I'd like it if you came every night."

At that moment, her mother and uncle stopped beside them. "It's time to go, Victoria," her mother said. She turned to Marcus. "We hope to see you again soon."

He glanced down at Victoria and smiled. "I'll probably come to visit tomorrow night if that's all right."

Victoria flashed him a big smile. "That sounds wonderful. We'll see you then."

He didn't mount his horse until Mr. Perkins's buggy had pulled away from the church. Then he climbed on and turned the mare toward Pembrook. It had been an unsettling day. The problems at Pembrook that Dante had warned him of were troubling enough, but he also found himself beginning a relationship with a woman he'd only known for a little over week. He had no idea how to address either matter.

❧

Two months later on a Sunday afternoon, Victoria sat in a chair underneath a tree in back of her uncle's store. She'd hoped the shade would provide some relief from the heat that stifled her in the upstairs living quarters, but it hadn't. If it was this hot in the middle of June, she dreaded what July and August would bring.

There wasn't a leaf stirring on any of the trees today. The still air pressed down on her like a great weight. She closed her eyes and listened—for a bird's call, the laughter of children playing up and down the main street, the nicker of a horse—but she heard nothing in the quiet afternoon.

She swished her hand fan in front of her face and let her mind drift to the church service earlier today. Over the weeks, she'd learned the names of all the families in the congregation and which pew they sat in each Sunday. Uncle Samuel liked to be about halfway back, and she could spot where they would sit the minute she walked in the door. She doubted if it took Reverend Luckett but a few minutes to make a mental note of who was absent from the service.

A smile pulled at her lips as she thought of Marcus, who had sat beside her for the past month at church. It had taken him a few weeks to get up the nerve to ask if he could join them, and she had been thrilled. His presence beside her made her pulse race, but she tried not to let her facial expression show what was happening inside her.

This morning as they shared a hymnal, his finger had accidentally brushed hers on the back of the book. He gasped and glanced at her as if begging her pardon. She smiled at him, slid her hand across the back of the book, and stroked his knuckle. It was a brazen gesture, and her mother would have fainted if she'd seen it. The reward of his blue eyes sparkling at her had made her overture worth it.

"Good afternoon."

Her eyes flew open at the sound of Marcus's voice, and she jerked up straight in her chair. The book in her lap tumbled to the ground, and Marcus knelt in front of her and scooped it up. He smiled as he handed it back to her.

"Marcus, you scared me. I didn't hear your horse. Where is it?"

"I tied my mare to the hitching post out front and walked around here."

She reached up and smoothed her hair back into the bun at the nape of her neck. "I wasn't expecting you this afternoon."

He glanced around. "And I didn't expect to find you alone without your mother or uncle around."

"They decided to take a nap, but I couldn't sleep. It's so hot upstairs, and there are only a few windows. Every once in a while we get a breeze off the river, but not often."

He dropped down on the ground beside her and stared at the back of her uncle's store. "I'm glad my grandfather put a lot of windows in the big house. It helps a lot in the summertime."

"That sounds nice. The summers in Mobile are hot, too, but our house had a small garden with some large shade trees. I spent a lot of time outside."

He stared at her for a moment. "You must miss Mobile a lot."

She shook her head. "I would have missed it more if I hadn't met you."

He directed his gaze to a sprig of grass and pulled at it. "I just happened to be there when you arrived. Now that you feel more comfortable in Willow Bend, I'm sure there are a lot of young men who would like to get to know you better."

A retort that she had no wish to see other men hovered on her tongue, but she bit it back. Marcus had been calling on her for the last two months, and his actions told her he liked her. She didn't know why he couldn't say the words. Was this going to be their relationship forever? They'd sit in her parlor with her mother and uncle in the next room while he talked about his crops and what he planned to do at Pembrook?

If that was all he wanted, she might do well to move on. The thought made her sad. Marcus had come to mean a lot to her, but she had no idea how he felt about her. He had sought out her company and had called on her at least twice a week and sometimes more, but he never spoke of personal feelings. Maybe he never would.

She had to do something with her life. If her relationship with Marcus was going to lead nowhere, perhaps she needed to follow through on her threat to return to Mobile. If Uncle Samuel would loan her enough money for passage and living expenses for a few months, she felt sure she could stay at the boardinghouse where she'd worked. Maybe her old job would be available. If not, she'd look for other employment. That's what she would do—she would return to Mobile and put all thoughts of Marcus Raines out of her mind.

She sighed. "If there are any young men who want to get to know me, they'd better hurry."

He tilted his head to one side and frowned up at her. "Why?"

Her hands trembled. She flattened them on her skirt and smoothed out the fabric. "Because I probably won't be here much longer."

His eyes grew wide, and his mouth dropped open. "Why? Are you going somewhere?"

She nodded. "I told my mother when we came here I didn't expect to stay long. I think it's about time for me to go back to Mobile."

He jumped to his feet. "I had no idea you were thinking of leaving."

She stood and faced him. "I've been thinking about it ever since we got here. I can't see anything here for me except ending up as an unmarried woman who's spent her whole life working in a general store and living above it. I want more than that."

"And you don't think you can find what you want here?"

She let her gaze wander over his face. "Not if it means living above a store."

"Victoria," he said, "I don't want you to leave. I would miss you."

She eased toward him. She opened her mouth and touched the tip of her tongue to her upper lip. "I'll miss you, too, Marcus. I think about you all the time."

He couldn't take his eyes off her lips. The longer he stared, the redder his face became. After a moment, he shook his head and backed away. "I have to go. I'll come back one night this week. Please consider your choices carefully before you make a final decision."

"I will."

He turned and strode around the side of the store. Victoria stood still until she heard his horse gallop away. Then she dropped down in her chair.

What had she done? As she thought back to what she'd said, her face burned. Her words sounded like she dared Marcus to do something to make her stay. Her mother had often warned her she was too impulsive, and she certainly had been today. If Marcus thought she was pressing him for a commitment, she'd probably never see him again. She had just scared off the one man who had ever shown any attention to her. All she could do now was follow through on her threat and begin making preparations to leave for Mobile.

The thought of being away from Marcus crushed her heart, and tears filled her eyes. She sank down in the chair and covered her face with her hands. What had she done?

❧

Marcus dug his heels into the horse's sides and galloped out of Willow Bend along the river toward Pembrook. He couldn't believe it. Victoria was going to return to Mobile.

There had to be something he could do to keep her here. For the first time in his life, he'd met someone who made him glad to be alive, and he didn't want to lose her. He gritted his teeth and groaned. If he'd never gone to see her that first time, he wouldn't be so unhappy now. He should have kept his distance and not discovered how her very presence made his pulse race. But he had chosen to go. Now he was going to pay for that choice.

If only he knew what to do. She said she didn't want to end up an unmarried woman still working in a store. He didn't know why she should worry. As beautiful as she was, some man would be happy to make her his wife. Anger roiled in his stomach at the thought of Victoria with another man.

What was it she had said? That when she arrived at Willow Bend it was as if he was waiting for her. He'd had the same thought many times.

He pulled back on the reins, and the horse stopped in the road. Marcus leaned on the saddle's pommel and frowned. She'd said she wanted more out of life than what she had at her uncle's home. But what if he could give her more?

Maybe it had been decided the day something made him go to the riverboat landing to wait for his cotton planters. He'd had no idea he would encounter a beautiful woman, but he had. Was there some way he could control her decision about leaving?

His mouth pulled into a smile at the answer that came to mind. Of course he could. He knew exactly what to do. Turning the horse around, he spurred the mare toward town.

Within minutes he was back at the store. He jumped out of the saddle before the horse had come to a complete stop. He looped the reins over the hitching post, clenched his fists, and strode toward the back of the store where he'd left Victoria.

She still sat in the chair, but her hands covered her face and her shoulders shook. Shocked at the sight of her crying, he slowed his step and crept toward her. When he stood in front of her, he knelt on one knee. "Victoria, what's the matter?"

She jerked her head up and stared at him with a startled expression on her face. "What do you want?"

He felt at a loss as to what he should do. "I came back to apologize for leaving so abruptly."

She pushed up out of the chair and stepped behind it. "There's no need for that. I'm all right."

He frowned. "No you're not. Did I do something to offend you?"

She shook her head. "You didn't do anything."

He wanted to step closer to her, but the chair blocked his way. "I came back to tell you that you're not going back to Mobile."

Her eyebrows arched. "I'm not?"

"No, you're going to stay here and marry me." He could hardly believe he'd spoken the words.

Her hand clutched at her throat, and she stared at him. "You want me to marry you?"

He reached out, grabbed the chair, and set it to the side. Then he stepped closer to her. "I would regret it the rest of my life if I didn't stop you from leaving. You don't want to end up living over a store. I have a beautiful home that needs a woman in it. I want you to marry me and live with me at Pembrook."

Fresh tears welled up in her eyes. "What about love, Marcus? Do you love me?"

He hesitated before he answered. "I haven't had any experience with love, Victoria. All I know is that you are in my thoughts constantly and that I feel more at ease with you than anyone I've ever known. I can't imagine my life without you. I'm a wealthy man, and I want to provide you with everything you need in life. When I think of all those things, I know I love you with all my heart."

"You've been in my thoughts since I first met you, too. I don't want to go back to Mobile. I love you, too, Marcus. I want to stay here and be your wife."

Her words stirred his heart. "My wife," he murmured. He'd never dreamed he would be able to say those words, and she'd also said she loved him. He reached out, took her hand in his, and kissed it. "Thank you, Victoria. You do me a great honor. Now that we've settled our wishes, I must ask your family's permission."

"Do you want to talk to them now?"

He shook his head. "No. I'll invite all of you to Pembrook after church next Sunday. I want them to see where you'll be living and be assured you'll be cared for. Then I'll speak with them. This moment has meant so much to me, and I wish it to remain between the two of us until then. Is that agreeable with you?"

"Yes, that's fine with me."

He took a deep breath. "There is one more thing, Victoria."

"What?"

He grasped both her hands in his and stared into her eyes. "You must promise you will never leave me."

Her eyes narrowed. "Why do you think I'd leave you?"

He rubbed his fingers across her knuckles. "My mother left me when I was small, and I've never had a woman in my life until you."

She didn't blink as she returned his steady gaze. "I promise I will never leave you, Marcus."

He exhaled, dropped her hands, and backed away. "Good. I shall be back tomorrow night to invite your family to Pembrook."

He turned and hurried back to where he'd left his horse. At the corner of the store, he glanced over his shoulder at her. She raised her hand and waved. He pursed his lips and nodded before he continued on his way.

When he'd awoken this morning, he'd had no idea he would be engaged before the end of the day. His father's words about how a woman couldn't be trusted flashed into his mind. Father had felt that way because of his wife's desertion. She had deserted not only her husband but her son as well.

For the first time in a long time, Marcus allowed the emotions he normally struggled to conceal to flow through his mind. He tried again to remember what his mother had looked like, but with his father's refusal to have her picture in the house, he had no idea. He allowed the vision he'd stored away in the hollow part of his heart to drift to the surface, and he smiled. Did she really have dark hair and blue eyes like he imagined, or was she blond and fair skinned? He had no idea.

He wondered if she was still alive and if she ever thought of him. Probably not. In all the years since she left when he was three years old, she hadn't attempted to get in touch with him. What was it about him that made her not love him? He'd struggled with that question all his life and was no nearer an answer now than he had been when he was a child.

His blood turned cold at the fear that Victoria would dislike living at Pembrook as much as his mother had. Victoria said she loved him and promised she would never leave him, but she might change her mind in the future. He would have to make her realize how much he loved her so that she would never want to leave him. He couldn't lose her, too.

Chapter 7

Victoria knew the big house at Pembrook would be beautiful, but she hadn't expected its breathtaking interior. She remembered looking at the house from the deck of the *Alabama Maiden* and thinking the only way she'd get to see the inside of such a house was if she worked in the kitchen. Now she was here because the owner of one of the wealthiest plantations in Alabama wished to ask her family's permission to marry her.

From the moment she and her family walked in the front door, she'd been overcome by the spacious rooms and the ornate furniture. She'd almost gasped aloud when Marcus opened the door to the dining room and she spied the long table draped with a white cloth and sparkling candelabras at each end. Even in the daylight, the flickering flames from the candles cast dancing patterns across the wallpaper that Marcus whispered in her ear had been ordered from France by his father. The massive sideboard that sat against one wall had been shipped to Pembrook from England. Her heart fluttered at the thought of sitting in this elegant room at the other end of the table, facing Marcus and presiding over the dinner parties they would give after they were married.

Her uncle swallowed the bite of ham he'd placed in his mouth, laid his fork on his plate, and glanced at Marcus, who sat at the head of the table. "You have a nice home, Marcus. Thank you for inviting us today."

Marcus leaned back in his chair and smiled. His gaze drifted around the room. "My grandfather built the house, but my father was the one who furnished it. I was a small boy during the war, but I've often heard my father talk about how thankful he was the Yankees never came to Pembrook. Of course, he'd hidden most of the valuables. So even with all the slaves gone, he had money after the war to get Pembrook back on its feet. And he did a great job."

Her uncle nodded. "He sure did. Now it's yours, and I'm sure you'll continue to make it successful."

Before Marcus could respond, the door to the kitchen opened, and the woman who'd served their meal stepped into the room and stopped a few feet away from the table. Her dark skin glistened in the candlelight. A red scarf tied at the back of her head covered her hair, but a few tufts of wiry dark hair stuck out over her ears. She stood with her hands clasped in front of her and her gaze directed at the floor.

Marcus glanced at her. "Yes, Sally?"

"I's wond'rin' if ya'll needs anything else, Mistuh Mahcus."

Marcus looked from Victoria to her mother and uncle. "Would you like anything else before Sally serves dessert?"

Victoria's mother laid her napkin beside her plate and smiled at the woman who'd cooked their meal. "No thank you, but everything was delicious."

The woman didn't look up but nodded.

Victoria turned in her seat to get a better look. "Sally, Mr. Marcus told me that you cook all his meals. He's very fortunate to have such a good cook."

Sally's eyes grew wide, and she darted a quick glance in Victoria's direction. "Thank you, ma'am."

Victoria smiled. "I can only echo my mother's words about how tasty everything was."

Sally opened her mouth to speak, but Marcus interrupted. "You can take these dishes and serve dessert now, Sally."

The woman scrambled to clear the dishes away from the table. In a matter of minutes, she had taken all of them to the kitchen and returned with dessert plates filled with apple cobbler. Victoria picked up her fork, cut into the flaky crust, and took a big bite.

"Mmm." Swallowing, she reached out and touched Sally's arm as she placed a plate in front of Uncle Samuel. "Sally, this is heavenly. I don't know when I've eaten better."

Surprise flashed in the woman's eyes, and she glanced down at Victoria's hand on her arm. Taking a swift step back, she distanced herself from Victoria. "Thank you ag'in, ma'am."

She turned and rushed to the kitchen. Victoria turned a questioning gaze toward Marcus. "Did I frighten Sally?"

He shrugged. "She doesn't talk much. You probably just caught her off guard."

Victoria stared at the closed kitchen door, but the woman didn't enter the room again. When they had finished their dessert, Marcus stood. "If you're through, let's go into the parlor where we can relax. Then I'd like to show you around Pembrook."

Marcus stood at the door and waited until they had all passed by before he stepped in front and led the way down the hallway toward the parlor at the front of the house. Victoria glanced up at the curving staircase that led to the upstairs as they passed and wondered what the rooms up there looked like. If they were anything like those she'd already seen, she knew she was about to enter into a life she never would have dreamed about.

In the parlor, Victoria and her mother sat down on the gilt-framed French sofa that faced a marble fireplace, and her uncle took a seat in one of the sofa's matching chairs beside them. She gazed up at the large mirror above the fireplace and the two pink lusters that sat at each end of the mantel.

She pointed to the lusters. "Marcus, those are beautiful. Where did you get them?"

He glanced up at the enameled, bowl-shaped candleholders with the tier of single-drop crystals hanging toward the base of each stem. "My father had them sent from Bristol, England. Do you like them?"

"Oh yes. They're the most beautiful I've ever seen."

He smiled and then stepped in front of the mantel, turned his back on it, and clasped his hands behind him. Victoria thought he'd never looked handsomer than he did standing there, his gaze almost caressing her face. He cleared his throat. "It's been a pleasure to have all of you here today. But I must confess that I have an ulterior motive in inviting you here."

Her mother looked at Uncle Samuel, who frowned at Marcus. "What is it?"

Marcus held out his hand to Victoria. "Will you please come stand beside me?"

"Yes." Victoria cast a nervous glance at her mother and rose to stand beside him.

Her mother and uncle didn't blink as she and Marcus faced them. Marcus took a deep breath. "First of all, I want to thank you, Mr. Perkins and Mrs. Turner, for letting me visit Victoria in your home for the past few months. During this time, we have come to know each other. I have also developed a deep feeling for Victoria, and she assures me that my affection is returned. I spoke with her last week, and we decided we would bring our wishes to you today." He reached out and clasped Victoria's hand. "I would like to ask your permission to marry her. I promise I will take care of her and provide her with everything she needs in life."

Neither her mother nor her uncle spoke for a moment. Mama licked her lips and let out a long breath. "Marcus, do you love my daughter?"

"I do."

She looked at Victoria. "And do you love Marcus?"

"I do."

Her mother glanced at Uncle Samuel as if she was struggling with an answer. Uncle Samuel stared at her for a moment before he directed his attention back to Marcus. "But you've only known each other a few months. You need more time before you make such an important decision."

Victoria shook her head. "It wouldn't matter, Uncle Samuel. Marcus and I love each other, and that's not going to change whether we marry tomorrow or six months from now."

Her mother directed a piercing look at Marcus. "Do you promise that you will always respect and take care of my daughter?"

"I will."

With a shrug she sank back against the pillows of the sofa. "Then I suppose I give my permission for you to marry my daughter. I hope the two of you know what you're doing."

Victoria released Marcus's hand and leaned down and hugged her mother. "Thank you, Mama. We do know what we're doing."

Her mother's arms circled her shoulders, pulling her tighter, and she whispered in Victoria's ear, "I don't want you to think I'm not happy for you, darling. I am, but it surprised me. You know there aren't many women who could capture a husband as wealthy as Marcus. You'll be well taken care of for the rest of your life. That's always been my wish for you."

"I know, Mama. Being married to Marcus is the best thing I could ever have imagined."

Her mother released her. "Then be happy. When will the wedding be?"

Victoria laughed and glanced at Marcus. "We haven't decided yet. When shall we get married?"

He smiled. "The sooner the better for me. How long do you need to get ready?"

Her mother stood up and grasped Victoria's arm. "Don't rush it, darling. I'm sure the people of Willow Bend will expect a big wedding for one of the county's most eligible bachelors. We have to make your dress and decide what we'll serve at the reception. Then we need to talk to Reverend Luckett and see when would be a good time to have it at the church."

Marcus frowned. "I don't want to have it at the church, and I don't want a lot of people invited. I prefer that we have it in the garden off the terrace at the back of the house. The flowering plants are beautiful this time of year."

"You don't want to invite our friends?" Her mother shot an incredulous look at Uncle Samuel, who hadn't said a word.

Marcus stepped closer to Victoria and gazed into her eyes. "I want this to be our time and your family's. Of course we'll have Reverend Luckett and his wife, and I'd really like to invite Dante and Savannah. But that's all."

Her mother's frown deepened. "But that will only be four guests."

Victoria sighed. It was so like her mother to want a big event. If given the chance, she'd probably plan the biggest wedding Willow Bend had ever seen. She smiled at Marcus and turned to her mother. "Those four people are Marcus's friends, and they're also the only people I know well. I think a small wedding right here where we're going to live is just what I want."

"Very well." The grumbled words told Victoria that her mother wasn't pleased. "But we'll still need some time to get your dress ready."

Victoria shook her head. "You sound like you're trying to put it off." She turned to Marcus. "When would you like to have the wedding?"

"It would be better for me if we have it before harvest. I think two weeks would be best. What do you think?"

Victoria nodded. "That's fine with me." She turned back to her mother. "Two weeks from today we'll have the wedding right here at Pembrook."

Resignation flickered in her mother's eyes, and she pursed her lips. Giving a slight nod, she glanced around the room. "I hope you'll be very happy here, Victoria. This is a beautiful home."

Victoria felt as if she'd burst with happiness. Marcus reached out and pressed her hand into his. She stared up into his face and smiled. "Are you as happy as I am, Marcus?"

"I'm happier than I've ever been in my life. I can't wait for you to really be home with me at Pembrook."

She let her gaze rove over the ornate furniture and the heavy draperies that hung at the windows. It looked like a picture she'd seen in a book once, but this was different. It was going to be her home, and she was going to be the mistress of this grand house.

Marcus had never seen a more beautiful day. Cooler temperatures had drifted into the area overnight, and the July afternoon felt more like a spring day. The shade from one of the big oak trees scattered at the edge of the garden covered the area where he'd placed the chairs for the wedding guests.

From the veranda, Marcus stared across the garden at the guests who'd gathered for the wedding. Victoria's mother sat in a chair, and Tave and Savannah stood on either side of her. As they talked, from time to time one of them would glance at him.

Mrs. Turner's lips pulled into a nervous smile every few minutes. She was trying to be happy about the small wedding, but Marcus knew she would have preferred a big one in town. Savannah and Tave looked just as uncomfortable. Weren't they happy for Victoria and him? His heart sank at the thought that they didn't approve of the marriage that was about to take place.

Dante, who stood next to him, leaned closer and grinned. "Your life is about to change. Are you scared?"

Marcus swallowed and took a deep breath. "A little."

Dante laughed. "You wouldn't be a man if you weren't. Don't worry, Marcus. Daniel and I are here to get you through this."

Marcus swiveled and turned to Dante. "Savannah and Tave look unhappy. Do they not want Victoria to marry me?"

"I don't think they're unhappy. They're just concerned," Dante said. "After all, you and Victoria haven't known each other very long."

"How long did you know Savannah before you married her?"

Dante laughed. "About the same amount of time you and Victoria have known each other."

"Your marriage has worked out well."

"Yes, but even when two people love each other, it takes a lot of work. Do you remember the conversation we had the day you came to me for advice about your feelings for Victoria?"

"Yes."

"Then you understand why we're all concerned. You're a good person, Marcus, and you've been coming to church. But as far as I know, you haven't accepted Christ as your Savior."

"No, I haven't."

Sorrow flickered in Dante's eyes. "Then I fear for your marriage. The Bible is very clear about the responsibilities of a husband. If you haven't turned your heart over to Jesus, there's no way you can fulfill the role that God has for husbands."

Marcus's face warmed, and he fisted his hands at his sides. "I love Victoria and I'll always take care of her. You don't have to worry about me."

Dante shook his head. "But I do. I know how difficult marriage can be even when you love a woman with all your heart. Just remember that I'm always willing to help you in any way I can. And so is Daniel."

Marcus gave a snort of disgust. "Yeah, he cornered me and told me the same thing before you arrived."

"Then I suppose there's nothing else we can say to you today except that we'll be praying for you and Victoria and wish you the best." Dante smiled and stuck out his hand. "Don't look so glum. This isn't a funeral. It's a wedding. This should be the happiest day of your life."

Even though Dante's words and those of Daniel earlier troubled him, Marcus knew this was the happiest day of his life. A beautiful woman who said she loved him waited inside the house. It seemed like a dream come true. Soon Victoria would be his wife. She would be a part of Pembrook, and he wouldn't be alone anymore. Almost as if his father stood next to him and whispered in his ear, the thought that Victoria might hate life on Pembrook and want to leave like his mother did flashed into his mind.

Before he could banish the idea from his head, Daniel stepped through the door that led from the house onto the veranda. He stopped beside Marcus and smiled. "Victoria is ready, Marcus. Shall we take our places?"

Marcus gulped and nodded his approval.

With a smile, Daniel clasped his Bible next to his chest and walked to the spot they'd chosen for the ceremony. Savannah and Tave sat in the chairs next to Victoria's mother as the men approached.

When Daniel stopped and faced the house, Dante moved to stand beside

Marcus. Taking a big breath, Marcus turned, clasped his hands in front of him, and stared at the door of the house. It opened, and Victoria's uncle stepped onto the veranda before Victoria emerged. She smiled at her uncle and slipped her arm into the crook of his.

Her uncle whispered something in her ear and bent down to kiss her on the cheek. Victoria murmured something before she directed her gaze at Marcus. Her eyes sparkled, and he thought his heart would burst at how beautiful she looked. It had nothing to do with the dress she was wearing or the small bouquet she carried. Instead, it was the connection he felt as her gaze traveled over his face. For the first time in his life, he felt as if someone was looking at him through eyes filled with love.

So that was how love felt. He'd never known, and now he saw it on the face of the woman who wanted to share the rest of her life with him. A chill passed over him, and he straightened.

"A woman will break your heart." His father had said that to him many years ago. It couldn't be true of Victoria, though. He loved her and wanted to make her happy.

He shook the thought from his mind and watched as she walked toward him. When she and her uncle reached him, he turned to face Daniel, who opened his Bible and began to read. Marcus couldn't concentrate on the words for wanting to glance at Victoria, but she kept her attention on Daniel.

" 'Husbands, love your wives, even as Christ also loved the church, and gave himself for it.' "

Daniel's words startled Marcus, and he turned his head to look at the preacher. He frowned. The command sounded as if it was very important, but he didn't understand. Was the Bible talking about the buildings where people met to worship? He'd have to ask Dante to explain this to him later.

For the remainder of the ceremony, Marcus felt as if he was in a daze. He knew he mumbled words promising to love, honor, and keep only to Victoria as long as he lived, and he heard her speak the same vows. He also knew when he slipped the ring he'd ridden to Selma to purchase on her finger, but he remembered little else.

"I now pronounce you man and wife," Daniel said.

Marcus stared down at Victoria's hand that he grasped and then raised his eyes to her face. She was smiling, and he thought he detected a hint of tears in the corners of her eyes. He stared at her a moment, not knowing what to do.

Dante leaned forward and whispered in his ear, "Why don't you kiss your bride, Marcus?"

He hesitated a moment, not willing to break the spell that could hardly make him believe this gorgeous woman had just married him. Then he leaned forward, grazed her cheek with his lips, and whispered in her ear, "I love you more than I've ever loved anyone before, Victoria. I can't tell you how happy you've made me today."

She smiled as he straightened and touched his cheek with her fingers. "I love you, too, Marcus. I'm honored to be your wife."

Daniel stuck out his hand to Marcus. "Congratulations. I hope you'll be very happy."

Marcus shook hands and turned to Victoria's mother, who'd stepped up behind them. She kissed Victoria on the cheek and smiled at him. "I pray you'll have a happy life together."

"As do I," Savannah said and reached out to grasp Victoria's hand.

Tave put her hands on Victoria's shoulders and stared into her eyes. "Remember to put God first in your marriage, and He'll take care of you and Marcus."

Marcus put his arm around Victoria's shoulders and drew her close to him. He looked at the people who'd come to witness their wedding, and his heart swelled with gratitude. Not only did he have a wife; he also was beginning to have friends.

He cleared his throat. "I want to thank all of you for coming to our wedding today." He glanced from Victoria's mother and uncle to the two couples. "I hope that not only Victoria's family but our friends as well will know that our home will always be open to you. Now if you'll come into the house, I believe Sally has baked a cake and has some cider made from apples grown in our orchard."

Victoria looped her arm through his as they walked toward the house. With his free hand, he reached over and covered hers, which rested on his arm. He'd never felt such a protective feeling in his life. He was determined to make her like her new life at Pembrook.

Chapter 8

Victoria stretched her arms above her head and wiggled her toes in an effort to wake up. She turned her head to stare at the pillow next to her. The indention where Marcus's head had rested was the only indication that he had slept there. The sun streamed through the big bedroom windows, and she wondered what time it was. From somewhere in the house a clock chimed, and she counted the sounds.

Her eyes grew wide, and she bolted upright in bed. Eight o'clock. She'd never slept that late in her life. Marcus would think he'd married a lazy woman.

She sprang from the bed, ran to the washstand where a pitcher and bowl sat, and poured some of the water for her morning bath in the delicate china basin. She hurried through her morning preparations and ran to the walnut armoire where her mother had hung her dresses yesterday. Pulling out a simple day dress, she slipped it over her head and hurried out of the room.

As she strode down the upstairs hallway toward the staircase, she studied each of the bedrooms she passed. Marcus had pointed out three last night and told her that her family was welcome to stay anytime. The memory of how attentive he'd been to her feelings the night before drifted into her mind, and she smiled. He wanted her to be happy at Pembrook, and she knew she would be.

She reached the staircase and started to step down, but a closed door directly across the hall caught her attention. She hadn't noticed it the night before, and Marcus hadn't mentioned the room. She wondered what was behind the door.

The smell of baking bread reached her nostrils, and her stomach growled. She'd hardly touched her food last night, and she was hungry. Undecided which to do, she glanced from the door to the direction of the tempting smells.

Curiosity won. She backed away from the stairs, walked to the closed door, and grasped the doorknob. It didn't open, and she pushed harder. Locked. That was the only explanation. Victoria backed away from the door and frowned. Why would Marcus have one of the rooms locked?

The aroma of frying bacon mingled with the baking bread drifted up the staircase, and her stomach growled. Victoria shrugged. She would ask Marcus later.

She dashed down the stairs, hurried to the kitchen, and pushed the door open. "Good morning," she called out as she entered.

Sally Moses whirled around from her position at the dry sink by the wall and gasped. A bowl she'd been in the process of washing slipped from her fingers and crashed to the floor. Sally's wild stare darted from Victoria's face to the pieces of shattered glass at her feet. She shrank against the dry sink and uttered a moan.

"I sorry, Miz Raines. I doan know what make me be so clumsy this morning."

Victoria stopped in amazement at the fear she saw in the woman's face. Did she think Victoria would berate her for breaking a bowl? Victoria smiled and stepped closer. "Don't apologize. It wasn't your fault. I shouldn't have startled you." She glanced around the kitchen. "It's just a bowl. Where's the broom? I'll help you clean it up."

Sally grabbed the bottom of her apron and dried her dripping hands on the fabric. "No'm. I clean it up. You go on in the dinin' room and sets down. I take care of this here bowl after I serves you breakfas'."

Victoria glanced over her shoulder and frowned. "Sit in the dining room? I don't want to sit in there and eat all alone. What time did Marcus leave?"

"Mistuh Mahcus, he leave early ev'ry mo'nin'. He tole me to fix you somethin' to eat when you woke up."

Victoria rubbed her stomach. "I am hungry, but I'm not going in that dining room. I'll sit right here at the kitchen table. That way we can talk while I eat. I want to get to know you better."

Sally bit down on her lip and shook her head. "I doan think Mistuh Mahcus want his wife to be eatin' in no kitchen. Not when you got that big table to set at."

Victoria laughed. "Exactly. It's a big table, and I'm not going to sit in there alone. Now tell me where you keep the plates, and I'll get one out for myself."

A slow smile curled Sally's lip, and she pointed to a cupboard. "They's in there. I'll pour you a cup of coffee whilst you gittin' a plate. Then I'll git you some biscuits and gravy and some bacon."

Twenty minutes later, Victoria pushed her chair away from the table and wiped her mouth on the napkin Sally had handed her. "That was delicious, Sally. I've never tasted biscuits that good. Who taught you to cook?"

A shy smile pulled at Sally's mouth. "My granny be the best cook at Pembrook. She learned me ev'rythin' I know when I was a little girl."

"Did your mother like to cook, too?"

Sally's body stiffened, and she reached for Victoria's dirty dishes. "I doan 'member my mama. Mastuh Raines sold my mama off when I was little."

Victoria frowned. "Sold her. . ." The truth dawned on her. Sally and her mother had been slaves. Victoria raised her hand to cover her gaping mouth. After a moment, she spoke. "Oh, Sally. I'm so sorry. I didn't mean to cause you pain by making you remember the past."

"I reckon I doan never forget it, Miz Raines. It be with me all the time."

"I expect it is. It must have been very hard for you to grow up without a mother, but you're fortunate you had a grandmother. What about your family now?"

"Well, my grandmamma died 'fore the war. When we was freed, me and my husband lived out to the Crossroads for a while. Then when Mistuh Raines start wantin' tenant farmers, we come back to Pembrook. Our son, he born here. Been here evah since."

Victoria smiled. "You have a son? What's his name?"

"James. He a good boy."

"I'm sure he is." Victoria watched Sally carry the dirty dishes to the dry sink and set them in a pan of water. "What can I help you do this morning?"

Sally tilted her head to the side and turned around slowly to face Victoria. A look of unbelief covered her face. "He'p me?"

"Yes. Now that I'm living here, I want to keep busy. How about if I help you with the noon meal? I can cook, although I know I'm not as good at it as you are. And I can wash dishes."

Sally's mouth dropped open wider, and she stared at Victoria. "Miz Raines, you cain't be a-workin' in no kitchen like hired he'p. You the mistress of this here house. Mistuh Mahcus won't like it for you to be doin' such as that."

Victoria laughed. "Don't be ridiculous, Sally. I worked in the kitchen of a boardinghouse in Mobile. I'll tell you what I'll do. I'll run back upstairs and make the bed; then I'll come back down here. You find me an apron while I'm gone, and I'll help you with the morning chores."

Sally shook her head. "Miz Raines, I doan think Mistuh Mahcus gonna want you a-workin' with me."

"Oh he'll be glad I found something to occupy my time. I have to find something to do. I can't sit in a chair all day long." She started out of the kitchen but stopped at the door and turned back to Sally. "I meant to ask you about a locked room upstairs. What's in there?"

Sally's lips quivered. "That's Mistuh Raines's room."

Victoria frowned. "Marcus's room?"

"No'm. His father's."

"Why is it locked?"

"Mistuh Mahcus locked it after his pappy died. He doan let nobody in there 'cept me ev'ry once in a while to clean."

Victoria nodded. "I see. Well, I'll be back in a minute."

She hurried through the house and up the staircase to the second floor. When she reached the closed door to her father-in-law's bedroom, she felt an urge to try the door just in case Sally had been wrong.

She grasped the doorknob in her hand and turned it, but the door wouldn't open. Victoria backed away from the door and stared at it. Why would Marcus keep the door locked and forbid anybody to enter? She would have to ask him about that.

≈

Marcus could hardly wait for noon. He'd wanted to stay home with Victoria this morning, but he knew he couldn't. The work on a plantation as large as his didn't wait for any man, and he had obligations.

As he'd ridden across Pembrook land all morning, checking on the fields of the various tenants, he pulled out his watch from time to time to see how much longer it would be before he could go back to the big house.

Victoria had been sleeping when he left, and he couldn't bring himself to wake her up. He sat beside the bed for a while staring at her and wondering how he became so lucky to get a wife as beautiful as she.

Ever since she'd agreed to marry him, he'd dreamed of how she would look as the mistress of the big house. Now he imagined her sitting in the parlor at Pembrook, maybe some kind of needlework in her hands as she waited for her husband to come from the fields. She would set her work aside, rise from her chair, and glide across the floor to welcome him home.

The thought made him yearn to see her. He pulled the watch from his pocket again. It wasn't yet noon, but that didn't matter. He wanted to see his bride. He turned his horse toward home.

When he arrived at the big house, he tossed the reins of his horse to one of the young boys who worked in the stable and hurried toward the house. His excitement grew as he stepped to the front door, pushed it open, and strode to the parlor.

At the entrance to the room he stopped and stared. Victoria was nowhere in sight. Laughter rang from the back of the house, and he frowned. Turning toward the sound, he moved to the closed door of the kitchen and paused. Victoria's laughter came from inside.

He pushed the door open and stood in amazement at the sight before him. Sally stirred a bubbling pot on the stove, and Victoria, the sleeves of her dress rolled up, was up to her elbows in soapsuds as she washed dishes at the dry sink.

Victoria glanced over her shoulder, and her face lit up when she saw him. "Marcus," she cried out, "you're home earlier than we expected."

"I. . .I wanted to see if you were all right."

She dried her hands on her apron and hurried across the room toward him. He glanced past her at Sally, who had turned to stare at him. She lowered her gaze, faced the stove, and directed her attention back to the cooking food.

Victoria stopped in front of him, stood on her tiptoes, and kissed his cheek. "I'm so glad you're home. Why didn't you wake me up before you left this morning?"

Marcus's heart plummeted at the sight of her. She looked nothing like the vision he'd had all morning. Tendrils of hair had escaped the bun at the back of her neck, and she brushed them out of her eyes. Spots of flour dotted her face, and the apron she wore sported a stain that looked like grease. He pulled his gaze away from her disheveled appearance and stared into her dark eyes. "I wanted you to sleep on your first morning here."

She arched an eyebrow and smiled. "From now on, you wake me up. I want to see my husband in the mornings. It's so sweet of you to be concerned for me on my first day here, but you needn't worry. Sally has taken care of me just fine. In fact, she has a wonderful meal cooked for us."

He glanced at the dishpan. "And you're washing dishes?"

She nodded. "I've been busy all morning. I made the bed, and then I dusted the parlor before I came in to help Sally with the noon meal. I love this house, and I can't tell you how wonderful I feel being here."

"That's good." Marcus looked at Sally again, but she hadn't moved. He took Victoria by the arm and nudged her forward. "I need to speak to you in the parlor, Victoria."

"All right." She started from the kitchen but stopped and called over her shoulder, "I'll be right back, Sally."

Marcus clenched his fists as he followed Victoria to the parlor. When they stepped into the room, he motioned her to sit in a chair and positioned himself to stand in front of her. She gazed up at him, and his heart pumped. How could he make her understand what he wanted their life to be at Pembrook?

He took a deep breath and raked his hand through his hair. "Victoria, what were you thinking going into the kitchen and working alongside Sally?"

The smile on her face dissolved, and her eyes grew wide. "What are you talking about, Marcus?"

"You are the mistress of this house, Victoria. I want you to remember that."

Victoria pushed up out of her chair. "I thought I was your wife and that my job was to take care of our home."

He blinked in surprise. "You are my wife, but I don't want you acting like the hired help. I don't need another worker. I need a wife who wants to make a home with me, preside over the table at dinnertime, conduct herself like a Southern lady of privilege."

She moved closer to him. "But I want our home to be our own special place. I can't be like a princess sitting on a throne. I have to be active in making our life happy. I'm used to working, Marcus, and I can't change that. Sally is the only woman here, and I want to be friends with her."

He drew back in surprise. "Friends with her? That's impossible."

"Why?"

"Because she's. . ."

"Not white?" Victoria finished the sentence for him.

He licked his lips. "Sally is a former slave who works at Pembrook now. You are the owner's wife. There is no place for friendship between the two of you."

Anger flashed in her eyes. "That's the most ridiculous thing I've ever heard. The war has been over for sixteen years. Don't you know that ended a lot of the old ideas in the South? I worked with women whose skin color was different than mine in Mobile, and I found I liked them. This morning I found that I like Sally. I can't ignore the fact that she's in this house, and I can't sit around all day waiting for you to come home. If we're going to be happy together, you have to let me be the person I've always been. Don't try to change me, Marcus."

"I just think you should remember the difference in your and Sally's stations in life. If you want friends, there are Savannah and Tave."

Victoria crossed her arms and glared at him. "They both live miles from here. How am I supposed to see them?"

"I'll have one of the workers drive you over in the buggy whenever you want to go see either of them. As far as Sally is concerned, you can't be friends with her. My father made it clear that there was a line between the owner and the workers at Pembrook. They're like children that we have to take care of. Remember that when you deal with Sally. Be firm with what you expect from her and don't become involved in her life."

She shook her head. "That's the most ridiculous thing I've ever heard. You sound like a slave owner from thirty years ago. It's a new day in the South, Marcus, and your father is no longer here. You have to make your own decisions and find your own way of dealing with life as it is now."

He regarded her for a moment. "Your mother said you've always been impulsive. For now, I see I can't change your mind. As you get used to life here and see how the tenants need guidance, you'll change your opinions."

She shook her head. "I wouldn't count on it." Her gaze softened, and she reached up and stroked his cheek. "I don't want to argue with you, Marcus. I love you with all my heart, and I want us to be happy. Please try to understand how I feel."

His heart pricked at the sadness he detected on her face. How could he deny her anything? "I want us to be happy, too. I love you so much, Victoria, but you have to understand you've entered a different world." He glanced down at her simple dress and the grease-stained apron. "How would you like to take a trip?"

Her eyes lit up. "A trip to where? You said we couldn't take a honeymoon trip until later in the summer."

"I know, but I've changed my mind. Maybe we need to get away from Pembrook for a few days and go where we can be alone and get to know each other. We could go to Selma and stay at the St. James Hotel, and we could shop for a new wardrobe for you. I want to buy you whatever you need."

She clasped her hands in front of her. "Oh Marcus, do you really mean it? We can stay in a real hotel, and I can shop for clothes?"

He put his arm around her and drew her close. "You can have anything your heart desires. I want you to know how much I love you and how proud I am to have you for my wife."

"When can we go?"

"How about the first of next week? That should give me time to make arrangements to be away."

She threw her arms around his neck and hugged him. "Thank you, Marcus. I love you."

He put his finger under her chin and tilted her face up. The lips that he'd dreamed about so many nights hovered right beneath his. He tightened his embrace as her arms circled his neck and pulled his head down until their lips met in a sweet kiss.

Chapter 9

With only one day left until their departure for Selma, Victoria was determined to finish the dress she'd started working on before her wedding. As she concentrated on the hem, she thought back to how wonderful the last few days had been.

Ever since her argument with Marcus the day after their wedding, she'd tried not to upset him. She was sure that once they had adjusted to living together, he would see how some of the ideas he still held to weren't reasonable.

In the meantime she still helped Sally, but she tried to be waiting in the parlor when it was time for him to arrive home. He hadn't said anything else, and she hoped there wouldn't be another confrontation like the one they'd had.

The sound of music drifted through the house, and she sat up straight. The needle she'd been pushing through the fabric jabbed her finger, and she cried out. A tiny drop of blood bubbled up on her skin. Frowning, she stuck the finger in her mouth in an attempt to ease the sting.

The music echoed through the house again, and she pushed to her feet. What was it, and where was it coming from?

She stepped into the hallway outside the parlor and listened. The sound of a low-pitched voice singing reached her ears, and she moved in its direction. Stopping outside the closed door to the kitchen, she put her ear next to the door and listened again.

Strumming on some kind of instrument accompanied a melancholy voice that moaned the words of a song like nothing she'd ever heard. " 'The river calls me home, ain't gonna stay no more. The river calls me home, ain't gonna stay no more. When I leave on that boat, it gonna drop me off on heaven's shore.' "

"Oh, that's good, James. You done make up one I like." Sally's voice drifted to her ears.

Victoria pushed the door open and stepped into the room. A young man who resembled Sally sat in a chair, and he held the strangest instrument she'd ever seen. "I heard the music, and I came to see what was going on."

The young man jumped to his feet and backed toward the door that led outside. "I's sorry, Miz Raines. I didn't mean to cause no problem. I jest come in here to wait so's I can walk home with my mama. Whilst I was here, I let her hear my new song. I won't do it no more, Miz Raines."

Victoria held out her hand. "No, don't go. I liked your music." She glanced at Sally. "Is this your son?"

"Yes'm. This be James. He likes to play music. He makes up songs all the time."

Victoria pointed to the instrument he held. "Is that a homemade guitar?"

James nodded. "Yes'm."

Victoria took a step closer and studied the strange device he held. "Would you tell me how you made it?"

James held out the instrument for her to see. "Mr. Perkins down at the store give me a empty cigar box, and I cut me a hole in the middle of it. I found a plank that Mistuh Mahcus done tore off the henhouse, and I whittled it down till I got the right size to nail onto the box for my handle. There was some old screen wire left over in a shed out back, and I made me some strings out of that. 'Course, first I had to make this here bridge to lift the wires up so they'd make a sound."

Victoria's mouth gaped open. "You made this all by yourself?"

"Yes'm."

"James, you're so smart. And the song I heard you singing, did you write that, too?"

"Yes'm."

Victoria ran her hand down the strings and plucked at one of them. The twang sent a thrill through her. "I've heard lots of musicians in Mobile, but I've never heard any song like the one you were singing. What kind of music is it?"

James shrugged. "I doan know. It just a kind of song my mama and pappy used to sing to me when I was a little boy."

Sally stepped forward. "Back when we was slaves, we'd get so sad sometimes we jest had to let out our feelin's in our songs. James's music jest the same kind we used to sing."

Victoria nodded. "It does have a sad sound. It seems to come from the bottom of your soul. I'm glad I heard you singing, James. It was very beautiful."

The front door of the house opened, and Marcus's voice rang out: "Victoria, where are you?"

She whirled around at the sound of her husband's voice. "I have to go now, but please come again and play for me. I've never heard such a haunting melody in my life."

Marcus stood in the middle of the parlor when she reentered the room. He turned and smiled at her. "There you are. I saw your sewing lying here and wondered where you were."

"I was taking care of something in the kitchen." She stopped in front of him and put her arms around his neck. "I can hardly believe that we're leaving on our trip tomorrow. I'm so excited. Did you see my mother when you went to town today?"

"I did. I told her and your uncle that we would be away for the next two weeks. They said to tell you to have a good time."

She tilted her head and directed what she hoped was a coy look at him. "Just being with you will make me enjoy the trip. Of course, the new clothes you've promised me will be nice, too."

He threw back his head and laughed. "Mrs. Raines, you make me so happy."

"And you do me, too, Mr. Raines."

He drew away from her. "I need to go out to the barn and see if I can find James before he goes home for the day. I want him to drive us in the buggy to the boat landing tomorrow. We're going to Selma on the *Montgomery Belle*."

"Then you don't have to go to the barn. He's in the kitchen."

Marcus stiffened, and he frowned. "You were in the kitchen with him?"

"Not just with James." Victoria picked up the dress she'd been hemming and sat down. "Sally was in there, too. I don't know if they've left to go home or not."

"Victoria, I have told you how I feel about. . ."

She frowned at him. "I wasn't doing anything wrong, Marcus. I heard some music, and I went to investigate."

"Music? What kind of music?"

She shrugged and reached for the thimble she'd set on the table next to the chair. "It was a song that James made up. It was really quite beautiful."

His eyes grew wide. "You were in there listening to music with Sally and James? Really, Victoria, have you not listened to a thing I've told you for the past week? You are to keep your distance from Sally and from James, too. The only conversation I want you having with them is when you instruct them in what you want them to do."

"And what if I don't want them to do something? What if I just want to talk to somebody or to listen to a gifted young man play a homemade instrument?"

He gritted his teeth. "Find something else to occupy your mind. Don't befriend the tenant farmers' families."

She held up her hand. "Let's not start this again. We're leaving on a trip tomorrow, and we don't need to leave with an argument hanging over our heads."

He exhaled. "You're right. But when we get back, we're going to settle this once and for all."

Victoria jumped to her feet, and the dress tumbled to the floor. "Yes, we are."

He stared at her for what seemed an eternity before he turned and stormed to the hallway. Victoria stood with her fists clenched for a moment before she dropped back into the chair. What had happened? One moment she and Marcus were speaking of their love, and in the next instant they were locked in a war of wills. How they were ever going to settle this disagreement she had no idea.

≪≫

Victoria stared at her image in the full-length mirror of their hotel suite at the St. James Hotel. The new evening dress with its white satin underlayer and pink silk overlay trimmed in pink roses and delicate lace had taken her breath away when she first saw it in the store. The scooped neck and short sleeves added a stunning look to the elegant garment. She'd never felt so beautiful in her life.

The door to the room opened, and Marcus entered. His eyes lit up when he saw her. "You look beautiful."

She bowed her head and curtsied. "Thank you, kind sir. Maybe I can persuade you to escort me to the dining room tonight."

"It would be my honor." He stopped beside her. "Do you mind if we have guests join us?"

"Who?"

"Matthew Chandler and his wife, Portia. I ran into them downstairs. Matthew's family owns Winterville Plantation, and he and his wife are staying at this hotel, too. They asked if we would join them tonight."

"That would be wonderful," Victoria said. "I'd like to meet Portia. Is Matthew a friend of yours?"

"I hardly know the man. His father is still in control at Winterville. I don't think Matthew stays there much. He met his wife when he visited family at Dauphin Island. They've been married several years."

"They sound interesting, but do you think I'm dressed all right?" She grinned and turned in a slow circle.

His gaze raked her from head to toe. "I've never seen anyone more perfect."

Two hours later, Victoria swallowed the last bite of her dessert, wiped her mouth on her napkin, and glanced across the table at Portia Chandler. She studied the tiny woman who had picked at her food throughout the meal. Victoria thought she had spent more time pushing her food around on her plate than putting any in her mouth.

Victoria leaned forward. "Portia, my husband tells me you grew up on Dauphin Island."

Portia's hand shook as she set her coffee cup in its saucer. "I did. Are you familiar with the island?"

"I am. I'd lived in Mobile all my life until we came to Willow Bend."

Portia nodded, and the long curls that hung from the back of her head bobbed up and down. "I heard that. You must miss Mobile a lot."

Victoria laughed and glanced at Marcus. "I thought I would, but then I met Marcus."

Matthew Chandler leaned over and circled his wife's wrist with his fingers.

Portia's already pale face grew whiter at his touch. "Portia feels the same way. Don't you, darling?"

Portia dropped her gaze to the tabletop and bit her lip. She nodded but didn't answer.

Victoria glanced toward Marcus, but a sudden movement of Matthew's hand caught her attention. Out of the corner of her eye, she saw Portia wince as if in pain, and that's when she saw Matthew's fingers tightening around Portia's wrist.

Startled, Victoria couldn't react for a moment. Then she pushed her chair back and jumped to her feet. "It's getting stuffy in here. Portia, why don't we go up to the balcony on the second floor and get some air. We can sit out there and watch the river roll by while we cool off." She turned to Marcus. "You men can do without your wives for a while, can't you?"

Marcus stood. "Of course. We'll come up later."

"Good." Victoria grabbed Portia's arm and pulled her to her feet. "This will give Portia and me a chance to get to know each other better."

Without speaking, Portia followed Victoria from the dining room, up the stairs, and onto the second-floor balcony overlooking the river. When they'd settled themselves in chairs, Portia turned to Victoria.

"Thank you."

Victoria arranged the skirt of her new dress around her legs. "For what?"

"For getting me away from him."

Victoria reached over and clasped Portia's hand in hers. "I saw him squeezing your wrist. You looked like you were in pain."

Tears stood in Portia's eyes. "I was, but that was nothing compared to what it is sometimes."

Victoria's heart pricked at the sadness lining Portia's face. "I'm so sorry. Is there anything I can do to help you?"

Portia shook her head. "No one can help me. I should have gotten to know him better before I married him. He seemed so sweet and kind when I first met him. Then after we were married, it was too late."

"Have you talked to Matthew about this?"

"Yes, and it's done no good. I even tried to talk to his father, which was a big mistake. I paid a high price for that. Matthew beat me so badly that my eyes were so black I didn't leave my room for a week."

Victoria wiped at the tears in her eyes. "There has to be something you can do. You can't live the rest of your life in fear of being hurt by your husband."

"I don't intend to." Portia took a deep breath. "One of these days I will disappear. When you hear about it, pray for me that I may escape the monster I married."

"I will."

Portia leaned forward in her chair. "And be careful, Victoria. You didn't know your husband well before you married him, either. Take care that you don't end up like me."

Victoria swallowed and nodded. "I will, but you don't have to worry about me. Marcus would never do anything to hurt me."

Portia tilted her head to one side. "I don't know about that. Matthew told me that Marcus's mother left his father because he was so cruel to her. Just watch out." She squeezed Victoria's hand. "Promise me that you'll be careful."

"I promise."

⁂

Victoria was still thinking about Portia an hour later when Marcus joined her on the balcony. He stopped beside her chair. "What are you doing out here still?"

She inhaled. "Enjoying the night and watching the river."

He held out his hand. "It's getting late, and I have a big day planned for us tomorrow. It's time we were going to bed."

She grasped his hand and stood to face him. "Marcus, you've never talked about your mother much."

He shrugged. "Because I don't remember anything about her. She left when I was three, and I never heard from her again."

"Did you ever ask your father why she left?"

"I did when I was little, but he always said the same thing. That she hated life in the South, that she didn't love him or me, and that she wanted to go back to her family. After a while I quit asking when I realized that she left and had no desire to ever see me again."

She stepped closer. "But you don't know that for sure. You only know what your father told you."

His lips thinned into a straight line. He stepped to the railing of the balcony and grasped the top with both hands. "My father wouldn't lie to me. He told me why she left. Why are you asking these questions about my mother?" He grasped the railing tighter as he spoke through clenched teeth.

"I thought there might be something that you don't know. Maybe she had a reason for leaving that you don't know about. If we could find her, she might want to come back."

He raked his hand through his hair and groaned. "I don't want to talk about this, Victoria. I hate my mother for leaving, and I don't want to ever see her again."

"But Marcus—"

"No!" He whirled and glared at her. "Don't you ever talk to me about my mother again. It is none of your concern."

Victoria bristled. "Just like being nice to Sally and the other workers at Pembrook is not my concern? It seems that you have very definite ideas about what I can and can't do."

He took a step toward her, but Victoria didn't move. "You're pushing me too far, Victoria."

She lifted her chin. "What are you going to do? Hit me like your friend Matthew does Portia?"

His frown dissolved into a look of total disbelief. "Is that what you think of me? That I would do something like that?" He shook his head. "My father told me that a woman will turn against you. It didn't take you long to do that, did it?"

Panic surged through Victoria as she stared at Marcus. Without realizing it, she had just inflicted a great hurt on her husband. She reached for his arm. "Marcus, I'm sorry. I speak before I think sometimes. I didn't mean to hurt you."

He shook her hand from his arm. "I think I'll go back down and sit in the lobby for a while. Don't wait up for me."

Victoria tried to stop him as he brushed past her, but he avoided her touch. When he walked through the balcony door to the hotel, she collapsed into her chair and released the tears she'd held back.

What had she done? Her mother's words about how impulsive she was flashed into her mind, and she groaned. But Marcus had been wrong, too. He'd treated her like she was an outsider instead of his wife when he'd refused to even listen to her concerns about why his mother left. He seemed to have the idea that what she thought made no difference. Then there was the problem with their differing opinions on how the tenant farmer families should be treated.

She had only been married a few weeks. This was supposed to be the happiest time of her life, but minutes ago her husband had looked at her as if she were a total stranger. Perhaps her mother had been right. She and Marcus might have needed more time to get to know each other, but it was too late to think about that now. For better or worse, Daniel had said, and now she had to find a way to live with those words.

Chapter 10

Two months later, the tension between Marcus and Victoria had increased to the point that at times he thought he would go out of his mind. He hesitated on the front porch of the big house before entering. He tried to stay away from home in the fields as much as possible, but today he was hungry. Not just for food, but for the connection he and Victoria had shared during the first days of their marriage. He longed to get it back, but he had no idea what to do.

He put his hand on the doorknob but couldn't turn it. What was she doing today? He longed to see her in one of the dresses he'd bought for her in Selma, but she hadn't worn one yet. Every day she put on one of her plain housedresses and worked alongside Sally in the house even though she knew how much it angered him. He'd even overheard some of the tenant farmers talking about how she'd walked to the fields where they were working to meet them.

Once he'd also seen her coming from the barn when he returned home early. When he questioned her at supper about why she was there, she'd responded that she wanted James to drive her in the buggy to visit Savannah. Her dark eyes had glared at him. "Am I permitted to use the buggy to visit my friends?" she'd asked. He'd mumbled his reply that she was free to use anything at Pembrook and then stormed from the table.

He had no idea how many times James had driven her to see Savannah or Tave, but he felt sure they must know by now how strained the relationship was between the two of them. Her mother and uncle had to be aware of it, too, because he hadn't been to church with her since their argument in Selma. Each Sunday James drove her to the church and waited until she was ready to come home.

She acted like she hated him, and he couldn't understand why. He only wanted to help her understand what was expected of her as the wife of Pembrook's owner.

Marcus opened the front door of the big house and stepped inside. She wasn't in the parlor, so he walked down the hallway to the kitchen. He stopped at the closed door and listened. Victoria's voice drifted from inside.

"James drove me to Cottonwood yesterday to visit Savannah."

"Yes'm. He tole me that." Sally's soft voice was barely audible. "You have a nice time?"

"I did. We sat on their veranda and listened to James play his music for us. He's really a gifted musician, Sally. Savannah thinks so, too."

"I's glad she likes my boy's music. I always thought they was nice folks over at Cottonwood."

"Oh they are. Savannah has been like a big sister to me, but she told me something that I was sorry to hear."

"What was that?"

"She said that Portia Chandler had run away from Winterville Plantation."

"What you mean runned away? Like she done took off and left her husband?"

"That's right."

"Why she want to go and do a thing like that?" Sally's voice sounded surprised.

A chair scraped across the floor, and Marcus wondered if Victoria had risen to come to the door. He backed away a few inches but stopped when her footsteps didn't come closer. "I told Savannah that I knew why she'd done it. When we were in Selma, Portia told me that her husband was very cruel to her."

"What you mean?"

"I mean that he hit her all the time. She told me that he had beaten her so badly that she was going to disappear one of these days. She asked if I would pray for her when she left."

Sally clicked her tongue in disbelief several times. "Where you think she gone?"

"Savannah said she asked one of the tenant farmers to drive her to town so she could go to the store. When they got there, the *Alabama Maiden* was docked and ready to go downriver to Mobile. She got on board and left. It seems Captain Mills is a friend of her family. So everyone assumes he was helping her get back to her family on Dauphin Island."

"I shore hates to hear that. I cain't imagine no man bein' mean enough to hit his woman. My Ben, he wouldn't never do nothing like that."

"I would hope not. To my way of thinking, any man who would do that deserves to be hung." Victoria chuckled. "But then, my mother thinks I'm too outspoken at times."

Neither woman said anything for a moment. Marcus started to push the door open, but Victoria spoke. "Sally, did you ever know Marcus's mother?"

The hairs on the back of his neck stood up at her words, and he leaned closer to hear the answer.

"I's jest a chile when she come here. I doan 'member much."

"Do you remember if she was pretty?"

"Oh, yes'm. My grandmamma say she 'bout the purtiest white woman she ever done lay eyes on."

"Do you know why she left?"

"No'm. Like I say, I was jest a chile then."

Marcus clenched his fists and backed away from the door. Victoria had told him nothing about Portia Chandler's leaving, but she had told the whole story to a hired worker in their home. Also she had asked Sally about his mother. How could she discuss his mother after he'd told her he didn't want the subject mentioned? Did his feelings mean nothing to Victoria?

He raked his hand through his hair and groaned. Seeing Victoria now wasn't a good idea. They both might say some things that they would regret later on. He turned to leave the house but stopped when he walked by the staircase. A thought struck him, and he turned to stare toward the upper level of the house.

Taking a deep breath, he grabbed the bannister and climbed to the second floor. He stopped outside the closed door to his father's bedroom. He had come often to the room in the past but hadn't entered since his marriage. He pulled his watch from his pocket and stared at the key that dangled on the chain.

He inserted the key in the lock and pushed the door open. A musty smell of hot air and dust tickled his nose as he stepped into the room and closed the door behind him. The room looked just as he'd left it. The carved walnut headboard of the bed reached toward the ceiling with its ornate crown moldings that came from France. The white crocheted cover on the bed had been made by Marcus's grandmother, who'd died when his father was small. He'd only heard his father mention her once and had often wondered what kind of person she'd been and if she was happy at Pembrook.

Marcus walked to the armoire, which matched the bed, and opened the door. His father's clothes still hung just as they had the day he died. He closed the door and walked back to the chair that faced the fireplace and sat down. His gaze traveled up over the marble mantel to the painting of his father.

With a sigh, he settled back in the chair, gripped the arms, and studied the picture. He thought of his stern father and how he had shown little emotion. Whenever Marcus had cried when he was little, his father had ridiculed him for being weak and ordered him to get control of himself. He made it plain that he would tolerate no tears from his son.

His childhood had done little to prepare him for the task of running Pembrook, and his relationship with his father had done even less to give him guidance in being a husband. He closed his eyes for a moment and thought of Victoria. He hadn't known what love was until she came into his life, but their marriage hadn't brought the happiness he'd expected.

He had to do something to make her realize how much he loved her. He pushed to his feet and strode to the door. Before he walked from the room, he glanced back at his father's portrait. *"Women only bring unhappiness into your life."*

He could almost hear the words his father had spoken so often.

That couldn't be true. Dante Rinaldi appeared to be a happy man who loved his wife. He wondered what Dante's secret was. Maybe he should talk with him and find out. Marcus hurried from the room and locked the door behind him before he rushed down the staircase.

An hour later, he rode up to the barn at Cottonwood and dismounted. A young boy appeared at the open door of the hayloft. "Is Mr. Rinaldi around?" Marcus called out.

The boy nodded and turned to call over his shoulder. "Mr. Dante. Somebody here to see you."

Dante stepped out of the barn and smiled. "Marcus, good to see you. What brings you to Cottonwood today?"

Marcus's face warmed. How could he speak of his problems to this man who always seemed so self assured? "I. . .I wanted to. . ."

Dante waited a moment. "Yes?" he prompted.

Marcus glanced up at the hayloft and wondered if their conversation was being overheard. He pointed toward the house. "Can we talk somewhere privately?"

"Of course." He turned and called over his shoulder, "Caleb, I'll be back in a minute." He walked toward the house, and Marcus followed. When they sat down on the veranda, Dante smiled. "Now what can I help you with today?"

"It's Victoria."

Dante settled back in his chair and arched his eyebrows. "Are you having problems?"

Marcus nodded. "She's so different than I thought she would be. She's made it a point to meet all the tenant farmers and their families and even considers them friends. She stays after me to do the same."

"And don't you want to know the people who work your land?"

Marcus straightened his shoulders. "I know them. I work beside them every day, but they can't be my friends. They're workers that I've hired, and all I want from them is an honest day's work."

Dante exhaled and leaned forward. "Marcus, you're young and just starting out to manage the plantation that was built by your father and grandfather. In their time, though, it was different in the South. They had slaves to work their land. I don't think your father ever accepted the fact that the people who came to Pembrook after the war were no longer slaves. He wanted to hold on to that old way of doing things. We can't do that anymore. If we want to be successful on our land, we have to accept the differences of the people who work it or we will fail."

"But, Dante—"

Dante held up his hand. "You're talking to an Italian who settled here.

Nobody wanted to accept me, and I had to work for years to gain their respect. I was determined that I would do everything I could to help the people on my land be accepted as worthwhile citizens of this country. Without them, we wouldn't have the workforce to plant and harvest the crops we need to keep the land productive. And we wouldn't be able to provide for our families."

Marcus chewed on his lip and frowned. "I never thought of it that way."

"I think Victoria probably sees it the same way. She knows God loves the tenant farmer families at Pembrook, and she wants to show them. Instead of criticizing her for it, you should be thankful you have a wife with a kind heart."

Marcus nodded. "She is kind, but she can make me so angry. This morning I heard her talking with Sally Moses like she was her best friend. She told Sally that Portia Chandler had run away from Matthew."

"That's right," Dante said. "We didn't get to know Portia well. Maybe because Matthew kept her so close to home. Don't make that mistake with Victoria. Love her and honor her as your wife." He paused for a moment. "And don't fault her for being friends with Sally. They spend a lot of time together like Savannah and Mamie do. Savannah thinks of Mamie more like a mother and loves her with all her heart. Victoria needs a woman to be close to at Pembrook. You should be happy that Sally is there to fill that need. All the farmers I know speak very highly of the Moses family. They say that James is a gifted musician."

"That's what Victoria tells me. She never misses a chance to ask him to play for her."

Dante laughed. "The way you're grumbling, you almost sound like you're jealous of the attention Victoria pays that young man. I suppose she does think highly of him. I've noticed that he drives her to church every Sunday. She's made it a point to see that he comes inside and listens to the service. Victoria told Savannah she couldn't stand to think about him not getting to go to church because he had to drive her."

Marcus's eyes grew wide. "He comes inside to the service? What have all the people said?"

Dante shrugged. "I'm sure there are some who aren't happy about it, but Daniel has let it be known that he'll not listen to any complaining about it. Of course James could go to church with his family if you'd drive your wife to church. We've been missing you. I know Victoria would like to have you come with her."

Marcus shook his head. "I don't know about that. I tried it before we married, and it didn't appeal to me. I always felt restless and sad when I left the service."

Dante smiled. "Maybe that's because God was speaking to you, and you weren't listening."

"What would He have to say to me?"

"That He loves you and wants to give you a good life. He's given you a wife who loves you, and He wants to bless your marriage. I remember Daniel reading the scripture at your wedding that tells husbands to love their wives like Christ loved the church."

"I didn't understand that," Marcus said. "How could Christ love a building?"

"It's not the building. It's all the people who are believers. He loved us so much, Marcus, that He died on the cross for our sins. He wants you to love Victoria with that same kind of love, so much that you would lay down your life for her."

"So that's what it means. I do love Victoria. I suppose we just have to come to some agreement about our differences." He sighed and pushed to his feet. "Thanks for your time, Dante."

Dante stood and grasped Marcus's hand. "Anytime you need me, come by. But let me caution you. You need to get your relationship with God right first. Then let God lead you in your marriage."

"I'll think about what you said."

They talked of the crops and harvesttime that was approaching as they walked back to the barn, but Marcus couldn't concentrate. His mind was on everything Dante had said to him today. Much of it he didn't understand. He needed a good relationship with Victoria, not with a God he couldn't see.

He was more confused now than he'd been when he arrived at Cottonwood.

⁂

The oil lamp on the table beside her chair cast a yellow glow across the shirt that Victoria was mending. She tried to concentrate on her stitches, but her gaze kept darting to Marcus, who sat in the chair next to her. He'd been reading a book ever since they'd settled in the parlor after supper. He hadn't said much during their meal or in the hour since they'd left the dining room.

She sighed and directed her attention back to her sewing. Her mind drifted back to her life in Mobile and how happy she'd been working at the boardinghouse during the day and spending her evenings with her mother. At the time, she'd thought her life very dreary, but now she remembered it with a longing that brought tears to her eyes.

Marcus glanced up from his book and frowned. "What was that?"

Startled, she looked up. "What?"

"You were humming."

Victoria frowned. "I was? I didn't realize it. What was I humming?"

"I don't know. It had a sad sound to it, sort of gloomy."

She gave a nervous laugh. "Then it was probably one of James's songs. They're all very melancholy and sad sounding. Sally says it's the kind of music the slaves used to sing when they thought about their lost lives after being brought to this country. They made up the songs they sang, and now James does, too. He says they used to call it blue music; now it's called the blues because of the way it makes you feel."

His gaze searched her eyes. "Is that how you feel here at Pembrook? Blue? Sad? Do you want to run away like Portia Chandler did?"

She gasped. "How did you know about Portia?"

"I overheard you telling Sally."

She frowned. "But I didn't think you came home today."

"I did, but I didn't stay. I had a lot of work to do."

She laid the shirt aside and stared at him. "I have to admit that my beginning here hasn't been what I thought it would be and that sometimes I'm sad because I don't think you love me. But I have never thought about running away like Portia did."

He closed the book he held and laid it on the table. "Victoria, I do love you. It's just that we have very different ways of looking at things. I'll try to be more understanding of your need to help the people on Pembrook land if you will make an effort to understand my feelings about keeping ourselves separate from them. I've never had anyone who said they loved me before, and I want to build a life here for just the two of us."

She shook her head. "That's impossible, Marcus. This house isn't a refuge for you to escape to at the end of the day and expect me to be waiting to offer comfort and love. Try to understand that I am not your mother, and I'm not going to leave you like she did. I want us to build a life together that includes everybody who lives on our land. I want us to be like Savannah and Dante."

"I want that, too."

She smiled. "Then we have a common goal."

He stood, pulled her to her feet, and wrapped his arms around her. Her heart pounded when he stared down into her eyes. "I love you, Victoria."

"I love you, too, Marcus," she whispered.

As their lips touched, she prayed this would be the new beginning she'd been wanting. Only time would tell.

Chapter 11

The rooster's crowing woke Victoria from a sound sleep on a cold December morning. She didn't have to glance at the pillow beside her to know that Marcus was already up and at the barn. Every morning he arose early to do his chores and then returned to the house to have breakfast with her. This arrangement had come about after their uneasy truce months ago when they'd decided to try to build a life together.

Marcus still didn't understand her friendship with Sally and James, but he didn't argue with her as he had done at first. He also had not accompanied her to church again, even though Daniel had visited several times and Dante had also encouraged him. She could only hope that would change in time.

On this cold morning, she snuggled underneath the covers for an extra few minutes before she went downstairs to help Sally with breakfast. Thoughts of Christmas drifted through her mind, and she smiled at the plans she was already making for their first Christmas together. Along with her mother and uncle, they had been invited to spend Christmas Day at Cottonwood with Savannah and Dante. The Lucketts and Tave's father, Dr. Spencer, would also be guests that day. She was secretly glad they had been invited to Cottonwood because Marcus wouldn't expect Sally to be at the big house that day. She would be free to celebrate with her own family.

She smiled when she thought of how close she and Sally had become since her wedding. Victoria had never had a friend like her, and she couldn't wait each morning to see her. By this time, Sally would have the big stove fired up and biscuits ready to go in the oven. Usually the smell of coffee drifted up the stairs, but not this morning.

The clock in the downstairs hallway chimed the hour, and Victoria sat up, a frown on her face. Something didn't seem right. She threw back the covers, jumped out of bed, and dressed quickly. When she entered the dark kitchen, her heart lurched. Sally hadn't arrived, and the stove's embers had burned down during the night.

Marcus would be back for breakfast soon, and there was nothing to eat. After lighting the lamps in the kitchen, she set about to rebuild the fire in the big cast-iron cookstove. Within minutes a fire blazed, and she had ham sizzling in a skillet and biscuits ready to go in the oven. By the time Marcus stopped at the back door to take off his boots, she had breakfast nearly ready.

A surprised expression flashed across his face when he stepped into the kitchen. "Victoria," he said. "I didn't expect you to be up."

"Sally's not here yet, and I've cooked breakfast for us."

He glanced at the food and back to her. A slow smile covered his face. "I do remember you telling me you worked in a boardinghouse. It looks good."

She waved her hand in dismissal. "Anybody can cook breakfast, but I'm worried about Sally. She's always here by this time."

Marcus nodded. "James is at the barn. He said Sally has been sick all night."

Victoria set the platter of ham on the kitchen table and gasped. "What's wrong with her?"

"He didn't say. Just said that she wouldn't be here for a few days." He glanced down at his hands. "I'll go wash up and then come back to eat with you."

"All right. I thought we might eat in the kitchen this morning instead of at that long dining room table. Is that all right with you?"

"That's fine."

She watched him step out to the back porch where they kept the bucket of water with its dipper and wash pan, but her mind was on Sally.

She couldn't concentrate on her food all through the meal, but Marcus ate like he hadn't had anything in days. When he finished, he wiped his mouth and smiled. "With Sally out, I may get to see some of your talents I haven't experienced yet. I can hardly wait to see what you'll fix for the noon meal."

She smiled. "I'll try to surprise you."

He rose and kissed her on the cheek. "You always do. I'll see you later."

Victoria sat at the table after he left and glanced around the kitchen. It seemed so empty without Sally. She pushed up from the table but grabbed its edge as a wave of dizziness swept over her. Her legs trembled, and nausea welled up in her throat. She dropped back into the chair, folded her arms on the table, and laid her head on them. She lay there until the nausea and dizziness had passed. Then she stood.

She would wash the dishes, change clothes, and go check on Sally. Maybe there was something she could do to make her feel more comfortable. As Victoria took a step toward the dry sink, the dizziness returned, and she wobbled. Maybe she should ask James to drive her to the Moses home instead of walking. She would check on Sally and be back in time to fix Marcus's noon meal.

An hour later, though, as Victoria sat by Sally's bed, she knew her friend needed more medical attention than she was able to give. Sally's body burned with fever, and the pupils of her eyes had no spark in them. Her breathing was shallow, and hacking coughs rattled in her chest.

Victoria tried to recall if Sally had seemed sick the day before and remembered that she had coughed for several days. She had also seemed tired, but she hadn't complained.

Victoria glanced up at James, who hovered nearby. "How long has she been this sick?"

"Ever since she come home yes'tidy. She was real hot and went right to bed."

"Why didn't you come get me, James?"

"I wanted to, Miz Raines, but Mama say I cain't go up to the big house and talk to you whilst Mistuh Mahcus there."

Victoria pushed to her feet. "That's ridiculous. Marcus wouldn't want your mother to suffer." She thought for a moment before she faced James. "We have to take her to the doctor. Can you pick her up?"

James's eyes grew large. "You mean go see the doctor in town?"

"Yes. We need to get her to Dr. Spencer's office right away."

James backed away. "I doan think Mistuh Mahcus gonna like me drivin' his buggy to take Mama to town."

Victoria glared at him. "It's my buggy, too, James, and I'm telling you to pick your mother up and put her in that buggy now, or I'll do it myself. Do you understand?"

James gulped. "Yes'm. I'll do it, Miz Raines."

Victoria grabbed two quilts from the bed and wrapped one around Sally when James scooped her up in his arms. She folded the other one and carried it to the buggy as she followed James outside. She climbed in the backseat and scooted to the far side. "Put your mother beside me, and I'll cover her up with this other quilt. I'll hold her while you drive."

James lifted his mother onto the seat and watched as Victoria tucked the quilt around her. Victoria glanced up. Tears stood in James's eyes. "Thank you, Miz Raines."

She pulled Sally closer to her. "Sally is my friend, James. I want to see that she's taken care of."

He took a deep breath. "I don't reckon there be many white folks 'round here would feel that way."

"You're wrong, James. Savannah and Dante Rinaldi would, and so would Daniel and Tave Luckett."

He nodded. "Yes'm, I 'spect they would, but not many more."

James jumped into the front seat of the buggy, grabbed the reins, and flicked them across the horse's back. Victoria thought about what James had said as they pulled away from the Moses house. She wondered how many people would have ignored Sally and her family's need because of the color of their skin.

She gasped and sat up straighter as a sudden thought flashed through her mind. In naming the people who would have cared, she realized she hadn't mentioned one name—her husband's. Her heart sank at the thought that she didn't know what Marcus would have done.

❧

Marcus had been so surprised when he walked into the kitchen at breakfast and saw Victoria cooking. He had to admit he enjoyed the quiet time spent with her at the big kitchen table as they ate. He could hardly wait to get back home and see what she had cooked for the noon meal.

But when he walked in the back door, the kitchen was dark and the cookstove was cold. Where could she be? "Victoria," he called out. There was no answer.

He climbed the stairs and checked the bedroom. The dress that she had worn at breakfast lay on the bed, and the door to the armoire stood ajar. Why would she have changed clothes in the morning? Maybe James knew.

When he strode into the barn, another surprise awaited him. James wasn't there, and neither was the buggy. With Victoria and James gone and the buggy as well, Marcus realized there was only one place to look for them—at Ben Moses's house.

He jumped on his horse and galloped down the road toward the spot where the Moses family lived. He knew Victoria enjoyed walking and had often walked Sally home after her day at the big house. Why hadn't she walked today if she went to check on Sally?

Marcus spied the horse and buggy outside the Moses house before he even pulled to a stop. Gritting his teeth, he climbed down and strode across the barren front yard to the door of the house. He raised his fist and pounded on the door. "James, are you in there?"

The doorknob turned, and Victoria opened the door. She smiled when she saw him. "Oh Marcus, I'm so glad you're here. Come in."

He shook his head and backed away. "Come outside and tell me what you're doing here, Victoria."

She glanced over her shoulder and grabbed her shawl that lay on the back of a chair. Pulling it around her, she stepped onto the porch. "Sally is very ill. James and I took her to see Dr. Spencer. He says she has pneumonia."

Marcus's mouth gaped open. "You took her to Dr. Spencer? Whatever were you thinking?"

Her eyes narrowed, and she tilted her head to one side. "I was thinking that she needed to see a doctor. I was right. Dr. Spencer said she was very ill when we got there. He wanted her to stay at his office, but she refused. He let her come home if she would have someone with her at all times for the next few days."

"How do they think they're going to do that? Ben and James both have work to do. They can't stay here and take care of her."

Victoria pulled her shawl tighter and straightened her back. "I know. I told them I would stay during the day, and they could take care of her at night."

Marcus felt like he'd been kicked in the stomach. "You? Oh no. You're not going to stay here and take care of that—"

"Stop it!" she yelled. "Don't you dare say anything vile against Sally or call her any names that I've heard from others since I've been in Willow Bend. She's been good to me. At times she's been the only one good to me at Pembrook, and I intend to take care of her."

"You're defying me?" he shouted.

"I'm only doing what I know is right. I. . ." She stopped and swallowed before she touched her hand to her forehead. "I—I don't feel well."

Before Marcus could say anything, Victoria slumped. He caught her in his arms before she hit the porch. He sat down and cradled her close to his body. "Victoria, Victoria," he whispered.

James rushed onto the front porch and stared down at the two of them. "What happened to Miz Raines?"

"She fainted. One minute she was fine, and the next she was falling."

"I'll get some water."

James rushed inside and returned with a cup of water. Marcus held it to her lips, but most of it ran down her cheek. "Was she all right when you went to town?"

James backed away. "I thinks so."

"What do you mean you think so? Did she say anything?" When James didn't answer, Marcus yelled, "Tell me!"

"I heered her talkin' to the doctor 'bout how she been feelin' bad, but I doan know what he say."

Victoria stirred and opened her eyes. She frowned and stared up at Marcus. "Wh–what happened?"

"You fainted." She tried to rise, but he held her tight. "James said you talked to the doctor. Are you ill, Victoria?"

She shook her head and pulled free of him. "No."

"I's glad you fellin' better, Miz Raines. I better go check on Mama."

Marcus waited for James to go inside before he stood and helped Victoria to rise. When she faced him, he took her by the shoulders and stared into her eyes. "Tell me what Dr. Spencer said."

She blinked back tears but didn't waver under his piercing gaze. "I'm going to have a baby, Marcus."

He gasped and let his hands drop to his sides. "A baby? When?"

"In June."

He waited for her to tell him how happy she was, but she clamped her lips together. When she didn't speak, he took a deep breath. "And how do you feel about that?"

She pushed a strand of hair out of her eyes and pursed her lips. "How do you feel about having a child by a wife who you think defies you, Marcus?"

He tried to identify the emotion he saw in her eyes, but it was no use. He didn't know if it was hate, loathing, or anger she felt. He reached out to her, but she backed away.

His hand drifted back to his side, and he turned away. It was no use. There was nothing he could say that would make her forgive him for the things he'd just said.

As he rode away from the house, he glanced back once, and Victoria still stood on the porch, watching him. His chest felt like his heart had been hacked into pieces. Victoria was carrying his child, and she had looked at him like she hated him the same way his mother must have when she left him.

His father had warned him, and he'd been right. From what had just happened between him and Victoria, it looked like they might be on the same course that his parents had traveled. However, he knew there would be one difference. Victoria would never allow him to keep his child if she left.

❦

On Sunday morning, Victoria hurried from the church and headed to the buggy where James waited for her. She'd almost reached him when she heard her mother call her name.

"Victoria, wait. I want to talk to you."

She stopped and forced a smile to her face as her mother came toward her. "Hello, Mama. How are you?"

"I'm fine, but I wanted to check on Sally. Dr. Spencer told me that you brought her to his office this week."

"That's right. She has pneumonia, but she's better today. I've stayed with her for the last three days, but she insisted I come to church today."

Her mother's forehead wrinkled. "What did Marcus think about that?"

Victoria glanced over her mother's shoulder and spied her uncle coming toward them. "Hello, Uncle Samuel. How are you?"

"I'm fine. Has your mother told you the news?" he asked.

Victoria's eyebrows arched, and she turned back to her mother. "What news?"

"Your uncle has sold his store."

The news almost sent Victoria reeling. "Sold your store? Who bought it?"

"Henry Walton," he said. "He's one of Dante's tenant farmers. His family used to have a store before the war, and he's always wanted one. We got to talking the other day, and I told him how I would like to retire. The next day he came back and offered to buy me out."

Victoria struggled to overcome her surprise. "B–but how did he come up with the money on such short notice?"

Her uncle chuckled. "Dante Rinaldi loaned it to him."

Victoria's chin trembled as she thought of the difference between Dante and Marcus. "Yes, I can see Dante doing that. But what are you going to do now, Uncle Samuel?"

He glanced at her mother and smiled. "Well, not only me, but your mother, too."

Victoria's stomach roiled. She had a feeling that she was about to hear news that wouldn't be good. "What are you going to do, Mama?"

She reached out and grasped Victoria's hand. "Oh, darling, the most wonderful thing has happened. Captain Mills has been calling on me whenever the *Alabama Maiden* docks, and we've become quite fond of each other. He's asked me to marry him and go to Mobile with him. Your uncle is coming there to live, too."

Victoria's eyes filled with tears, and she shrank from her mother. "But you can't leave me. I'm going to have a baby."

"A baby?" Her mother's high-pitched cry carried across the churchyard, and several people turned to stare. She grabbed Victoria and hugged her. "That's wonderful. Of course I'll come back when the baby is born and stay with you for a few weeks. Is Marcus happy?"

"He's happy," Victoria whispered. "When is the wedding?"

"He's arriving when the *Montgomery Belle* makes its upriver voyage next week. We'll be married in Willow Bend and board the boat when it goes back downriver two weeks from now."

"Two weeks?" Victoria's lips trembled. "That means you won't be here for Christmas."

Her mother reached out and grasped Victoria's hand. "No, but if we can have the wedding at Pembrook, we can combine it with an early Christmas celebration."

"Of course we'll have the wedding at Pembrook, but Christmas won't be the same without you there."

Her mother waved her hand in dismissal. "It may seem strange at first, but you're going to Cottonwood on Christmas Day. You'll have Savannah and Tave to spend the holiday with you."

Victoria swallowed the lump that formed in her throat. She'd have her friends, but if things didn't change between her and Marcus, he might not even want to celebrate Christmas.

"But I've never been away from you before. I don't want you to leave me here."

Her mother put her arms around Victoria and pulled her close. "Please be happy for me, darling. When your father died, I was sure I'd never find love again, but I have." She released Victoria and stared into her eyes. "If I didn't feel you were well cared for, I would never go back to Mobile. But you have a very rich husband and a beautiful home. And now you're going to have a child. What more could you want?"

Victoria bit her tongue to keep from unleashing the pent-up emotions that surged through her body. Ever since Victoria had been a child, her mother had talked about how she wanted her only daughter to marry well. And to many people it probably looked like Victoria had made a perfect match. In her heart, though, she knew better. Something was missing from her marriage, and she had to find out what it was. Right now, the big house at Pembrook was a desolate place.

Ever since Sally had been sick, Victoria had risen early and fixed Marcus's breakfast as well as something for the noon meal, but she left the house before he came from the barn. Neither of them talked during supper. As soon as he'd eaten, Marcus disappeared into his father's room and didn't come out until the next morning.

Victoria had stopped at the closed door to her father-in-law's old room several times, but she couldn't bring herself to knock. Marcus didn't appear to have any desire to talk with her, and she wouldn't push herself on him.

When her mother and uncle left for Mobile, she would be all alone at Pembrook. Now she sensed how alone Portia Chandler must have felt. Her hand touched her stomach. She wasn't alone. By the summer she would have her child.

Victoria smiled and hugged her mother. "Then we'd better get busy planning your wedding."

Chapter 12

Victoria had never experienced a Christmas like the one she spent at Cottonwood. A tall spruce tree stood in the parlor, its branches decorated with strings of dried fruit, popcorn, and pinecones. Snowflakes that had been fashioned from white paper dangled from the top of the tree to the bottom. Vance had made a great show of pointing out the ones he had cut and those his sister had created.

Victoria settled back in a chair near the parlor fireplace and moaned with happiness as she recalled the holiday meal they'd just devoured. "Christmas dinner was delicious, Savannah, even though I'm sure all of you tired of hearing me talk about my mother's wedding."

Tave shook her head. "I thought it was a beautiful wedding. They looked so happy."

Savannah turned from stirring the logs in the fireplace and smiled. "I was go glad you invited us. Your mother was beautiful, and her new husband couldn't take his eyes off her."

"She did look happy," Victoria said. "I was upset when she first told me she was getting married, but I want her to have a good life like she thinks I have with Marcus."

Savannah's eyes grew wide. "Is there a problem between you and Marcus?"

Victoria fought back the tears in her eyes. "It seems we don't think alike on a lot of things, and I can't do anything to please him. Right now he's angry with me because I've taken care of Sally since she's been sick."

Tave scooted to the edge of the sofa. "What kind of problem has Sally's illness caused between you and Marcus?"

For the next few minutes Victoria told her friends how strained her relationship with Marcus was. "Now I'm going to have a baby, and my mother is gone. I feel so alone."

Savannah and Tave glanced at each other before Savannah spoke up. "We thought there was a problem. You seem to think that Marcus is the one at fault, and I'm sure he bears responsibility for some of your problems. But you must remember that there are always two sides to every story. Perhaps you've been so determined to have your own way that you haven't thought about his feelings."

"His feelings? I don't even know how to understand him. He thinks himself so superior to all the people who live on Pembrook land. He can't stand it because I like Sally and James, and he gets so angry if I visit any of the tenant farmers' homes. I've tried to tell him that they are part of the Pembrook family and we need to treat them with respect. He won't listen to that, though. He just says that's not what his father thought."

"My father and his father knew each other," Savannah said. "I can't say they were friends because Marcus's father didn't seem to want friends. He ruled Pembrook and its people with an iron hand. I imagine Marcus had a hard time growing up with a demanding father and no mother. Have you ever thought that he might just want to be loved by someone?"

Victoria's face grew warm. "Well, he has told me that I'm the only person who's ever loved him."

Tave reached over and touched Victoria's arm. "Do you love him?"

She thought about the first days of their marriage and how happy they'd been. "Yes, I want us to be happy, but we look at life so differently."

Savannah and Tave exchanged quick glances before Savannah spoke. "Victoria, I know you attend church every Sunday, but was there a time in your life when you accepted Christ as your Savior?"

Victoria clenched her fists in her lap and thought back to the day when she was twelve years old and sat in church, listening to a sermon about how God gave His Son for everyone's sins. That day she had asked Christ into her heart and had promised to live for Him. But had she? Her thoughts had centered on herself instead of what she had vowed that day.

"I did accept Christ years ago, but I suppose I haven't really placed a lot of importance on it in my life."

Savannah knelt in front of Victoria. "Then you need to read your Bible and pray. You need to ask God to turn you into a vessel full of His love and help you show it to others, especially Marcus."

Tave nodded. "Marcus hasn't been taught about God's love. Until he understands it and you recognize the importance of it in your life, the two of you are going to see things differently. If you truly are one of God's children, you have the task of bringing your husband to Christ, Victoria, and you can't do it by doing things that make him angry. You have to approach him in love."

"How can I do that when he treats Sally or James or any other worker at Pembrook with a total disregard for their feelings? Am I supposed to smile and bow down to him?" Victoria's nails dug into her palms from her clenched fists.

Savannah frowned. "Of course not. Just remember what Jesus said about turning the other cheek. Without being angry, tell him that you're sorry he doesn't understand how his words can hurt someone. Tell him you love him and that you're going to pray that God will give him a new awareness of how to treat others. Then you have to pray for him."

Tave arched an eyebrow. "Do you pray for Marcus, Victoria?"

She dropped her gaze. "No."

Savannah leaned forward. "Marcus has a big responsibility at Pembrook. Try to look through his eyes and see what his life is like. Examine the way you treat him, and then try to ease the burdens he must feel at times."

Victoria straightened her shoulders and stared at her two friends. "You make it sound like the success of my marriage depends on me."

Tave and Savannah exchanged smiles before they looked back at her. "That may be true," Tave said. "Are you willing to make the effort and see if you can be happy, or are you going to continue the way you have been and remain miserable?"

She didn't move for a minute. Her gaze flicked back and forth between the two women. Tears flooded her eyes. "I want us to be happy."

Tave nodded. "Good. Then renew your relationship with God, read your Bible about what is expected of a wife, and begin to fulfill that role in your home. No more acting like the impulsive child that Marcus married. Be the woman he wants in a wife."

Victoria thought of the Bible that lay on the table next to her bed. It hadn't been opened in months. Her heart pricked as she realized that she had work to do if she ever expected to be happy at Pembrook.

She reached over and grasped the hands of her two friends. "Thank you. This is the best Christmas gift you could have given me."

They squeezed her fingers. Savannah leaned closer to her. "We'll be praying for you, too, Victoria. Your mother may be gone from Willow Bend, but you're not alone."

A new resolve flowed into her heart as she stared at Tave and Savannah. Both of them appeared to have happy marriages, and they wanted the same for her. For the first time she realized that many of Marcus's problems stemmed from the fact that she had neglected her relationship with God. That was something she needed to remedy first. From now on, she would let Marcus see God's love in her actions.

⌘

After the meal he'd just eaten, Marcus drifted on the edge of sleep in Dante's office. The drone of Dante's voice as well as Daniel's and Dr. Spencer's floated around in his mind as if he inhabited the most tranquil place he'd ever visited. His head nodded forward, and he jerked upright. Had someone spoken to him? He glanced around at the three men, who grinned back at him.

"Having trouble staying awake?" Dante's eyes sparkled as he asked the question.

Marcus straightened in his chair and gave a nervous laugh. "Please forgive me. After the good meal your wife served, I couldn't stay awake."

Dr. Spencer rubbed his stomach. "I know what you mean. Christmas at Cottonwood is always a special event. Tave and I have been coming for years, even before she and Daniel married."

Daniel nodded and groaned. "And I always feel like I can't move after dinner. Savannah and Mamie always make everything extra special."

Dr. Spencer turned to Marcus. "Speaking of Mamie makes me think of Sally. How is she doing?"

Marcus shrugged. "All right, I guess. She came back to work this week. I want to apologize to you, Dr. Spencer, for Victoria bringing her to your office."

A look of surprise flashed across Dr. Spencer's face. "Why would you apologize?"

"Because Sally is the wife of one of my tenant farmers."

Anger flashed in Dr. Spencer's eyes. "Haven't you learned anything in the years since the war? I thought I was through dealing with that kind of attitude around here, but maybe I'm not. I treat every sick person who comes to me no matter what color their skin is. You need to take a lesson from your wife and act like you care for the workers at Pembrook. Sally and her family have worked hard to make life good for you. You need to repay them by at least seeing that they get medical attention when they need it."

Daniel reached out and laid his hand on Dr. Spencer's arm. "My father-in-law gets carried away sometimes, Marcus, but he's right. We're all equal in God's sight."

Marcus stared at the two men and then at Dante. "I'm sorry if I've upset you, but I wasn't brought up to feel that way."

Dante leaned forward in his chair and propped his arms on his knees. "I know you weren't. Your father and I had conversations similar to this several times while he was alive, but he never would listen to what I said." He stared at Marcus for a moment. "Do you remember the warning I gave you last summer at the church picnic about the grumbling I'd heard from your tenant farmers?"

"Yes."

"They talk to the men who live at Cottonwood, and they love and respect Victoria very much because she cares about them. They don't respect you, Marcus, because they say you're trying to run the plantation with the same stern manner your father used. It's a new day in the South, and all they want is to be treated fairly and appreciated for what they do for you." Dante took a deep breath. "The same way that Victoria needs to be appreciated."

Marcus jumped to his feet. "You don't know anything about what goes on between my wife and me. I've given her everything a woman could want—a home, more clothes than she can ever wear, freedom to visit her friends anytime she wants. And what does she do? Defy me at every turn."

Daniel and Dante both rose. Daniel sighed. "We're not condemning you. We want to help you. The two of you seemed so in love when you married."

"I do love her."

Dante studied him a moment. "I think you do, Marcus, in your own way, but not in the way Christ meant for men to love their wives. Do you want to have a good marriage?"

"Yes."

"Then you have to come to understand several things," Daniel said. "First of all, you have to realize that God loves you and wants to give you peace and happiness, but you have to come to know Him. When you do, you'll begin to see people differently than how you view them now, and you'll understand how God wants you to be a better husband to Victoria."

"Dante, you've talked to me about accepting Christ before, but I've never seen a need for it." Marcus struggled to control his anger. "Do you think I'm a bad husband?"

Dante shook his head. "I don't think you're a bad person, Marcus. I believe you want to do what's right, but you don't know how. When you come to the point that you recognize the need for Christ in your life and ask to be forgiven for your sins, you'll see a whole new world open up to you."

"But I don't know how to do that."

Daniel smiled. "I have a Christmas present for you, Marcus." He walked over to Dante's desk and picked up a Bible. "I brought this for you today. I've marked passages that I want you to read. They'll help you understand how Christ loved you so much that He died on the cross for you."

Marcus chuckled. "You make it sound like He died just for me."

Daniel nodded. "He did. The Bible tells us to believe on the Lord Jesus Christ, and He'll come into our hearts and never forsake us." He handed the Bible to Marcus. "Read the passages I've marked, over and over until you understand that kind of love. Then read the places I've marked about how husbands should love their wives. It will all become clear to you. Will you do that?"

Marcus hesitated a moment before he reached for the Bible Daniel held. "I will."

Dante smiled. "Good. And one more thing. When you feel like Victoria doesn't understand your point of view, don't get angry. Be patient and tell her that you love her and try to explain why you feel the way you do. Communication is so important in marriage."

"Marriage is difficult under the best of circumstances," Daniel said. "It takes a lot of work and a lot of compromise to understand how the other person feels. Now that you're going to be a father, you're adding new responsibilities. You want your child to have a happier childhood than you did, don't you?"

For the first time it struck Marcus how his life was about to change. He would have a child who would look to him for all his needs. He thought of Dante and how Gabby and Vance adored their father. He wanted that, too, with his son or daughter. He didn't want his child to experience what he had growing up.

"Yes, I want my child to be happy."

Dante pointed to the Bible in Marcus's hand. "You have the guide right there that can help you solve every problem you encounter. It's not always easy, but once you turn your life over to God, He'll be there with you."

Marcus stared at the Bible. He'd never had one before. What would his father think of his reading the book? It didn't matter. He had to do something to repair the damage he and Victoria had done to their marriage. And they had to try to make Pembrook a happy place for the child they were going to have.

Maybe Dante and Daniel were right. Reading the Bible might be a start, but he didn't have much faith that it would work.

⏤⏤

On Christmas night, Victoria sat in the parlor of her home alone. Marcus had disappeared into his father's old room shortly after they'd eaten a light supper, and she hadn't seen him since. That was two hours ago.

During her time alone, she'd thought of everything Savannah and Tave had talked to her about today. She had even brought her Bible down from upstairs and sat in the parlor, reading as she tried to find a way to try to reach her husband. As she flipped idly through the pages, a passage in Hebrews caught her attention, and she read it. When she finished, she reread the passage. *"Let us hold fast the profession of our faith without wavering; (for he is faithful that promised;) And let us consider one another to provoke unto love and to good works."*

The verses made her heart sink. She had not held fast to her profession of faith. Instead, she had married a man who didn't share her beliefs and didn't understand her love and concern for other people.

How many times in the last months had she berated Marcus because he didn't agree with her instead of telling him of God's love for him? Her impulsive manner and sharp tongue had displayed no kindness. Guilt for her actions flowed through her. She clasped her hands and bowed her head.

"Oh God," she prayed, "help me to be kinder to my husband. Tell me how to show him Your love through my actions. I promise You, Lord, from this day forward I will hold fast to my profession of faith. Give me the words and the actions to show Marcus Your love."

She raised her head and thought of Marcus alone in his father's room. What did he do all the hours he spent there? Laying the Bible aside, she rose from the chair and walked to the staircase. Her knees trembled as she put her foot on the first tread and lifted her head to stare toward the upper floor of the house. She took a deep breath and mounted the stairs.

When she arrived at the closed door to her father-in-law's room, she raised her clenched fist and knocked. "Marcus, are you in there?"

Through the paneled door, she heard the sound of footsteps approach, and the door swung open. Marcus's eyes held no emotion as he stared at her. "Victoria, what do you want?"

She breathed a silent prayer that God would give her the words to speak to her husband. She smiled. "I wanted to tell you what a wonderful Christmas our first one together was. I enjoyed the day at Cottonwood, and"—she reached to the collar of her dress and touched the brooch she'd pinned there—"I love my Christmas present from you. I've never had a piece of jewelry as beautiful, and I wanted to thank you again."

He gazed at the brooch for a moment before he looked into her eyes. "And I liked the socks and scarf you knitted for me."

"I hope so. Even in Alabama it gets cold on January mornings. I thought some heavy socks and a scarf around your neck might help you stay warm."

A small smile pulled at his lips. "Thank you for thinking of me."

She blinked back the tears that wanted to fill her eyes. "I think about you all the time, Marcus. You may not believe that because of the way I act sometimes. I warned you before we were married that I was impulsive, and I know I've said things to hurt you. I'm sorry for that. I hope you'll forgive me."

His eyes grew wide. "You want me to forgive you?"

She moved closer to him. "Yes. I haven't been as thoughtful of you as I should be. After all, you're the most important person in the world to me. I love you, Marcus, and I want us to be happy."

He reached out and took her hand in his. "I want that, too. I haven't been as understanding of you as I should have been, and I'm sorry about that. But I do love you, Victoria, and I'll try to be a better husband." He glanced over his shoulder, but she couldn't see what he was looking at. "Dante and Daniel gave me a Bible today with some passages marked for me to read. I've been trying to understand them, but so much of it is strange to me."

"I've been reading my Bible, too. Maybe if we studied it together, we could discuss it and see what God wants to tell us."

His grip tightened on her hand. "I don't know anything about God. Will you help me learn?"

A tear slid down her cheek. "That's what I should have been doing all along instead of arguing with you because we didn't think alike. I want you to know God."

"Thank you."

She reached up and caressed his cheek with her hand. "Marcus, I miss you so much at night. Do you have to sleep in your father's room?"

He pulled her hand to his mouth and kissed her palm. "Do you want me to come back to our bedroom?"

"Yes."

He wrapped his arms around her and pulled her closer. "I never should have left. Please forgive me for that. I want to be with you all the time."

"I want that, too."

"Wait a minute." He released her, walked back into the room, and blew out the oil lamp on the table. When he stepped back into the hall, he held a Bible in his hand. He wrapped his free arm around her shoulders and smiled down at her. "This is the best Christmas I've ever had."

Her heart pounded in her chest as she stared up at him. "Me, too. But something tells me this is just the beginning for happier times at Pembrook."

Chapter 13

On a June afternoon six months later, Victoria stepped onto the veranda of the big house at Pembrook, put her hands in the small of her back, and stretched. She'd stayed in bed longer this morning, secretly enjoying the first pangs of impending labor.

She hadn't told Marcus of her discomfort before he left because the baby wasn't due for two more weeks, and he had too much to do in the fields to spend his time worrying about her. Besides, Sally was with her, and her mother would arrive in three days on the *Alabama Maiden* to spend a few weeks. This morning, however, she waited, enduring the erratic pains that had come and gone since early morning, until she could be sure it was time to send for Dr. Spencer.

Now as she lifted her face to the warm sun, she thrilled at the thought that her baby would be born today. She could hardly wait to hold him. She'd been sure from the first that it would be a boy, but Marcus said he'd be happy with a girl.

She smiled as she thought of all the changes that had taken place at Pembrook since Christmas night when she and Marcus had started on their journey of reconciliation. They had carried through on their decision to study the Bible and had devoted several hours each night to reading and discussing God's Word. That time spent together had repaired the brokenness of their marriage, and she treasured those moments.

Over the past months, she had grown in her understanding of the importance of God in one's life, and Marcus had slowly come to an awareness of his need for God. Her happiest moment had come a few months before when he had finally accepted Christ. As a new believer, he spent a lot of time talking with Daniel as his new way of looking at life took root in his soul.

His continued remote attitude toward the tenant farmers and their families hadn't improved, and that worried her. Sally and James were the exceptions. For the past few months, he'd seemed to come to an appreciation of all they did for Pembrook. Perhaps the absence of Victoria's mother had made him understand how important Sally's attentive care of Victoria was to her. He also had come to understand Victoria's love of James's music.

In February when Victoria had mentioned how she wished James had a real guitar, Marcus had told her to order one from Montgomery if she liked. James had been overwhelmed when the instrument arrived, and he'd spent hours ever since playing for Victoria.

A disappointment to Victoria had been the departure of two families from Pembrook. One had taken Henry Walton's place at Cottonwood, and the other one had gone to Oak Hill. Marcus had soon found other tenants to take their places, but she sensed he was saddened by the loss of the two families who'd been there for years.

She had prayed about it and had received peace about the problem. In her heart she knew it was just a matter of time until Marcus would be able to let go of the old ideas of the past and would embrace all the residents of Pembrook as he had Sally and James.

Victoria closed her eyes and inhaled the sweet smell of the roses that bloomed beside the house. Life had never been sweeter, and she'd never been happier.

"Miz Raines, you out here?" Sally's voice from the back door caused her to turn.

"I'm here, Sally. What is it?"

"I don't need nothin'. Just wanta keep my eye on you. Now doan you go wand'rin' off nowheres. I done promised Mistuh Mahcus I be lookin' out for you."

Victoria laughed. "I'm not going anywhere. I just came out for a breath of air."

Sally stepped onto the veranda and studied Victoria. "You feelin' all right?"

Victoria rubbed the small of her back again and frowned. "I don't know. I'm having some pain in my lower back."

"Show me where you hurt." Sally's eyebrows pulled down across her nose.

"Right here. It's—" Victoria's mouth dropped open, and she placed her hand on her stomach.

"Miz Raines, what the matter?"

"I—I just had my first hard contraction," she stammered. "I guess it's time to send for Dr. Spencer."

Sally took her by the arm and guided her to a chair on the veranda. "You sit down right here. I gonna run to the barn and tell James to get Mistuh Mahcus. Then I'll git you in bed. I be back 'fore you knows it."

Victoria eased into the chair and watched as Sally hiked her skirt up and ran toward the barn. She couldn't help but giggle at Sally's long legs skimming across the ground. She looked up into the sky and said a prayer of thanks. It wouldn't be long before she'd be holding her baby, and she couldn't wait.

∽

Marcus sat beside the bed where Victoria lay and held her hand. His heart thumped so loudly in his chest he was afraid she might hear, but she didn't seem to notice. The clock in the downstairs hallway chimed, and he bit down on his lip. James had left to get Dr. Spencer hours ago, and he hadn't returned. What could be keeping him?

"Why didn't you tell me you weren't feeling well before I left this morning?" he asked.

Victoria ran her thumb over the top of his hand. "I knew you had a lot planned today. I didn't want to upset you before I knew for sure what was happening."

On the other side of the bed, Sally wrung the water from a cloth and mopped Victoria's face. "This here gonna make you feels better, Miz Raines."

Victoria gasped and squeezed his hand. After what seemed an eternity, she relaxed and smiled at Sally. "Thank you, Sally. That feels good."

Sally nodded. "I 'member what I feel like when my James born. Now doan you worry none. Sally gonna be right here wit' you till that little baby git here."

"Thank you, Sally. I don't know what I would do without you." She turned her head and smiled at Marcus. "And thank you, too, for sitting here beside me. I feel bad that you had to come home."

He leaned forward and kissed her on the forehead. "And where else do you think I'd be? I gave James instructions he was to come for me the minute anything happened. I'm going to stay with you until Dr. Spencer gets here. Then I imagine he'll make me leave. But for now, I'm right where I want to be."

She smiled. "And where I want you to be."

The front door of the house opened, and Marcus could hear footsteps on the stairway. "I believe Dr. Spencer has arrived."

Sally rushed to the bedroom door and opened it just as the doctor appeared in the doorway. He strode into the room, set his bag on the floor beside the bed, and bent over Victoria. He took Victoria's hand and smiled down at her. "Sorry it took me so long to get here. I was out on another call, and James had to wait until I returned. But I'm here now and ready to go to work. Are you ready to become a mother?"

"I am. I've been waiting for this day."

"Then let's see what's happening here." He looked over at Marcus. "It's time for you to say your good-byes for a while. Sally and I will take over now. Go on downstairs and wait in the parlor while I examine Victoria. I'll come down in a little while and tell you how things are going."

"All right." Marcus stood and leaned over Victoria. "I won't be far away."

She smiled up at him. "I'll be fine. I'll see you later."

As he gazed down at her, the reality of what was about to take place filled him with a fear like he'd never known in his life. Victoria was about to endure pain and suffering like she'd never known, and he was scared. Masking the terror that filled his heart, he bent over her again and kissed her on the cheek. "I love you."

She gazed up at him, and in her eyes he saw love shining for him. He'd never seen that from another person, and suddenly he wanted to do anything he could to make what she was about to endure easier. But he couldn't. All he could do was pray to the God he was just getting to know.

An hour later at the sound of footsteps on the staircase, Marcus rushed to the parlor door. Sally stopped at the bottom as he approached. She grasped the bottom corner of her apron and rolled the fabric between her fingers.

"What's wrong? Where's Dr. Spencer?" Marcus asked.

She pointed upstairs. "He still with Miz Raines. He done asked me to go find James."

"Find James? Why?" Sally tried to step around him, but he blocked her way. "Sally, what's the matter? Why does he want James?"

"He want James to go fetch Miss Tave over to here. He say she done helped him birth babies before, and he need her. He say the preacher can sit wit' you." She backed away. "I's got to go, Mistuh Mahcus. He say I need to hurry."

Marcus stepped aside. "Of course. Tell James to saddle the fastest horse and ride to Daniel and Tave's house as quickly as he can."

"Yas suh. I will."

When Sally disappeared out the door, Marcus looked up at the staircase landing. He had to find out what was going on up there. He stepped onto the first tread and then hesitated. Dr. Spencer was alone with Victoria at the moment, and he didn't want to pull him away from her. With a sigh he stepped back to the hallway and reentered the parlor.

The Bible he'd been reading at night with Victoria lay on a table beside one of the chairs, and he picked it up. For now all he could do was place Victoria and Dr. Spencer in God's hands. He opened the book and began to read.

It was only a few minutes before he heard Sally rush back up the stairs, but Dr. Spencer didn't appear in the parlor for another hour. When he did, he stopped at the door. "Marcus, may I speak to you for a moment?"

Marcus closed the Bible and pushed to his feet. His heart sank at the worried expression on Dr. Spencer's face. "Of course. Come in."

Dr. Spencer walked into the room and stopped in front of him. "I'm sorry I haven't gotten down here sooner, but I've been busy." He motioned to the chairs. "Why don't we sit down?"

Marcus's body trembled in fear of what Dr. Spencer was about to say. He dropped into a chair, and Dr. Spencer sat down facing him. He scooted to the edge of the seat. "Most times babies are born without any problems at all, but sometimes something that no one expected happens. I'm afraid we have a problem."

Marcus grasped the arms of the chair and squeezed. "What kind of problem?"

Dr. Spencer exhaled. "The baby is breech, Marcus. Do you know what that means?"

He swallowed back the fear that knotted his stomach. "Yes. I've seen calves that are breech."

"I'm sure you have, and you probably know that there are several ways this can occur. In Victoria's case, the baby is lying crosswise instead of head down as he should be."

The words pounded into Marcus's head. The vision of the cow that had died giving birth flashed into his mind. "What are you going to do?"

"I have tried several times to turn the baby, but I haven't had any luck. I don't want to try too often because it's hard on Victoria. Of course, we're just in the beginning hours of labor. I may be successful later."

"And if you're not?"

Dr. Spencer's mouth pursed. "Let's not talk about that. For now I'll concentrate on keeping Victoria as comfortable as possible and see what happens. I've sent for my daughter. She's helped me at times with problems such as this. I also told Sally to ask James to go to Cottonwood and bring Mamie. She's assisted many women in childbirth. I imagine Savannah will come with her. So you will probably have some company before long."

"That's all right. Maybe it will keep my thoughts occupied."

"Would you like to see Victoria before everybody gets here?"

Marcus jumped to his feet. "Yes."

He followed Dr. Spencer up the stairs and into the bedroom. As he walked to the bed, he glanced at Sally, who was still applying cool cloths to Victoria's head. He nodded to her as he bent over Victoria.

"Victoria, are you awake?"

Her eyelids fluttered open, and she smiled. She reached up and grasped his hand. "Marcus, you came back to see me. I'm so sorry you're all alone downstairs while Sally and Dr. Spencer are with me. Are you making it all right by yourself? If you're hungry, Sally can go downstairs and fix you something to eat."

"I'm not hungry, Victoria." Her concern for his welfare brought tears to his eyes. "Don't worry about me. You just concentrate on getting our child here."

She smiled and closed her eyes. "I will. I can hardly wait."

Her face contorted into a mask of pain, and her head thrashed on the pillow. Her groan chilled his blood, and he whirled around toward Dr. Spencer. "What's happening?"

Dr. Spencer stepped forward. "It's another contraction. You'd better go now."

Marcus stumbled to the door but looked back at his wife writhing on the bed. With tears streaming down his face, he ran from the room and down the stairs. He slammed the parlor door and fell to his knees.

"Oh God," he cried, "don't make her suffer like that. Please help her deliver that baby."

He prayed for long minutes, but his heart received no answer. He relived every cross word he'd ever said to her and begged God to forgive him and give him a chance to make her happy. Finally, exhausted, he rose from his knees, slumped in a chair, and pulled his watch from his pocket.

Six o'clock. According to what Victoria told him, she'd already been in labor twelve hours. How much longer could this last?

⨎

Marcus's question hadn't been answered at midnight. Nothing had changed in Victoria's condition according to Dr. Spencer.

He sat in the kitchen, his elbows on the table and his hands on either side of his head. Dante poured a cup of coffee and set it in front of him. "Drink this, Marcus."

Across the table, Daniel nodded. "You need to eat something, too. Sally and Mamie fixed a good supper, but you hardly tasted anything."

"I can't eat," he protested. "Not with Victoria up there dying."

Dante slid into the chair next to him. "Dr. Spencer hasn't said she's dying."

He straightened and looked from Dante to Daniel. "We've worked with animals all our lives. You know as well as I do what happens when one of our animals can't give birth. They die, just like Victoria is going to." He burst into tears and covered his eyes with his hands. "Why is God doing this to us? I thought you said when I became a believer, He'd take care of me."

Daniel reached over and grasped Marcus's shoulder. "I said God would be there with you even during the tough times. We don't know what God's plan is for Victoria. Right now we have to trust that He's going to make things right in the end."

Marcus jumped to his feet, and his chair clattered backward to the floor. "In the end? What does that mean? I don't think God cares. I think He's punishing me for all the years I ignored Him, and now He's going to take my wife and child to pay me back."

Daniel and Dante both stood. Daniel shook his head. "God's not in the business of paying people back for their mistakes. He wants to give them hope for the future. Victoria would be upset to hear you talking this way."

"God's here for you, Marcus. You just have to open your heart to His comfort," Dante said.

Marcus shook his head. "Then where is He? I haven't. . ." He paused and tilted his head to one side. "What's that?"

Dante frowned. "What?"

"That singing. Don't you hear it?"

The three of them stood silently for a moment before Marcus strode from the kitchen. "Somebody is singing in front of the house. Who is it?"

He rushed to the front door, threw it open, and stepped onto the front porch. He stumbled to a halt and stared wide-eyed at the scene in front of him. The Pembrook tenant farmers, their wives, and their children stood in the front yard, their faces lit by the lanterns they carried. James stood at the front of the group and strummed his new guitar as the people lifted their voices in song.

A haunting melody rose from the assembled crowd as they sang of a chariot that would come and take them home. The singers stared at the ground, and their bodies swayed in time to the music that seemed to flow from the depths of their souls. Marcus moved slowly down the steps until he stood by James, who played as if he were in his own world.

When the song ended, Ben Moses stepped forward, his hat in his hand. "We doan mean to be causin' you no problem, Mistuh Mahcus, but we come 'cause we hear Miz Raines ain't doin' too well."

"No she isn't, Ben."

A low moan rippled through the crowd, and Marcus let his gaze travel over the group. Ben cleared his throat. "Miz Raines been mighty good to all of us ever since she come to Pembrook. My Sally might of died if 'n she hadn't taken her to the doctor." He pointed to one of the men. "And Charlie there, his little girl been larning how to read 'cause Miz Raines been a-helpin' her. And when Lester's wife be sick, she done come day after day and brung them food to eat. And she's done lots more. Too much to tell, I reckon. She been there for us when we needed her, and we jest wants her to know we's here for her."

Ben's words stunned Marcus. Victoria had never told him all the things she'd done for his tenant farmers. Now as he stared at them in amazement, he realized how much they loved her. He remembered the day that she arrived in Willow Bend. As he'd ridden into town with James, he'd wished that he had a relationship with his tenant farmers like Dante had with his. Now he realized that God knew that day what he needed to do to make his wish come true, and He had sent the answer in the woman who arrived on the *Alabama Maiden*.

Tears filled his eyes, and he reached out his hand to Ben. The man stared at it for a moment before he grasped it. "Thank you, Ben, for telling me what my wife means to all of you."

"You welcome, Mistuh Mahcus."

Marcus faced the crowd. "I want to thank all of you for coming tonight. This means more to me than you'll ever know. I hope to show you in the days ahead how much I appreciate this and all you've done at Pembrook. Without you, it wouldn't be the great plantation it is. Now take your children home and get some sleep. I'll see you tomorrow."

Ben shook his head. "Nah, suh, I 'spects we be stayin' right here 'til we know 'bout Miz Raines."

"But that could be all night."

"That's all right," Ben said. "We gonna sit right here and pray for Miz Raines. You can come out and tell us when she out of danger."

"B—but it's cool, and there are children here. If you want to stay, come in the house where it's warm."

"Nah, suh. We be all right out here."

Marcus glanced around and saw the determination on the faces of everyone. "Very well. Thank you for your prayers. I'll come outside as soon as I know anything."

He walked back onto the porch where Dante and Daniel waited. "I just realized that God has been here all along. I just haven't been able to see Him."

Entering the house, he saw Sally and Mamie waiting in the hallway. "Sally," he said, "please round up every quilt and blanket you can find and take them to the people outside. I don't want them to be cold. And make sure that everyone has plenty of food and water as long as they are here."

A slow smile spread across Sally's face. "Yas, suh, Mistuh Mahcus. Doan you worry. Sally gonna take care of ev'rythin'."

He didn't know what was going to happen, but he did know one thing. God hadn't deserted him, and whatever happened, He would be there with him.

Chapter 14

The clock in the hallway chimed six o'clock, and Marcus jerked awake. Daniel snored on the parlor sofa, and Dante lay on the floor. Marcus had no idea how long he'd slept, but it couldn't have been more than a few hours. He'd looked out the window at three o'clock, and the yard was still filled with people.

He stood up and tiptoed to the window. A look outside told him that no one had left. He rubbed the back of his neck and sniffed. The smell of coffee drifted into the room. He followed the tantalizing aroma to the kitchen, where Sally and Mamie appeared hard at work preparing breakfast for everyone.

Sally looked up from rolling out biscuit dough when he walked in. "Mistuh Mahcus, kin I gits you somethin'?"

"No thanks, Sally. I smelled the coffee and thought I'd get a cup."

She turned to walk across the kitchen. "I'll wash my hands and git it."

He held up a hand to stop her. "There's no need to stop what you're doing. I can get it."

Sally cast a surprised glance at Mamie and returned to her work. When he'd poured the coffee, he walked back to the hallway but stopped at the sight of Dr. Spencer coming downstairs. He set the coffee cup on a table and met him at the bottom of the steps. "What is it? Has something happened?"

Dr. Spencer shook his head. "No, but I need to talk with you, Marcus. I think we have to do something."

Marcus grasped the end of the bannister to support his shaking body. "What?"

Dr. Spencer motioned him into the parlor. As they entered, Daniel and Dante both opened their eyes. Daniel sat up on the couch, and Dante jumped to his feet. "Is something wrong?" Daniel asked.

Dr. Spencer shook his head. "I need to talk to Marcus. Maybe you two should leave."

Daniel stood up, and both turned to leave. Marcus held out his hand. "No, don't go. You've been with me through this ordeal, and I want you to hear what Dr. Spencer has to say."

Dr. Spencer took a deep breath. "Very well. I've tried and tried to turn the baby, but it won't move. Every time I do, it weakens Victoria. I don't think she can stand much more of this. She's been in labor for twenty-four hours now, and

336

she's almost to the point of wanting to give up. This concerns me."

Marcus's heart felt like ice. "Give up? You think she wants to die?"

"I'm afraid so if something doesn't happen soon."

"What else can you do?" Marcus asked.

Dr. Spencer hesitated before he spoke. "I haven't mentioned my last option yet, and I'm not sure I even want to use it. But it may be the only way to save at least one of them. If something doesn't change, we're going to lose Victoria and the baby."

Marcus heard the words, but he couldn't move. Lose Victoria and his child? *Please, God, don't let that happen,* he prayed. He took a deep breath. "Then what's our last option?"

Dr. Spencer chewed on his lip before he spoke. "I recently read about an operation that a doctor in Tippecanoe County, Indiana, performed about a year and a half ago. The woman couldn't give birth, and the doctor made a lengthwise incision in her stomach downward from her naval. Then he made another incision in the uterus and delivered the baby that way. I won't go into all the details, but I feel this is the only way to save Victoria and the baby."

Marcus tried to still his trembling hands. "How dangerous is it?"

Dr. Spencer pushed his glasses up on his nose. "I won't lie to you, Marcus. I've never done this operation before. I don't think either the outside or inside incision will be hard to make, and I think we'll be able to get the baby out safely. I don't know about Victoria, however."

"You think she might die?" His voice was barely above a whisper.

"I don't know. Once I have the baby out, I will need to sew up both incisions. I don't know how long it will take me or how much blood she'll lose. But I do know this is the only option left to us."

Marcus sat still for a moment. He didn't want to think about having a baby without Victoria. But she was going to die if they didn't attempt the operation. He took a deep breath.

"Very well. I want you to do the operation."

Dr. Spencer nodded. "Do you want to talk to Victoria before I sedate her?"

Marcus started forward. "Yes."

He followed Dr. Spencer up the stairs and into the room once more. When he approached the bed, his heart lurched at her pale face. Her dark hair, matted from perspiration, fanned across the pillow. He knelt beside her, and Dr. Spencer stood on the other side of the bed.

"Victoria, can you wake up a moment?" he asked.

Her eyelids fluttered open, and she turned her head to stare at the doctor. "Yes."

He smiled and patted her arm. "It won't be long before your pain will be over. I've talked to Marcus, and we've decided you need an operation to deliver your baby. I'm going to put you to sleep so you won't feel anything. When you wake up, you'll have your baby. How does that sound?"

She licked her lips. "That makes me happy."

"I've also brought you a visitor. Marcus is here," he said.

She turned toward him and frowned. "Marcus? Is it you?"

"Yes, I'm here. Don't try to talk. Just rest. This is all going to be over soon."

She reached her hand up, and he grasped it. Her eyes blinked as if she had trouble focusing. "Is my mother here yet?"

"No, not yet. She'll be here soon, though, and she can hold her first grandchild."

She squeezed his hand tighter. "Tell her for me. . . ."

"What is it you want me to tell her?"

"That I love her. That I've always loved her."

A tear trickled from his eye. "You can tell her yourself when she gets here."

She closed her eyes and shook her head. "One more thing. Promise me."

"What? I'll promise you anything."

Pain flickered in her eyes as she looked up at him. "If I die, take care of our son. Don't teach him the things your father taught you. Listen to Dante and Daniel, and teach our child about God. Teach him to love all people. Will you do that?"

His chest felt as if his heart had shattered into pieces. "Don't talk like that, Victoria. We're going to raise our son together."

"No." She tried to push up in the bed, but he put his hand on her shoulders to restrain her. She lay back against the pillow and gasped. "Promise me you won't do to him what your father did to you. Promise me."

"I promise, Victoria. I promise." Tears ran down his cheeks.

She smiled and closed her eyes. "I love you, Marcus."

"I love you, too."

He pushed up from the bed and stumbled from the room. At the bottom of the steps, he spied the front door. He opened it and walked to the porch. As he walked toward them, the people rose from the quilts where they'd sat all night.

Tears ran down his face, but he didn't care. He faced the people whom Victoria loved. "Dr. Spencer is going to perform an operation to see if he can deliver the baby. He's never done this before. Please pray that God will be with him."

Without speaking, the people sat back down on the ground in silence. He looked around the group for a moment before he sat down on the ground next to James.

"Play your music for Victoria, James. Let her know how much she's loved."

James began to play, and the tune pierced his heart. Blues, Victoria had called James's music. It was first sung, she'd said, by the slaves as they reached out to God for deliverance. Now it filled his soul as he reached out to God and begged Him to spare his wife and child.

Thirty minutes later the front door opened, and Savannah ran onto the porch. "Marcus, come quick."

His heart pounding in his ears, he jumped up from the ground and raced to the porch. "What is it? Is Victoria all right?"

She smiled and motioned him into the house. "Dr. Spencer is still working on Victoria, but there's someone you need to meet. Your son."

Sally stood at the bottom of the staircase, a blanket bundled in her arms. The blanket moved, and a shrill cry pierced the room. Marcus stumbled forward and stared down at the baby Sally held. He swallowed and looked up at her in disbelief. "Is this my son?"

She held the baby out to him. "Yas, suh. This heah yore baby. And he 'bout the purtiest one I ever seen."

Marcus reached for the baby but then thought better of it. "I've never held a baby before."

Dante and Daniel, who stood beside Sally, laughed. "You'd better get used to it," Dante said.

He attempted to control his shaking arms as he reached out and took the child in his arms. A feeling like he'd never experienced washed over him as he stared down at his son. From now on this child would depend on him, and he had made a promise to Victoria. No matter what happened, he intended to keep that promise.

He blinked back tears and smiled. "I want to go show him to all the people outside. There's a new life at Pembrook, and I want to share it with them."

Marcus tucked the blanket around the baby and stepped onto the front porch. "Dr. Spencer is still working with Victoria. So keep praying for her, but I want you to meet my son. Please step up here and see him."

The tenants looked from one to another as if they didn't know what to do. Ben and James stepped forward, and then the others followed. As they each came to look at the baby, Marcus felt for the first time that Pembrook was really beginning to feel like a home. Now all he needed to make it perfect was Victoria.

⟨∾⟩

Two months later on a hot August day, Victoria and Sally stood in the middle of the empty bedroom that had once been occupied by Marcus's father. Her mother had slept here during her visit, which had stretched from two weeks into two months. Now with her departure for Mobile, the time had come to convert the room into a nursery. Victoria glanced around the bare room. "Do you think we've missed anything, Sally?"

Sally propped her arm on the broom she held and shook her head. "No'm. I thinks it's all gone, and I'm glad. You been working too hard a-cleanin' this here room out. You still not well."

Victoria laughed. "How many times are you going to say that? I'm perfectly healed. Dr. Spencer said so."

"Well, he may be the doctor, but I doan knows that you needs to be doin' all this liftin' and cleanin'."

"You're beginning to sound like Marcus. The two of you would like to still have me in bed, but my son is now two months old. And I feel great."

Sally smiled. "He a real sweet baby."

Victoria nodded. "I think so, too. But I'm afraid Marcus is going to spoil him. He can't stay away from him."

"He gonna make a good daddy." Sally pointed to the marble-topped dresser that sat against the wall. "Did we gets ev'rythin' outta there?"

"I think so, but maybe we should check."

Victoria walked over to the dresser and pulled each of the drawers out one at a time. When she pushed the bottom one back in, she frowned and glanced at the decorative carving that ran across the very bottom of the piece of furniture. It appeared to be loose at the top. She put her fingers on the bottom of the carving and pulled it toward her to see if it held. To her surprise, the long piece of wood pulled forward to reveal a hidden drawer.

"Look at this," she called out. "There's a hidden drawer in the bottom of this dresser."

Sally moved behind her and stared over her shoulder as Victoria pulled the drawer all the way out. "Well, I done cleaned this here room a lot of times, and I never knowed there was no drawer there."

When Victoria had pulled it out as far as it would go, she stared down at the contents that appeared to be letters of some kind. She opened one, and her eyes grew wide at the signature scrawled at the bottom. Laying it down beside her, she scooped up the remaining letters and shuffled through them. There had to be at least a hundred in the drawer, and they were all from the same person.

Her hand shook, and she stared up at Sally. "Is Marcus in the barn?"

"Yes'm. He was a little while ago."

"Would you go get him and tell him I need to see him right away? It's an emergency."

Sally took one look at Victoria's face and bolted from the room. Within minutes Victoria heard Marcus's footsteps pounding on the staircase. Breathless, he ran into the room. "Sally said you needed me right away. What is it?"

She pointed to the letters scattered about her on the floor. "I found a secret drawer in your father's dresser. Inside were all these letters. Some of the older ones are addressed to your father. Some that are postmarked years later are addressed to you."

He frowned. "Letters to me? Who from?"

She held out her hand to him, and he walked to where she sat. "Oh, Marcus. They're from your mother."

His face paled, and he dropped to the floor beside her. "My mother? I. . .I don't understand. What do they say?"

"I don't know. They're for you to read first." She turned her head at the sound of the baby's cry. "I have to go feed the baby. Why don't you read them and tell me what they say?"

His lips trembled, and he glanced back down at the letters. "All right."

Victoria left the room and closed the door. As she walked to the bedroom where they'd placed the cradle for now, she prayed for her husband. She hoped words written by his mother years ago would at last bring healing to the wounds he'd suffered as a child.

Three hours later, however, Marcus still hadn't emerged from the room. She'd passed by the door several times and heard him walking about, but she hadn't wanted to disturb him.

She glanced out the kitchen window at the sun setting and wished he would come out. Sally had left for the day, supper was ready, and little Spencer lay on the pallet she'd placed in the corner of the room. She walked over to the baby she'd named after the doctor who'd saved their lives and picked him up.

"Have you been a good boy today?"

The baby gurgled, laughed, and squirmed in her arms.

"He's beautiful, isn't he?" Marcus's voice from the doorway startled her, and she looked up.

"Yes he is." She waited for him to enter the room.

When he stepped nearer, she couldn't tell what he was feeling from the expression on his face. "I read the letters."

"And how do you feel?"

He raked his hand through his hair. "I don't know. I may struggle with that answer for a long time."

She took his hand and drew him toward the table. When they were seated, she positioned the baby in her lap and turned to him. "Do you want to tell me about it?"

He nodded. "Yes. The first thing I learned is that my mother didn't leave Pembrook voluntarily. From her letters I gathered that my father was cold and cruel to her, not at all what she'd thought when they first met. He considered her his property and practically kept her isolated here. She wasn't allowed to go anywhere or have any friends. She was expected to cater to his every wish and be at his beck and call. Evidently if she didn't please him, he would lock her up for days at a time and was even abusive to her at times."

Victoria's heart broke with each word. "Oh no."

"Finally, she got up her nerve to tell him that she hated him and wanted to leave. She said she would take me and go back to her family. He accused her of being unfaithful to him and told her she would never see me again. He had the sheriff, who was a friend of his, come to Pembrook and drag her from the big house into a wagon that transported prisoners. Her letters were filled with hate for him at how she screamed and begged him to let her have me, but he laughed and slammed the door. The sheriff drove her to Selma and put her on a train to Montgomery. From there she traveled on to Boston, where her family lived."

Victoria reached across the table and grasped his hand. "Marcus, how awful. What about the letters to you?"

"As you know, she wrote those later. She said since I was older and could read, she hoped that some way one of them would fall into my hands. Most of them were written on my birthday, and she told me how much she loved me and that she was praying we'd see each other again someday."

Victoria frowned. "But the letters must have stopped at some time. I wonder why."

"I know why," he said. "The one with the last postmark was sent when I was about twelve years old. She wrote because my father had sent her a letter saying that I was killed in a riding accident. He even sent a copy of my death certificate."

"How could he get a death certificate for someone who was alive?"

"You didn't know my father. He could get anything he wanted. Anyway, that last letter was so sad. She told him that any link between them was gone, and he would never hear from her again. She ended by telling him that God was helping her cope with my death, and she could only pray that someday he would come to see how he'd ruined all our lives."

Marcus pushed up from the table and paced back and forth across the kitchen. He raked his hand through his hair. "How could he have been so cruel? He forced her to leave and then told me over and over how she didn't love me and didn't want to take me with her. I grew up without any love, and she was in Boston without me to love her back."

The baby stirred in her lap, and Victoria jiggled him around. "What are you going to do?"

He stopped in front of her, knelt, and wrapped his arms around both of them. "I'm so thankful that God's given you and Spencer to me, but there's a piece of me missing. After all these years, my mother may not be alive, but I have to find out. If she's still living, I have to bring her back here to see her grandson. Do you understand?"

Victoria smiled at him. "Of course I do. Go to Boston. Find your mother and bring her home."

Chapter 15

On a chilly October day Victoria waited inside the store that had belonged to her uncle until a year ago. She transferred Spencer from one arm to the other and tried to smooth the wrinkles out of her skirt.

"Do I look all right?"

Savannah held out her hands to Spencer, who giggled and leaned toward the woman he knew so well. "How many times do we have to tell you that you look beautiful? Your mother-in-law is going to be so happy to see you that she won't care what you're wearing."

Tave, who stood on the other side of Victoria, chuckled. "You'd think royalty was coming with all the preparations you've been making."

"But I want her to feel good about coming back here. She left under such terrible circumstances. I want her to feel welcome."

Savannah bounced Spencer in her arms and smiled at him. She glanced at Victoria. "What did Marcus say in his letter?"

"He said he'd had a difficult time finding his mother. You know he's been in Boston for over a month. There was no one living at the address that was on the letters. It took him some time to find anyone in the neighborhood who had known the family or what happened to them. He went house to house in the area for days until he found a woman who'd been friends with his mother. She had an address where she thought he could find her."

Tave's eyes grew wide. "What happened when he went there?"

"A woman opened the door. He said for a moment he couldn't speak. Then he asked her if she was Elizabeth Raines. She told him she had been once but hadn't used the name in years. When he told her he was Marcus, she almost collapsed. From what he wrote, it was a very emotional reunion. And now she's coming back to live with us at Pembrook."

The low musical rumble of the *Montgomery Belle*'s whistle pierced the afternoon quiet, and the three women rushed to look out the door to the river landing. The tall smokestacks of the steamboat drifted into view, and Victoria reached for Spencer.

"They're here. Let's go."

Savannah jerked the door open. "Go on to the landing. You need to have a private meeting. We'll wait here for you."

Victoria held her son close and hurried across the street. She halted at the top of the bluff and watched as the big boat slid into its docking place and stopped. Within minutes the gangplank was lowered, and deckhands began to swarm ashore with baggage and goods.

Victoria scanned the decks for a glimpse of Marcus and his mother. Then she saw them. Marcus waved and leaned down to whisper to the woman beside him.

Marcus's mother looked small standing next to Marcus. Her head barely came to his shoulder. Her gray hair was pinned up underneath a wide-brimmed hat that matched the black traveling dress and coat she wore. Even from far away, Victoria could see the curling smile that reminded her so much of Marcus.

She watched as Marcus took his mother's arm and guided her across the gangplank and up the bluff to the top of the landing. When they stopped in front of her, Marcus's eyes devoured her and Spencer before he turned back to his mother.

"Mother, this is my wife, Victoria, and my son, Spencer."

Victoria stepped closer. "Welcome home, Mother Raines. I can't tell you how happy I am you're here."

Tears flooded the woman's blue eyes as she looked from Victoria to Spencer. "Victoria, I understand I have you to thank for finding my letters of long ago."

Marcus leaned over, kissed Victoria on the cheek, and took Spencer from her arms. Victoria smiled at the frail woman facing her and grasped her hands. "I know you left under terrible circumstances and you've had years to think about it. But I've prayed that you can let all of that go and enjoy being here. We want you to be a part of our family and share the love that lives at Pembrook now."

"When I left Alabama, I prayed I would see my son again someday, but that hope was destroyed when I thought he'd died. Now God has answered my prayer of long ago."

"You're home now, and that's all that matters," Victoria said.

Marcus handed Spencer back to Victoria. "I want the three of you to stand there for just a moment."

He walked a few steps from the landing and turned to face them. Victoria and her mother-in-law exchanged questioning glances. Victoria tilted her head to one side and stared at him. "What are you doing, Marcus?"

"I was just thinking how quickly one's life can change. A year and a half ago, I stood right here and watched a beautiful woman get off a steamboat. That woman is now my wife. I have a son. And today I have the mother I've wanted for years. God has brought a lot of blessings to me on this river."

Marcus came toward them, his arms outstretched, and drew the three of them close. "I never thought I could be so happy. God has blessed me more than I ever could have imagined."

Victoria stood on tiptoe and kissed her husband's cheek. "You're right. God has been good to us. I think we're going to have to teach James some new songs. There aren't going to be any blues around Pembrook from now on."

A Letter to Our Readers

Dear Readers:

In order that we might better contribute to your reading enjoyment, we would appreciate you taking a few minutes to respond to the following questions. When completed, please return to the following: Fiction Editor, Barbour Publishing, Inc., P.O. Box 719, Uhrichsville, OH 44683.

1. Did you enjoy reading *Alabama Brides* by Sandra Robbins?
   ❑ Very much. I would like to see more books like this.
   ❑ Moderately—I would have enjoyed it more if _____

   _____

   _____

2. What influenced your decision to purchase this book?
   (Check those that apply.)
   ❑ Cover   ❑ Back cover copy   ❑ Title   ❑ Price
   ❑ Friends   ❑ Publicity   ❑ Other

3. Which story was your favorite?
   ❑ *The Columns of Cottonwood*   ❑ *Blues Along the River*
   ❑ *Dinner at the St. James*

4. Please check your age range:
   ❑ Under 18   ❑ 18–24   ❑ 25–34
   ❑ 35–45   ❑ 46–55   ❑ Over 55

5. How many hours per week do you read? _____

Name _____

Occupation _____

Address _____

City_____ State_____ Zip_____

E-mail _____

RED ROCK WEDDINGS

THREE-IN-ONE COLLECTION

BY
LAURALEE BLISS

Love triumphs in Utah as three separate women learn that God always has the best in store for His children when they allow him to lead.

Contemporary, paperback, 352 pages, 5.1875" x 8"

CHRISTMAS ROMANCES

A BILTMORE CHRISTMAS
ISBN 978-1-61626-419-2
by Diane Ashley, Sylvia Barnes, Rhonda Gibson, Jeri Odell
Four sisters find work at the Biltmore Estate during its heyday.
Will the Vanderbilts' tradition of Christmas hospitality help
bring romance into each of their lives?

CHRISTMAS AT BARNCASTLE INN
ISBN 978-1-61626-438-3
by Susan Page Davis, Darlene Franklin,
Janelle Mowery, Lynette Sowell
Each Christmas the Barncastle family transforms its sprawling Victorian bed
and breakfast into a fantasy world that is fertile ground for
the development of four modern romances.

CHRISTMAS BELLES OF GEORGIA
ISBN 978-1-61626-480-2
by Jeanie Smith Cash, Rose McCauley,
Jeri Odell, Debra Ullrick
Love finds four separated sisters when and where they least expect it, in these
tender tales of Christmas romance set in a quaint Georgia town.

A QUAKER CHRISTMAS
ISBN 978-1-61626-479-6
by Lauralee Bliss, Ramona K. Cecil,
Rachael Phillips, Claire Sanders
Christmas is a simple matter among the Quakers of the historic
Ohio River Valley, but can it be a time to welcome love into four households?

PRICE: $7.99 Each
5.1875" x 8" / 352 pages / Paperback

Available wherever Christian books are sold.